4—

RED CARPETS
& WHITE LIES

LEA**BLACK**

RED CARPETS & WHITE LIES

a novel

BEAUFORT
BOOKS

RED CARPETS & WHITE LIES

Library of Congress Cataloging-in-Publication Data On File

For inquiries about volume orders, please contact:
Beaufort Books, 27 West 20th Street, Suite 1102, New York, NY 10011
sales@beaufortbooks.com

Published in the United States by Beaufort Books
www.beaufortbooks.com

Distributed by Midpoint Trade Books
www.midpointtrade.com

Printed in the United States of America

Cover Design by Michael Short

Hardcover: 9780825307485

TABLE OF CONTENTS

CHAPTER 1

RED CARPET RIDE

> I know the event is sold out but I have a
> potential donor willing to spend $100K on
> a table!!! Call me!

—Lauren

Leigh Anatole White raised her face to the soft, slightly salty air and closed her eyes. Tonight was the night that Miami socialites had waited for all year, and the scene was perfectly set for it. Stars shone brightly in the clear night sky. Waves dumped froth just beyond the hotel's lights. The air was drained of humidity, a rarity here, and a warm breeze played along the beach. Leigh could almost hear her partygoers making frantic calls to their stylists, begging for extensions. Even clip-ins a shade off would do! What woman wouldn't want to take advantage of such a climate, and accentuate her look with long, flowing hair moving gently against her bare back in the breeze? And with all those cameras around!

The thought brought Leigh back down to earth. She had work to do—and anyway, she'd held the pose long enough for any onlookers.

Leigh's Charity Ball gala, a benefit for troubled teens held at the Ritz Carlton South Beach, was tonight's hottest ticket in town. To Leigh it was more or less business as usual; but to some of Miami's finest, the gala would be the party of their lives, that crowning opportunity to see and be seen on the red carpet of a city known for its never-ending-party lifestyle. Carefree Lifestyle limousines lined up for five blocks, anxiously waiting their turn to cruise up in front of the Ritz. As they opened their doors, camera flashes hit their passengers' faces like a slap and a kiss, flattering and uncomfortable at the same time. Beyond the red carpet, crowds of pretenders lined up too, hoping to slip through the barricades and have their lives magically turned around, at once and forever.

Miami Beach, the setting of this jewel of opulence, was fresh and full of itself, and Leigh loved it. The beaches here were like no other beaches anywhere. Just walking Ocean Drive and seeing the shore in the distance was as good, if not better, than actually being on it. All day the shops, tattoo parlors, restaurants and newsstands buzzed with the energy of hippies, professionals, hung-over tourists and hookers. In the street, motorcycles, bikes, sports cars, cabs, walkers and skateboarders drifted in the sea breeze, and bobbed in and out of clouds of sweet, sticky green weed smell. The sights of white sand beaches with blue water, bikini bodies and boy toys, joggers and roller-bladers, combined with loud music and the smell of the ocean, gave you the feeling that in this place you were connected to every other beach in the world.

Now, as the evening set in, all the energy of the city seemed concentrated at the front entrance of the five-star hotel at the heart of Miami's world-famous, one-of-a-kind playground, South Beach—Miami Bitch, as some called it.

The mob of photographers behind the ropes at the edges of the red carpet were all eyes and elbows, and jostled each other ruthlessly for the best locations. For the paparazzi, getting that prized "money shot" had everything to do with obsession, aggression, ego and luck. A celebrity in a beautiful dress was worth something; some part of the same celebrity sliding unintentionally *out* of that dress was worth a lot more. A skirt blowing up like Marilyn's in a sudden sea breeze? Huge. And what about the great celebrity photo of the early 21st century—a shot of So-and-So climbing out of her Range Rover, panties nowhere to be found? Priceless.

This, of course, was only outside. With security tight and asses tighter, most of the press was barred from the hotel's Grand Ballroom, where the main event took place. Leigh welcomed society writers there; after all, most of them knew how to behave. But the rich and famous look about as bad as the poor and anonymous after eight hours of nonstop drinking; and after Leigh had caught the *Entertainment Tonight* crew filming the split down the back of Jane Fonda's gown, most cameras had been off-limits inside.

Only Miami's royalty were invited to this magical night of fine cuisine and cocktails, haute couture, and tits and ass, and they knew from the beginning that they were in for a rare experience. Even the invitation process was over-the-top. Leigh's guests each received a $250 handmade invitation, designed by the prestigious firm Natural Impressions, that was the size of a magazine cover and encrusted with pave diamonds. When the sunlight hit it, it could be seen from a block away. Only a small number of these invites were made, and only one in the history of the gala—the victim of a vicious divorce, as rumor had it—ever made its way to a resale shop.

Each invitation was hand-delivered—on a Sterling silver tray donated by Christofle—by a gorgeous, rock-solid 6'3" German muscle man. Having been driven to the prospective guest's home in an exotic car donated by Warren Henry Motors for the occasion—sometimes a Lamborghini Veneno, sometimes Mr. Henry's own 1934 Rolls-Royce Phantom Coupe—the beef-slab would then walk ceremoniously up to the front door in very tight black slacks, a red bow tie and white gloves, and no shirt, showing off a perfectly tanned, perfectly oiled, perfectly shaved chest and abs to match. Along with the invitation he brought champagne, $1200 of Marky's caviar presented in a small Baccarat dish, and a single, long-stemmed yellow rose. Legend had already sprung up about the outlandish stud's wavy, light-brown hair, which irresistibly tempted both women and men to run their hands through it; and about the great distances from which neighbors could hear women squealing when he arrived with his goodies. Forget the Publisher's Clearing House van; this guy was hotter than money!

Yet money, after all, was the name of the game. The sheer opulence of the invitation was Leigh White's way of saying, "You and I both know you can afford a big donation for the kids," and the message was received loud and clear. The people who got it weren't just rich or society-savvy; they were the "professional guests," the people who knew the way the game was played. They knew how to get that invitation. They knew how to walk a red carpet. They knew where to look when the flashes went off. They knew it was all theater, and they rose to the occasion in revealing dresses, beauty-queen poses and blinding smiles. The smart ones did their homework, and dressed with the background in mind: they knew the photographers loved complimentary colors. They also knew that this was the charity event where money talked, and the amount they spent would speak volumes about them. Here, if they donated enough, their ride on the magic red carpet could get them one-of-a-kind, career-changing press.

For everyone else, no amount of money was enough to buy their way through the door. Of course, this didn't keep them from going to great lengths to try, or stooping to great depths when they failed. Many who would later claim they'd partied at the Charity Ball until 5 a.m. hadn't been there at all; and those for whom they spun the lie—equally disappointed at having missed out—never questioned it. Some of Miami's wannabes, high-powered couples hoping to rise in society, would plan trips out of town in order to avoid the embarrassment of not being invited. Some barricaded themselves in at home all weekend, drapes closed, hiding from the same "in" crowd they hoped one day to join, and the press they hoped one day to court.

As for that press, Leigh's attitude was that, as long as they didn't chase away her guests, any press was good press, and more press was always better; so they were always the first to arrive on gala night. *People Magazine*, *In Touch* and *E! Entertainment* were given the royal treatment. Andy Cohen was coming to tape for his "Watch What Happens Live!" show, and South Beach was already abuzz with Andy sightings. Editors and writers from every magazine in the South were there, along with representatives of local and national newspapers, television stations, websites and blogs. At first, Leigh had balked when a housewife from Muncie with a fashion blog had requested press credentials. But her Charity publicists had insisted, and soon Leigh understood why. One great sentence from a usually uninteresting blogger could take over cyberspace and create undreamed-of fame. So what if it only lasted fifteen minutes? It was fodder for the next fifteen minutes, and the fifteen minutes after that. Poor Andy Warhol, Leigh had mused—the interwebs had really made a mess of his principle.

The promise of positive national publicity was how Leigh pulled in her big performers and celebrity guests. Those who already had a good name wanted to maintain it, and those who didn't, often wanted one desperately. It was a lesson Leigh had learned early in her gala-giving days, and she was no fool about it. She and her team scoured celebrity sites, pouncing on those who had recently wrecked their car drunk or picked up a low-end hooker now bent on revenge. In their dazed, post-popular state, they were apt to give her a sheepishly quick "yes" when she asked them to perform or show up at a benefit for kids at risk; and backing out was not an option when you said yes to Leigh White.

Consequently, the guest list was nothing short of fabulous. Celebrities like Eva Mendes, Aretha Franklin, Taylor Hicks and Alex Rodriguez were mingled in among tonight's biggest donors. It was a very eclectic group; here one might expect to see the Rock and Rush Limbaugh rubbing elbows. The more gracious local celebrities stopped for interviews with the national media, hoping to extend their appeal. Out-of-town celebrities, true to reputation, walked right past the local reporters and photographers, driving them crazy. Interns working the event slipped their favorite bloggers in for a question or two—and Leigh made sure even these small-timers were kept happy. Hell, they'd be running *People* next week!

The A-listers and major players arrived early, as arranged by their publicists, to be sure they got prime page placement in all the major publications. Watching these celebrated people and socialites walk the red carpet was an amazing sight. Among the glamorous divas who evidently imagined themselves walking down a couture runway or the long carpet at the Oscars, there were always a few with husbands or "walkers," not unlike the parading trainers at the Westminster Dog Show, whispering words of advice and encouragement to them through clenched smiles as they passed. And the inexperienced were always easy to pick out. Leigh spent five minutes watching a young woman in a flowery Nicole Miller gown sticking her short, heavily muscled leg out in a childish impersonation of Angelina Jolie. Truth be told, though, no one spent too much energy knocking these awkward newcomers. If you were there at all, you were somebody, and somebody special. The Charity Ball wasn't entirely devoid of fellow feeling.

***

Leigh White, the Queen of the Night and founder of the Charity, considered herself a sort of cheerful dictator when it came to producing her gala. Well—"hostess" was what she preferred to be called, and in keeping with her title, she paid close attention to every detail. She had been the first to arrive, walk the red carpet and speak to the press line; and she would be the last to leave, stepping gingerly over puddles of liquor and tipped-over signs.

She positioned herself at the end of the red carpet for the arrivals. No one held a more strategically perfect ground than she, to see or be seen; and from this vantage she had a bird's-eye view of every celebrity, guest and press member. She'd given strict instructions to her volunteers and to the press as to how they were to behave tonight, chief among them being *Focus on the big donors.* Every guest was to feel like the most important person in the room, but the sales directors of Range Rover, Grey Goose Vodka and American Express were actually up there. Leigh had planned this evening for months, plotting out which celebrity she wanted photographed in front of which sponsor's logo, what drinks would be offered—and *not* offered—to whom, and so forth. It was the little tactical details like these that ensured the Charity Ball's sponsors returned each year; and though this was to be her last gala, she wasn't about to do it any differently.

Now, looking on at the groupies behind the velvet ropes around the Ritz's driveway—at the endless flash of their cameras, and pens and paper waving in the air for autographs—Leigh felt a contented yet melancholy stirring in her heart. She had planned galas for years, and planned this one for months; she had grown used to this moment, when she could look out on the crowd writhing at her doorstep and think to herself, after all her careful preparations, *It's go time.* Only now, go time was time to go, too. The planning for this evening's gala had occupied so much of her energy over the past months, Leigh had barely had time to reflect on the finality of her decision. Now that it was here, the reality of it crowded in on her. It had been a miracle each year to see all the struggling, arm-twisting, infighting and argument culminate in the Charity Ball, a night as beautiful and magical as any in Miami legend. Despite her experience, it had amazed Leigh each time. And though she knew in her heart that she was ready to move on, Leigh found herself wondering if she would ever find the same kind of excitement elsewhere. Not to mention the kids—who was going to provide for them?

Enough of that, she said to herself, shaking off the feeling. There would be time for honest reflection later. For now, it was time to welcome the crowd.

Katie and Billie Parker, two of the best-known local celebrities expected, were the first to arrive. As soon as their limousine door opened, the mob of photographers started yelling—but not for both of them.

"This way! This way, Billie!"

"Big smile, Billie!"

"Billie, one more please, this way."

Billie, a renowned fashion designer used to the limelight, looked relaxed and completely at ease. By contrast, his wife Katie's silicone smile—puffy Botoxed lips covered in Tom Ford Black Orchid—seemed painted on, and her makeup thick and airbrushed. Nothing on her face moved, nor did she depart one inch from her course. Dressed extravagantly in a backless silk gown with diamonds dripping from her ears, collarbone and wrists, she stayed glued to her husband's side, determined to ride the wave of his popularity right along with him—or past him, if she could.

To capture a bit of celebrity by being seen with her husband and his celebrity friends and models was, increasingly obviously, Katie Parker's number-one priority. The energy of the red carpet thrilled her, and even the cosmetic paralysis of her face couldn't keep in her excitement when a photographer's assistant asked her to step away from her husband. Finally—they wanted an individual photo! She stepped quickly away from her husband and assumed her best red carpet pose—hand on hip, one leg pushed forward.

With nary a word of acknowledgment, the photographer's assistant stepped around her and set up a quick shot with Billie. Fuming, Katie pulled away and walked up to Sarah, the gala publicist, who was dressed in a black number designed by none other than Katie's husband. Thinking Katie was going to comment on this, Sarah began to greet her warmly—but Katie had other ideas.

"Never mind the dress," she spat, gesturing at the photographer's assistant who'd pulled her away to snap Billie alone. "Who does *that* little bitch think she is?"

Turning back from the cameras, Billie got an earful of the venom his wife was spewing, and grabbed her arm. He hoped her anger was coming from ignorance; after all, she was a small-town girl, and this had to be overwhelming for her. But lately he'd had his doubts; it seemed all Katie cared about were the cameras. "Keep smiling," he hissed in her ear, smiling resolutely as they continued up the carpet.

Leigh laughed to herself, having caught the whole spectacle. Billie had really unleashed a beast! If Katie ever got any real attention, or achieved any relevance, what true colors would show through? Only time would tell; but Leigh knew it couldn't end well. When she looked at Katie, she saw big ambitions behind those flat, soulless eyes. The girl was up to no good.

The next locals to the red carpet were Dr. Howard Johnson and his wife Dixie. These were real friends and supporters, and Leigh welcomed them with genuine excitement.

Dr. Johnson, psychiatrist to the rich and famous, was a much more popular man than his appearance would suggest. Everything about him screamed average, from his thinning hair to his thickening physique; still, everyone wanted to be friends with him, in hopes of meeting some of his celebrity clients. Despite his friendliness, however, Dr. Johnson was very professionally discreet, and seemed a difficult man to get close to.

His wife was another matter. Five-foot-two with eyes of blue, and an effervescence to match her penchant for champagne, Dixie Johnson was an irrepressibly sociable woman who lived for gossip. In the rare event that talk itself wasn't enough to make a friend out of her, a glass or three would do the trick; and long habit had taught her never to turn down a new acquaintance. Today's stranger was tomorrow's juiciest confidant; and with Dixie by the Doctor's side, everyone with a smile knew they could at least squeeze into a photograph with the odd pair, and put themselves one degree closer to somebody who mattered.

Right behind the Johnsons, as though in counterpoint to their friendly familiarity, came Sassy and Jacques. Jacques, the mystery man of the evening, was as new to the scene as any plus-one to the Charity Ball had ever been. Everyone wanted the story behind this tall, dark, and handsome man on Sassy's arm. He seemed exotic and delightful, with a fabulous French accent that rang like music.

Sassy, though a more familiar player on the Miami scene, was hardly any better known herself. She was one of the most aggressively cutthroat high-end realtors in the city, and, as is sometimes the case with people in such competitive professions, she kept her cards very close to the vest. She had an almost masculine ease about her that had long proven irresistible to men, particularly the "bad boys" she seemed to go for; but she favored dates and one-night stands over relationships, and truth be told, nobody really counted her among their close friends. Jacques seemed an exception to this rule, but nobody knew him well enough to draw any conclusions. For all anyone knew, she was just using Jacques for a professional come-up of some sort—but then again, he might be doing the same.

At any rate, Jacques was definitely the type that caught the eye of every woman at the event—howsoever happily married—and half the men to boot, and Sassy obviously knew enough to flaunt him. Leigh greeted them graciously, hoping to herself that whoever he was, Jacques would have big bucks to bid at the auction.

"Leigh!" Sassy yelled, in her theatrically friendly voice. "What a great job you've done! Meet Jacques Mercier, my boyfriend. He's new here, from France. We're in love!"

Leigh looked at the couple, a Mona Lisa smile dancing at the corner of her lips. Did Jacques really not know *anything* about Sassy's reputation?

"Hello, Jacques," Leigh said. "Thanks for coming. What brings you to Miami?"

"I'm an art dealer," replied Jacques. "Miami's the perfect place to be, especially now, where anyone and everyone in the art world comes for Art Basel."

"Ah, excellent," said Leigh approvingly. Maybe he *did* have some money to throw around! The art market was notoriously fickle, but the guy certainly looked like he did all right; perhaps he was a player after all. "Our auction's got some beautiful things this year—I hope you approve."

He looked around with an appraising eye. "How much money do you expect to raise tonight, if you don't mind my asking?"

"Oh, with any luck, this party should raise a few million," Leigh said. "But it's never enough, really; we've got a lot of struggling kids out there. I don't know how it is in your country, but ever since Bush ruined our economy, no one has done a thing for them. All the government programs were cut, and people are still struggling. So open your wallet tonight, Jacques—we have a Ferrari you could bid on!"

"I'll see what I can do," laughed Jacques, "but I'm sure I'll be upstaged by *this* crowd." He scanned the mob around them. "Quite a lot of beautiful women, eh, Sassy? Who was that very tall blonde?"

He really is new here, Leigh thought. "That'll be the one and only Diva Lorraine Manchester," she said, laughing, as the crowd went wild.

"The drag queen I told you about," said Sassy, with a wink.

"Impressive," said Jacques, but with a disapproving sneer. "She is just as beautiful in person as she is in the photos you showed me. What a waste! If she weren't so tall I would never believe she is really a man. I'm shocked that she is so…socially accepted here."

"Oh, darling," Sassy laughed, holding him a little tighter, "get over it. Lorraine is a charmer. Everyone loves her."

"Charming to you, maybe," Jacques answered quickly, with a cautious look. "If she gets close to me, she should watch out. I'll wipe that hot-pink lipstick off those big puffed-up lips of hers.—His?—Whatever."

Leigh was startled by this sudden hostility. "Surely there are drag queens where you're from, Jacques?" she asked.

"Please—the French *invented* drag queens," said Sassy, rolling her eyes.

"Where I'm from, men are men," said Jacques, passing over Sassy's remark with continental hauteur. "My friends would never accept him, her, it—*that.*"

"I don't hear anyone asking you to go to bed with *her*," Sassy shot back, tugging Jacques toward the entrance. "We'll see you inside, Leigh."

Jeez, thought Leigh, watching them go; *that jerk better be good and rich!* To say things like that about anyone—much less a friend of hers! Hopefully he wouldn't be so conservative with his cash later. Even if he wasn't there for the kids, he seemed like he might be the type to show off if it might get him laid. Not that he'd have that problem hanging out with a woman like Sassy. That was one woman who knew what she wanted, and always had a plan to get it.

That was at least one similarity between Jacques's new girlfriend and *this* one, Leigh smiled to herself, turning to watch the famous and fabulous Lorraine Manchester beginning her own night-long red-carpet moment. No stranger to local fame, this legend in her own mind had already whipped the crowd into a frenzy with her appearance, and was now working them hard with a practiced barrage of kisses and disses. Lorraine was one of Leigh's longer-standing friends at the event tonight, but Leigh knew better than to try talking to her now. She'd have to catch the Diva inside, where there'd be fewer cameras rolling.

As Lorraine posed for photos and signed autographs for her fans, Leigh watched the press photographers turn to their next target. Promoter and party boy Mitchell Hudson had just arrived, surrounded by his usual entourage of tall, gorgeous girls—all model-perfect with beautiful smiles, incredible hair, hot bodies, and near-unnoticeable Botox and silicone. Waxed and exfoliated, puffed and buffed within an inch of their lives, the whole coterie were dressed as if they'd just stepped off the runway—or, knowing some of them, out from under the bedsheets—and the press absolutely ate it up. Mitchell, no less polished in appearance than his human accessories, but a good deal more accomplished in banter, was careful to field all their questions.

Well known and well liked, the young playboy made an entrance as casually as if he'd practiced it in in the mirror all day. He thought of himself as a host and concierge to the rich and famous, a sort of nouveau Hugh Hefner—and nobody questioned him. He'd certainly done his part in making *this* party happen in years past. His philosophy was, fill a room with pretty girls and liquor, and the money guys will start throwing dough around like confetti—and it always worked like a charm. It seemed too straightforward to be true; but then, even in Miami some things were still straightforward.

Posing for photos with Mitchell and his babes, Leigh knew he'd delivered again. Their group was already turning a *lot* of heads, and Leigh could almost see the rich bachelors in the crowd thinking over some of the ways they might get the girls' attention off of Mitchell and onto themselves. Fortunately for the Charity, their imaginations were pretty limited. With them, fancy sports cars and $250,000 Audemars Piguet watches were the norm; they'd have to bid big to stand out here. As for the girls themselves, who knew what they thought, or how much they were in on Mitchell's real motivations? Did they really "think" at all? They always seemed pretty surprised and flattered whenever Mitchell made a move on them; but then again, that might just be what they knew he wanted. It was always difficult in this town to truly know who was zooming whom; and Leigh was sometimes sure she saw hidden depths in the smile of one or another of these Lollipops of the Night.

"Great crowd, Leigh," said Mitchell, already looking around to see if the babe grass was any greener on the other side of the red carpet. Jesus, the kid had a chronic hard-on, Leigh thought; you could practically see him sizing up his next threesome. Hardly past sundown, and the guy already had a fiesta going on down there.

"Takes one to make one," said Leigh, glancing approvingly at his entourage. "Welcome to the Charity Ball, ladies—champagne's just inside."

"Has Scarlett arrived yet?" she heard Mitchell asking a door assistant as he passed. Laughing, Leigh cut in.

"No, Mr. Hudson, Ms. Ruiz has not arrived yet," she said with mock formality.

This was always the first question Mitchell asked at the door wherever he showed up. Leigh knew the same went for Scarlett. You'd think the two promoters were married, rather than rivals; but then, the rivalry had always seemed to be a pretty happy one. Scarlett had a hankering for the ladies that rivaled Mitchell's own, and Mitchell referred to her as "the little muff diver" whenever she was out of earshot. But despite their competitiveness, the two of them always had more than their share of beautiful women around. Some of these were invariably of a persuasion they couldn't persuade themselves, and in these cases, they'd save face by feigning indifference and sending the babe in question over for the other to enjoy. It was what Mitchell called "living a balanced life," and it worked wonderfully. Each liked feeling like the other was indebted to them; and though in reality both of them were too high up on the nightclub food chain to be threatened in any real way by competition, their like-mindedness—Mitchell was in it for the money and sex, while Scarlett was in it for the sex and money—and sexual incompatibility obviously made each of them feel more relaxed in the other's company. Their frequent fights over women and celebrities were like a friendly formality between them, a shared language that underlay the obviously false camaraderie they affected in public. In their world of shallow connections and fake friendships, their rivalry was probably the closest thing to real intimacy that either had ever experienced.

"You bring that one for her?" Leigh whispered in Mitchell's ear, with a nod toward the stunning dark-eyed blonde at his right. Blondes with long, straight hair—and not too much going on underneath it—were Scarlett's favorite.

Mitchell pretended not to understand—something he was

remarkably good at—and was saved by an assistant running up to Leigh.

"Mrs. White, Mr. White is arriving now," she said, lowering her walkie-talkie.

"Brad!" called Mitchell, taking the opportunity to pull away.

"Hello, Mitchell," said Brad White, shaking the promoter's hand briefly before turning to his wife with a loving look. "And hello you too, whoever you are."

"Sir, are you on the list?" Leigh said, her poise breaking for just a moment into a broad grin. Ten years in, and her husband never failed to make her smile.

"I was hoping to charm my way in," said Brad as they hugged. "Hello, darling," he whispered. "You look lovely."

"So far, so good, anyway," said Leigh with a laugh. "Just seven or eight more hours to go."

"No time at all," said Brad, flashing his handsome smile. "Shall we go in?"

"Just a minute—I need a photo with the King and Queen of the Ball," Mitchell cut in, grabbing the arms of two of his girls and positioning himself front and center. The five of them stood for a few shots, then Mitchell rallied the rest of his coterie with a few practiced gestures, and they all went in.

***

The over-the-top Emilio Robba–decorated cocktail reception doors opened to loud gasps from outside and the music of DJ Tracy Young from within. Tracy was dressed in an incredible electric-blue vintage Yves Saint Laurent velvet pantsuit that perfectly set off her chic, short hairdo, but not many in the crowd took notice of her as they rushed the lounge area. The legendary DJ Tracy—who'd been catapulted to fame by Miami's Queen of Nightlife, Ingrid

Casares—was as connected as any of them. She'd spun for a ton of celebrities, including Madonna, who'd had her spin at her wedding to Guy Ritchie. ("Not that *that* had turned out so well!" Leigh had joked, when they'd brought her on stage.)

The corridor outside the Grand Ballroom had been transformed into a Miami nightclub scene of breathtaking opulence, with pockets of soft lighting, exotic flower arrangements spilling across coffee tables and deep white couches where partygoers could sink down, drink, and sink down further. It was a "been there, seen it all" crowd, but from the first glance they knew they were in for an evening that would go down in party history—provided anyone were able to remember it afterward.

As Leigh walked through the cocktail reception lounge, she felt as though she were in a scene from a James Bond movie, or perhaps the beginning of a particularly artsy porno. The women were all resplendently dressed, and the men pretty evenly divided between white dinner jackets and sleek black tuxedos. Flashes of light sparkled over guests' heads from thirty Baccarat crystal chandeliers. Flashes of that sweet perfume—*Eau de Ganja,* as Leigh called it— drifted through, accentuating the room's classy elegance with a more familiar note.

Some of Miami's finest designers had collaborated on the redesign and decoration of the space for tonight's event, and Leigh herself could hardly believe the transformation. The room had started out as a huge, bland hotel corridor—about 8000 square feet, right off the hotel's Grand Ballroom—the first sight of which had filled her with a creeping horror. It had been so restrained, so antique— she couldn't imagine, at the time, how anyone could give such a drab space the look she'd had in mind for it. Yet the designers had risen to her challenge. Now it was voluptuous yet modern, over-the-top yet familiar, with oversized beds covered in white velvet in between the low couches, overstuffed white pillows, silver candles, bright sprays of flowers and dramatic glass and silver statement pieces from every top-of-the-line designer showroom in town. The long hall caught the vibe of the progressive, edgy Miami night scene perfectly. It would have rivaled any nightclub—including Ingrid Casares's own monumental Liquid, the club of all iconic clubs—for ambiance and sophistication. No one would have guessed by the look of it that it had been a passageway only a few weeks earlier, or that it would be one again in a matter of days.

During the two-hour cocktail party, the drinks flowed and the crowd glowed. The room filled up quickly, and the guests, most of them schmoozers by profession if not by nature, got down to the serious business of partying. To aid them in their intermingling, the long hall had been divided with white velvet ropes into four sections: "VIP," "Celebrity," "Corporate" and "South Beach." Everyone could come and go as they pleased, but they were each given a wristband at the door that suggested which themed area they might start their evening in, in order to meet up with friends and acquaintances from similar walks of life.

The VIP area was all candles, silver sculptures and white peonies. As one would expect from its name, it filled up very quickly.

The Celebrity area, decorated with twinkling stars, mirrors and disposable cameras, was where most of the press gravitated. This was convenient for the actual celebrities, who almost all avoided it.

The Corporate section offered minimalist furniture, high-end cigars and decanters of Grey Goose vodka and single-malt Scotch to its inhabitants, who looked on with a mixture of distaste and envy at their neighbors, as they were used to doing.

The South Beach section, by far the wildest, boasted pedestals with go-go dancers in micro-minis, waitresses dressed like Playboy bunnies, nude mimes painted white, and colorful sex toys strewn across the overly broad beds—in short, pretty much exactly what South Beachers would expect.

Strolling along the corridor between sections, beginning to make her rounds, Leigh bumped into Katie Parker by the "Celebrity" section, making her late entrance after dallying on the red carpet for more photos and fame-stalking. Leigh had to admit, she looked terrific: her backless black gown put her in perfect contrast to the white-on-white corridor. If she weren't so obviously out to have her picture taken, she'd have been a photographer's dream.

"Hi, Katie," said Leigh warmly. "I saw you on the red carpet earlier; that's such a beautiful dress! Where's your husband gone off to?"

"Oh, he's around somewhere," Katie said, eager to get back to her favorite topic, herself. "You don't think it looks a bit too plain for me?"

"The dress? No—of course not! What makes you think that?"

"Well, I just—oh, excuse me, Leigh! I think this gentleman wants to talk to me—?"

A photographer had approached them, and was raising his camera for a shot.

"I'm from the *Miami Herald*," he said. "Do you mind if—"

Before he could utter another word, Katie subtly pushed Leigh aside and struck a dramatic pose. A beautiful, renowned woman in an elegant dress—it was exactly the kind of shot the paper loved to run! Katie was practically on the edge of orgasm.

"That's great," said the photographer, snapping off a couple of shots. "And can I get your name for the byline?"

"My—!" The orgasm had quickly become a cramp. "I'm Katie Parker!" she barked.

"Ah. The designer's wife?"

"Of course, the designer's wife!" She rolled her eyes dramatically.

"Great, great. And I assume that's one of your husband's designs you're wearing?"

"Listen—" Katie began, but abruptly stopped herself. A glimmer of limelight had just shone into her brain.

"As a matter of fact," she purred, "it *isn't*. I love his work, of course, but I don't want to be defined by his work; sometimes it just isn't what I want at an event like this." She rolled her eyes again in mock embarrassment. "I make my *own* decisions in that department—a woman needs her independence, you know."

"Of course, yeah!" The photographer had jumped at the bait, and was already fumbling his notebook open. "Whose design is it?"

Leigh watched Katie lean in conspiratorially with the photographer to tell him, as though it was their little secret. Now her photo was sure to be published, and probably prominently, too. You had to hand it to Katie Parker; she was proving to be quite a natural at this "fake it 'til you make it" business. Leigh even caught herself wondering who the designer might be.

"Nice work," she said, as the photographer wandered off.

"I try," said Katie sweetly.

"Hope Billie's okay with it."

"Oh, he'll get over it! Besides, he—oh, there he is now!"

Billie was wandering by at a little distance, smiling absently to himself. To look at him, you'd think the man was quite pleased with his lot in life. Truth be told, he was thinking about the gorgeous model he'd just bumped into at the bar. They'd met briefly on a *Vogue* shoot once, and when he'd touched her hand just now to say hello, sparks had flown. He hadn't wanted to linger there, but now he was earnestly wondering which section she might be in. She was South American of some kind, with dark hair cropped into bangs, playful, exotic eyes and a smoky voice. He wondered what his name would sound like, moaned over and over by that voice. Somewhere in the background of his fantasy, he could hear—just barely—an annoying, shrill noise.

"Billie! *Billie!* The music must be too loud; he doesn't hear me."

Like parents don't hear their screaming baby after a while, Leigh thought. "It's ok, go on—I'll catch up to you two later."

Katie was already off, and in Billie's ear. "Billie, I've been *calling* you! Did you notice that guy from the *Herald* photographing me? It's about time they realize who the real star in this family is, ha! Billie, wipe that silly grin off your face—am I really that hot tonight—?"

A little ways down the corridor, near the "Corporate" section, Leigh saw Lauren Altamira, her best friend and one of Miami's hottest high-end realtors, out of the corner of her eye. Catching Lauren's glance, she waved her over.

"There's the Mexican royalty I was looking for," Leigh said. "You look fabulous. Can I guess?"

"Give it a shot," said Lauren sarcastically. She always wore Valentino to Leigh's galas, and pretty much every other occasion.

"Ummm…Valentino."

"Bingo! But lest you think you have me all figured out, Mrs. White, the diamonds are by Jeffrey Rackover, and this diamond clutch is Hermès."

"Whoa, lady, look at you!"

"Hey, it's why I love to work! Speaking of which, have you run into Sassy yet? She's after my clients, and already working the room like a thousand-dollar hooker."

"Lauren, be nice," Leigh said. A nasty little rivalry had sprung up lately between the two women, and Lauren had been getting a bit obsessive over it. "Don't think about that tonight—please!" Leigh scanned the crowd behind Lauren. "No husband this evening, huh?"

"No—again," Lauren sighed. "That's what I get for marrying a mad scientist, I guess. I love the man; but God, is he a private person—too private, if you ask me!" She laughed.

"Nice that *someone* still is," Leigh said, spotting Katie Parker, husband in tow, weaving through the crowd like a shark after blood.

"I know, I know. Around here, Francisco's a rare breed. It'd just be nice to have him along at these things once in a while. I feel like I hardly ever see the guy. Sometimes it feels like we lead separate lives."

Leigh knew that had as much to do with Lauren's high-powered work ethic as anything else, but that was a conversation for another time.

"Well, every marriage has its ups and downs, doesn't it? And it's not so bad a problem to have. At least your husband's a brainiac, and not a drug addict or pervert or something. Anyway, never mind that tonight—enjoy yourself! And help me pick some pockets."

"Ok, ok. I'm going to circulate."

The two women did a little secret high five, as only close friends can, and Lauren disappeared into the crowd.

As if she'd been awaiting her turn in the rotation, Dixie Johnson appeared. She moved in for a hug, and Leigh remembered why they called Dixie "the Double D."

"Faaaaabulous party, darlin'!" shrieked Dixie.

"Well, *you* certainly seem to be having a great time," Leigh said. A few glasses in, and Dixie's twang always returned as her sense of decorum fled.

"How could Ah *nawt!* These sections yew've got set up—what a *great* ahdea! Though Ah seem to've lost mah husband in one of 'em..." she trailed off, looking around for Howard.

It was a good thing Dixie had married a shrink, Leigh thought; short of a saint, she couldn't imagine who else could handle the little firecracker. Black-belt shopper, master gossiper, world-class drunk—not exactly the combination of every man's dreams! But Howard loved her, and if he had any problem with her habits, he never let on. Nor did Leigh, for that matter. Dixie always brought the party, and Leigh loved her for it—especially on gala night. She and Howard could be counted on to keep the bids up, and even to bid themselves, if all else failed.

"Well, Dixie, if anyone can part a man from his money, it's you," Leigh said, holding Dixie's shoulders for emphasis—and to keep the woman steady. "Help me get them to bid tonight, ok?"

"Of koorse, darlin'—yew know Ah'll do mah part," Dixie drawled, her expression becoming somber. Abruptly she swayed and giggled self-consciously, grabbing a chair for balance. She could never keep a straight face for long.

"All right, enjoy yourself! I think I saw Howard over by the 'Corporate' section; I'm sure he knows a few people there."

"Thanks, babe! See ya soon. And don't worry about us—we'll get them big spenders spendin', all right!"

For a moment Leigh's mind wandered. The energy of the party filled the room, but the music and conversation all seemed to fade as she looked around and took stock of the scene. Her friends and guests all wandered the room as though in slow motion, drinking and talking amongst themselves; looking at them Leigh felt a strange self-awareness come over her. Seeing her friends all at once, noticing them like this, was almost jarring, like noticing her own breathing. Where had they all come from, these people in her life? Where would these friendships take her, and where would they all end up? How many of them would still be her friends a year from now—or next month, for that matter?

She was jerked back to reality from this little daydream by the familiar yet strange sight of a large, overly made-up head parting the crowd on its way toward her.

"Hey, Leigh!" the Diva Lorraine Manchester yelled from across the lounge. "You want a good laugh?"

"Always," smiled Leigh.

"I saw little Billie Parker being interviewed for *Deco Drive* earlier, on the red carpet. You know that boy always brings the fashionistas flocking! So I graced his interview with my presence—"

"While they were filming?"

"—of course, darling—and apologized for not wearing one of his men's suits to your gala tonight. Oh, the crowd loved *that* little zinger; bet it makes it onto Andy later!" She said this with a straight, albeit very made-up, face.

"Ha! Very witty. But why does something tell me you had another motive?"

"When do I not? I've been waiting for little Billie to offer me one of his men's suits, but he never seems to get the memo! I may have to schmooze with him and his little wife-thing later, just to make sure the point gets through."

"Just don't go vanishing on me! You know I need you to help with the auction."

"Of course, darling, of course—but—the suit! Brandon West-brook needs to look good too, beautiful."

"He's going to have a hard time keeping up with you."

"Don't they all, darling, don't they all—an occupational hazard of mine! But Brandon does have a leg up, you know."

And with that, the Diva winked broadly and sashayed off.

Leigh watched her go, wondering as always how the Diva did it. She was in Chanel—vintage, couture Chanel—from head to toe, and dripping with pearls under three wigs she'd managed to stitch seamlessly together. Her four-inch Donald Pliner beaded shoes and handbag had been made custom for her, just for this occasion. How *did* she afford such fancy clothes? And how did she get them to fit? Vintage rarely fit modern women, much less modern men. And Brandon's body—when he appeared as Brandon—never seemed especially slim or effeminate. Like many things about her theatrical friend, it was shrouded in glamorous mystery.

An assistant calling her name shook Leigh out of her reverie.

"Mrs. White? We have some last-minute adjustments for the auction—would you like to come take a look?"

No rest for the weary! But it'd be over soon.

"Of course," Leigh said, smiling. "Let's go."

***

In the shopping section of the Miami Nightlight lounge, the guests were still mingling about, chattily checking out the silent auction items. Billie Parker stood at the bar, waiting for a cocktail, while Katie ostentatiously pretended to add her name to one of the bid sheets. The hot guy standing nearby looked like the type to go for a girl with money, and it was no secret Katie had a thing for the young hot ones.

"Katie, there you are!" Lorraine Manchester's voice rang out.

Katie whipped around and smiled conspiratorially at the Diva. The two had met at a party one night not long ago, and had slipped away from Billie to enjoy the available young men and party favors that paved the streets of Miami. If Katie had known just how well connected the Diva was, she would no doubt have made a nuisance of herself; but as it was, she only knew Lorraine Manchester as a local drag queen, so the two had been able to have a pretty good time together.

"Hello there," said Katie, trying to sound cool. "What are you doing here?"

"I'm on the charity committee, darling," purred Lorraine. "Didn't you know? I'm in with the top brass, babe, and I hope you're bidding on everything. If you're not, I can give you a lesson or two on how to spend Billie's money—but I have a feeling you're doing just fine in that department."

"You're so evil!" smiled Katie. "That's what I love about you."

"It would be," said the Diva. "Where's that hubby of yours?"

Katie noticed that Billie was no longer at the bar, but she couldn't see where he'd wandered. "He's probably just gone outside for a smoke," she said.

"Well, that's convenient for you," said the Diva. "We getting into any trouble tonight? There's always an after-party."

"I think tonight is going to have to be strictly business," Katie sighed. "I have an image to build up, you know—and a lot of the right people are here."

"Cagey Katie, always scheming! Don't think I don't know when you have something up your sleeve, darling. And—oh, but I *must* run for now, darling; if they're dimming the lights, there's something I'm supposed to be doing soon. Bye for now, Miss Katie!"

The lights were indeed dimming quickly as the two parted, and the crowd drew in their breath all at once. Something was beginning.

A beautiful voice emerged from the darkness and a surprise guest star, Plácido Domingo, stepped into the light. As he wound masterfully through "Neesun Dorma" from Puccini's *Turandot*, spotlights slowly came on, revealing pairs of Cirque du Soleil acrobats performing a synchronized dance in front of each of the six sets of closed doors that led into the Grand Ballroom. The song crescendoed hypnotically as the crowd stood spellbound.

As the music came to its dramatic end, the acrobats threw open all twelve of the ballroom doors at once and vanished through them. A collective gasp ran through the crowd.

On the other side of the doors lay the most beautiful, enchanting room of twinkling lights, exotic blooms and sparkling gold any of them had ever seen. Dining tables lay ready throughout the huge room, set for a lavish supper. It was miraculous, unreal-seeming. It was Hollywood in the Thirties, with nothing missing but Fred Astaire.

Watching from the ballroom as her elated guests poured through the doors, Leigh Anatole White blinked back tears of happiness. She had worked so hard for this night, and it had paid off; she had pulled off another "Ah-ha!" moment, in a city that expected one or two a day. It was her job to think of everything, to have everything under control—but it still always surprised her when things came off as planned.

Yet there were bigger surprises in store for Leigh White; and as the rich and famous and beautiful streamed from table to table, searching for their own names among the place settings, nobody— least of all herself—could have foreseen the disaster brewing.

CHAPTER 2

BLACK AND WHITE IN HEWITT, TEXAS

> Can you let me know who to contact?
> I have a young kid –troubled, at risk –
> needs guidance before he ends up in jail.

—Sharey

At 4:30 in the morning, Leigh got into the limo and sank down for the ride home. Brad followed her in, exhausted and dazed from the long hours of schmoozing, handshaking, smiling and drinking. At events like that you already felt drunk just being there, and most of the conversation had driven him to top off. Plus he'd been too busy to get anything more substantial in his stomach. As he would later joke, it was the most expensive dinner he'd ever ordered, and he'd not gotten to take one bite.

But he was as proud as he could be of his wife. The Charity Ball had been an outrageous success, surpassing the previous year's event in both starpower and money raised. Leigh had worked her magic once again on the stage of the Grand Ballroom; and the schoolkids would have a robust operations budget for next year, as well as a nice chunk of change for the endowment.

Leigh sank even deeper into the limousine's soft leather seats, put one Christian Louboutin six-inch-heeled black pump against the other and used her toe to pull them off. She was beat, but content. It had been immensely hard work producing an event of the Charity Ball's caliber, but her satisfaction at being able to help those troubled kids was difficult to put into words. It reached to the depths of meaning in her; to places in her past and experiences in her upbringing that few would have guessed lay behind the powerful fundraiser and socialite they thought they knew. Given all that had gone into transforming Leigh into the woman she was now, it was hardly surprising that she could transform a bland hotel hallway into a Miami nightclub, or build up the Charity Ball from nothing as she had; but that was a story that few had heard, or would believe if they had.

***

Leigh Anatole was born without fanfare in the small town of Hewitt, Texas, to a Cherokee Indian father and a mother rumored to be a descendent of the Union general William Tecumseh Sherman. This last rumor was never quite confirmed within the family, because no one boasted of it in public—not in the South, anyway.

Hewitt was a one-horse town, of a population probably fewer than 5,000, counting the grandchildren that came to visit. It was also a pretty uniformly conservative, Southern Baptist community, where the biggest event in town was the potluck lunch that followed church on Sundays. Every woman in town spent days pondering whether to bring Frito pie, King Ranch Casserole or cornbread muffins as their "covered dish"; Leigh's grandmother always brought a Texas-sized bowl of fresh fruit salad sprinkled with pecans and shredded coconut, a pan of her country fried okra with stewed tomatoes, and enough gossip to satisfy anyone looking for it.

No one ever left a Sunday potluck without a full belly and a headful of the local news. In the summers, when it was over a hundred and the air didn't move, ladies brought their hand fans, wore their biggest-brimmed straw hats and, once they sat, went immobile themselves. The heat would be so intense, cream lines would appear on the faces of some of the women where their make-up separated and caked, transforming their prim and pious Sunday faces into jigsaw grotesques. But no one cared. This was *the* place to be on Sunday afternoons in Hewitt; and even if you hadn't found Jesus, you pretended you had in order to fit in there. Only sinners stayed home.

Her early upbringing taught Leigh the golden rule, and she lived by it. She was closer to her grandmother Annie than to her mother, and in the eyes of the former, she could do no wrong. "My baby Leigh is special," her grandmother would repeat daily; and whenever Leigh was around, she would beam and praise her, calling her things like "brilliant," "beautiful," and "absolutely perfect." For many children such soaring praises prove a burden impossible to live up to; but for Leigh, they rang through her heart and kept her steady and strong.

Leigh's brother, on the other hand, earned no praise from Grandma Annie. He got the exact opposite. How much this was the cause, and how much the result of his behavior, it was difficult to say; but one thing was certain: Gerald Anatole was more than a handful, almost from the beginning.

Gerald was tall, with a medium build and thick, light brown hair with natural blonde highlights. He was clean-cut and manicured, always dressed in jeans with rolled-up cuffs and white T-shirts; and naturally charming, with a James Dean look and an edgy James Dean reputation to match. Yet in those days, as still in places, the charm that dripped from Southern men could often turn to violence in a flash—perhaps a curse inherited from their long history battling heat, bugs, Indians, Yankees, booze, boredom and women—and Gerald was every bit this sort of Southern gentleman.

For him, the Golden Rule was that he should treat everyone the way *he* thought they should be treated. His sense of right and wrong was not black and white, but grey—and grey in many shades. He could be the sweetest person one minute, and the next he would be found fighting and rolling drunks for cigarettes as they lay passed out in the street. One day he'd bring his grandmother flowers; the next, he'd steal a chain out of her jewelry box to hock at the local pawnshop. The money he got from such callous endeavors, he'd spend on beer and diapers for his ne'er-do-well friends and the stray kids and petty criminals he hung around with. On Sundays, while Leigh sang in the church choir, Gerald would roar across town to the other side of the tracks, to the seedy section of town that Grandma Annie always warned Leigh away from—the home of poor trailer trash, men who never left their corner, pot-smoking teenagers and families who lived by their wits to make ends meet in cockroach-infested shacks.

Gerald and Leigh's parents had divorced when they were young children; and Gerald had taken it especially hard, growing accustomed to rage and despair as regular emotional occurrences. Their mother worked long hours, and usually came home tired and irritable. She would take this out on Gerald, often quizzing him relentlessly as though he were on the stand for a crime. Being older, Leigh stepped up as surrogate parent; and feeling the tension and instability of life at home with Mom, she tried to keep the two of them out of their house as often as possible.

Grandma Annie's house, a few blocks away, became their refuge. This house was a home; it was clean and calm, and the meals—roast beef and potatoes, meatloaf, gelatin molds with suspended orange slices, baked beans, stuffed cabbage rolls—came regularly. Yet its peaceful environment only encouraged the growing dichotomy between the two siblings. Here, Gerald had the quiet to work on his schemes, and Leigh became accustomed to lying for him. She hated doing this, but he was her baby brother, and the love she felt for him was unbreakable. She spent hours trying to convince him not to venture back over the tracks. When none of it worked, she decided she needed to try another tactic. She'd led a sheltered life with their grandmother, and it never occurred to her that following Gerald to the bad side of town would change her life forever. She only hoped he might get in less trouble with her around. But what she saw that day introduced her to another world, and showed her things she would never forget.

She saw families living in tarpaper shacks and dilapidated dirty sheds, where not even a riding mower should have been kept. She saw children living alone, their parents dead or in jail for God knows what, in abandoned houses that seemed no more than piles of two-by-fours. She saw the same children hustling for change on the street, or hanging around in doorways with expressions at once pleading and hostile. Gerald told her the older ones sometimes sold themselves. After all, he said, people had to eat.

Teenage girls, some of them with babies, met her eye with a thousand-yard stare usually found on the faces of traumatized soldiers. Prenatal care was unheard-of here; these babies were often born on car seats and kitchen tables, with nary an adult—much less a doctor—around to help. Inside the falling-down shacks lining the road where they stood, Gerald told her, the conditions were truly unbearable. Roaches flooded the kitchens. Children awoke covered in bug bites and even rat bites, which festered into raging infections. Bedbugs, scabies and lice were ever-present. Families lived there, three and four to a bedroom, many without heat in the winter or air conditioning in the summer. Babies sat in soiled diapers for days, screaming. Many of the dads who were still around were drunks, drug addicts, or teenagers themselves.

Leigh realized then and there that life wasn't fair. She knew she deserved no more than the poor kids on the wrong side of the tracks; life had simply placed her in one set of circumstances, and them in another. And somehow, deep inside, this was where her brother—still a child himself—felt he belonged. It broke her heart, but she didn't know what to do, short of getting herself and Gerald out of Hewitt altogether.

Not long after this, Gerald was caught hanging out with a friend who had shoplifted some beer. Gerald was innocent of the crime—for a change—but when the cops interrogated them, the friend blamed him. This accusation landed Gerald, still a minor, in a juvenile-delinquent detention center, where "rehabilitation" was the term for an intensive instructional program in theft, violence and con artistry. The entire center was, in point of fact, a school for crime; and Leigh was shocked at the stories Gerald shared in his letters. An eleven-year-old stabbed a seventeen-year-old for his high-tops. Another boy died in a puddle of his own vomit, with guards and fellow inmates standing by. It was an outrage to Leigh; what should have been an opportunity for the detainees was instead an advanced education in crime.

Leigh was terrified for her brother's safety, but in a way his incarceration liberated her to follow her own path. Hewitt has since come up in the world—even to the point of being ranked #44 by *Money Magazine* in their "Top 100 Places to Live"—but in those days, Leigh knew it was a town to escape from, and determined to find a way out at any cost. During the time her brother was away, she worked hard at her singing, dancing and piano lessons, and soon landed a scholarship to the University of Texas at Austin—a liberal, creative oasis in the middle of a tough state full of tumbleweeds and

Republicans—and a summer job teaching dance lessons at the city's popular Arthur Murray Dance Studios. She left town the day after her high-school graduation, with two hundred dollars in cash and everything she owned packed in a ten-year-old two-door sports car given to her by her grandparents.

For Leigh, college was more than an escape plan; it was a chance to have a new life, to reinvent herself. Yet her first "summer job" in Austin would prove just as crucial, and occupy her throughout college and beyond.

Even then, Arthur Murray Dance Studios were known throughout the country. They were *the* place for well-to-do young men and women to learn how to ballroom dance, and lessons weren't cheap. Aside from the teenage children of the wealthy, most of the other students there were rich housewives who enjoyed the attention of the boy toys who comprised a good number of Leigh's teaching colleagues. Many of these were gay and funny, and aside from widening Leigh's small-town perspective, they proved friends she'd keep for life.

Straight men, too, came to dance with the beautiful female instructors, and Leigh quickly became one of the most popular among them. Most of them were socially awkward young men who wanted to use dance as a way to transform themselves socially and gain the confidence to pick up women. They couldn't tell their left foot from their right, but had ample money for lessons and were eager to please a pretty instructor. In Leigh's mind, these were the best students. Any progress they made was a reason to add more classes—which meant more sales. It seemed the more her students danced with her, the more they wanted to dance with her. Every one of them felt he was Leigh's favorite—she had that way about her.

At her new job, Leigh shook off the small town dust in a hurry. She was sharp, and caught on fast to the ways of business. After three days of working for a few bucks an hour teaching students who paid hundreds of dollars for her lessons, she negotiated a larger hourly wage and commission on her sales. It was her first taste of self-reliance in business. Glorying in it, she vowed never to be financially dependent on anyone else ever again.

Still, she made it her mission to help those she could, including Gerald, their mother, their grandparents, and even Gerald's friends on the streets. When her grandmother's second husband abruptly passed away, Leigh worked three jobs and sent money home. Along with the money, she always included instructions to take care of Gerald; she wanted in particular to ensure he graduated high school.

Leigh never took time off, and spent her holidays working. During her spring break, she would work as a cocktail waitress or take on extra hours at Arthur Murray. With all this going on, Leigh had little time for play in her life, but was happier than ever. Her grades were good, she was saving money, and she had men at school and work constantly trying to win her over. Aside from her increasing beauty, she had a maturity that set her aside from most college girls and made men see her from the beginning as a prospective girlfriend or wife.

She saw most of them, however, as her next paying dance lesson. She had no idea how attractive she was becoming, and thought little of the fabulous gifts she received from her dance students. Unbeknownst to her, the studio was awash in affairs and "friends with benefits" arrangements, and to many of her students she was the highest prize worth pursuing. Yet she was completely blind to all of it. She never took any of her would-be suitors seriously, or spent any time with them outside of work. She appreciated their gifts, and wondered if all men were always so generous, but could hardly conceive why they were giving them to her, beyond the fact that they liked her, and were thankful for the extra dance lessons and the confidence she gave them. Every once in a while, one of them would look a little too deeply into her eyes, or overenthusiastically grind against her pelvis; but she always chalked it up to a love of dancing or two left feet.

Yet her complete obliviousness to their overtures, and to her own beauty, only made Leigh more attractive. It dawned on her from time to time that others thought her attractive; but she never ceased to see herself as ordinary, or to value her accomplishments and independence over others' superficial compliments. Beauty was fine, she often thought, but it didn't put food on the table. "Pretty is as pretty does," her grandmother had always taught her; and the lesson stuck.

After four years of intense study and work, a deeper, more self-assured Leigh moved to New York City. There she rented a small apartment, and with recommendations from the Austin studio, landed a job with Arthur Murray Studios in Manhattan. Within weeks of taking her new job, she was introduced, through one of her students, to a man in the jewelry business who took her on as a sales assistant.

Leigh had a passion for jewelry, and learned the business quickly. She met wealthy clients, mingled with jet-setters, traveled the globe. She flew to Paris first-class, stayed at the Plaza Athenée, and ate at La Stella, Maceo and Septime. Throughout it all she never spent a dime of her own money—there was always a man there to pick up the check.

While selling jewelry night and day and weekends, one of her best clients, a well-known chemist, suggested she try a line of skincare and cosmetics he had developed. If she liked them, he said, she could sell it to her jewelry customers. She agreed; and several months later, he'd developed four skincare products and a lipstick line for her. Leigh was overjoyed. She vowed to sell, sell, sell—and she did exactly that, paying him back his investment in half the time expected.

Leigh continued to sell her jewelry and beauty products, auditioning for QVC outside Philadelphia and becoming one of their star on-air sellers. The ingredients in her cosmetics were the best the world had to offer, and Leigh had an eye for color that women adored. In a matter of months, a big distributor offered her a worldwide distribution deal that would land her products in major department stores, including Harrods of London. She couldn't say no.

***

Miss Leigh had made the big time. She was at the top of her game, traveling a couple of hundred thousand miles a year, wearing beautiful clothes, and living a life of success and luxury.

Yet still she had no airs about her success; she assumed it was all simply a natural result of hard work. She also understood that it came with great responsibility. As a businesswoman, she made sure to keep abreast of current affairs and the stock market, politics and social issues; and she soon became a news junkie, hooked on CNN and MSNBC. Despite her toughness as a businesswoman, she also kept a huge place in her heart for the kind of people she'd met with Gerald back home, on the wrong side of town.

Intrigued by an invitation to an ACLU dinner, Leigh did a bit of research and discovered the keynote speaker was an unknown lawyer talking about civil rights, human rights and the unfairness of the criminal justice system. Remembering what had happened to her brother so many years ago, she felt stirred to go.

The speaker, an attorney named Brad White, was electrifying. Leigh hung on every word. She'd never heard anyone speak so eloquently about the lost people of the world. Everything he said seemed to resonate with her own experience and ideals. When he spoke about how "you can get just about as much justice as you can afford" in America, Leigh recalled all of her brother's friends who'd been in and out of juvenile detention centers and jails because they'd had no parents, no guidance and no money. The government had let them down, and others had been too busy with their own affairs—or just too busy trying to survive—to make any real difference.

After the dinner, she walked right up to Brad, introduced herself and started in on all that was wrong with the system. The attorney was noticeably taken aback. He'd been a lawyer for twenty years, and took these evenings in stride as part of his work. Most of the guests were simply dressed-up social butterflies with their own superficial agendas, and he rarely socialized with them. But there was something about this woman. As the guests were leaving, he asked her to join him at the bar for a drink. He ordered vodka and she ordered Scotch—Macallan 25, at sixty-five dollars a shot—and they settled in.

When the bartender kicked them out at 2 a.m., they exchanged numbers and email addresses, and said their goodnights. Leigh drove home, energized by their discussion and listening to CNN the whole way. The presidential debates were a few weeks away, and Leigh was obsessed. She was thinking fearfully about what was at stake in the upcoming election as she walked into her apartment—where she was surprised to find a message from Brad waiting on her computer, inviting her to lunch tomorrow. Without a second thought, Leigh emailed him back. Lunch—of course—the Ritz, one o'clock. When Brad got her reply (he would later tell her), he laughed to himself in excitement. Finally, a woman who was used to calling the shots!

The next day, Leigh showed up for lunch dressed like a fashion model who'd turned the wrong way down the catwalk and ended up at the Ritz. She never dressed to impress anyone but herself, but something in this man made her want to. He was different from the men she was used to meeting in the style business, fashion-plate types so flashy and self-involved they no longer saw the real world beyond their reflections. High-end jewelry buyers, fashion mavens and marketing professionals usually had a fairly developed sense of style about them, and a swagger to match. They often had stylists, and always wore designer clothes. They understood dermabrasion and the science of collagen well; they got manicures regularly, and—when they had to be poolside—pedicures as well.

Brad, on the other hand, wasn't quite Madison Avenue or quite Wall Street. He didn't have perfect style, by a long shot—he showed up for lunch in a tie with a fish design on it—but he had potential. When Brad talked, the world stopped. From the moment they sat down, Leigh knew: meeting Brad White would be the real "before-and-after" moment of her life. Again the conversation was dynamite—so much so that neither of them touched their food—and they'd scheduled another date long before they parted company.

After a few dates, Leigh and Brad quickly became inseparable. Whenever Brad talked, Leigh Anatole—known for her non-stop energy—stopped and listened; and despite his nerves of steel in the courtroom, Brad White's heart raced every time Leigh walked into a room. They espoused the same charities, took up the same causes. They'd slip away and lock themselves in the bathroom at parties, oblivious to the long line forming outside, and only emerge after a good interval, their faces flushed and that bottom-of-the-sea sex smell floating behind them like Chanel No. 5. It was as if the two had been one all along.

A year later, Brad and Leigh were married. Brad had chased her, but it was Leigh that caught him. Their marriage was based on love, but the union was almost like a corporation, with each possessing talents that complemented the other's perfectly. With his brilliance and her entrepreneurial talent, he became one of the top lawyers in the country, and Leigh sold her business to raise the twin boys that came along soon after. They bought a beautiful home together in

Miami, and worked hard to make it a happy place for their sons, their friends and their love.

Leigh threw herself into her adopted city, and its life became her own. It was said that if she'd continued to devote the energy and determination to capitalism that she had turned to charitable causes, she'd be a Fortune 500 CEO; but her heart was elsewhere, and she had to follow it.

Her brother drifted in and out of her life. Over the last few years they'd lost contact, and finding herself unable to keep the connection alive on her own, she'd found a new outlet for her protective feelings in her growing charity work. Yet the charity brought her into contact with more than just people in need. As she ventured deeper into the community, fundraising for local initiatives and building her dream of a school for at-risk youth, she met hundreds of new people: doctors and lawyers, jewelers and art dealers, realtors, surgeons, bored wives and excited mistresses. There were so many different ways of life here, so many ideas of happiness and meaning; and Leigh reserved her own judgment and worked with them all. She tried to understand everyone she came in contact with, to learn their histories and their motivations, and help them where she could. It was the kind of selflessness that had always worked for her, and her Charity Ball had been a testament to its continued success.

Now, some nights—such as tonight, exhausted as she was—even Leigh herself would lie awake, and wonder just how she had made it so far. She had a wonderful husband who loved her, a track record in business to rival any CEO's that would keep her financially independent for life, two perfect sons, and a wardrobe fit for a queen. She pinched herself constantly to be sure it was real—as one found oneself doing so often in this strange town. She'd grown used to the city's rhythms of gossip and secrecy, truth and falsehood; and her mastery of them had brought her to a place she'd never imagined for herself. Yet she was far from done; her retirement from the Charity Ball would only mark the beginning of her next chapter. What adventure would life bring her next?

Filled with all the quiet excitement of that question, she sank into contented sleep.

CHAPTER 3
THE DOG OF THE HAIR THAT BIT HER

Meet me at the Yacht Club at noon.
No hats! Can't wait to hear your gossip…

—Leigh

"**W**e have to meet for lunch!" a familiar voice screamed out of the phone, the morning after the gala. "You'll never guess who's leavin' town to adopt a foreign baby! That girl thinks she's Angelina; but Gawd, Billie ain't no Brad Pitt—!"

Leigh was intrigued by gossip—though she never had much time for it—and was addicted to Dixie's stories in particular. That woman always had the best dirt! It had made a sort of post-gala tradition for them over the last couple of years to get together and swap secrets. Not that they didn't do that often enough; but the gala always gave them a burst of fresh material. Plus, the morning afterward Leigh could actually take the time to enjoy it, and let the stress seep out of her along with the previous night's champagne.

Still, Leigh knew not to invite Dixie to her home for these little sessions, as far as that would be from prying ears. Dixie's enthusiasm far outweighed her tact, and with even the smallest scrap of gossip to pore over, she would never fail to overstay her welcome. So Leigh arranged for them to meet at the restaurant at the Yacht Club, a regular hideaway whose beautiful dining room overlooked Biscayne Bay. Every table had a view of the turquoise bay, where dolphins flashed in and out of view and multimillion-dollar boats stretched as far as the eye could see; and Leigh loved the Lenox china, Baccarat wine glasses, and Cristofle silver that the white-gloved serving staff flourished there. But more important than these little touches was the place's exclusivity, which turned off most eavesdroppers. Non-members were allowed in Tuesdays through Fridays, but few took advantage of the fact, which usually made the restaurant a great place for her and her friends to dish dirt. The Bal Harbour shopping crowds could be avoided here; as could the Bal Harbour waiters, whom everyone in Miami knew were insatiable gossips. It was widely suspected that many of them sold the secrets they overheard at work to the tabloids, and Leigh couldn't have any of that. Sure, gossip was for sharing—but not with just anyone.

"There's my freeeeend!" Dixie yelled as Leigh came in. *So much for the day-after detox,* Leigh thought. From the way she stood up, it was obvious Dixie had already had several cocktails today. It was surprisingly busy in the restaurant this afternoon, too, Leigh noticed with a jolt of disappointment; she'd have to try to rein Dixie in a bit.

"Hellloooo, Leigh," she slurred, trying to air-kiss Leigh before she sat down.

"Sorry I'm late," Leigh said nonchalantly. "Traffic over the causeway was bumper-to-bumper. I didn't notice anyone gnawing on anyone else's flesh, though." The two women laughed at the memory of the Miami Cannibal, the city's most inexplicable criminal.

"Have some wine," Dixie ordered cheerily, as she poured a healthy serving of Chardonnay into Leigh's glass. "I have *much* to tell."

"Dixie, how long have you been here? Did you start drinking at home?" Leigh asked softly, looking around the packed dining room.

"Never mind that, honey!" Dixie looked at Leigh and leaned in closer to whisper. "Katie Parker has a *whole* plan! She's anglin' to become more famous than her husband and dump him, and she's got a game goin' to generate publicity for herself. A *bay-bee!* Ah tell ya, that bimbo is *way* slicker than Billie Parker ever imagined. She's gonna tell everyone she's going on a cruise, and she's comin' home with a *bay-bee!* A cute li'l thing she saved from a life on the streets, you know." Dixie snorted loudly, dug her finger into her armpit and adjusted her bra, a habit she repeated unconsciously no matter where she was or who was looking. "A real Mother Theresa, that Katie!"

"My God," Leigh said. "Does Billie know?"

"Of *koorse* not. Ah heard it from Howard."

"Katie goes to him too?"

"Oh, no—but she must've told *someone* who does. And it's a damn shame; while she's layin' plans to rack up publicity 'saving a child,' her poor husband's in *mah* husband's office, spillin' his guts about how anxious he is to get rid of that new gold-digging, social-climbing wife of his. She's gonna look like a saint, saving babies! He'll never be able to leave her; the press would be too much." Dixie shook her head profoundly and took a deep pull of her Chardonnay. "Who said this here stuff was buttery?" she wondered into the air.

"That really is too bad—but hang on a minute, Dixie." Leigh looked around the club and leaned in closer. "How exactly do you know what he said to your husband? Surely Howard didn't *tell* you—?"

"Of *koorse* not!" Dixie laughed again. "He's far too perfessional fer that."

"How, then?"

Dixie leaned in conspiratorially over her wine. "Well, sweets, Ah just listen to his tapes every once and again."

"What?" Leigh choked. "You can't do that, Dixie!"

"Sure I can. And I do."

"He records all of his sessions?" Leigh asked.

"A lot of 'em," Dixie smiled.

"But that means—"

"Yup, it sure do," Dixie said proudly. Her voice dropped. "Ah know everything about *everybody*, dear."

"Ladies? My name is Charles," began the waiter, who had appeared as if by magic.

"We're—er—not quite ready, Charles, thank you," Leigh tried to reply calmly, though the waiter had visibly startled her. She smiled broadly as he walked away, suddenly suspecting Charles the waiter might be one of those eavesdropping Bal Harbour types, and struggling to maintain her composure. Listening to patient tapes—! Leigh had grown to love Dixie's stories about her husband's famous patients, but had never asked her where they'd come from; she'd always assumed the good doctor just let a colorful detail loose once in a while, after one drink too many. Now that Dixie had told her, the guilty pleasure suddenly looked a good deal guiltier. This wasn't gossip—this was reporting! And the trouble Dixie might get herself and Howard into for spreading such confidential information from such high-profile clients—! A lot of celebrities didn't have much reason to back down from civil suits like that, and if enough of them got together on it, Howard would be finished.

"Dixie, I hope for your sake you aren't telling too many people about this kind of stuff," Leigh said, when the waiter had gone.

"No, no, darlin', only you—so far!" Dixie laughed, raising her glass. Relieved, Leigh clinked glasses with her.

"Does Howard know?" Leigh asked.

"Oh, noooo, no, no," Dixie said. "He'd have to notice *me* to notice what I was doin'!" And she let out a big belly laugh.

"But Dixie, he'll divorce you!" Leigh said, laughing too in spite of herself.

"Only if he finds out, darlin'!" Dixie whispered, and they both cracked up.

"We'd better hurry up and order," said Leigh, "so we can gab without the big ears of the waiters." She'd noticed their waiter hovering around, cringing in concentration whenever Dixie spoke up. Privacy, nothing; it was like a spy movie in here! They might as well have gone to Bal Harbour after all.

"Let's just order the special," Dixie said. "We probably won't eat it anyway. I can never eat when I'm dishin'."

"Or drinking! Wouldn't want to kill that buzz," Leigh said.

"To the buzz!" Dixie shouted, and they touched glasses again, belly laughing loudly now.

"As long as Ah have mah wine to keep me company, I'll be fine," Dixie said sincerely, as she threw her arm in the air and waved the waiter over. *She really shouldn't wear sleeveless dresses,* Leigh thought.

"Ladies? Are we ready to order?" said Charles the waiter deferentially, and they ordered. When he'd gone again, they leaned back in.

"Leigh, the Katie and Billie thing is right out of a Jackie Collins novel. Gawd, I love the way that woman writes," Dixie chuckled, and took another sip before going on. "Anyway, not only is Katie plannin' to forge a marriage that so-and-so couldn't escape from— what's that magician's name? Houdunit?—anyhow—*but* Ah hear she wants to take over Billie's clothing empire, too! Can you believe it, that woman wants to host her own television show and be in the magazeeenes! That's her plan, but I can't see it working, especially because—"

"Oh my God, what a *surprise!* Is that Leigh?" came a loud voice, and the two women turned abruptly to see Lauren Altamira walking across the restaurant towards their table.

Leigh and Dixie froze, speechless. Leigh felt like she'd just been busted. What were the chances of Lauren showing up at the Yacht Club during their lunch—and in the middle of such a juicy piece of gossip, too? Well, one thing was for sure: it had to stop here. Leigh knew they couldn't talk about the Doc's clients in front of Lauren. She'd never been much of one for keeping secrets, and she knew almost as many Miami power players as the two of them did.

As usual, Lauren was dressed to kill. She had on a Valentino suit, a Van Cleef classic Alhambra chain of clover leaves and diamonds, and 4-inch Brian Atwood platform pumps, and was carrying an Hermès Red Kelly Croc bag. Remembering her manners, Leigh stood up to hug her friend.

"Lauren, what a wonderful surprise! Do you two know each other? Dixie, this is my dear friend Lauren—Lauren, my friend Dixie. I can't believe I didn't introduce you last night!"

Dixie, who seemed a bit unhappy with the uninvited guest, shook her hand and said a limp "hell-low."

No helping it, Leigh thought. "Now, Lauren, sit, and tell me how you tracked us down."

As Lauren stood by the table, a waiter whispered up behind her and slid a chair against the backs of her legs.

"Oh, I just happened to—" Lauren started, then stopped herself with a laugh. "Okay, okay. I bribed your cook with coupons for a spa day at the Biltmore," she confessed. "I was desperate! You weren't answering your cell, and I needed to talk to you." Lauren shrugged her shoulders and grinned. "Then I was going to wait and do some shopping in the meantime, but—ugh, those Bal Harbour bitches in their haute couture and hats! You can't walk into a boutique in the afternoon without running into a hundred of them in there, taking up all the air."

"Amen, sister," Dixie laughed in surprise. "Ah think Ah'm gonna like this one, Leigh. Do you need a drink, Lauren?"

"Absolutely."

"Amen again! Hey, Charles in Charge," Dixie cried to the waiter, "more Chardonnay!" And the three women settled in.

"So what's eating you, Lauren?" Leigh asked, once they'd had a chance to clink glasses again.

"It's just—last night was the *worst!*" Lauren spat out.

Leigh looked like she'd been slapped. Lauren backtracked.

"Oh no, no, Leigh—I didn't mean it that way. The *party* was superb!" Lauren rubbed the top of Leigh's hand conciliatorily for a moment, before gripping it with an almost painful intensity. "But there's a thief in our midst," she hissed, "and it's that bitch Sassy! Excuse me a moment."

In the stunned silence following her outburst, Lauren calmly passed her wine to Dixie and called Charles back to the table to order an extra-dry Beefeater martini with three olives. *So it's reached that point*, Leigh thought. Lauren only drank hard like this when she was really agitated; but at such times, she seemed to run on the stuff. It was a good thing she preferred the garnish she did; those olives were probably the only nutrition she'd get all day.

While the drink was being prepared and served, the three of them sat quietly—a rare and not altogether comfortable occurrence. Once Charles had vanished, though, Lauren didn't wait to pick up where she'd left off.

"Sassy Davilon, my dears, is a vulture. She never met a client she wouldn't wrap those collagen-inflated, dick-sucking lips around, especially if it closed a deal. But she isn't just a whore, she's a predator—a stalker! She shows up everywhere I am, and steals my clients right out from under my nose. She posts all kinds of messages on my Facebook page, and then, when I try to keep it professional and civil, I end up looking like a loser, and she looks like the hot bitch at the party. Everyone thinks she's so cute and risqué—but it's no laughing matter when she steals a client ready to close on a 6.5 condo, is it? She stole the client and the deal! And what about Jacques? The man's brand-new in town. Last time I looked, he was *my* client, and things were looking great. Then suddenly, BOOM! he's on Sassy's arm and 'they're in love.'" Lauren said this last bit looking like she'd just taken a deep whiff of Limburger. "No wonder he can't be bothered to return my calls—and we practically had a contract!"

"That's frustrating, agreed," Leigh said, "but don't you think you're letting this get to you a little too much? Nobody thinks you're a loser, and from the looks of you"—she gestured to Lauren's impeccable outfit—"you're hardly suffering for clients."

"It's the principle of the thing," sniffed Lauren, tugging self-consciously at her diamond chain. "She's hasn't been here too long, but she ought to know better. Professionally speaking, it just isn't done."

"Well, it sounds to *me* like there may be something deeper than the job at stake here," Leigh suggested gently.

"What do you mean?"

"I mean, it's just been under your skin so badly lately—is everything okay with Francisco? You did say something at the gala about that."

"Ugh, that's another story," said Lauren.

"What's going on?"

"I don't know, really; it's weird. It's not exactly that he's distant. It's more like I don't see him much, and when I do, he's sort of—different."

"Different how?"

"Ummm…performative, maybe? Like he's really aware of himself while he's doing things."

At this, Dixie perked up.

"While he's doin' what *sort* of things?" she asked with a mischievous grin.

There was a beat. Lauren was obviously flustered. Dixie, ever the kind-hearted soul, backtracked.

"Oh, don't worry about it, honey, Ah know it ain't my business. Ah'm sorry to pry! But hell, if your man Francis is actin' performative *there*, Ah could certainly think of worse problems. At least he's still performin'!" She took a deep swig of her Chardonnay and smiled. "*Mah* husband practically hasn't touched me since mah last birthday!"

Lauren was stunned. *Welcome to Dixie Johnson,* thought Leigh.

"Lately, all he does is work," continued Dixie, looking earnestly at her new friend as if she might have an answer for her. "He comes home late, goes straight to his study, and when he knows Ah'm asleep, he gets into bed." Lauren shifted uncomfortably in her chair.

Leigh broke the silence. "Now, Dixie! You're not giving the whole picture here. Howard dotes on your every word, and does everything he can to make you happy."

"Ah know, Ah know!" Dixie slurred loudly. "But Ah'm alone every night, and bo-ored. Ah got nothing to do but drink and shop online! Well, and a couple of other things." She winked at Leigh and toyed with her glass. "I do love that UPS boy! He brings me stuff Ah don't remember buying—it's such a lovely surprise when it arrives." She stared into space, smiling.

Taking the chance to change the subject, Lauren turned back to Leigh.

"In any case, Leigh, you've got to help me with this Sassy bitch. I know you know her—better than the rest of us do, anyway! Where does she get her clients? How does she always manage to take mine? Is it really just that she's seducing them, or could there be something else going on there? I know you think I'm paranoid, but she really seems like she's gunning for me."

"Okay, okay, stay cool, Lauren," said Leigh. "I'll look into it a bit and see if her connections are really credible, or if she's just a babe on the prowl."

"Bitch in heat, you mean," Lauren blurted. Dixie laughed uproariously.

Leigh's phone was vibrating on the table. *Saved by the bell,* she thought, looking at the text. "Sorry, but I'm going to have to go, ladies. I told the Board I'd meet with them if they had time today, and they've just texted—they need to know how much money we raised last night, and I need to give them my news."

"Your news—?" asked Lauren.

"That this was my last fundraiser," said Leigh nonchalantly. "I'm done!"

"No!" both other women shouted at once.

"Yes," Leigh countered.

"Are yew sure?" asked Dixie, crestfallen.

"Absolutely."

"Wow, that really is news," said Lauren. "And too bad! But it makes sense. You had a really great event last night—it'll be good for you to go out on top." She called for the check and laid her black American Express card on the table. "I ought to be going too; after all, I invited myself!" She laughed. "It was lovely meeting you, Dixie."

"Yes, lovely," Dixie slurred, drifting back from Leigh's bombshell into her spectacular buzz once more.

"Dixie," said Leigh significantly, as Lauren was signing, "we'll have to get together another time soon. I'm sure you have a thing or two more to tell me! But I'm so glad you got to meet this one, who I blab about so much. I'm sure you two are going to love each other."

"Don't yew know it!" Dixie drawled agreeably, and the three women walked together to the restaurant door.

CHAPTER 4

DOUBLE D AT THE HOWARD JOHNSON'S

> That Lauren is really somethin' huh?
> Call me.

—Dixie

Dixie wasn't satisfied with her and Leigh's little lunch rendezvous. They'd hardly gotten to dish at all, and Lauren's entrance had thrown her for a loop. She liked Lauren, that was for sure; but she wasn't quite sure what to do with a woman of such a cool—what was the word? Demeaning? Demeander? Ah, Dixie couldn't remember.

Anyway, Lauren had a detachment about her that was alien to Dixie's warm sensibilities. She seemed able to dish, moan and swear with the rest of them, then wipe her mouth like royalty and walk away unperturbed. Opening up to someone like that never felt quite right afterward, especially when the wine wore off; and what she'd said to Lauren about her marriage came back to her now with a pang. She'd have to be a bit more cautious in the future.

And after all, Leigh was right—she'd made her marriage sound worse than it was. Howard was a wonderful man, and Dixie knew very well that she still loved him. But even though he'd been home in the evenings more often than usual lately, there was an absence lately, a dull ache where she wanted to feel loved. It seemed he had come to take their partnership for granted, and with all her exuberance, Dixie found herself at a loss with how to say it to him. It never seemed worth the pain it would surely cause him to hear it, so Dixie had put it off and put it off, and come to find a new excitement in keeping it to herself. There was nobility in secret-keeping, she felt, especially for one so unused to it, and for such a good cause; it felt good to know she bore the strain of their marriage alone.

Of course, there were some marital stresses that couldn't be borne alone; and that was where Danny came in.

As with many of the things he bought for his wife, Howard had hired the young chauffeur as a concession to one of her bad habits—in this case, drinking and driving. He knew there was nothing he could do to change her, even if he'd wanted to; and far preferred that she be kept safe in her vices than that she hurt herself pretending for his sake not to have them. And there was an element of guilt in it for him as well; if he could not be there himself to keep an eye on his wife, the least he could do was provide her with someone who could. But Danny was able to do more than drive Miss Dixie, as he had proven more than willing to demonstrate.

One afternoon, after a particularly indulgent dish-dealing lunch with Leigh, Dixie needed help getting into the house. Danny, ever the eager hand, was gentleman enough to bring her all the way to her bed; and finding her somewhat reluctant to stay put, applied a few tested methods of keeping her there. The lady of the house responded in perfect keeping with his attempts, and tipped him handsomely on top of it.

From that time forward, the faithful chauffeur's alliance was entirely with Dixie. Still a young man, he stood ready at a moment's notice, and didn't mind working overtime. Howard called him daily to check up on his wife, and it never seemed to occur to him when he came home that she'd ridden on more than the backseat of their Audi that afternoon.

***

Dixie's husband had trained at UCLA, one of the top schools for clinical psychiatry in the land. When he'd graduated, he'd logged thousands of hours of psychoanalysis with patients of all types, and managed to build up a patient base among Hollywood's top stars. It's said that the bigger the star, the larger the ego; and Howard found this applied to the superego, the id and all their problems as well. Unlike many other patients, however, most of his high-powered clients didn't seek quick fixes or cures. They wanted something rarer in the celebrity world: a trusted confidant with whom they could share secrets and fantasies that they wouldn't dare tell anyone else. Howard proved better even than that. In addition to his ability as a listener, he had a unique gift for making his patients feel it was okay to be the way they were—a trait practically impossible to find in their world. He soon became an indispensable part of many famous lives.

For a lower profile among the L.A. gossip hunters, Howard had always kept his offices at home. This was very much appreciated by his patients, but far more so by his wife, who had quickly found ways to listen in on his sessions. Dixie marveled to hear the famous voices through the walls as they shared their most intimate secrets and perversions. When Howard moved his practice to Miami and got an office away from home—anticipating a lighter workload and more time to enjoy the tropical climate and lots of golf with his wife—

Dixie had found herself disappointed in the beginning. Yet his reputation followed him, and even at triple the rates he'd charged in L.A., he soon had more work than ever. More importantly to Dixie, many of his patients followed him too, staying on as phone clients; and since the Doctor wasn't getting any younger, he made it a practice to record all of his sessions and listen to them again at home before he made his notes and prescribed medications.

During one of Dixie's long drunken rambles through their house, she had gone into Howard's office. She'd known at the time that she was breaking a sacred rule of their marriage—never snoop— but she wasn't exactly in her right mind, and it didn't exactly feel like a marriage. His session tapes were the first thing she'd looked for, and her excitement when she'd popped the first one in to listen to it was enough to drive all other thoughts from her mind.

Indeed, the thrill she felt listening to Howard's tapes was matched only by the thrill of telling Leigh about what she'd heard there. With this information she was a gossip goddess, a queen of the startling revelation. Obviously, the privilege came with its risks. For Howard to find out what she was doing was unthinkable. He'd cut her tongue out, or kill her, or even make her give up drinking— she was sure of it. She couldn't imagine the hugeness of the rage he'd feel if he knew she was listening to the tapes, much less telling Leigh about them. Listening to them was a sin; gossiping about their contents was a full-blown crime. But Dixie just couldn't stop herself.

Now, creeping into his office, she was fascinated all over again by the rows and rows of color-coded cassette boxes. She leaned in, squinted, read the name "BLACKBIRD" on one, and pulled it out. This was one she hadn't heard yet. Turning it over and over in her hands, she looked down and saw Howard's small recording machine on his deck. Having told herself the first time was just a one-time indulgence of her curiosity, she hesitated—but only for a moment.

To hell with all that sanctity of marriage crap, Dixie thought jubilantly as she popped in the tape. She put on her husband's earphones and punched Play.

A deep male Australian voice filled her ears. This Mr. Blackbird certainly sounded familiar, but she couldn't quite place where she recognized him from.

"I *can't* stop, mate," he was saying. "I can't. I just yell, 'Go Russ! Go Russ!' when I fock. Can't turn eet off! Sure, I'm pissed. Pissed outta me mind! Some burd told the press. Then another burd, and another. I couldn't *believe* that focking shit." He went on for a while, transitioning into a few self-congratulatory party stories and an excited rant about the sexiness of fat women. Howard's voice came on over the Australian's, intoning a Gregorian chant of psych-speak, in the midst of which Dixie could recognize a few well-worn phrases. "Repressed, childish sexuality… mother-worship… boundary difficulties… trouble sharing… compulsive… narcissistic self-aggrandizement through storytelling… quite a few unstated substance-abuse issues…"

Dixie smiled and changed the tape. In the next she recognized the voice of a local billionaire, renowned for his house full of glass-top furniture and stunning views. His voice was low, and got even lower as he described the sexual frenzy he felt when young girls would mess up his house, strip and squat on his furniture. Some would let him lie underneath the glass-topped coffee table for free. Others asked him for money. But all of them obliged him.

Again, Howard's baritone came in over his patient's voice. "Classic case of coprophilia…particularly interesting, though, because the typical coprophile most often likes to defecate on others. Here, not only does he choose to be defecated *upon*, but he has provided *completely* for his contradictory compulsion for cleanliness, and its adjoining germ phobias…quite unique, really."

Since Dixie didn't know what "coprophilia" or "defecation" meant, she was thinking about the low, rough Australian voice as she slipped her LELO Inez Gold Vibrator out of its purple presentation box. Dixie had ordered this 24-karat gold-plated bliss of a dildo, priced at $15,000, off a late-night cable television shopping channel. She'd vowed to herself to use it once and return it. But she just couldn't. The thing was a wonder: it held a two-hour charge and could provide the sexy sensations of hot or cold on command. "Pleasure dots," tiny gel-covered diamonds on its surface, worked like a charm on her. She came fast and hard every time.

Dixie found the tape of the Australian again, put it back in and hit Play, settling back into her husband's Aero chair. She pulled up her skirt and found the "glory hole" in her Spanx. That was what she and Danny called it when they played "Spanx Time"—one of her favorite pastimes with the chauffeur. Danny would lift her skirt and slide his finger through the girdle structure's slit, teasing her to almost unbearable excitement. Spanx were a spanking good time with the lights out! Holding the slit open, she slid the LELO in.

The pleasure dots tickled her all the way up, just like the French ticklers she'd used as a teenager. She turned the sleek machine to its lowest vibrating speed, moved the knob to the "warm" setting, leaned back and went into a zone. Her vagina tingled, the lips swollen and lush, as she worked the LELO back and forth. Even her Spanx scaffolding couldn't contain her. Too bad the good part of the Australian's session came to an end before she got off; soon it seemed all he wanted to talk about was his nanny growing up, and how soft and fat she'd been.

She leaned forward, vibrator pressed against her pubic bone, and swiveled the chair around again to her husband's tapes. Most of them were quick listens, but that was all right with her now. She listened to one on which a young, rich party girl bemoaned the large, fat penis of her new rapper boyfriend. She loved the hipness of having a black boyfriend on the red carpet, but that bazooka of a dick was gonna wreck her! He'd once tried to put his bazooka in her ass and, as she told the good Doctor in a raspy whisper, "There was no way *that* was happening."

Awk, Dixie thought. *No anal!* She selected another tape, and put it in the player. The dildo was beginning to chafe, but her vagina loved the edge of orgasm. She'd learned to keep herself there for a quarter of an hour, a Cirque du Soleil move for a woman her age.

She hit Play and an older male voice filled her ears. He was telling the Doctor about a time he'd gotten caught in his fetish. He'd been riding his second wife-to be when his first wife had walked in, said, "I can't believe you got someone else to do that for you too," and left. He'd been so startled, his mask had fallen off! It had been so embarrassing.

Dixie smiled and shivered. She couldn't guess how long she'd been listening. Yet still she wanted more. More secrets. More vibrations. More tales of strange secrets and furtive sex—more!

***

Leigh left the Yacht Club that day with white flashes of sun and the heat of midday Miami pounding down on her. She stood at the valet station searching for her Chanel sunglasses as her hybrid came up the horseshoe drive. Leigh hated the Lexus, but after she'd been rear-ended in her BMW convertible, Brad had insisted she get a safer car. She slid into the driver's seat and hit the gas. *Hybrids or golf carts,* she thought as she drove off—*which has the better pick-up?*

Leigh was still red-eyed and dry-mouthed from lack of sleep and abundance of champagne. Why had she agreed to this meeting the day after her gala? The board meeting would only be a rehash of the financial gain from last night, which could have waited. Well, that and her big news—which really could have waited, too. And then she remembered she had agreed with the Diva to go to an anniversary party for Mynt, a hot Miami club, tonight—ostensibly to celebrate her gala's success, but really to celebrate the Diva herself. Her stomach was filled with acid and her head began to pound at the thought of going out again. *Middle age is a war against exhaustion,* Leigh thought. But she'd promised the Diva she'd be there, and Leigh White did what she said she'd do. It was a rare, old-fashioned, small-town Texas trait that set her apart in the endless hustle of Miami's "I'll do that if nothing better comes along" mentality. Besides that, she'd wanted to do something special for the folks who'd helped her in the gala office, and especially for Jeffrey, the best employee who ever lived. The man was a superhuman in assistant form, and she knew he was looking forward to tonight. There was no backing out.

Leigh was greeted by the Board of Directors as if she had just carried off a winning performance on *American Idol.* Her heart beating with a sudden nervousness, she sat in the stale conference room listening to them recap the huge financial success of last night's gala. More than 750 moneyed guests had attended; and between ticket sales, silent auction bids and donations, the evening had raised a couple of million dollars. It was the best pull in the history of the gala.

As the room beamed with the news, Leigh stood up. *Now's as good a time as any,* she thought.

"Everyone," she said, and the room turned to her, "I have an announcement of my own to make. With last night's gala having been such a success, I hope it'll be easier for you, as it was for me, to know that it will be my last. The last nine years have been very rewarding and a lot of fun, but a lot longer than I ever anticipated! With all your commitment and talent, I'm sure you'll continue on with great success. Thank you."

Gasps ran around the table, and the Board exploded in disappointment. Some of them begged her to reconsider. Leigh sat quietly, shaking her head from side to side, tears at the corners of her eyes.

The Chairman of the Board stood.

"Leigh, we cannot thank you enough for what you've done for these children and for this city. We're devastated to lose your passion and skill, but if it's time for you to go, we understand. And we reserve the right to call you when we don't know what to do!" The room burst out in emotional laughter.

Leigh blushed and looked down at her hands. She hated to disappoint, and hated not to deliver. But this year, she knew she needed to take care of herself. She was simply worn out, and both she and her businesses suffered when she threw herself so fully into fundraising. Never mind the family she had to take care of! It was the only decision she could make, and she was happy for her resolve.

Now that the news had been broken, a wave of exhaustion washed over her. A 5-hour energy shot wasn't going to cure this feeling: she needed sleep, and lots of it. Hopefully she'd have time for a power nap before the club tonight.

Fortunately the other Board members were friends; there would be time for further talk later. She excused herself quickly as the meeting broke up, and made her way out of the stale conference room.

CHAPTER 5

DRAGGING THROUGH LIFE

> Call me. I got JOOSY gossip.

—The Diva

Awakening from his daily four-hour nap, Brandon West-brook took off his navy-blue satin eye mask and welcomed in the Florida sun. His California king bed, piled with goose down pillows and a 1500-thread-count Pratesi comforter, was like a cocoon in the frigid apartment: Brandon set the thermostat to 50 degrees year-round, electric bill be damned.

He reached for the bedside table, grabbed his phone and checked for messages. His friend Randy had picked up some South Beach guys and awoken six hours later, bent over the sofa with something in his ass. *Probably an English cucumber,* Brandon thought idly as he read the message. Randy, a notorious freak, was partial to the English cucumbers, and understandably; they were so much smoother than the regular cukes, with no wax on the skin to slow things down. He'd have to call Randy back and get the details later.

Right now he needed to begin the ritual by which college-educated, well-traveled Brandon Westbrook transformed himself into Diva Lorraine Manchester, ruler of the hottest nightlife city in the world and confidant of A-listers from Hollywood to London.

He slid his iPod onto his speakers, and a long list of female pop artists and torch-ballad singers lit up. Brandon needed no coffee upon waking; the music always energized him. And when he needed the extra pick-me-up later, he'd do a bump—and we aren't talking the bump and grind. Nobody understood how much performers gave, and a little coke was fair compensation for the energy they showered on the untalented.

He touched "Etta James" on his playlist and began to sing along as he rolled from the California king.

Brandon kept the music pumped up loud. The apartment of the glamorous Lorraine Manchester ought to sound like a club, he always thought; the music of her favorite icons, past and present, was just the thing she needed to get into character. Brandon's iPhone played everything from showtunes to disco queens, soul sisters and pop—and Brandon knew every word to every song.

Time flew during the next three hours of preparations, as it always did. One by one Brandon fantasized himself as Diana Ross—Dolly Parton—Barbra Streisand—Eartha Kitt. He listened to Gaga and one Madonna song—his favorite—"Like a Virgin." He imagined his alter ego Lorraine at the Super Bowl, performing wild aerobic dances in thigh-high boots and singing to millions of screaming fans.

Lighting gardenia-scented candles and filling the bathtub, Brandon pulled together his outfit du jour while the water ran. Winding through the maze of his tiny duplex apartment, he sang while pulling jewelry from boxes and drawers and styling Lorraine's wig.

Without an inch to spare, Brandon had stacked, hung, layered and stuffed the wardrobe and accessories of a star diva all around him. Clothes, wigs, makeup, padded bras and fake boobs, lotions, girdles and costume jewelry lay everywhere. His bedroom was a giant closet with a bed in the center; his closets were shoe-closets. If he rolled over too far in bed or raised his head up too high, his flaw-lessly well-cared-for face got nicked by rough petticoats, sequined scarves, metal girdle stays or loose chandelier earrings—which would require an extra facial that day at the Ritz Carlton's spa, just over the Causeway. There seemed to be only one empty space in the whole apartment, and it stared at him accusingly. That was the space on the wall by his bed where the fabulous oil portrait of Diva Lorraine would go, once Arturo was done with the damn thing. It was supposed to have been done before he left for Europe; when he got back, Brandon would most certainly be dropping by to give him an earful. *Maybe a mouthful too,* he thought mischievously to himself. After this long a wait, his money ought to be worth more than a painting—even a painting of Diva Lorraine.

Still belting out the tunes, Brandon pulled Lorraine's gown for tonight's event off of one of the many clotheslines hanging throughout the apartment, and hung it up carefully in the bathroom on a pink satin hanger. He hung it over the tub, just high enough to give his long legs room to be raised up and shaved, but low enough to let the steam from his bubble bath smooth out every wrinkle. No ironing needed for this drag queen! All that was needed was a bit of ingenuity—and voilá.

This bath is better than Valium, Brandon thought, as he sank into the tub. He relaxed and imagined himself as Lorraine on stage, electrifying a nightclub crowd. Four hours from now, she'd be doing just that. Brandon was a perfectionist where Lorraine Manchester was concerned, because Lorraine paid the bills. She had to be prepared for any performance. Whether it was lip-syncing or host-essing, Lorraine always delivered the goods, looking camera-ready and glamorous from head to toe. No one knew for sure when that "big break" might come and she would become a national star. And Lorraine knew it was coming. For now, Miami was a dress rehearsal.

As she lounged in scented bubbles, scenes from last night's gala ran through Lorraine's mind. Katie Parker! Now *that* was one crazy girl—and a perfect party buddy. Katie loved the male models, and so did she. Lorraine replayed her red carpet walk and tried to recount how many poses she'd struck, how many photos were taken and with whom. And that Jacques character—ugh! He had recoiled when Lorraine leaned in to kiss both of his cheeks, which had offended her. She'd deviously whispered a sexual innuendo into his ear and swayed off on her six-inch heels. *For God's sake,* thought Lorraine, *the man's dating Sassy, a woman who's never waxed her mustache right.*

Through the pumped-up music Lorraine heard the phone ringing, her lifeline to the outside world. She certainly couldn't see through her windows any longer; the closet was too full, the room too steamy.

"Hello," purred the Diva into the receiver of her rhinestone-covered cell phone. She always held it in her left hand—accented with Lee's Press-on Nails, in hot pink of course—even when in the tub. "This had better be important, because I'm ready to walk out the door!"

Lorraine, of course, was far from ready. This was only her standard line, letting everyone know how in-demand she was. Brandon Westbrook still sat naked, bony knees pulled up to his chin, looking nothing like a glamorous diva—but that was none of Lorraine Manchester's business.

"Leigh, my darling!" she said in her finely tuned voice. "I've been meaning to call you with some juicy gossip, but I must run or I'll be late." This was another of the Diva's go-to lines. Lorraine Manchester made it a point never to be on time, and loved to make a spectacular, fashionably late grand entrance in front of the crowds of nightclub groupies waiting to get in.

"I am *so* happy you're coming to see me at Mynt tonight. I look fabulous, of course. You know I *always* take special care to look gorgeous for this crowd. You never know what celebrity might show up, and I'm not going to let any one of them upstage me!—Of *course* I've got you and your group on the guest list. You know I always take care of my Leigh, and everyone will be kissing up to you so you'll probably be sent champagne too.—How many in your group? Six—no problem. I'll alert the media that Leigh White and her entourage will be at Mynt this evening. Say eleven o'clock?" Lorraine glanced at the clock and gave a cry of theatrical despair. "Okay, gotta run! See you later, love! Love you!"

Going through her seemingly endless wardrobe and deciding on the perfect outfit for each occasion was one of the highlights of Lorraine's daily life. Now began in earnest the magical makeover from which the beautiful and glamorous Diva would emerge. The whole process was somewhat like watching a fuzzy caterpillar transform itself into a glamorous butterfly.

First, the biggest platinum-blonde wig in her collection—one that added six inches to her six-foot frame—was chosen, touched up and set aside. This hand-made, ready-styled wig, one of more than two dozen, was one of Lorraine's finest creations. Not everyone had the talent to combine three wigs into one fabulous up-do, much less one styled well enough to stand up to the scrutiny of photographers and fans outside of one of Miami's top spots.

Singing along with the Broadway diva Linda Eder, Lorraine got on a stepladder and reached for her Jean Paul Gaultier dress, still damp from the steam. While it was drying she painted on her beautiful face with incredible care, accessorized her eyes with two pairs of long false eyelashes, and accented it all with voluptuous hot-pink lipstick and high-shine lip gloss.

Now it was time for the trick that every successful cross-dresser had to master: the Tuck.

There are seemingly as many ways to do the Tuck as there are drag queens wanting to make a YouTube video. The real problem, of course, is the balls. No one wants to see a bulge in a woman's crotch—or at least, not many people do. Most drag queens force their balls so far back, those two shy egg-shaped wonders are virtually nestled between their legs. This is a move that causes some discomfort, but much confidence: testicles tend to stay put there.

For a while, Lorraine had instead used a gaff, a pair of tight spandex panties or bikini bottoms, to corral her man bits in a slightly less forcible way. Her gaff had been specially designed for her by her beloved Versace; and truth be told, it had given her a terrible prickly heat. But oh, Gianni! When South Beach lost the great man to a gun crazy, Gianni's gaff made Lorraine too sad, and she'd returned to the low-tech, old-school drag tuck. It was then that her career had really taken off, and she'd never donned the gaff again. Still, she'd kept it in her panty drawer, and touched it every day for luck. It was orange—a beautiful Hermés orange. Just the color excited her.

Over the years Lorraine had developed her own special tuck-nique, and now brought it to bear with practiced skill. First, she took a roll of Charmin and unwound three or four feet of it. Cupping her scrotum, she then pulled the balls up against her stomach, and began to wrap the tissue around her penis. Last, she pulled the entire balls/penis/toilet paper construction down and back towards her butt crack and stuck it in place, running tape up the crack and onto the lower back as needed. All told, it was an extremely stable arrangement. This was one reason among many that she generally avoided drinking too much at her functions; getting everything out to pee was a major production. She'd trained her bladder to hold it for hours—a skill she considered a professional necessity.

After a few other necessary appurtenances—tape on the chest for cleavage, fake breasts, fishnet nylons, a Jennifer Lopez–like silicone butt-and-hips enlarger—came the now-dry gown and corset. The silk corset had been designed for Pamela Anderson by Gaultier himself; Lorraine had added a few inches of lace down the sides and voilá, it fit. The dress was equally flawless, as were the hard-to-find four-inch Jimmy Choo stilettos she chose to set it off. Pamela, one of her best girlfriends, would have been proud of this glamor-puss tonight.

Next, Lorraine added jewelry to complete the magic. The process of creating the custom "copied" Chanel pearl earrings had been complicated: Lorraine had taken three pairs of matching Chanel earrings and painstakingly glued them together, adding feathers and crystals for more drama. If Coco Chanel could make a statement, Lorraine Manchester could make a bigger one. Because of their size and weight, the earrings had to be safety-glued to Lorraine's ears. She always carried her glue with her—along with tape and safety pins—for any fashion emergencies. She really had become a pro at the art of glamour.

Last came a set of long, pointed hot-pink nails that perfectly matched her lips, the wig and its adjustments, a spritz of Chanel No. 5 and a classic Chanel quilted handbag with trademark gold chain—one of many Lorraine had borrowed from Leigh White's closet while visiting. *Wonder if Leigh had noticed?* she always laughed to herself when she looked at it.

Now, standing in front of the full-length mirror, Lorraine Manchester looked at the beautiful image staring back at her. With stilettos and hair, the Diva stood 6'9" tall—and all of it fabulous.

Her legs were perfect, her hair just right. The completed ensemble looked like the work of a team of professional stylists. Giving a theatrical twirl, she felt the gown swing naturally around her in a graceful motion.

Coco Chanel had been quoted as saying, *Before you walk out the door, look in the mirror, and take one thing off.* The Diva had a different creed: Look in the mirror and add two things. Taking one last look in the mirror—her favorite place to look—she kissed it and told her reflection how gorgeous she was, then paused to touch up her lips and eyes with just the subtlest hint of sparkle. Having completed this last step of her ritual transformation, the Diva Lorraine Lancaster sashayed confidently to the door.

She would drive herself; real divas enjoy their privacy and independence on the way to a performance. For years the Diva had folded herself into the tiny interior of a Honda hatchback, blonde hair pressed against the inside roof and windshield, and could be seen speeding not-quite-fabulously up and down Biscayne Boulevard on her way to and from each grand appearance. She now drove a Range Rover, the low seat and high ceiling of which spared her hair from being smashed down. The side and back windows were tinted, too, restricting the paparazzi to clear shots of her through the windshield. This had been a big decision: leave the glass clear, to allow for more photos, or tint it as a star would? In the end she'd opted for stardom. Whenever at a crossroads, the Diva generally resolved it with the answer, WWSD—What Would a Superstar Do?—and it had been the right decision. Now she could fantasize herself as Britney Spears on the run, whenever someone shot her driving.

Once inside, Lorraine popped in one of her custom CDs and sang at full volume to "Ain't No Mountain High Enough," feeling at the top of her game. She'd come a long way since her days of knock-offs and borrowed gowns; now her world was one of haute couture and designer favors. No longer working for tips, she now earned up to $2500 a night whether she performed or not. The long club lines she'd once stood in were now hers to bypass; velvet ropes dropped all over town for the Diva to step over in her grand entrances. Now she was a VIP host, entertainer extraordinaire, occasional DJ and confidant to the rich and shameless. She was the only one whom her success could not have startled; yet it was really not such a strange thing. After all, times had changed, and her brand of over-the-top appearance was only the essence of what everyone else wanted in their heart of hearts. Things were bigger and better now, and more was the new black.

***

At ten on the dot, the Diva made her entrance at Mynt.

In her mountain-high platinum wig and modified Chanel, Lorraine made quite an impression. She had the perfect backhand wave, copied after royalty waving from balconies to shouting crowds below, and employed it to great effect. Smiling and waving as though the crowds behind the velvet ropes had been waiting for her all along, she created her own red-carpet moment—as she always did. Her self-assurance was infectious, and this crowd was eager to play along.

Entering the club, she passed bodyguards, doormen, ropes and chains. All the way she threw kisses to the crowd and smiled for the photographers—even if there weren't any photographers. She'd learned that to fake it was to make it, and to act like a star was to be one. She even sometimes hired burly men—usually lovers, ex-lovers or lovers-in-waiting—to act as security. Nothing said "celebrity" like giant, scowling bodybuilders following you everywhere!

The buzz about the Miami nightclub's anniversary party had not been overplayed. Right inside the door the Diva ran into Paris

Hilton and Lindsay Lohan, ignoring each other, and P. Diddy with his entourage. If only Ingrid Casares had been there—she always liked to impress the nightclub maven—but Ingrid, she was told, was out of the country.

For the club's big night, Lorraine Manchester played hostess to the wild crowd. Her over-the-top, ridiculously exaggerated and exuberant, to-hell-with-tomorrow femaleness always cheered people up. She stopped at the bar, flirted a bit with the buff boy toys and showed some of the cleavage that had taken fifteen minutes of her ritual makeover to create. She also ordered her usual cocktail: champagne with a whole strawberry as a garnish, which she could sensually suck or lick when she needed to win over a big tipper. Some of these were sure to be at the end of the runway-shaped stage tonight during her song-and-dance number.

She'd made her entrance with her usual fashionable leisureliness, and now it was less than ten minutes until show time. She waltzed around the nightclub, making sure to bat those big, dark eyelashes as she bumped and grinded her way to the back of the stage.

From behind the stage's screen, the Diva scanned the crowd, looking for celebrities and any of her rich friends—or rich soon-to-be friends. These parties were sort of like church: no one ever really wanted to go, but once you were there, well, you just got into it. Would this be a typical night where she'd do her stage show, work the VIP section, pose for photos and sneak out as soon as she could? As it would have surprised even her friends to know, Lorraine usually got home by five a.m.—when, that is, she wasn't tempted to hit the after-hours clubs. The most popular after-hours club for the locals, and the Diva's top late-night hangout, was a spot called Twist, right in the heart of South Beach. House, the more famous and over-the-top Wynwood spot, was a lot of fun too; but where House was a place to visit, Twist was home. If you were gay or just loved hanging out with the gays, Twist was the place to be; it gave off the vibe that the highly styled and accomplished gays in Miami had paid their dues and now had a home for themselves. That said, most often Lorraine simply went home at the end of the night. It was better for her skin, and her image. Always leave them wanting more…!

The moment before she went onstage, she glanced over and made eye contact with Katie Parker. Normally Lorraine didn't talk to Katie unless there was something in it for her, but this time Katie was surrounded by boys, and people with boys were always good to know. Lorraine waved, and Katie waved back excitedly. The handsome young man draped around Katie's shoulders, who waved too, was certainly *not* her husband; but Katie sure was enjoying his attention. Well now! Tonight would definitely be interesting now. Katie seemed not to care that Lorraine had seen her cuddling this boy toy; but then, Katie seemed to have no idea that Leigh and her friends were on their way. The Diva imagined a somewhat less enthusiastic wave out of little Mrs. Parker when *they* ran into each other. Hopefully it'd shake Katie up a bit about being spotted around town; maybe then she and Katie could work out a trade.

The Diva smiled and stepped onstage. The crowd, already worked up, exploded into applause as she sashayed across, the first pulsing beats of her opening track—"If My Friends Could See Me Now"—blasting out of the club's speakers. She *owned* this song! She owned all of them.

Tonight's going to be incredible, she thought.

CHAPTER 6

WE OWN THE NIGHT

Text when ur outside. I'll part the crowd.

—Scarlett

Tonight's going to be intolerable, thought Leigh.

She tried to dismiss the thought from her mind. She'd just have to make the most of it—she had to support her friend the Diva, and tonight was really important to Lorraine.

The Diva had called her several weeks before to make sure she'd attend tonight's party, and she'd agreed. At the time she had thought the anniversary show, with its fabulous crowds and blowout atmosphere, would be a perfect reward for her staff, and a welcome relief from the never-ending drama of producing the gala. Yet now she was more than questioning her decision. What had she been thinking? After last night she was aching for a night free of drama, and in South Beach, gossip and innuendo lurked behind every velvet rope—especially where the grand Diva Lorraine Manchester was scheduled to perform. If there was no drama, the Diva would find a way to create some—after all, in any attention is good attention in show business!

Rumor had it that the Mynt anniversary would be glamorous and raw, even by Miami standards. The nightclub was already quite a hotspot for celebrity connections. Its owner, entrepreneur extraordinaire Romain Zago, was not only eye-candy himself, but made half of a hot item with supermodel Joanna Krupa, and the two of them had recently brought attention to the club with their appearance on a hit reality show.

Lorraine, accordingly, had worked the phones for months in her usual way. First she'd locked in her A- and B-list friends for the guest list. Then she'd diligently alerted the media, providing the names of every national and local celebrity that had agreed to attend. Finally she finished the circle by sending the A- and B-listers a full roster of the reporters who'd be covering the Mynt party, along with a synopsis of their recent coverage and where they'd be setting up their cameras to cover the arriving stars. Translation on both fronts: "Don't forget the publicity needs of Lorraine Manchester, and she won't forget yours!"

Despite being a regular on the social circuit, with her face ever in the pages of local glossies, Leigh rarely made appearances at nightclubs, except when they were somehow related to her charity. The Diva had offered, as always, to arrange everything for her and her party; but Leigh knew well that she'd be too consumed with her own grand appearance to do any such thing, so she called ahead just to be sure everything was set. Luckily, Scarlett Ruiz was also working the party that night. Leigh knew Scarlett could always be counted on to welcome her and hers with a VIP table and the best champagne in the house.

Brad had gone out of town this afternoon to meet with some

clients on an important case, so on this occasion she had her assistant Jeffrey with her. It was too bad Brad couldn't join her, but she was always happy to have Jeffrey along, whether Brad came or not. The tall, gay Australian looked like a Ford model, and dressed as impeccably.

Leigh and Jeffrey walked arm-in-arm through the front door and into the pounding, pulsating atmosphere of the club. The entrance was a scene in itself. Dressed-to-be-seen cliques were lining up outside the door: a young Japanese-looking man in a leather coat right out of "The Matrix" with a pair of models, both in cutoffs, tube tops and six-inch strappy platform sandals; two couples—the women in matching Missoni dresses and the men in black suits with pencil-thin ties—chatting quietly; a group of club kids fidgeting in silence, rubbing their fingers together compulsively as the molly kicked in. Everyone knew the drill: be chic, be fabulous, be edgy; stand out; see and be seen; do what no one else is doing. The line stretched around the block—mostly young people, but with some not-so-young people scattered in too, smoking and talking and flirting and hoping their Marc Jacobs bags, wedge booties and rayon-blend hi-lo dresses were enough style to open the ropes for them. Youthful breasts in cheap strapless dresses usually helped; but in a scene like this, the odds were against the anonymous.

Scarlett waited at the door to welcome Leigh, who rushed in past the photographers yelling at her.

"Leigh, you look great as always," Scarlett purred, looking prim and incredibly sexy at the same time in her sleek black dress. "I've reserved a private skybox that overlooks the whole scene," she said, giving Leigh a fist bump and a wink. "It's the best view in the club."

"Oh, Scarlett—thanks! My gala staff will love it," Leigh smiled.

Scarlet was no dummy. She knew that just getting Leigh out to a club was a big coup. Nobody could do that. If Leigh got stuck with chain-smokers, drunks, pill poppers or in-crowd hangers-on, it would definitely not be good P.R. She wanted Leigh happy, and the word out and about how great the new club was.

"Absolutely no problem," she said. "And we have all of them on the list, for whenever they arrive."

"That's perfect; thanks again."

"You know, there's a rumor, Leigh"—Scarlett leaned in toward Leigh and spoke under her breath—"that you're quitting the gala. Let me be the first to try and change your mind! You inspire us all."

Even though Scarlett preferred younger celebrity-type women, Leigh had never been able to shake the feeling that Scarlett had a thing for her. In between the endless flattering comments Scarlett would make, Leigh always caught her eyes on her cleavage. But Leigh was too shrewd to take any notice of it. Scarlett had helped out massively at her gala every year, and could always be counted on to deliver an A-list crowd.

"I'll walk you to your box and come back to join you when Lorraine goes onstage," Scarlett said as she ushered Leigh and Jeffrey past the ropes and into the crowded club, casting searching looks left and right along the way. Beyond the fact that it was her job to know exactly who was in the room and where they were, Leigh knew she was also anxious—as always—that Ingrid Casares would show up and upstage her. Scarlett had been trying to top Ingrid for years, but she knew as well as anyone that it would never happen; Ingrid was an international nightclub icon and best friends with celebrity royalty.

The VIP skybox she'd reserved for them was on the second level, overlooking the stage and first level of the club with an incredible view. Say what you would about her, Scarlett never disappointed. Everyone in the packed club stared at them as they were escorted in to the best seats in the house.

Jeffrey, whom Scarlett was obviously ignoring, held onto Leigh as they worked their way through the crowd. Ignoring people was a trademark of Scarlett's, but it always seemed to give her particular pleasure to pretend gay guys weren't there. In Jeffrey's case this was even more the case, since he was just an *assistant*—but Jeffrey, for his part, didn't mind laughing it off. He knew he had Leigh's ear and she always trusted what he said. The rest of these society people were insecure, shallow, little minds in Jeffrey's book—and he knew his book counted.

"This is fabulous," he yelled in his Australian accent over the thumping music. "We can see everything!" He rushed into the skybox and looked out over the edge at the club below.

"I'll send someone over to open the champagne," Scarlett said to anyone but him, as she guided Leigh into the skybox.

"Thanks—this is great, Scarlett," replied Leigh, at bit embarrassed at all the attention they were getting from the crowd and Scarlett.

"Enjoy yourselves! I'll be back soon," Scarlett said as she disappeared into the crowd.

"This is incredible, my Queen—simply fabulous!" Jeffrey gushed again. The reference to "Queen of Miami" always made Leigh cringe, but his excitement was infectious.

"I'm glad you like it, Jeffrey."

"Like it? Oh, I could *live* in this skybox; it gives me the whole picture at once. For instance: I take one look at the crowd, and guess who I see sitting at a table, surrounded by a group of the hottest model boys you've ever seen?"

"I give up. Who?" said Leigh, who stood staring at a woman waving at her, and trying to make out who she was.

"Katie Parker—and her husband is nowhere in sight!" said Jeffrey, as excited as an ornithologist filling out his list of "Birds I Have Seen."

"I think we may have another problem to deal with," said Leigh, as she recognized the wild waving woman walking towards her through the crowd. "We're being attacked by Dixie. Again! Goodness, I just left that woman six hours ago. Prepare to jump ship!" Leigh laughed at her little joke, but inwardly was a bit perplexed. Dixie certainly hadn't been invited to Mynt tonight, and Leigh didn't know how she might have found out that *she* was even going.

"Leigh, darlin'!" Dixie yelled, as she approached their VIP section. She sloshed into the skybox as if it were her own, and made herself right at home. "It's about *time* you arrived. Ah've been havin' cocktails at the bar, waitin' for you."

"But—how did you know I was coming?"

"Why darlin', you told me yourself today!" Dixie yelled. Even in their private box, shouting was the only way anyone could be heard over the music and the hysterical party crowd. "Ah knew it would be a great time, so Ah called up some people and invited myself. Ah knew you wouldn't mind; the more the merrier, right?"

"Of course I don't mind," replied Leigh, inwardly kicking herself. "I would have invited you myself, but I had no idea that you'd come out this late."

Though Dixie was Leigh's good friend, Leigh would never have invited her here if she hadn't been too tired to think. Dixie was more than a handful, and would undoubtedly drink way too much. Leigh was already tired, and didn't want to babysit Dixie into the bargain. Still, she thought (trying to look on the bright side), at least she wouldn't have to drive Dixie home. No doubt that driver of hers—more like a loyal beagle than a man—was waiting patiently for her, staring out the back windshield from time to time. Perhaps he was anticipating a treat for his patience.

"You've got the best box in the club. Let's toast!" Dixie screeched, as she grabbed one of the glasses the waiter had just poured for Leigh and Jeffrey.

"Thank you," Leigh said with a smile, as the waiter handed her the other glass and poured a third for Jeffrey. It was hard to be mad at Dixie; she was adorable and harmless, and a pretty entertaining drunk sometimes. Still, better safe than sorry. Leigh signaled the waiter and discreetly whispered into his ear. "Just so you know," she said, "we all dilute Dixie's drinks when she's in play, so please—keep the ice coming!"

"Here's to good friends!" Dixie shouted, barely waiting for Leigh to clink her glass before she tossed back the bubbly. "Who else is coming, anyhow?"

"Besides the rest of my staff, I'm not sure," replied Leigh. She'd phoned a few friends who'd provided above and beyond the call of duty for the gala, including Mitchell Hudson; she'd also called Lauren. Mitchell had promised he'd make an appearance but Lauren had begged off, since she had an early showing appointment in the morning. "I'm sure we'll run into more people we know," she added, suddenly remembering Jeffrey's observation. "Jeffrey, what did you say you saw Katie doing just now?"

"This is *so* great," Jeffrey said, turning from his view to join the two ladies. His face said it all—he could hardly contain his glee. "Katie Parker is making out with what must be one of the hottest male models in the world. I really should take a photo; I'd never have to pay for another Billie Parker suit again!" He beamed and poured himself another glass of champagne.

"*Where* are they?" shrieked Dixie. "Ah've *got* to see that!" She rushed over to the railing, practically stumbling over Jeffrey. "Come on now, Jeffrey, get over here and show me!"

"I wanna see too," Leigh announced, as she joined them at the railing.

"Second table from the front," said Jeffrey, as he pointed briefly down across the first floor. He'd taken out a small digital camera, and was focusing in for a picture. "Here, just let me—there. That's one picture the camera whore *won't* want taken!" he said, shouting with laughter.

"Where are our binoculars?" quipped Leigh. "I'd love to see where all those hands are. This is better than any opera!" They all burst into laughter again.

"Jeffrey, Ah'm shocked," gasped Dixie in mock surprise. "That camera idea is something *Ah* would do. You're usually so shy and reserved—Ah'm so proud of you! You're finally getting with the program."

"It's the champagne talking. Here, have some more, Leigh," he said, as he poured for both Dixie and his boss. He chuckled to himself; he enjoyed encouraging Dixie's drinking.

"Somebody important must've just arrived," Dixie announced. "Look at all the flashes at the entrance. It's probably some local, Diddy or Mickey Rourke. I've seen them two around town so many times, Ah'd be more excited to see my pool boy!" *She's not fooling anyone,* Leigh thought. Dixie was as celebrity-obsessed as a teenager.

Suddenly, Mitchell Hudson appeared in the crowd. Grabbing the arms of a pair of gorgeous blonde models who had suddenly materialized on either of side of him, he walked them to the top of the stairs so that everyone could see him. From there he looked down, saw Leigh, and gave a little smile and a wave.

Leigh waved back, wondering for the umpteenth time how anyone could live a life so grounded in the groundless. For nightclub promoters, appearance was all. Their jobs were mysterious, they relied often on very tenuous celebrity and press contacts, and they often cost nightclub owners more in freebies for the rich and famous than the ensuing P.R. was worth. To do what they did required balls of steel, a gambler's heart and constitution, a natural sense for what would impress people, and zero shame. Still, when they were good, they were really good. They didn't become legends by simply packing the house, but by packing the house with the *right* people—and Mitchell was on his way to becoming a legend. He was the go-to promoter, reliably filling clubs like Mynt and Liv—which held hundreds—with quality crowds.

Two photographers followed him and his beautiful entourage as they made their way through the crowd back to Leigh's skybox. Mitchell walked slowly, stopping here and there to chat and have his photo taken with the celebrities in his path. Nobody worked a room like Mitchell, except perhaps Scarlett; and she had the advantage of tits that got her in the door with both men and women.

After a brief back-and-forth with Ariana Grande, who was in town for a sell-out stadium performance—and who was finally old enough to be in the club legally—Mitchell entered the skybox with a flourish, as if the entire scene had been blocked and rehearsed beforehand. His arms went out as he walked over to Leigh. Kissing her on both cheeks, he then turned her towards the waiting photographers and positioned her to his right in one smooth, balletic motion. Another swift gesture and he'd placed the two models on his left. He turned to the photographers, who snapped photos until he waved them away, apparently satisfied they had the shots he wanted them to have.

"Mitchell, I'm so glad you came," said Leigh as the waiter poured again for everyone.

"Oh, of course—it's always nice to see you out, Leigh."

"Now you've done it," Jeffrey yelled from the railing. "Katie Parker must've seen the photographers—she's on her way up to our table!" He was clapping his hands as he turned to look at the now-full skybox. "This is getting better and better."

"There's no room for Katie," sighed Leigh. *And not just in terms of space,* she thought.

"Oh, she'll probably leave anyway when she finds that the photographers have left," Jeffrey laughed.

"I imagine she's probably coming to explain away all the male models at her table," Leigh said.

"Shall I send some more down to her table, with the photographers?" asked Mitchell. "I'd rather she were photographed with her party than with any of us!"

"Not bad, Mitchell," laughed Leigh. "What do you call that little maneuver?"

"That one's called 'Photo Revenge,' and I am gooood at it." He smiled like a pirate, winking broadly at Leigh.

"Yes, that'd be brilliant!" Jeffrey cheered. "Let's send the photographers down to her table—that'll draw her off the scent. And we'll see whether she'd rather be photographed in a compromising position, or not photographed at all."

"She's already headed this way," Dixie announced, happy about the drama but unhappy she was being ignored. "She's like a wildebeest followin' lightning—she runs toward the flash!" She laughed at her own exotic simile. "We probably could have made it through the night without a visit from her, if it weren't for them photographers."

"Dixie, be nice," admonished Leigh. "Billie donated money and fashions for every charity event I ever did, so we have to try not to upset Katie too much."

"*Did?* Yew used the wrong tense there, Leigh," Dixie said. "Ah know you said you'd decided already, but we can't live without that fabulous gala."

Before Leigh could answer, Katie Parker was upon them.

"Leigh, darling!" Katie shouted as she entered the skybox. "I never expected to see *you* out at a club like this!"

"Obviously not," slurred Dixie.

"Hello, Katie," said Leigh, welcoming her into the skybox.

"Is Billie here with you?" she asked pointedly.

"No, Billie's at the factory," cooed Katie. "I'm here with some of his models from today's photo shoot. We're having *so* much fun." Katie eyed the two beautiful models by Mitchell's side, and a dark look came over her. She was still insecure about her looks, and very uncomfortable around picture-perfect young women—especially if they didn't reek of silicone and lipo. These two were natural beauties, thoroughbreds at that; and they made her visibly uneasy.

"Good evening, Mitchell," she purred, kissing him on the cheek. "I can see *you're* having a good time, too! Just stay away from my table with those girls of yours; you know I have to protect my male models. They represent Billie's new Fall line, and I'm afraid those two would eat them alive! We had a big photo shoot today, you know—it's my responsibility to reward them, so I brought them out for a night on the town."

"Of course, sweetheart," Mitchell replied, chuckling to himself. "I'll send the photographers down to take some photos of you all." He smiled at her, then turned back to Leigh, mouthing the word *"reward?"* in mock horror.

"Oh, great—I'll head down there in a minute," said Katie, oblivious. "Anyway, what are *you* doing out this evening, Leigh?"

"I'm just here to see Lorraine Manchester perform," said Leigh. "I'm never out this late."

"Who are you here with?" asked Katie eagerly, hoping to catch her in a compromising situation.

"I'm here with Jeffrey," said Leigh. "Jeffrey, you know Katie Parker." Jeffrey had been stealing sidelong glances at Mitchell's two beautiful models, who he was convinced were into each other.

"Hello, Katie," Jeffrey said, smiling broadly. "Is that Matt Champion sitting down at your table? He's my favorite model."

"Oh—you saw me at my table?" Katie replied, looking a little embarrassed. "Yes, that's Matt. Do you want to come down and meet him?"

"Yes—er—yes, I do," Jeffrey blurted. He was rarely flustered by anything, but tonight had him at its mercy.

"Why don't you go down to Katie's table with her," Mitchell said suggestively to Jeffrey. "I'll send the photographers down."

"Thanks, Mitchell," Katie said as she kissed him one more time. "And maybe you should come down later and visit, yourself," she added seductively. "But without those girls."

"Now, Katie," smirked Mitchell. "What would Billie think?"

"Like I said, Billie's at the factory," she snapped. "He wants me out having a good time. It's good for business. Besides, I'm only—"

"Ladies and gentlemen," the announcer's voice boomed out over the speakers. "Mynt nightclub is proud to bring you the internationally acclaimed performer, Diva Lorraine Manchester!"

"See you later," Katie said abruptly as she rushed out of the skybox and back to her table below, leaving behind a cloud of cheap perfume. *She must have been feeling like a whore in church up here,* Leigh thought.

"I'll stick around," Jeffrey said, returning to his senses. "I'd rather not be introduced to any boys by that one—even if they are hot, and very tempting."

Leigh, Dixie and Jeffrey stood at the railing and watched the drag diva perform, dancing and lip-syncing to Beyoncé's "Put A Ring On It." Mitchell and his girls took the opportunity to sit and snuggle on one of the skybox's luxurious couches. Leigh looked down, amazed once again that Lorraine could cause such pandemonium among the crowd with her performance. While Leigh enjoyed the show, it was definitely not her scene. She didn't like late nights, or crowded nightclubs with all their primping and pretense. That kind of thing had never really been her cup of tea; and tonight was pushing even Miami standards. The sound was deafening, and the crowds frantic with excitement. Pairs and threesomes of every combination of genders were practically stripping each other on the dance floor. There was probably already more booze spilled on the bathroom floors here than most other clubs saw vanish down their patrons' throats in an evening. And all the selfies—did anyone here have any shame, or sense?

She watched Katie slinking back to her table of male models, and wondered if she'd end up in bed with one tonight. Katie had a reputation of playing with the boys whenever her husband was out of town or working. He certainly seemed to be doing both a lot lately. Leigh wondered if he knew how busy his wife was keeping herself in his absence.

"Leigh, look over there at that back table," Dixie screamed, pointing to one of the tables behind Katie's. "Isn't it that Sassy bitch from the gala? The one poor Lauren was so upset about stealin' her clients out from under her?"

"Oh, God," said Leigh. "Yes, that's her all right—and she's with Jacques, her new 'soulmate.' I can't believe it; what are *they* doing here? Lauren is going to *die* when I tell her."

"And who are those short, dark fellas with them?" Dixie asked bluntly. "Friends of hers, I guess?"

"I guess they must be, from how they're acting; I've never seen them before, but they all seem quite cozy."

"Whoo! Well, they sure are gettin' personal with the gal! Guess this Jacques ain't the jealous type, eh?"

Leigh grabbed her phone from her purse and was ready to dial Lauren's number. Then she realized Lauren wouldn't be able to hear a thing. And it was a bit much to text right now, anyhow. Pity! It'd have to wait. But this was a night for the midday gossip brigade, if she ever saw one! First Katie and her boy toy, and now Sassy in some sort of sexy scrum with Jacques and two mysterious foreign-looking men! Tonight was the gift that kept on giving.

"Your gal Sassy's makin' out like a dog in heat!" Dixie drawled before downing another glass of champagne. She turned to Leigh with a beatific grin on her face. "Leigh, Ah have *so* much fun whenever Ah'm out with yew. Yew always let me join the party!" She turned back around to face the club floor and yelled, "Go, Katie!" at the top of her lungs, then turned to smile at Jeffrey and gave him a fist bump. Jeffrey was having a great time too, deviously pointing his camera in every direction and laughing deliriously to himself. The two exchanged Mona Lisa smiles, eyes sparkling.

"They're making a show of their own!" Jeffrey shouted with glee, his head spinning with gossip. "I've got some good pictures of it, too. This is too good! I don't even know who they are, but the crowd is sure starting to pay attention to them, now that Lorraine's finished. What a performance! Here, pass me that bottle."

"I can't wait to call Lauren tomorrow," said Leigh as Jeffrey poured another round of champagne. "She's going to be *furious*. That Sassy really is like a dog in heat! It's a good thing Lauren wasn't here tonight, or we might've gotten to witness a murder along with everything else!"

She and the others laughed at her little joke, but she knew it wasn't far from the truth. Lauren would happily arrange to have Sassy run out of town, if there was a way she could do it without getting her hands dirty.

"Darlings!" the Diva Lorraine Manchester exclaimed as she entered the skybox, ducking to protect her high hair. "Did you all love my show?" She'd changed from her skimpy Gaultier stage outfit to a dramatic long red gown covered in red feathers, six-inch rhinestone heels and tassel earrings. A red boa framed her colorful, wrinkle-free face. Given the constant interchange of makeup that face went through every day, the smoothness of her skin always amazed Leigh; but she attributed it all to Sudden Youth Skincare and a good night's sleep.

"You were fabulous," said Leigh, as she held out her arms. Lorraine rushed to give her a hug. *No air kisses for true friends!* as the Diva always said. "The crowd loved you. I hope you're getting paid well."

"No club could ever pay me what I'm really worth," quipped Lorraine. "But it's a living and a life, love." Lorraine looked at Leigh smiling. "Now, tell me you're going to stay and have some fun, aren't you? Especially now that you aren't working that charity! I can't *believe* you've resigned!"

"How does everyone in this town know what happens *before* it happens?" Leigh laughed. "And I'm not buying this 'social media' crap—I left that meeting only a few hours ago! But yes, I'm done with the gala, and I'm done watching you perform too!" she added playfully. "I have a long day tomorrow, and it's way past my bedtime."

"Well, you can't leave until we get a photo together, at least," announced Lorraine, as the club photographer entered the skybox. "Now Leigh, you stand on this side, and Jeffrey darling, you stand on my left."

The Diva posed, ordering the photographer around like her personal paparazzi.

"Yes, now another—good—a sharper angle now—yes—perfect! Thank you darling, you can go now," she told the photographer. "Don't forget to email me copies!" The photographer nodded eagerly, and retreated into the crowd. Miami photographers had long since learned that Lorraine's orders were to be followed closely, if they ever wanted to photograph her or her many famous friends again.

"What happened to Dixie?" asked Leigh when he'd gone.

The Diva looked around in puzzlement. "Who, darling?"

"My friend Dixie Johnson," Leigh explained. "She was watching your show with us, and suddenly disappeared just now. I hope she's okay. She's had quite a bit to drink."

"There!" Jeffrey yelled, practically jumping up and down. "Dixie's down there beside that couple making out. There's a photographer there taking photos of them, and they're really into it!" He cupped his hands around his mouth and started cheering like he was watching a couple of Real Housewives slinging woe.

"What's happening?" asked Leigh, with a sneaking suspicion. "Let me see."

Sure enough, Dixie was standing next to a photographer taking photos of Sassy and Jacques and the two darkly tanned, short men. At that moment Dixie turned and saw Leigh watching and she smiled up at Leigh and gave her the signal to call her. The sly devil! She'd probably tipped the photographer generously to shoot Sassy, Jacques and friends, and to email her copies of the pictures tomorrow that they could pass on to Lauren. That was thinking on her feet—and drunk, too! That Dixie was something else!

Well, she had the right idea leaving, anyway, Leigh thought. It was time to go, and the shorter the goodbyes, the better. Scarlett had promised to make an appearance during Lorraine's show, but she probably had her hands full with this crowd. Mitchell had disappeared during the show, too; so Leigh said her goodbyes to Lorraine and signaled to Jeffrey.

Leigh held onto the security escort as they made their way through the crowd. She only stopped once, to gape at a scene that made her wish she was snapping photos herself.

Mitchell leaned against a wall making out with one of his blonde beauties, his hands firmly planted on her ass. Scarlett, her back to him, was making out with the other and being vigorously felt up in turn. Mitchell had once again come prepared, and the infamous rival promoters had made their détente for the evening.

In the midst of everything else, it was actually pretty sweet.

CHAPTER 7

THE NIGHT OWNS DIXIE

> Did you see Dixie out last night? I still hadn't seen her when I left this morning.

—Howard

Leigh was fighting to get to the surface when her consciousness kicked in and she heard her phone ringing. Brad rolled away from it and groaned.

"Hello?" Leigh murmured into the receiver.

"Leeeeeeeigh," a familiar voice slurred on the other end.

"Dixie!" Leigh shouted, waking up instantly. She could hardly hear Dixie over the background noise; where *was* she?

"Yeah, it's mee. Ah need your hepp, honey," Dixie said slowly. Her drawl was almost incomprehensible. "Ah'm in this jail and ever'bodee's hollerin'."

"All right, all right," Leigh said, sitting up. "What's going on?"

It was clear that Dixie had her panties in a big knot as she told Leigh—in between gulps of air—exactly what had happened.

Danny, her driver, hadn't been at the car when she'd left Mynt. She didn't know where he'd gone, and couldn't reach him on his phone. Nevertheless, she was more than ready for bed; so after waiting for him for a while she'd taken the extra key from underneath the driver's-side mat and set out to drive herself home. She'd been doing fine until she jumped a curb in Indian Creek Village, the private island off the Miami shore where she and Howard lived. She'd been picked up by the cops, and a local gas-station attendant was now trying to tow the car out of the fountain where it was wedged.

"All right, just wait!" said Leigh when she'd finished. "I'll be there right away. Stay calm, and don't talk to anyone." Leigh knew this was an impossible directive for Dixie; but she also knew, from being married to a lawyer for so many years, that anything Dixie said would be a problem later.

"Brad," she said, pulling up the covers, "Dixie is in jail, and we need to go bail her out."

Brad was used to Leigh's time-for-business tone—there was no room for debate when that tone came out—so they grabbed their things without a word and headed out for the county jail. On the way, Brad put in a call to a bail bondsman and they stopped at a 7-11, where Leigh bought three large cups of black coffee.

"Sweetie, there's no reason for you to have gotten Dixie a cup," Brad chuckled as Leigh got back into the car. "It'll be hours before she gets out of jail."

Leigh couldn't believe what she was hearing.

"What do you mean, hours?" she said incredulously.

Brad explained that by the time the bail bondsman got there and posted bail, the sun would be high in the sky—never mind the fact that there was a four-hour minimum wait in the county jail, no matter what the detainee had or hadn't done.

"Well then, why did we rush out the door?" Leigh asked.

Brad raised an eyebrow at her.

"Well," said Leigh finally, "I know you're in the middle of a big case and have a really big day in court tomorrow. Just drop me at the jail. I'll wait for Dixie. You can send the driver over to pick us up later."

Brad, ever the gentleman, tried to mask his laughter. "Honey, you obviously haven't been to a county jail lately. Let's get on our way, huh?"

They left the 7-11 and drove off. It seemed to take forever to get to the jail, but it was really only half an hour of increasingly unpleasant driving. The closer they got, the seedier the neighborhoods became. Leigh saw low-riders with rolled-down windows, their drivers flicking cigarettes out the windows as they yelled at women on the streets. Despite the early hour, the loud bass beat of rap music caused entire blocks to thump, and some hangers-around were already smoking pot.

I'm glad I left the house without makeup and jewelry, Leigh thought, anticipating the scene ahead. Her heart was pounding and her palms were clammy with sweat. She looked over at Brad. He was taking it all in stride.

"Honey, does any of this make you nervous?" Leigh asked.

Brad chuckled. "Guess I'd be in the wrong business if I answered yes."

They pulled into the parking lot, and Leigh was never so happy to see so many cops. As they entered, she pulled her hood up over her ponytail and walked in behind Brad. "No hoodies if you are seeing a prisoner!" she heard one of the cops say. Leigh had no idea why this should be the rule, but pulled her hoodie off quickly.

Inside the jail, the atmosphere was something beyond her comprehension. Brad had tried to warn her what it was like, but his warnings were nothing like the real thing. The noise, the yelling, the crying, the stench, the filth, the sheer numbers of people behind bars were overwhelming. Everything smelled sharply of urine, with high notes of vomit and feces. The stench of booze and cigarettes oozed out of the pores of the inmates' tattooed skin. Some looked and smelled as though they'd been here for days without a shower or a change of clothes. There were no whites showing in anyone's eyes, only a veiny red.

Brad calmly looked at his wife. "Honey, take a deep breath— you're looking pale. Are you okay?"

Leigh nodded yes. *I'm not taking a deep breath in here*, she thought, and put her hand across her face. Brad asked the guard if he could have a word with his client, and was told to take a seat. He and Leigh looked at each other as if to say, *No thanks, we're standing.* Leigh thought to herself, *The only thing I want to touch in this place is the inside of my shoes, and I plan to burn them along with this sweat suit when I leave.*

The whistles and catcalls soon started up. "Hey you, pretty girl—look over here!" called a huge man, rattling the iron doors and cackling out loud. Brad approached the desk again and asked if they could be directed to the women's section of the jail.

A fat female officer in combat boots came over and said, "Sure, follow me."

Brad and Leigh followed the officer down two corridors and across a waiting room to the women's section of the jail. Brad asked the desk clerk if he could see his client, and gave Dixie's name; whereupon she looked up and pointed. Leigh looked over and there was Dixie, sitting amidst a group of about a dozen women, gabbing away like she was at a charity tea party. *She must really be wasted,* Leigh thought to herself. Leigh walked over and made eye contact with her.

Brad stepped past Leigh and spoke directly to Dixie. "Dixie!

You'll be held for about three more hours, and there's a bail bondsman on his way."

Dixie turned to her new friends. "Wait here, dears; Ah'll be right back!" she said, and walked across the cell to where Brad was standing. There she burst into tears.

"How can Ah keep this from Howard?" she wailed. "Will all mah friends find out?" Mascara poured down her face as she wiped the tears away. Reverting to a feral state at the sight of her tears, her newest friends started to harass her.

"Hey, white lady! Don't do the crime if you can't do the time!"

"Who are these fancy friends of yours?"

Leigh tried to console her. "Dixie, you're just going to have to ride this out a while. There's nothing we can do to get you out in less than three or four hours."

"Ah'm scared, Leigh," Dixie told her though the bars. "Ah've been sitting in the corner bah myself, but they started harassing me, sayin' Ah think Ah'm better than 'em, and pokin' fun at me. They think Ah think Ah'm too good to talk to 'em, and told me Ah'd regret it. They got in mah face with horrible bad breath and gold teeth; they're scarin' me, Leigh! Ah've been trying to talk to 'em, but Ah can't understand much of what they're sayin', and Ah'm sure it ain't good! Ah'm tryin'—Ah'm pretendin' to be freends with 'em. Ah just—oh, I just don't know what to dew! You've *got* to hep me, Leigh, pleeez!"

As Dixie and Leigh huddled in a corner, whispering through the bars, Brad was at the desk, calling to check on the bail bondsman. The other women in the cell were still yelling at Dixie.

"Hey girl! Get your chubby ass over here."

"You too good to talk to us? You gotta talk to that fancy friend of yours?"

"You don't like pretty girls like us?"

"We go to parties, too! We pretty! We fun!"

Dixie turned away, wiped at her tears and went back into the center of the lion's den. Leigh walked a few feet away, and leaned up against the wall to watch and listen. She heard the loud talking, the laughing, the bickering, the screaming, the raving insults. Dixie sat back down, and from a distance Leigh could see the sobering fear in her eyes as she held back tears and tried to chat with her cellmates once more.

Suddenly, an image of Gerald washed over Leigh. She'd spent time in jails before, but they'd been small-town jails where the sheriffs were used to having the same suspects—namely, her brother and his friends—behind bars every weekend, over and over. This place made the Hewitt jail look like a YMCA.

Yet with this thought came another familiar feeling as Leigh was again struck by the unfairness of it all. The women in here, like Gerald's friends, had probably never had a chance. Born poor, they'd stayed that way; and life for them was nothing but disappointment, crisis and abuse. They talked tough—probably fought tough—but in their eyes Leigh saw the same hopeless, thousand-yard stare. Many of them had simply been broken by misfortune. Gerald used to say that some people preferred prison to not having a roof over their heads; in this place the thought was beyond Leigh's comprehension. Suddenly the far-off pain of her childhood came welling up in Leigh's heart, and tears came to her eyes. What was Gerald doing right now?

Brad came to her, and said the bail bondsman was on his way. Leigh was shaking; her heart raced and her head spun, random useless thoughts crowding into her head for no reason. *Wow,* she thought, *if I were ever thrown in here, I couldn't handle it! How did Gerald go through it so many times? And how did Dixie get herself into this mess?*

After hours spent waiting, breathing in the rank, moist air and attempting to console their friend, Leigh and Brad met the bail bondsman, and Dixie made bail and was released. Holding her head high and fighting back tears, she went to the desk to check out and sign for her jewelry, handbag and personal items. A few minutes later, she was sitting in the back of Brad's luxurious Mercedes in her Chanel suit. Before they left she slipped off her four-inch pumps, leaned out the car door and placed them gently on the asphalt.

"Why are you leaving your shoes behind, Dixie?" Brad asked.

Dixie burst into tears. She explained, between swipes at melting mascara, that when she was in the cell, if the women wanted to pee, there was a hole with a drain in the center of the floor. All the women were expected to stand in a circle around the girl peeing, turning their backs to give her privacy. Sobbing as she continued, Dixie told them that this drain seemed to be clogged and over-flowing all the time. As a result, everyone tracked everything all over the floor.

"My Manolos smell like pee—I never want to see them again!" she sobbed, as though this were the source of all the world's hor-rors. In a rush she told them about the feces on the wall, the hooker who'd tried to French-kiss her and the cop who had handcuffed her so tight it made her wrists swell up black-and-blue. When she was done, she looked down at her Hermès scarf and, as if as an afterthought, threw it out the window.

"It smelled like jail too," she explained miserably.

Having exhausted herself, she sat silent for a few minutes, still wiping away tears and mascara and trying to get her story straight for Howard. Together, the three of them decided that the best thing for her would be to go to the Whites' house, shower there, borrow some of Leigh's clothes and take a nap before she went home. She'd text Howard to say she was at Leigh's, had stayed there last night, and would be home later; and would apologize that she'd worried him.

It was now close to midday. Howard wouldn't be home for hours, Dixie said, so she'd hopefully have time to get the car into the garage for repairs and find Danny. She couldn't imagine what had happened to him; she tried his cell phone again from Leigh's phone, only to get his voicemail. He'd sure never done this before—and when *she* was through with him, he wouldn't ever do it again!

CHAPTER 8

BERGDORF DOESN'T CARRY BABIES, MA'AM

> On shopping trip. Will bring you back something special.

—Katie

As Dixie dealt with her return home across town, Katie Parker and her cotton mouth were preparing to board a plane for Indonesia.

It had been a complicated arrangement to make, but her reason for it was every bit as simple as Dixie Johnson's report had made it sound. She was going to adopt a child.

After about a year and a half of plotting—and reading about Angelina Jolie's adoptions and the press she'd gotten—Katie was on her way to adopt a tsunami kid. Katie knew she needed that orphaned child as much as it—he—needed her. Her pre-nup with Billie would kick in soon; and without a child, she was vulnerable.

Katie realized now that she'd been naive when she married Billie. It had never crossed her mind that he'd married her for any reason other than true love. But now, having come around a bit to the other side of things, she wondered. Had he married her image and not her? Was her whole role here to promote "family values" for his brand? She now suspected she had been a pawn. While he was creating an image for himself he may have thought a trophy wife was necessary. But the new, hugely successful Billie—maybe he didn't so much need that starry-eyed, tabloid-obsessed little girl he'd hoped to groom into the perfect wife. When he'd finally achieved the success he wanted—when his clothing took hold in middle America, where those family values were essential—he would no longer need her.

Billie had certainly already made a name for himself, and his designs had earned him a fair amount of press. His name appeared in the society columns regularly, with and without Katie. But he'd made a mistake; he'd obviously allowed her way too much time to think, and had not paid nearly enough attention to her. In short order, Katie had gone from spoiled to scorned, and had plenty of time to think over what she was going to do about it.

No one noticed how she had changed into a beautiful woman, or appreciated her new dresses, longer extensions, higher heels and exfoliated, Pilates-forged body. All those horrible promotional tours—all those dinners with the financial backers, and the phony press conferences! Katie had had enough. Why was it that she was always invited on the promotional tours in those little towns in the middle of nowhere, but was left sitting at home while Billie went to the A-list events in Manhattan? It wasn't the life she had signed up for; but having had a taste of money and glamour, she wasn't going to settle for the small-town life she'd had before. She was no pawn in someone else's game. She was a queen with a plan, and she was sticking to it. But she knew she would have to work fast.

She'd communicated secretly with an adoption agency for a year. Having looked into her and her husband's finances and histories, the inspectors from the agency had come to her house only once. Brandon Westbrook, on hiatus from a Diva Lorraine tour, was happy to act as Katie's husband. For once, he said, he could make himself up as a man—and he did a smashing job at it. He'd looked the part, he was a great actor, and he picked up the hint of the feminine in Billie brilliantly.

Katie got the call the day after the gala. It was time for her to meet her child. Billie had left the same evening on a trip to New York, to entertain the buyers of America's top department stores; and Katie knew he wouldn't miss her.

The boy's name was Suharto. He was three and a half. A huge tsunami wave had picked him up and deposited him safely atop a Coke machine, taking the rest of his family who knows where. It was as if he had just fallen from the sky: not a single relative or neighbor had since stepped up to identify him.

Now he would become Billie Jr. on paper, so as to leave no question that he was the designer's son. For some added American cache, Katie figured she'd nickname him "Jack"—as in "Jakarta," she laughed to herself. She'd made the deal through channels upon channels, so it would all check out. Her husband never questioned the many expenditures she'd made in the process; a few perks to the accountant made sure of that. All told, Little Billie cost more than four Birkin bags—but Katie knew it was the smartest money she'd ever spent. You had to spend it to make it sometimes; and the boy was marriage insurance, plain and simple.

Katie figured she had a year or so to keep Billie in a trance that would let that pre-nup deadline come and go. She knew that he had always dreamed of a son—a namesake, at that—and she had good reason to hope that little Billie Jr. would fast become the apple of his eye as the clock ticked and she implemented her plan. She'd been legitimately unable to deliver one for him, so it was plausible enough that she might decide to buy one to make him happy.

Leaving a wife was usually forgiven, but it looked pretty bad when a man broke up a family just to save a few million dollars. And a family with such a politically correct child—forget it! *That* wasn't an image a well-known designer would ever want to paint for his public, even if he couldn't stand his big-spending wife and her not-so-discreet boy toys. Anyway, he'd come around eventually to her view of things. He had an image to uphold, and she was part of the package, whether he knew it or not.

It's my time, she thought proudly as she strutted through the airport doors. *Billie's just going to have to get with the program!*

***

Steve Senkew liked this line of work.

Granted, it was very different from what he'd done before. Night-and-day different. Even a few years into it, he still made the comparison; which, with an ability like his, was unavoidable. It was hard not to compare the present with the past, when you had a photographic memory; the past was that much more present to you. But after years of seeing the sorts of things he'd seen on the force—and without the ability of most cops to forget—it was a welcome change.

Plenty of cops went into private-investigator work, but few had been as lucky in their connections as he had. Most of those he knew worked for courthouses or insurance companies, and spent their dull days tracking people down to serve them subpoenas, or looking into suspicious claims. Some were a bit luckier, and were hired by the wealthy to find out whether the companies they invested in were legit. Those guys had it pretty good—or their expense accounts did, anyway. But either of those lines of work would have bored Steve stiff. Imagine poring over reams of insurance claims and company records all day, and not being able to forget any of them!

No, the kinds of things Steve now saw on a day-to-day basis were *much* more interesting to see, and to remember later. Cheating housewives, energetically screwing their gardeners; runaround husbands, getting head from their secretaries; secret drug addictions, sex addictions, gambling problems, fetishes, you name it—if it was something you could imagine hiding from your spouse, it was something Steve Senkew was paid, very handsomely, to catch you doing. The more trivial the secret, it seemed, the more Steve got paid to sniff it out. There was simply nothing like marital distrust to make people shell out without hesitation. And marital distrust was a very brisk business in Miami. Steve had a few clients in other parts of Florida, but they were mostly personal referrals; certainly, he had enough here to keep him more than comfortable.

And oh, the things he'd seen!

As a cop, his flawless memory had plagued him. The everyday horrors of the job—shootings over nothing, corpses fished up from the bay, children with nowhere safe to go—all these visions and events stayed with him forever, with the unspoiled clarity of the first time he'd seen them. Yet now he rarely regretted what he saw. In comparison with those ultimate social evils, the petty deviancies of rich married couples were practically comical. There wasn't much to laugh at about a double homicide, or a missing person; but an aging executive, straining to keep his boner straight enough for a hooker to snort a line off of it? There was quite a lot to laugh at *there,* indeed.

Steve had been hired by businesspeople, politicians, celebrities, heirs and heiresses. Some hired him to dig up dirt; others, to make sure nobody else was digging up theirs. A group of three siblings hired him to find their long-lost father, only to discover that one was married to him. One well-connected husband and wife, both of them secret bondage enthusiasts, had each hired him independently, to make sure the other wasn't following them—to the dungeon they both frequented. Many of his clients were high-profile, and again—the higher the profile, the pettier the problems seemed to become.

Take the guy Steve was working for now: a fashion-designer husband, out to get a handle on his grasping, fame-obsessed wife. Sure, the wife was a liar, and a cheater, and a pretender, and an opportunist; but it would have taken a pretty blind man not to have noticed that before now. The woman had been messing around on her husband for months now, and her hard-working hubby had only just caught on. The only reason he'd found out at all was that *he* was fooling around on *her*, and had wanted some concrete evidence to use in kicking her to the curb; but when Steve had started tailing her, he'd found her indiscretions extended to far more than the occasional nightclub make-out session.

Now she was on her way somewhere, for reasons unknown. It was clear she was flying internationally—Steve had dug up recent credit-card expenses not only for an international flight, but for a passport renewal—but to what country, and for what purpose, it was harder to find out. That's what Steve was doing here today, waiting in the damn airport terminal while the beautiful day passed by outside. He glanced at his watch, and wondered again how long it would be before he saw her.

Then, as if on cue, she appeared.

Steve saw her walking through the airport lounge at a furious pace, and despite her long overcoat *(he'd seen it four days ago, lying folded on their couch)* and huge sunglasses, his infallible recognition was triggered. He stood up, newspaper in hand, and calmly followed her. She must have been in a hurry to get her things together this morning, he reflected; it had been late *(4:13 a.m.)* by the time she'd left that bartender's apartment *(car service, black Excursion, Florida plates, R79 7WC)*, and she couldn't have had her things packed already.

She was heading for the International Departures. Where might she be going? It probably wasn't for long; she only had a smallish bag with her. She stopped for a coffee, and he pretended to read the departure times. He'd already looked at them once; that was enough to have them all for as long as he'd need them. It was a good thing her husband had had an inkling of her travel plans, and was rich enough to buy him a ticket just to get him past security today. Too bad he hadn't known the destination, though; it was pretty clear she wasn't going to Winnipeg. Ah well, he'd just have to follow her to her gate. Maybe she was meeting someone there.

Nope—she was going in alone. Admittedly, some days the business was a little dull. Still—United 9641, to Jakarta? *That* was a surprise, anyway. Steve had seen a lot of affairs, but not too many carried out in Southeast Asia. Well, his work here was finished; he wondered what the hubby would make of *this* info.

He scanned the airport idly as he walked back out into the Arrivals area. When he was a cop, he'd spent hours scanning crowds for the smallest sign of suspicious activity. A lot of cops did that, of course; but then, most of them wouldn't remember every face later, in case something did go down. There were a few telling signs, though—mainly the same signs of any preoccupied person: nervous looks, sniffing, sweating. Some people nodded to themselves, as though steeling themselves for something. Others—well, now, this guy was doing it, right here.

Steve studied the man as he paced back and forth, a concerned look on his face. Hell of a face, too—regal-looking, European, very handsome. Impeccably dressed in a dark-blue suit and silk tie, he certainly stood out among the regular schlubs at the airport. And he made quite a contrast to the guy he was apparently meeting, too: small, good-looking but slightly soft-around-the-edges, about thirty, also vaguely European-looking, in jeans and a T-shirt. It was a strange pair. Suit-and-Tie was annoyed with Softy, that was for sure; right off the plane, and Softy was already catching hell.

Steve looked over at the flight information: British Airways 1588, from Madrid. Now *that* was an interesting-looking pair! If he'd still been a cop, he would've stuck to their heels.

But then—he smiled happily to himself—he wasn't.

CHAPTER 9

PLUS-ONES

> On my way. Running late. Can't wait to catch up with you at lunch!

—Lauren

When Dixie had been dropped off at home after her stint in jail, Leigh crashed and slept for what seemed like a week. She was aware of Brad coming and going for his big case; but other than that, she spent the next few days in a haze, burying herself in her Portuguese linen sheets, eating, tidying up her papers and taking off-and-on "congratulations on the amazing gala" calls. All of her closest friends understood her exhaustion and left her alone.

All, that is, except her best friend Lauren.

Today she'd somehow agreed to bring chaos into order and lunch with her dear friend, who "needed to talk." She knew this meant that she'd probably spend the entire lunch listening to Lauren complain about work; and from the moment she walked through the door at Carpaccio—dressed in her usual classic style, accessorized with lots of big jewelry and a colorful Hermès scarf—she had the distinct feeling of impending doom.

The Bal Harbour restaurant itself was an odd choice. With all the out-of-the-way places around the shops, why would Lauren have picked a place so crowded, and so far-and-wide famous for people watching, for their lunch? Leigh would much rather have gone somewhere more intimate, but it was Lauren's lunch, and Lauren's call. Ah well, Lauren was a dramatic girl; maybe she had reasons for wanting to be out in the open.

"Table for two—I believe the reservation is under Altamira," she told the hostess.

"Yes, of course," the hostess smiled. "Your friend and her companion have already arrived. I had to move you to a larger table to make room for the extra guests, but she said that wouldn't be a problem."

"Thank you," Leigh replied, her stomach twisting as she followed the hostess in. What did she mean, "extra guests"? Who on earth had Lauren brought along with her?

"Leigh, darling," Lauren shouted from her seat at the table, bringing another little grimace. Leigh hated making a scene. Lauren stood as she approached the table, and nudged the man at her side to stand as well. When Leigh saw who it was, she knew their lunch wasn't going to be the girl-to-girl chat she'd imagined. She also realized in a flash why Lauren had chosen such a high-profile, see-and-be-seen place to bring them.

"Hello, Lauren," Leigh smiled, air-kissing each cheek. "I see you've brought a guest."

"Yes—you remember Jacques, of course?" Lauren gushed in her "everything is wonderful" voice. Jacques inclined his head regally as he greeted her, showing his upper-class Spanish nose to full effect.

Leigh had heard that the position of the hump in such a nose literally betrayed its bearer's true nationality and class, and this guy looked the part. He was perfectly barbered and beautifully dressed, with manicured nails and David Webb cufflinks. His shirt was obviously custom-tailored, and starched to the point that it rustled when he moved. Lauren, never to be upstaged in this department, was dressed in a beautiful Valentino suit—her version of office wear—and an armful of bracelets, all from Cartier and all gifts from her husband. In other words, she was dressed for war.

"I hope you don't mind that I invited Jacques to lunch," Lauren went on blithely. "He's new in town, and shopping for a Miami home. You might have met him with Sassy at the gala."

"So nice to see you again," Jacques said, his voice dripping with charm befitting a gigolo, or a soap-opera villain.

Leigh was stunned for a brief moment, but recovered herself by dropping into Hostess Mode.

"Hello again, Jacques! Lauren didn't tell me we were having a guest for lunch; I *love* meeting Lauren's friends." In truth Leigh knew all of Lauren's friends by now, and the comment was a dig at her friend. As all of her close friends knew, Leigh didn't like lunching with strangers. It meant she had to be "on." With Lauren alone, Leigh could say anything; and they usually used lunch to dish on all their friends. So what was this man doing here? From what Lauren had said, he'd already dumped her professionally—and maybe other than professionally—for Sassy. What was Lauren up to?

"Sit and have some wine, darling," purred Lauren. "Jacques is moving to Miami, and hopes to open a gallery here. He's an international art dealer—aren't you, Jacques?" Lauren turned to him as if she were holding a microphone for an interview.

"Yes, I'm here in Miami checking out the scene," Jacques added with a smile. "I've been here, of course, but never with anything but a passing interest. But Miami is filled with art collectors, or so I've heard—most of my experience with them has been through other dealers in New York and Berlin. And it's such a beautiful place! I'm positive I could be very comfortable here."

"Oh, I can assure you Miami has a wealth of art collectors," Leigh replied. She could see why Lauren was obsessed with losing Jacques as a client, or however she'd lost him. He was a handsome man, urbane and presumably educated. Still, though, Leigh couldn't quite get over the way he said the word "comfortable." He made it sound insinuative and dirty. Leigh turned to Lauren and gave her a phony smile. "So, Lauren, who are the *other* guests I hear are coming?"

"Didn't Dixie tell you?" asked Lauren in surprise. "She phoned me this morning and said that you'd told her about our lunch, and asked if she could join us. I thought since Dixie was going to be joining, I'd bring a friend too." When Lauren saw the expression on Leigh's face, she realized she'd made a mistake. "Did I do something wrong?"

"Why, no, darling," replied Leigh, choking back her reaction. "The more the merrier. Where's our waiter?—I need a drink."

"Waiter!" shouted Lauren, now in trouble. She turned back to Leigh and spoke under her breath. "But Leigh, isn't Dixie your friend?"

"Yes, of course she's my friend. But—" Here Leigh, being the lady she was, stopped herself. "It's nothing," she went on. "I was looking forward to lunch with you, and I don't recall mentioning it to Dixie. But I'm so glad you took it upon yourself to make it a party." She smiled and turned away from Lauren to speak to the waiter.

Fortunately the waiter was a sensitive type, and the drinks arrived with lightning speed.

"So, Leigh," said Jacques once they'd toasted, leaning in, "you mentioned Miami's wealth of art collectors. You seem particularly

well connected; surely many of these collectors must be friends of yours?"

"Yes—yes, a few of them are," said Leigh, suddenly feeling cagey.

"Perhaps you might introduce me to one or two," said Jacques. "After all, connections are everything in this business."

"I'm sure that would work out wonderfully," said Leigh; then, without quite knowing why, she added, "though quite a few of them are often out of town."

"As collectors so often are," said Jacques unctuously. "I believe I met a few at your charming gala the other night, however. Whose card did I take—? A Mr. Arriaga, I believe?"

"Of course. Hernan and his partner, Fabio Lopes, are wonderful designers, and very astute art collectors."

"Ah yes, I remember meeting Mr. Lopes as well. That would be Mr. Arriaga's—*design* partner, I presume?"

Leigh remembered this particular ugly qualm of Jacques's, and determined to needle him. "Yes, and partner in the *usual* sense as well," she said. "They're very talented, very charming—and very dear friends of mine," she added pointedly.

Jacques smoothly recovered his smile. "Wealthy friends, at that."

"Most of the guests at my galas are."

"Of course. Much of our brief discussion was about—their—collection. Do you happen to know who assists them with it? I couldn't find a tactful way to ask, when I met them."

Leigh instinctively tensed up. She didn't know much about art collectorship, but she could tell a behind-the-scenes business question when she heard one. Lauren wasn't the only one at the table with a hidden agenda!

Before she could answer, a familiar screech resounded through the restaurant.

"Haahhh there, Leigh!"

Dixie blew in like a tipsy hurricane, firing air-kisses in every direction and settling in at once. Leigh was surprised at the relief that washed over her.

"Lauren, darlin', so nice to see you again. And who's *this* handsome fella?"

"Jacques Mercier—it's a pleasure to meet you, Mrs. Johnson."

"Dixie, please! And the same goes, Ah'm sure. But did we meet before? Ah don't believe Ah remember—"

"Giving me your last name? Forgive me; I must have heard it at the gala the other night. I was there, with—"

"Here, Dixie, let me fill a glass for you," Lauren cut in.

"Well, if yew in*sist*," smiled Dixie innocently, before turning her attention back to Jacques. "Now, what *is* that accent yew've got, darlin'? Russian?"

Leigh smiled as the two fell into a flirtatious back-and-forth. For once, Dixie's domination of the talk was welcome, and lightened the mood considerably. She bounced Jacques's over-the-top charm back at him and then some, and somehow managed to keep him from getting a word in edgewise at the same time. Lauren was obviously trying to turn things around to business with Jacques, but even she seemed happy to let Dixie carry on for a bit. There'd be no shop talk with *that* Southern belle around!

Leigh was beginning to feel positively relaxed when a throaty voice from behind her cut through Dixie's pleasant Southern drawl like a knife.

"Well, isn't this a cozy little group! Leigh, darling, you didn't tell me you were having a party."

Even if Leigh hadn't recognized the voice, she would have known who it was from the look on Lauren's face. She turned around.

"Hello, dear," she said, giving Sassy her hand but not standing up.

Sassy's idea of office wear was a bit revealing, to say the least.

Full cleavage leaped out over her low-cut neckline, which looked like it was competing with the hem of her girdle-tight to see who could show more. *Hardly out of the ordinary for that one,* thought Leigh. Like Melanie Griffith in *Working Girl,* Sassy had always had a mind for business and a body for sin—or at least she thought she did.

"You know, I'm so glad to see you here, Leigh," replied Sassy, pulling up a chair between Dixie and Jacques. "I know you're probably working on your next gala, and I wanted to volunteer my services." She put her arm casually around Jacques's shoulders, hardly looking his way as she did so.

"No," Leigh said, perhaps a little too bluntly. "I'm actually out of the gala game, as of this year. Even so, it was so nice of you to stop by and say hello."

"Yes, enjoy your lunch," Lauren fumed, "whoever you're here to meet."

"It was so lucky to run into you—I was out shopping," Sassy said, completely ignoring Lauren's comment.

"Sassy, darling," snapped Leigh, a little perturbed to have yet another unwanted guest at the table. "My fundraising days are behind me. I'm taking a break but I do appreciate your offer—and I'm sure I'll need help with something else that I can call you about." She hoped this would get Sassy to leave; but now it was her that Sassy was ignoring.

"I'm so glad all of you are getting to meet Jacques," Sassy chirped, turning to Lauren and tightening her grip on Jacques. "You know he's my client and then some! I'm showing him some more property tomorrow, as a matter of fact." Leigh thought she saw Sassy mouth something at Lauren, whose face immediately went red and puffy.

"Now, Sassy," Jacques cut in. "There's no reason for attitude. I'm new in town, and am enjoying meeting everyone. Surely we can get along! Let's at least offer my lovely lady a drink," he added to the rest of the table, and made puppy-dog eyes at Sassy. Lauren looked as though she might puke bullets.

"Hey, yeah, come on and have a glass of wine and join the party," said Dixie to Sassy with a twinkle in her eye. "Ah'm Dixie, the one you ignored when you sat down." She was a drink away from being drunk, and loved the new action at the table.

"Sorry, love—hello, I'm Sassy," said Sassy, offering her hand to Dixie.

"Ah can see that! Nice to meet you, darlin'," slurred Dixie. "Now, could you pour me some more, after you pour yourself a glass? Our waiter seems to have disappeared, and—"

"I'll take care of that, Madam," said the waiter, who had been standing behind Dixie the entire time. With a flourish he produced a glass for Sassy, making her a part of the table whether they liked it or not.

"Thank you, darlin'," slurred Dixie, grabbing at the waiter's leg as he poured. "Be a dear and bring us another bottle, will ya?" She turned to Leigh and held up her glass. "To my dear friend Leigh— Ah'm havin' the best time."

"Yes, to Leigh," said Lauren through clenched teeth.

Leigh looked at Dixie, then at Lauren. The dynamic had changed: with Sassy and Jacques along, even her two best friends were enough to send her back to bed with a migraine and an icepack. She *had* to figure a way to get Sassy out of here, at least—and the sooner the better.

Dixie, however, wasn't in on the plan.

"Now Jacques," she said, turning to the handsome Frenchman again, "Ah know Ah've heard about yew before, but what was it you said you did?"

"I'm a high-end art dealer, specializing in private collections."

"Haahh-end, eh? And just how haahh-end are we talkin' here?"

"Well, I've just put together a small collection for Jay-Z and Beyoncé to shop at Art Basel," Jacques replied nonchalantly. "A nice mix of Old Masters—drawings, mainly, for the cultural caché—as well as some abstract expressionists and African art. They've been collecting the Mandé people's sculpture lately; they love the heart-shaped faces and rounded bellies. Apparently, Beyoncé's trying to get pregnant again," he threw in with a knowing smile.

In spite of themselves, the entire table had leaned in at the word "Jay," and now let out an appreciative gasp. Not only did Jacques seem to know his stuff—he had an inside scoop on the King and Queen of Pop!

"Well," Dixie said appreciatively. "If Jay and Bey are buyin' from you, you must be quite the go-to art guy!"

"Oh, he certainly is," said Sassy, before Lauren could speak up.

"I do the best I can," said Jacques with a showy modesty.

"Excuse me," announced Lauren. "I must go to the ladies' room. Leigh, would you like to join me?"

Leigh hated public restrooms, but Lauren obviously needed her. The look on her face fell somewhere between "seasick child" and "serial killer."

"We'll be right back," she said, smiling at Dixie. She knew it was dangerous to leave these three alone at the table, but if Sassy wouldn't take the hint to leave, she supposed this was the next best thing.

"How am I going to get rid of her?" screamed Lauren under her breath, as soon as they entered the ladies' lounge. "I *told* you that bitch has been stealing my clients—and now she has the nerve to stop by our table and flaunt her affair with one of them! I invited him to lunch to try and get his business back—the *right* way, with my legs together! I deserve that commission, Leigh, I really do. He was my client way before Sassy stole him—remember, she met him through me, the slut! Seriously, though, what can I do?"

"Well, for one thing, we'd better not stay in here too long," said Leigh. "Who knows what'll happen with those three out there! Dixie's a lot of things, but discreet isn't one of them." She looked hard at her friend. "And what are you doing using Sassy's sneaky tactics, anyhow? Bringing Jacques around unannounced, to work on him at lunch with me? It's not worth it, even if you're doing it for professional reasons. That's beneath you, Lauren. Next thing I know, you'll be wearing fuck-me pumps and Forever 21 mini-tube dresses that out-cleavage Sassy's."

"You're right, you're right," Lauren laughed. "I'm just so *mad* at that bitch, it's making me nuts! I really just thought I could get him back as a client this way, but my cleavage failed me!" She laughed again. "Let's go back."

"All right—but keep your head! We'll just get the check and leave. Let's wrap up this uncomfortable lunch; I'm miserable. Now I need a nap because of you! I thought we were going to have a relaxed girls' lunch, and you bring me to Carpaccio to flaunt it in front of some guy."

"I know, I'm sorry. I thought by asking Jacques to lunch in such a popular spot, with you, it'd help me gain his trust. Sassy's connections have got to be so much trashier! And the guy's the ideal client. Supposedly he has a whole fleet of cars, and is quite a successful art dealer. I was hoping he'd realize Miami is ideal and spend a few million on a home here. And then Sassy ate him whole. Or he's eating her hole, I don't know." Both women let out a big laugh.

"The whole thing just makes me sick," sighed Lauren when they'd had a moment to collect themselves.

"Then *leave* it," Leigh said. "Don't take the dishonest moves of your opponent and make them your own. It's completely beneath you. You *have* lost Jacques, and you'd better accept it; he's deep into Sassy, whatever that means. Meanwhile, unlike her, you have a reputation to maintain. Take the high road! It's easier on the wheels, and has fewer gutters."

Just as they were about to walk out of the ladies' lounge, Dixie stormed in.

"Lauren, honey, you'd better get back to the table, and quick," Dixie shrieked. "That Sassy gal has her hands all over your friend! Ah had to excuse myself; she was practically climbin' into his lap!"

Lauren and Leigh exchanged a quick grimace.

"Remember—the high road," said Leigh.

"The fuckin' high road," repeated Lauren.

They walked back to the table slowly, smiling like nothing was going on; but their smiles dropped quickly when they got there. Lauren grabbed Leigh's hand and gasped.

"They're gone! They're gone and she's won," wailed Lauren miserably.

"The nerve of that bitch," Leigh added before she sat down. "Didn't even leave a tip for the wine she drank!" She grabbed her own glass and drained it off.

"She really will stop at nothing!" said Lauren. "God, fuck her— and fuck him too, the horny idiot."

"They've probably just gone off for a little afternoon tryst," said Leigh. "It probably has nothing to do with business. You should call him later, and keep it professional. Don't let Sassy get to you. She's the loser, not you. Tell him that if she fails to find him a home, he can still call you. Leave the door open."

Leigh looked at her friend, hoping she'd made her feel a little better; but they both knew the truth. Sassy had wrapped her legs around Jacques and wouldn't let go. This was one business deal that reeked of bedroom drama.

"They gone?" asked Dixie as she returned to the table. "Good thing—them two need to get a room, and fast! Still, Ah had such a great time, darlings. As usual! Lunch is on me—Ah've already taken care of the check."

"Oh, Dixie, you shouldn't have," said Leigh.

"Hell, why not! We didn't eat anything anyhow." Dixie laughed. "You know, Ah still can't find Danny! Marie's callin' me a car service. Oh, we must do this again real soon." She bent to kiss Leigh and nearly fell over. "Oh dear, Ah'd best be going—the ol' balance is actin' up again." She blew a kiss at Lauren and stumbled out of the restaurant.

Leigh looked at Lauren and smiled. "See? Some people have real problems." The two laughed. Then a serious look came over Lauren.

"Oh, Leigh, you *have* to have your gala again next year," she said earnestly, placing a hand on Leigh's shoulder. "My business always suffers this time of year, and I find potential clients there every time."

Leigh raised an eyebrow. "Like Jacques?" she said.

"Never mind him," said Lauren. "Seriously, Leigh—please. I need that gala." The two stood up and turned to walk out. When they were outside, Leigh stopped.

"You know, I *have* been reconsidering my decision a bit," admitted Leigh. "But not because of the needs of the Miami real estate market."

"Really? What happened?"

"I saw some people in jail—a project for Brad," Leigh added quickly, to keep Dixie out of the story. "It made me feel the same need to help that I've always felt. I just—I don't know how else to do it right now."

"Leigh, it's what you do best. You've been at it so long, you're a natural at it. And it helps so many people—myself included! Just think about it, okay? Even just one last one? None of us are ready to see you go."

Leigh handed her voucher to the valet in silence. The two

friends stood in thoughtful silence as the car was brought around. Then, as she was getting in, Leigh paused. *I really must need a nap,* she thought. *It almost sounds like a good idea.*

Brushing the thought from her mind, she waved goodbye to her friend.

"We'll see, Lauren. We'll see."

CHAPTER 10

THE BENEFIT OF THE DOUBT

> Please please please can you be here at 630 to walk the red carpet? It would really help the cause!

—Gena

Try not to judge. Try not to judge.

Leigh usually didn't have to say such things to herself, but tonight it had already become her mantra. She had agreed to attend her friend Gena's fundraiser tonight—Gena's first effort in that direction—and in her usual fashion, she'd pulled out all the stops to ensure it had a good showing. Not only had she convinced Brad to attend with her, but she'd also called most of her friends to encourage their financial support. Now, thinking of how her friends might see what she was seeing, she fought to keep down a cringe. Hopefully they would have forgotten, during the two months that had passed since her last gala, what a *real* fundraising ball was like.

Try not to judge.

Guests at her own annual gala entered via a red carpet at a

designated entrance, to the flash of paparazzi's cameras. Tonight's event was held at the Gansevoort Hotel in Miami Beach; and its guests, as she was currently discovering, were to enter through a crowd dressed in sweats, on their way to a gym next to the ballroom on the second floor.

"I can't believe Gena didn't arrange for a separate entrance," she said as she bumped her way through a trio of oblivious muscle-heads.

"I think it's funny," laughed Brad, who held her arm and led her through the gym-going crowd. "And actually, I kind of prefer it to the red carpet."

"Of course *you* would; you hate having your picture taken," Leigh said. "Still, it isn't the first impression I'd want for my guests, especially if I were—"

"Leigh, darling, I'm so glad you're here," shouted Lauren, who was already standing in line at the check-in table next to a group of lost-looking tourists in loud polo shirts. Dressed in a gorgeous black strapless Valentino cocktail dress that offset her long, thick auburn hair—and a necklace of round diamonds set in lacy platinum that Leigh was sure she'd seen for forty grand in a Tiffany catalogue—she looked as though the tourists' shirts might sunburn her.

"Lauren! You look beautiful. And you've got Francisco with you! Hello, Francisco."

"Nice to see a friendly face," said Lauren's handsome husband with a grin.

Lauren leaned in close. "This event is *atrocious,*" she whispered. The two women exchanged hugs as their husbands shook hands and made "here we are again" faces.

"Why, what's wrong?" asked Leigh under her breath. "And why on earth is there such a long line at the check-in table?"

Lauren looked at her as if to say, *You know exactly why.* Leigh cringed again. Certainly, the art of the check-in, so crucial for setting the tone of the night, was not on exhibit here. Guests at Leigh's events were greeted with champagne on silver trays and checked in immediately, if they weren't recognized on sight by the trained door staff. Here, the guests had to line up to prove they'd been invited, and waited, drink-less, while slow and disorganized volunteers pored over their lists. Not a great way to start, with someone whose money you were after—this would almost guarantee that most of them would begin the night grumpy, and end it with paltry donations.

"It would never happen at one of *your* galas," Lauren said. "I can't believe we had to share the entrance with those stupid tourists and sweaty people. In Spandex! For a minute there, I almost felt overdressed." They laughed out loud together.

"Ah well, I'm sure we'll have fun once we get inside," said Leigh, trying to be optimistic. "There'll have to be drinks there! And anyhow, the event's for a good cause, so it's important we support it."

"Francisco and I'll go find out where we're seated," Brad said, already walking away with Lauren's husband. "I'll try to find us some drinks, while I'm at it."

"Thanks," smiled Leigh back at him.

"How hard did you have to twist *his* arm to come tonight?" Lauren asked.

"Oh, no more than usual. So, a fair amount." They laughed. "How about yours?"

"The same, really. He's still been strange with me lately, but he seems happier, and a lot less reclusive. I told him it meant a lot to me that he come with me, and he agreed immediately."

"That's great," said Leigh. "Wonder what the strangeness is about, then? Maybe he's planning a surprise for you."

"Maybe! Things have definitely been better lately in…you know."

"Oh?"

"Yeah." Lauren smiled mischievously. "I mean, he still seems a little weird—*performative* is really the best way to put it! Like he's trying to impress me, or something. But lately…I don't know. He's been telling me to do certain things, and wear certain things, and stuff like that…and I've actually been getting kind of into it. It's been pretty hot with him, to be honest."

"That's terrific!"

"Yeah, it is." Lauren's face flushed. "Anyway, I'm glad you guys both came tonight; Brad's the best."

"I'm very lucky,"agreed Leigh, as they walked into the sparsely decorated ballroom. "Brad *is* the best! Now let's find some champagne before I get stressed out."

Before they could move, though, she heard a voice calling her name.

"Leigh! Good evening—Leigh!"

The milling crowd parted, revealing Gena Evans, the evening's hostess. The sight was, as usual, a little jarring. Gena was one of those cosmetically enhanced society ladies who, after uncounted surgeries, look at once decades younger than their millionaire husbands, and decades older than they really are. It was a strange effect of all that cutting and Botox, and one Leigh could never understand anyone consciously going for. Fear of age seemed to trump consciousness, for some. Yet aside from that strangely artificial face, Gena was always proper and well dressed, and this evening was no exception. She looked elegant and streamlined, in a floor-length St. John knit accessorized with understated Van Cleef gold jewelry and a diamond brooch she'd bought during the Elizabeth Taylor estate auction at Sothebys. Leigh had always known her to be inoffensive and unemotional—a well educated, perfectly bred, beautifully dressed bore with coiffed hair and a canned laugh. She was a fixture on the same society circuit that Leigh generally avoided, aside from soliciting potential donors; and should be well used to this crowd. But this was her first effort at producing a fundraiser; and even through her flawless outfit and immobile face, she was obviously a bit flustered.

"Leigh, darling, I'm so glad you could attend my little fundraiser!" she said a little too loudly, coming in to greet them. "And hello, Lauren—I'm glad you were able to join her."

"Hello, Gena," Leigh replied. "I'm so glad you invited us. I generally spend so much time working on my gala that I don't have much time for other charity events; I'm glad I have more time now."

"I heard," Gena said, with an effort at a dismayed look. "It's *so sad* that you're retiring from it."

"Yes, well, we'll have to—"

"I made sure your table was right in front," Gena said proudly, looking around as a photographer approached. "Where's your husband? We should really get a photo."

"I believe he's looking for our table," Leigh said, thinking to herself that this was the perfect place *not* to have her photo taken. While she was quite accustomed to the flash of photographers, she hadn't planned to be photographed here and directly associated with Gena's train-wreck. Sure, she'd called in some of her friends to ask their support—after all, it was for a good cause: an after-school program for underprivileged girls. But Gena had been one of her gala donors, and if her photo appeared in the press for tonight's event, she'd be expected to attend everything for every other donor who'd ever attended any of her galas. Fortunately, Gena didn't press the point.

"I'm so sorry for the confusion at the door, by the way," she said, her face turning pink. "When I booked the ballroom for this event, the gym hadn't opened yet, and no one told me we'd have to share our entrance with a group of…perspiring gym enthusiasts."

"Ah, don't sweat it, Gena. It's a charity; people will understand. It looks like you have a nice turnout."

"Yes—thanks to you, I have a nice group of big spenders," agreed Gena. "Let's just hope they can stand to open up their pockets in this economy."

"I'm sure they will. Hey, I'm going to mingle, and I'll come back when I find Brad, okay?"

"Absolutely, darling," Gena said, already turning to follow the photographer through the crowd. Leigh knew she'd be looking for recognizable faces, regulars in the *Miami Herald's* society column. At least, she should be. Since this was her first attempt, she needed all the press she could get.

"Oh my *God!*" shrieked Lauren suddenly. "There's your friend Dixie over there. Or should I say *stalker?* Does she go everywhere you do?"

"Actually, I gave her a call to join us at our table," Leigh replied, looking around for her. These days she knew if she didn't invite Dixie, she'd invariably show up anyway. Besides, Dixie wasn't exactly a stalker—she was more like a loyal fan without any other real friends.

"Who's she got with her?" Lauren asked. "Surely that's not her husband."

"That's odd," Leigh said, scrunching up her nose in confusion. "I'd assumed Dixie would bring her husband Howard, but for some reason she seems to have brought her driver instead."

"I'm just glad she *has* one, at the rate she drinks," laughed Lauren.

Leigh was about to say something, but thought better of it.

"Oh, Leigh," shrieked Dixie, as she crossed the room, "there you are. I thought you'd never get here."

As usual, Dixie had already had her share of champagne; and was pawing at arms and butts trying not to fall down as she walked up to Leigh. She wore a bright-red chiffon dress that looked a bit like a designer knock-off—probably something purchased online during one of her drunken shopping sprees. Be that as it may, she sure didn't stint on the jewelry; if they'd auctioned off what was around Dixie's neck—all diamonds and rubies—they could probably keep the girls' program running for another year.

"Hi, Dixie," said Leigh, as Dixie grabbed her for air kisses. She was glad to see Dixie; with her at their table, the event would at least be entertaining. "No Howard tonight?"

"Oh, he ain't the type to frequent things like this," Dixie said with a dismissive wave. "Ah'm his only charity! And he's neglecting me as usual. He actually told me to bring Danny as my date!" Dixie laughed uproariously. "If he only knew," she whispered confidentially. "Tonight's the first time Ah've seen Danny since Ah was in… well, *you* know. Ugh!" She shuddered at the memory of it.

"Forget that, Dixie," Leigh said. "Forget it like those shoes you left in the parking space! You look lovely tonight."

"Well, maybe Ah do! You know, Leigh," she added, smiling, "this is *nothin'* like your gala. Whoever organized this should be shot."

"No comment," said Leigh uncomfortably. Dixie was right, of course; but Leigh couldn't believe she'd actually said it. "I'm sure—"

But Dixie had turned from her to draw off Lauren for a moment, and was whispering something in her ear. Lauren face brightened strangely, as though Dixie had goosed her. *What could she be telling her?* Leigh wondered.

"Leigh—phew, I thought I'd never make it back," laughed Brad, easing through the crowd. "I only just made it to the front to get our table number. Francisco's grabbing drinks for Lauren and him." He passed a flute of champagne to Leigh, who quickly put down the one she'd already taken from one of the passing waiters. *Ever the dutiful husband!* she laughed to herself. He looked extra handsome tonight—his Armani suit, vintage Versace tie and wavy salt-and-pepper hair made him look at once formidable and cool.

"There you are, darling," she said, "and not a moment too soon! This crowd is not at all what I expected; I'll be surprised if Gena raises any money at all."

"Why so?" Brad asked. "Aren't there any bigshots here?"

"Oh, this group's only interested in having their photos taken and seeing who else is here. No one's even bidding on the silent auction items. I really feel bad for Gena." That much was true; Leigh was genuinely concerned. If anyone knew how much work went into these events, it was her. Still, she knew never to donate any of her time to charities that were so shallow, all photo ops and egos. Leigh's events had superficial elements to them, sure; but at bottom they were all about the real deal: donations. Big ones.

"I'm sorry to hear that," Brad said. "But listen, I think we'd better get to our table." He looked around cautiously. "I just saw Billie Parker outside with his wife Katie, posing for a photographer that was following them around. Katie caught me and asked about you, and made me promise that we'd pose with them for a photo!" With a smile, he tossed off the rest of his champagne and gave his empty flute to a passing waiter.

"You wouldn't let such a thing happen to me."

"Of course not, darling. Shall we?" Brad asked, taking Leigh's arm.

"My knight in shining armor," Leigh laughed. She was a pro at maneuvering her way through crowds like this, but was always pleased when her husband took control.

"You know, Lauren," Leigh said quietly, as they found their seats, "tonight feels like it might have been a mistake after all."

"You've got *that* right!" Lauren laughed.

"You know that isn't what I mean."

"I know. But it isn't your fault it's such a mess, honey."

"I know, I know." She frowned. "Just—just tell me my gala

wasn't ever like this. This is just a photo-op for social climbers!" Leigh felt bad saying it, but she was upset by the spectacle of the evening. Dinner hadn't even been served yet, and it was almost 10:30.

"Leigh, this is nothing like your gala," Lauren said, placing her hand on Leigh's shoulder. "You know that. Poor Gena doesn't have a clue. She needs a charity to rescue *her!* From what I've seen, this isn't even a real money crowd."

"I wonder how many other tables are full, like ours?" Leigh said softly to Lauren. "If Gena gave away most of her tables to people she hoped would bid in the auction, she might go home owing money instead of making it."

"Your head's too much in the game. Try to forget about it and enjoy yourself."

Try not to judge. Try not to judge.

It was easier said than done. Poor Gena! Leigh inwardly vowed to pay for their table herself, even though Gena had offered it for free just to get her there. It was just the right thing to do. *God,* she thought, *I wouldn't offer a free seat to the Queen of England at my gala. That just isn't how charity events work.*

As she looked around, Leigh could see a few familiar faces. Dottie and Dr. Anderson, regular contributors to her charity, were seated at the table next to theirs. Dottie waved and looked a bit uncomfortable as her husband gestured wildly, trying to get the attention of a waiter.

"I hope you had cocktails outside," yelled Dixie across the table. "Apparently they're a little short-handed tonight."

Not one to be caught out in the dark, Dixie had three glasses in front of her. From her drawl and pink-tinged complexion, Leigh guessed she was on her fifth or sixth already. Only Dixie could have managed to sneak so much out of the cocktail party—most of the others were still waiting for drinks.

Brad sat on Leigh's right, and Lauren sat on her left. Francisco, returning with a couple of glasses of champagne, made a face as he saw his seat next to Dixie. He was in for an earful of Southern charm, and he knew it.

Before she could start in on him, Leigh leaned across to her. "Dixie—where's Danny?"

"Oh, he's around somewhere," Dixie whispered back. "Hopefully he hasn't found another woman to drive." The two women laughed.

"I'm starving," said Francisco.

"I'm sure now that we're all seated, the waiter will be here soon," Leigh said, trying to be upbeat. She knew it was wishful thinking the moment she said it. By the looks on the faces of the guests who'd already been seated a while, service wasn't high on the list for the evening's event. Now that they were seated, Leigh noticed their centerpiece seemed a bit tattered, like it'd already been used for another event.

Poor Gena! After all this work, it was rather sad. Granted, Gena would be the first to make a snide comment at someone else's event, if everything wasn't perfect. But she was now one of the few who truly knew what went into these events, and Leigh felt a certain sisterhood for her. Energy was everything at these things, and the energy here was against her.

"Now you see why people rave about *your* gala, dear," whispered Brad, leaning over so no one else would hear. "Though frankly, I'm surprised the Gansevoort hasn't made a better effort—everyone loves the hotel, and this event could showcase their banquet services. The place is usually so amazing; what a miss!"

"Well, at least we're all sitting now," Leigh said. "There's—wait, Gena's going to say something."

"My apologies, everyone," said Gena, standing to address the crowd. "The wine that was donated for the event just arrived.

Apparently the waiters were hiding in the back—they were embarrassed that there was no wine, and didn't want to serve dinner without it." A nervous laugh ran through the crowd.

"Bad service due to excellent service," joked Francisco quietly. Lauren giggled and punched his arm.

"But now that we have it," Gena went on, "we're going to get started! Thanks for your patience, and enjoy your dinner."

She smiled broadly, her calm exterior threatening to crack. As she turned, Leigh noticed a tiny stain at the base of her spine. Poor Gena was sweating! *This is really not her night,* Leigh thought. Some people were just meant to be guests.

The waiters finally served the room-temperature wine, and dinner was underway. The only one who seemed not to mind the delay was Dixie; who, on some strange impulse, had insisted on refilling her glass of champagne from the others she'd corralled in front of her, and who now kept the waiter busy refilling her wine glass. Warm or cold, wine was wine in her book.

Hunger had left everyone a little on edge, and the table conversation was a bit stiff. Lauren urged Francisco to talk about an algorithm he'd been working on in his spare time—something about predicting population densities in middle-sized cities—but Francisco seemed less eager to talk about it than anyone else was to hear it. In turn, Francisco asked Brad about the case he was working on; which, Brad was sorry to tell them, was strictly confidential. Leigh almost asked Lauren how *her* work was going; then, coming to her senses at the last moment, remembered that she didn't want to get her started about it for the hundredth time.

Always encouraged by silences, Dixie filled the air with enthusiastic descriptions of Leigh's last gala and the ones before it, and painful comparisons between those and Gena's.

"Can you imagine, asking me to show my invitation! That

woulda never happened at one of Leigh's galas."

"Ah've seen a lot of dining-room chairs, butcha know when I really understood what good upholstery was? Leigh's gala."

"You see that? He walked right past me! And my glass is as dry as a bone. You know, at Leigh's gala, we were treated nothin' like this."

Finally, everyone at the table seemed to turn to Leigh.

"So, about what we were talking about the other day," said Lauren. "Have you *really* decided never to have another fundraiser? I mean, it's up to you, of course—but I'd rather stay at home than attend another one like this."

"I'm sure she's doing the best she can," muttered Leigh, hoping to change the subject.

"Come on, Leigh," Brad cut in. "Even your very first fundraiser was better than this fiasco, by far." Diplomatic attorney that he was, Brad usually held his tongue in such things; but the evening was obviously going to be a bust.

Lauren gestured at a no-name singer in the corner, lip-synching to a music track while everyone ignored her.

"Poor—um—singer," she laughed, "whoever she is! You know, even during dinner, I think our favorite diva Lorraine would have been a better choice." It was true; Lorraine would have kept the place packed and the crowd happy, under any circumstances.

"Anyway, Leigh, what's your charity gonna do without money from your gala?" asked Dixie.

"Hey, that's a good point," Lauren cut in. "You can't let those kids down! Never mind us; though if it hurts me to lose you, it's got to hurt them more. And you know how many prospective clients I get every year from your fundraiser—it's one of my best networking events. If I have to depend on events like this, I really *will* lose all my business to—"

"So *that's* why you come to my gala, huh?" Leigh asked, trying to keep a straight face. "It's just a networking opportunity?"

"No, no—I mean, it *is* that, but not *just* that," Lauren replied. "Leigh, you know what I mean. This event is just so…déclassé. Like you said, it's packed with social climbers out to get their photos taken. Your gala is something special. It's hard for us to see it go."

"I get it," said Leigh. She looked down at the table, and grimaced. The plain white tableware was chipped; the lame daisies in the centerpiece were drooping. The whole sight depressed her. She looked up and watched Dixie almost fall from her chair trying to get a waiter's attention. The room was slowly but surely emptying.

Miami has come to this, she thought.

Suddenly it occurred to her that it was exactly what Miami *would* be coming to, if the Genas of the world were allowed to run the show. Sure, she had great intentions, and she'd tried her best; but she had no idea how much work was involved, poor thing! It just wasn't a job you could do halfway, and that's how she'd done it. Everything at this fundraiser was slapdash and half-thought-out. A gala took passion, commitment and hard work. It took someone who was willing to work 24-7 to make it happen. This—this was just phoning it in. But so much of the world was. It was the schools, the economy, the prison system, everything. Damn, was she sick of the world phoning it in! But what was *she* doing about it—?

She stood abruptly. Sensing something was wrong, Brad stood too.

"What is it, honey?" he asked.

She took a deep breath, exhaled, hesitated.

"Brad, do you…I mean, would you mind…"

Her husband stared into her eyes.

"Happy wife, happy life," he said with a grin. "You know that's my motto."

The two stood smiling at each other for a long moment. Leigh looked around at the faces of her friends, tilted up expectantly at her. She couldn't believe she was going to say it.

"I'll do it," she said. "I'll do one last gala, and I'll make it spectacular. If I'm going out, I want to go out with a bang."

The rest of the table cheered.

CHAPTER 11

IT BEGINS...AGAIN

> Gena's gala! I had to drive through Jack-in-the-Box on my way home to get something to eat.

—Adrienne

Leigh sat up in bed and looked at her alarm clock. She'd over-slept without meaning to, for the first time in years. Granted, it wasn't long past eleven; but Leigh was used to getting up at seven every morning for her breakfast cup of green tea.

She felt dazed, foggy. How much had she had to drink last night? Well, never mind that—it was time to take stock of things. It was Saturday, so the kids were at home. No, wait, they were at a friend's. Brad would be—*ohhh*. Right. She remembered that she'd told him—and everyone else at the table—that she'd be doing another gala. There had been someone else too; who was it?

Adrienne, she suddenly remembered. It was Adrienne Adams.

She'd run into the snippy editor-in-chief as they were leaving that terrible benefit late last night. Adrienne was known and respected around Miami—though not necessarily liked—for her work at *Ocean View Magazine*. She had the reputation of an Anna Wintour wannabe, but without Anna's brains, experience or talent. She was also a size 12, which was as much an aberration in Leigh's world as it probably was in Anna's.

Leigh had shared the news that she was back in the gala business, blurting out that this would be her biggest, bestest gala ever. She had also—the memory came back to her in a cold rush—agreed to do an interview with *Ocean View,* if the charity was featured on the cover. She couldn't believe she'd said it. She didn't want to be on a magazine cover—she didn't really even want to produce another gala! What was she thinking? In a moment of champagne-fueled ego, she'd spoiled her plans of returning to business, running her company, traveling for work and taking a few exotic vacations. *I'm a fool,* she thought.

Before she could even make it out of the bedroom, her cell started ringing.

"Good morning, this is Leigh," she said, putting on her pleasant phone voice. Only her closest friends had her cell number, so she didn't hesitate to answer—even with calls marked PRIVATE, like this one. Who could that be, she idly wondered.

"Good morning, Leigh, I hope it's not too early to call," a sharp voice said. Leigh was struggling to place the voice just as the caller announced herself. "It's Adrienne Adams, dear—I just wanted to follow up on our conversation last night. Your friend Dixie gave me your cell number, and told me she was sure you wouldn't mind me calling."

Dixie! Just as Leigh was about to lie and tell Adrienne she didn't mind the call, a tone let her know she was getting another call.

"Adrienne—lovely to hear from you—can you hold for a second? I'm getting another call." *Who could be calling this early on a Saturday morning?* she thought as she picked up.

"Leigh, it's Dixie," Dixie said breathlessly. "I ran into Adrienne Adams from *Ocean View Magazine* last night after you left."

"Yeah, I know," said Leigh, cutting Dixie off abruptly. "She's on the other line. You gave her my cell number? *Really?* Now I'll never be free!" Of course, Leigh wasn't really mad. It looked better for Dixie to have given out her number, than it would for her to have done it herself. She was still shocked that she'd agreed to a cover story, though.

"Leigh, I'm so sorry," Dixie whispered.

"Dixie, let me call you back," Leigh replied curtly. "I'll call you back as soon as I'm finished with Adrienne." She'd knew if she kept her hanging a bit, she could probably guilt Dixie into volunteering her time for the charity—or even better, making a big donation. She took a breath and clicked back over to Adrienne. Cover story or no, what on earth could the editor want with her on a Saturday morning?

"Sorry," she said. "It was actually Dixie letting me know that you'd be calling."

"No problem," answered Adrienne. "I just wanted to schedule a meeting for Monday. We need to finalize our plans for your cover story and photo shoot. I wanted to make sure that *Ocean View* has an exclusive on the gala, as you indicated last night."

Leigh felt a sudden chill run down her spine. Even with all the wine she'd drunk the night before, she was positive she hadn't agreed to an exclusive.

"Now, Adrienne," she started, hoping to charm the editor. "You know I can't promise an exclusive. I'm promoting a charity—a fundraiser—and I need to generate as much press for it as possible." An *exclusive?* What was the woman thinking? It was enough to commit to the cover. Who did this Adrienne woman think she was, anyway?

"Leigh, I'm not talking exclusive coverage of the gala. I'm just talking an exclusive interview with you and your husband, talking about your part in Miami society—fundraising and the whole social scene. Surely you don't think I'd ever demand exclusive coverage of a charity gala! That would be so selfish—and, well, redundant for our readers."

Oh, right, Leigh thought. She knew that if Adrienne could get exclusive coverage of the gala, she would. Not only that, she'd attach the magazine's name to the event and promote it as if *Ocean View* had produced the entire affair—all while contributing nothing but the magazine's name and a little media coverage. It was an old P.R. game, and Adrienne should have known she was too savvy to fall for it.

"Well in any case, Adrienne, why don't we talk about all this next week?" she said sweetly. "I'm running late for a kids' birthday party, and I have presents to wrap." Hopefully this would get the editor off the phone.

"Of course, darling," Adrienne said, trying to sound light and charming herself. "Why don't we have lunch on Monday, and we can discuss it then?"

Why would she want to meet so quickly? Leigh thought. The editor's insistence caught her off-guard; what was she so eager about? Still, she knew enough about the magazine business to know that Adrienne would hound her until she scheduled a meeting. She'd have to capitulate for now—but on her terms.

"Monday it is," replied Leigh. "How about noon at the Palm?"

This was an invitation to the age-old game, engaged in by serious power brokers around the world, of "Lunch Chicken." In this noble contest, the two parties each compete for a lunch spot closest to their own office. The one who drives the shortest distance to make their meeting wins. It was a subtle form of one-upmanship, and it was childish as hell; but Leigh didn't care. It was like a duel: if she was going to be forced into lunch with this woman, then she was going to pick the place and time.

"The Palm," Adrienne said hesitantly, taking up her end of the game. "Actually, I was thinking of—"

Leigh quickly cut her off. "I always lunch at the Palm on Mondays," she said.

"Oh—okay, the Palm it is, then," agreed Adrienne. *Funny, I thought I'd get more of a fight out of her,* Leigh thought. "I was going to suggest Scarpetta, at the Fontainebleau," Adrienne went on, backtracking. "The menu is excellent, and if you haven't chosen a location for the gala, I thought you might consider the Fontainebleau. I know everyone there, and could help you arrange it. But if you prefer the Palm this time—"

Adrienne was smart. The Fontainebleau was an excellent choice for the gala but Leigh couldn't let her control the terms of the interview. Lunch was the entrée to the story.

"Yeah, I'm a bit hooked on the Palm," Leigh insisted. The Fontainebleau was an excellent choice for the gala, she had to admit; but it was way too early to let herself be swayed by Adrienne, even with that connection. Besides, didn't Adrienne think she had her *own* connections at the Fontainebleau? Phillip Goldfarb, the iconic hotel's highly respected president and CEO, was a friend of Leigh's. "I'll take a rain check on Scarpetta—though it sounds like a lovely option."

Her phone buzzed again. It was probably Dixie calling back. *Saved by the bell,* Leigh thought. She was already getting anxious about the interview; she had to find a way to turn this whole ordeal around! She'd have to figure out how to make the story about the charity, and not about her and Brad; that kind of personal attention always made Brad uncomfortable. "Listen, Adrienne, I'm getting another call and my boys are waiting. I'll see you on Monday at noon, right?"

"Right," said Adrienne. "Bye now, dear—don't talk to any other magazines before we talk!"

"Bye," said Leigh, then clicked over to the other call. "Hello?"

"It's me. Are you home?" asked Lauren on the other end; then, without waiting for a response, she went on. "Of course you're at home. It's Saturday morning, and you were out drinking late. You naughty girl! I'm so exited about the news, and of course you can count on me again to volunteer. Oh, I wanted you to know I ran into Adrienne Adams last night at the valet and she asked me if I'd be available for an interview. I wanted to make sure it was okay with you before I said yes—you don't mind, do you?" Lauren finally took a breath.

"Lauren, wait just a minute," Leigh said, rubbing her temple. She was used to her friend being direct, but this was a little too much, too quick and too early. "Why would you have to ask *me* if Adrienne wants to interview you? You've never consulted me before on any of your press."

"Oh, you don't know?" replied Lauren. She spoke more slowly, realizing Leigh had no idea what Adrienne had cooking. "Adrienne is planning on interviewing some of the people close to you that are connected to the charity gala, for the cover story in *Ocean View*. There might even be a photo shoot of some of your friends, and possibly we'll—"

"Hang on—back up a second," Leigh snapped. "What's this about an interview? You mean she's going to interrogate people about *me?*" Leigh was definitely awake now, and her blood was beginning to boil. She had barely agreed to an interview herself, and now she was finding out her friends were already part of this. "No, no—this isn't happening; I'm going to put a stop to this. This is supposed to be about the charity, and it's turning into a society column! I won't allow this kind of bait-and-switch."

"Wait a minute, don't get mad at me," Lauren cut in. "I'm just telling you what Adrienne told me. Besides, I'm the one who should be upset with *you*. I thought we were best friends! I was shocked to hear from Adrienne, rather than you, that you were signed to do a cover story."

"*Signed?* I can't believe this woman. I ran into her while I was leaving Gena's charity, less than—not even seven hours ago! Of *course* she asked about the gala, and casually offered me a cover story about the charity. I'd had one drink too many, and I said yes. I really didn't think much of it; obviously I wasn't thinking. Now it sounds like she's really running away with it. What have I gotten myself into? Lauren, please tell me I haven't made a huge mistake. I'm feeling the pressure already."

"Darling," Lauren laughed, "don't you realize how much publicity you'll get for the charity and your gala? It's going to be grand for you!" *For me, eh?* Leigh thought, knowing well who Lauren was *really* thinking about. Lauren loved getting press; it was good for her business.

"I'm just—I'm concerned about the angle the magazine might take. When I agreed to this, I envisioned a little interview with just me, talking about the charity and the gala. If Adrienne is going to be interviewing my friends, I have to think she has another angle."

"Well, so what? You haven't got anything to hide."

That much was true. Leigh's was one of the few charity galas where all the money actually went to the charity. No one else made a red cent from the event; everything was donated or sponsored.

"True," Leigh agreed. "I don't really know why I'm reluctant; I just have a bad feeling about this."

"I'm sure it's just nerves! But don't worry about it; it's just press! Anyway, Leigh, we'll have to continue this another time—I'm running late for lunch with Dixie."

"Dixie? That's a surprise! Guess you guys hit it off, eh?"

"Yeah; she has some dirt for me, apparently."

"Always! Well, tell her I said hi—or wait, scratch that. Let her think I'm mad at her a little longer. She's the one who gave up my cell number to Adrienne."

"She did you a favor, then!" laughed Lauren. "Talk to you later, babe."

Leigh hung up. She'd been pacing back and forth during her whole conversation with Lauren, and gotten herself all worked up. Now she sat back on the bed and looked at the clock. It was almost noon; she couldn't believe she'd been on the phone for such a long time.

Fortunately, Jeffrey was coming this morning to organize her home office. She could tell him about her plans for the gala then, and maybe he could do a little research to find out what Adrienne might have in mind. He could also craft a strategy for her to use at her Monday lunch meeting with Adrienne. Like most powerful men and women, Leigh didn't enter a room without first being briefed on the other important attendees, and any alliances that needed to be encouraged, formed or strengthened.

The phone rang again. This time, at least, she knew who it was.

"Hello, Lorraine," Leigh answered. "I guess you've heard the news too."

"Well, hello yourself, Miss Cover Girl," sang the Diva.

Lorraine had been involved with Leigh's charity for years. Being the media darling she was, she loved any attention she could get from the press; and when she'd first volunteered for the charity, Leigh (and everyone else) had assumed that Lorraine was only in it for the photo-ops and press. But she'd proven everyone wrong. Both Lorraine Manchester and Brandon Westbrook had worked as hard as anyone else on the committee, and volunteered their services wherever needed. Brandon showed up for most of the work on the gala committee, and Lorraine worked her celebrity connections to get items for the silent auction. Still, Leigh knew that if there was an opportunity for press—particularly a photo-op for a glossy publication like Ocean View—Lorraine would be there with bells on. Her biggest bells.

"Okay, who have you talked to, and what have you heard?" asked Leigh. She knew that Lorraine wouldn't hold anything back, and would enjoy telling her every juicy little part of it. "Does everyone in town know that I'm producing another charity gala?"

"It was on Page Six this morning!" Lorraine cried, with a howl of laughter. "Well, Page Six hasn't picked it up yet, but that can be arranged! Just let me make a phone call."

"Not yet," Leigh implored. "I'm not ready yet. I just made the decision last night, and the craziness has already started."

"Well, aren't you the lucky one," Lorraine purred. "Wouldn't you have been disappointed if no one cared?"

"I know, you're right. You always say there's no such thing as bad publicity. I think it might just be everyone else's expectations that are making me anxious."

"Well, love, I just wanted to congratulate you. I'm so excited! We're really going to do this one over the top."

"Absolutely," Leigh said. The Diva's encouragement always made her feel better. Why shouldn't she settle into it? Like Lauren said, she had nothing to hide; and besides, this was her last gala. It had to be her biggest and best. She decided to take the bull by the horns.

"Listen, Lorraine. The cover story is going to be a good start, but we're going to need to lock in our celebrity appearances and auction items early if we're going to pull this off. It's our tenth anniversary, and we're already a couple of months behind."

"Say no more, darling. I'll make a few phone calls today, and get back to you later. I want to come over soon anyway—I have photos to show you from my David LaChapelle shoot. I went all the way to Hawaii for it, and I *do* look gorgeous in them."

"I have no doubt. Talk to you later, dear."

"Ciao, love!"

Leigh chuckled to herself as she hung up. With anyone else, she'd suspect exaggeration in such claims; but there really was no one better at marketing than Lorraine Manchester. The Diva had fans worldwide, high and low; and not only did she have hundreds of photos of herself with celebrities, but she kept in regular contact with all of them. It was pretty remarkable, when you thought about it. Leigh herself had a lot of contacts, but she could hardly keep in touch with them all by herself. Speaking of which, where was—

As if on cue, she heard Jeffrey's voice in the hall.

"Leigh, are you in there?" he called, knocking on the bedroom door.

"Yes, I'm here, come on in," she said, grabbing her robe from the chair on the way to the door. *Almost noon, and I haven't even left the bedroom!* she thought in disbelief.

"Morning," trilled Jeffrey, breezing in through the door.

"Morning, Jeffrey," she said. Leigh rarely welcomed guests into her bedroom, much less let anyone see her before she combed her hair and put on a little makeup; but Jeffrey was more than family—he was her right hand. "Sit down, dear. I have some news."

"Could it have anything to do with the announcement of your next charity gala?" Jeffrey smiled. "Or could it be your agreement to appear on the cover of *Ocean View Magazine?* If the latter, I do hope it involves the news that everyone close to you—including yours truly—is being tapped for interview, for the feature that Adrienne Adams is writing for that same issue. Speaking of which, your office phone has been ringing off the hook all morning—and on a Saturday! You've already had calls from"—he swiped through notes on his phone—"Adrienne herself; Greg Lotus's assistant—

apparently Greg's the one set to shoot the cover (how'd you get him by the way?—oh, never mind, moving on); a stylist named Inga; the manager of Scarpetta at the Fontainebleau, who wants to set up a special luncheon for you and your gala committee; your twins' tutor, who wants to *volunteer* for the gala committee; that Sassy Davilon woman, who also wants to volunteer; separate calls from Lynn Martinez from *Deco Drive* and Louis Aguirre from *The Insider;* a very distinguished-sounding man with a heavy accent called Jacques, who says he must speak with you immediately about art for the charity; Kamal from *Haute Living Magazine;* several other charities; and your husband, who went to the gym and tried calling your cell, but it was busy. Now then," Jeffrey said with a smug smile, "what is your news?"

"I—I'm giving up green tea," she laughed, sitting back on the bed.

"Well, that *is* news." He grinned at her. "And may I ask why?"

"These times call for coffee, Jeffrey. Black, hot, caffeinated coffee."

"I'll be right back," he said, rushing back out the door.

CHAPTER 12

DIXIE BRINGS THE DIRT

> Sorry 2 miss u! Was out w/ new friends.
> Where's the car?

—Danny

Lauren was surprised at herself.

Why was she so nervous to hear what Dixie had to tell her? Leigh was right; that Jacques guy had really gotten under her skin, to make her dread even to hear dirt on him—and practically from a stranger!

Still, she had to hear what it was. Dixie had insisted it was something she'd want to hear, and seemed to have reasons she couldn't just tell her at Gena's gala. Lauren hoped it wasn't just Dixie's way of glomming onto her, like she'd already glommed onto Leigh—but that was a mean thing to think. Maybe the woman *was* lonely; you couldn't blame her for wanting to make a new friend.

Of course, it was hard to feel sorry for her when one found her like this, Lauren thought as she walked into Mariposa, the lovely restaurant at the Neiman Marcus, finding Dixie chatting high-spiritedly with a waiter and one of the hostesses at a corner booth. The three looked as though they'd been friends for years. *That woman will gossip with anyone,* Lauren said to herself. *Hopefully her new friends haven't gotten her too drunk already.*

"Hi, Dixie," she said, approaching the table.

"Lauren!" screeched Dixie, rising up to kiss her wetly on both cheeks. "It's so"—*smooch*—"good"—*smooch*—"to see yew! Darlin', this is Suzanne, and this is Bobby—Bob, or Bobby, love? Bobby? All right—Suzanne and Bobby, my dear friend Lauren. We were just dishin' on some of the clientele here! Bobby just waited on a politician the other day—who was it, Bobby?"

"Paul Ryan and his wife," said Bobby with an eye-roll. "Lousy tippers."

"Ain't it the way with the *really* rich ones?" Dixie said, shaking her head.

"Always," said Suzanne.

"Well, it's lovely meetin' the two of yew," said Dixie. "Be a dear and get my friend a glass, will ya? We've got some dishin' of our own to do!"

"Absolutely, Dixie," said Bobby. "I'll be right back."

The two women sat. Dixie reached across and took Lauren's hand in hers.

"Ah'm so glad you could join me, Lauren," she said. She seemed remarkably sober; Lauren realized she hardly recognized her that way.

"Of—of course," Lauren replied, a little disarmed.

"Ah just had something Ah thought you should hear about—something about that Sassy gal, Ah think Ah told you before."

"You did, yes."

Bobby returned to the table. They sat quietly as he poured a glass of Chardonnay for Lauren and left.

"All right, well," said Dixie conspiratorially, "you know mah husband's a psychiatrist, right?"

"Yes," said Lauren.

"Well, Ah don't know if Leigh ever told you, but Ah—well—on occasion, Ah have been known to listen to some of his session tapes."

Lauren's eyes went wide, and she almost choked on her wine.

"Dixie, that's really serious," she said. "You know you can get in huge trouble for that, right? *He* can get in huge trouble for that."

"Ah know, Ah know," said Dixie impatiently, "Ah don't do it *that* often; and anyway, Ah'm tryin' to cut back! But that's not the point, anyhow. It's just how Ah heard what Ah wanted to tell you about."

"I'm not sure I should listen," said Lauren doubtfully.

"Oh, hush, dear—Ah'm not gonna tell you any names! The guy whose tape it was ain't anyone we've heard of anyway, Somethin' Cavalleri. Ah had to look up who he was online; he's some sorta high-profile crook who went to jail years ago for fraud, and has been advisin' politicians ever since."

"What's he going to your husband for?"

"Oh, he's a closet-case—he wants someone to talk to about bein' gay, without outin' himself to all his connections."

"Okay—go on."

"Well, so he's talkin', and somehow Sassy's name comes up. Ah think maybe he saw her in the street a bit ago. Turns out he knows her, but in some kinda shady way—apparently neither of 'em wanted to talk to the other, or so he's tellin' Howard. Sounds like it was just sorta an awkward moment; he didn't go into it too far."

"Okay…" Lauren couldn't see where this was going, but she was definitely intrigued.

"So then he mentions the guy Sassy's with. He describes him and everything; it's that Jacques fella of yours. And he laughs and says—and Ah quote—'*He obviously didn't know the first thing about who he was with, but Ah'll tell you: whoever the guy is, he's in way over his head with* that *one!'"*

Lauren sat thunderstruck. Dixie took a big sip of her wine and went on.

"Then Howard asks him somethin' like, *'With what you know about her and her past, how did it make you feel to see them together?'* And the guy just laughs, and says, *'Well, he'll find out about her soon enough—Ah can't believe he hasn't already!'"*

Lauren found her voice. "And—?"

"And, nothin'! They changed the subject, and that was all they said about it!"

"You've got to be kidding me. That was *all?*"

"That was all."

The two women sat in silence a moment while Lauren digested the mysterious information Dixie had just given her.

"Okay, so… if this Cavalleri guy's gay, he obviously isn't talking about the usual kind of connection with Sassy," Lauren reasoned, "so it must have to do with a criminal past."

"Exactly!" Dixie said excitedly. "And there was somethin' else that made me think that, too."

"Oh?"

"Yeah; Ah was gonna tell yew that next." Dixie took a sip of her wine. "Yew know Ah have a driver, Danny."

"Yes—?"

"Well, a while back, Ah was at a party with Leigh—some club's anniversary or whatnot—and Danny, well, he didn't show up to drive me home that night."

"Ouch. How'd you get home?"

"Ah, uh—Ah took a cab—but never mind that; it ain't important! The important thing is, when Ah talked to him later about it, Ah'll tell you how it was; it was just the littlest detail."

"All right then, go ahead."

"Well, so Ah asked him, 'What on Earth were yew up to, Danny? Ah've got a mind to fire yew.' 'Well,' he says, 'Ah met some fellas, and we had a little bit to drink, is all, and Ah'm sorry, ma'am, and it won't happen again.' 'Well, that's all right then,' Ah said (cuz Ah always appreciate it when people are honest), 'but what fellas were they, anyhow?' 'Some Mexicans,' he says; and Ah said, 'Mexicans? Are yew sure they weren't Cubans?'—cuz we do have quite a few of them around. And he says, 'No, ma'am—Mexicans—specifically speakin', fellas from Mexico. Like when you're chewin' on the worm, you know; *and* a Fraanch guy,' he says, 'by the name of Frarrah!'"

Lauren was confused. "Frarrah?"

"That's what *Ah* said!—'Frarrah, Danny? Are yew sure? Cuz that sounds like an Arab name to me.' And Danny says, 'Well, maybe that ain't right, then; he was definitely Fraanch. And I said, 'What was his name, then?' And he says, 'Well, we were all callin' him Frarrah something, like it was part of a Fraanch name.' And we went back and forth about it for a while, and Ah thought he'd lost it, and Ah told him so, in so many words. But to make a long story short, Ah remembered your freeend Jacques, and Ah remembered that song about Frarrah Jacques too—Ah guess it *is* a Fraanch name after all! So Ah said, 'Danny, yew sweet fool! Was the man's name *Jacques?*' And he says, 'Yes, ma'am, that's it! Frarrah Jacques, and his Mexicans!'"

"But—what on Earth does all this have to do with Sassy?" Lauren asked.

"Now, darlin', cool your jets," scolded Dixie. "Ah'm gettin' to that! Well, Leigh's assistant Jeffrey had sent me some pitchers he took at the party, of this and that—it ain't important what, but let's just say he got some real doozies! There was a few of Katie Parker with a whole gang a' boy toys; talk about incriminatin'! She was makin' out with this one, and touchin' that one, and them two had hands on her legs—they might've been playin' Twister at that table! Hopefully those pitchers'll come in handy soon; Ah'm sure Billie doesn't know. And then there was a few where—"

"*Sassy!*" cried Lauren in exasperation.

"Well, if yew didn't keep interruptin' me," said Dixie testily. "As Ah was about to say: Ah was lookin' through these pitchers, and Ah found a couple Ah'd taken of your Sassy gal from that same party, with all sorts of Mexican fellas humpin' all over her! Now I figure they musta been her freeends, and after what Danny said, Ah'll bet you *she's* the one who set 'em on your pal Jacques, to get him drunk!"

"That…actually *does* make sense," Lauren admitted. She looked darkly at the table. "I *knew* that woman was crooked! But what could she be doing with Jacques?"

"Ah don't know, but she's gotta be takin' him for a ride somehow," Dixie said.

"That wouldn't be too hard, given how much she's got him wrapped around her finger," Lauren said angrily. "And I've been so hard on him! We have to find out what she's up to. That guy whose tape you listened to—there aren't any other tapes of him, are there?"

"No," Dixie lamented. "Ah checked."

"And there's no way you could find out from Howard—?"

"Oh, Gawd, no! Even if Ah could ask him without lettin' on about the tapes, he'd never tell me—that stuff is *confidential*, you know!" Dixie took another swig of wine.

"Well, I've got to warn him somehow," Lauren said. "Even if he did dump me for Sassy, he doesn't deserve to get screwed over. Maybe if I tell *him* about the tape—"

"No, no, *no!*" Dixie cried, barely recovering her glass. "You *cain't* tell anyone! If it got back to Howard how you found out—" She looked sick.

"Well, what the hell am I supposed to do to help Jacques, then?"

"Ah don't know—but you cain't do that!" Dixie pleaded. "Ah'm sorry; Ah just thought Ah should tell you, so you knew somethin' was up. Shame he's new in town, and doesn't have more freeends to look out for him. What if we asked Leigh? Ah bet she'd know what to do."

Lauren snapped her fingers.

"That's it!" she said. "Leigh's gala!"

Dixie was confused. "Ah don't follow ya."

"I'll tell him Leigh's doing one more gala—maybe he'd want to provide artwork for it, for the auction. That'd give him some business aside from whatever that whore's got planned for him, and put him on his feet in Miami, so it'll be harder for her to get at him." *And put him back in my pocket, hopefully,* Lauren thought to herself.

"Ah gotcha!" said Dixie excitedly. "And we can put the ahdea in Leigh's head too, and talk him up to her."

"Would you do that too, then—?"

"Oh, of *koorse!* That way we wouldn't have to say nothin' about the tape—it's perfect!"

"All right, that's what we'll do, then," said Lauren. "Ugh—I can't *stand* the thought that he's hanging around that snake right now!"

"Well, if she's workin' on him like this, it's at least better for yew that you haven't sold him anything," Dixie offered. "Better wait until he's out of the devil's clutches before you make any deals with *that* fella!"

"In a way, I guess you're right," agreed Lauren. "We need to get him out of this, before anything else." She sighed. "You know, I think I need a refill."

"Testify!" cried Dixie, and they waved Bobby over.

Once the waiter had gone, Dixie leaned in again. "Y'know, Ah meant to ask yew," she said gently, "how's your husband situation going, with—ah—Francesco?"

"Francisco."

"Yeah, that's the one. Ah remember you sayin' before that things had been a bit tough lately—?"

Lauren wasn't used to being asked questions so directly, but there was something about Dixie's homey straightforwardness that inspired her trust.

"I don't know," she said. "Things have been better lately, I guess. He still seems a little weird, but it *is* better. It's hard for me sometimes; he's a very secretive person in general, which I have a hard time getting. Sometimes it drives me nuts. I mean, he has a computer I'm not supposed to touch—he's working on an algorithm on it."

"An algo-what?"

"Exactly. Some sort of nerdy program—hardly the kind of thing I'd even care to look at! But being told I can't mess around with it just makes me want to. We're very different people, that way."

"Well, Ah'm hardly the one to talk about *that,*" Dixie said. "Ah can't even keep out of my husband's session tapes, and that's illegal!" The two women laughed. Lauren was glad she'd come along; despite her shortcomings, this Dixie character was all right.

"So…what else have you heard on those tapes?" she asked, with a wry smile.

Dixie chuckled.

"Settle in, darlin', and Ah'll tell ya a thing or two," she said. "But first"—she waved to the waiter again—"Ah think we'd better have Bobby leave the bottle on the table, don't yew? We may be here a minute."

CHAPTER 13

CLAWS CÉLÈBRE

> Katie is stalking Adrienne. Call me.
> But not between 3 and 5. My waxer is 2
> DIE for. She even gets my no-no place!

—The Diva

Katie Parker had been calling Leigh for weeks.

When she'd come back with her new baby, the publicity storm had been predictably intense, and predictably short. She'd made arrangements while she was away for a media reception on her return, and arrived home dressed strategically like an upscale parishioner from a wealthy church: grey plaid Dior suit with white pocket scarf; short, single string of South Sea pearls; Chanel shoes and quilted handbag; Philip Stein white, gold and grey crocodile wristwatch. She hadn't looked particularly comfortable holding her new baby—her "rescue," as she seemed to think it was appropriate to call him, between attacks with the Sani-wipes—but that was what her entourage of caretakers were for. Unfortunately, she also hadn't thought to tell her press contacts when her flight was delayed, so most of them had left by the time she got there; but her arrival made it onto a few style blogs nonetheless.

After that, the media had run with the "fashion designer and wife adopt beautiful Asian baby" story—but only so far. After all, as had been said, the two were nowhere near Brad and Angelina's level; and even if they had been, the embarrassing truth was that Brad and Angelina had already done it. Katie's desire for publicity, unfortunately, was not matched by her creativity.

When the media storm had died down, everyone knew it was only a matter of time before Katie's next scheme would come to light. With the upcoming *Ocean View* story and all of Adrienne Adams's behind-the-scenes dealing, Leigh suspected it would have something to do with her.

But then the calls started coming.

For a while she'd ignored them, promised to call Katie back, or put her on hold until she hung up. Katie was persistent, but usually too temperamental to persist through more than a few snubs. But this time Katie had really stuck with it, calling three and four times a day. What could she be up to?

She had no sincere interest in the charity, that was for sure. Whatever she was after, had to be motivated by self-interest. She probably knew that Leigh was onto her boy-toy habit, and might suspect that Leigh knew where some of her bodies were buried. Not that *that* was any mean feat; Leigh could sight dick tracks like a safari guide, and this girl had them all over town. There was the *Ocean View* story; but word was, Adrienne had already called Katie. She wouldn't be asking for Leigh's permission, like Lauren; there wasn't much that got between Katie and an interview, or any press for that matter.

Leigh decided she'd better call Katie and get a pulse. If nothing else, it'd get the woman to stop hounding her.

***

"Katie! It's Leigh."

"Well, hello, Leigh," Katie answered, a distinct layer of sarcasm coating every word. "I'm glad you finally found time to return my calls."

"I know, I'm sorry it's taken me so long to get back to you—I've been crazed with all the gala preparations."

"Interesting that you should call me now," Katie went on, as though Leigh hadn't spoken. "It doesn't have anything to do with the fact that Adrienne from *Ocean View* is interviewing me for your feature, does it?" She laughed lightly. *That Katie sure gets right to the point,* Leigh thought to herself.

"Oh, is she? I hadn't heard," said Leigh.

"Mm-hmmm,"Katie said. "Billie and I were having dinner a couple of nights ago at Nobu, and Adrienne happened to be sitting at the next table. We got to talking, and your name popped into the conversation." Katie paused to let the information sink in. "Of course, I told her we were *close friends,* and that Billie and I had attended your charity gala for the past few years. Naturally she was interested—her article, and all."

"Yes, we're so appreciative of the magazine helping promote the charity," Leigh said, trying to stay calm. What she really wanted was to reach through the phone and strangle the little bitch. She'd probably stalked Adrienne to weasel her way into an interview. How dare this silly woman involve herself in the article, and pretend to know anything about the charity? Of course, there wasn't much danger there, Leigh thought; all she'd want to talk about was herself. But if she decided that it would help her to lie about Leigh…

"Oh, Adrienne's a doll," Katie went on. "We hit it off right away. Of course she wanted to hook up with Billie too, but I didn't want to bother him with it while he's working on his new line for next season. That's far more important than a silly magazine article, or a charity.

Besides, I told her I wouldn't mind interviewing for the both of us."

"Very selfless of you," said Leigh.

"I thought so," Katie laughed. "Anyway, Leigh, I was hoping we could get together and chat before my interview with Adrienne, but it's taken you so long to get back to me, and I'm meeting with her today at two. We're going to have our interview over lunch."

"How nice," Leigh said, still seething. "I'm sure you'll have a lovely lunch."

"We're having lunch at Joe's Stone Crab," Katie boasted. "It's not one of my favorites—so touristy. Adrienne chose it; it's near her office."

Now this was getting on Leigh's last nerve. How dare she be so snooty about Joe's Stone Crab? She'd probably never even heard of the restaurant before marrying Billie; she certainly wouldn't have been able to get a table there.

"Very nice," Leigh said again through gritted teeth. "I'd stop by, but I think I'm overbooked this afternoon."

"That's a pity," said Katie. "Anyway, I'm going to be wearing one of Billie's designs. I know that Adrienne will probably want to photograph me, and the timing is coincidental, after all—Billie's promoting his new women's line. I figured I'd give her a taste at lunch. You know, it's because of me that Billie got into women's apparel in the first place!"

"I doubt she'll want to photograph you at lunch," Leigh said, astonished at the woman's idiocy.

"Who knows? One always has to be prepared," laughed Katie. "But Leigh, I almost forgot—one of the reasons I've been calling is about your own photo shoot with the magazine." Her voice was suddenly serious. "I'm sure you've heard I have a new jewelry line—?"

"I think I remember hearing that," Leigh said, tensing up. *Here it comes,* she thought.

"Oh, it's only a little hobby of a project, of course, but it's going *so* well. I was thinking of donating something wonderful for your silent auction; but I thought you might also want to wear some of my designs for your *Ocean View* shoot."

Leigh was stunned. That Katie thought she could trade on the charity to promote Billie's fashion line, was already ridiculous. Did she really think she was going to push her tacky jewelry the same way? Leigh was so taken aback by the woman's selfishness, for a moment she couldn't think of how to respond.

Katie, however, didn't wait for her answer.

"You know," she went on carefully, "Adrienne is *very* interested to hear what I'll have to say today. And you know these journalists—such sensationalists! They hardly care about fact-checking anymore."

Leigh almost dropped the phone.

"Are you—just what are you saying, Katie?"

"Oh, nothing, dear—nothing. Only asking, *politely,* whether you wouldn't mind wearing some of my designs for your cover photo, and in the article."

Leigh bit her tongue in fury. Adrienne had told her that she might ask around for a quote or two for the feature, but hadn't said anything about full interviews, especially with people like Katie who had almost nothing to do with the charity. Perhaps she'd need to make time for lunch today, after all. *Okay, get a grip,* she thought, remembering the old cliché. Learn to fake sincerity—once you can do that, you've got it made.

"That's very nice of you to offer, Katie," she said, struggling to control herself. "And that's wonderful that your jewelry line is doing well! I really don't know how you do it."

"Yes, well," said Katie hesitantly.

"No, really! Being a mother doesn't seem to have slowed you down at all! Designing by day, clubbing by night—I don't know when you find time for little Billie! You must have the energy of a teenager."

"Little Billie is fine," Katie snapped. Now this was the Katie that Leigh knew so well. "I'll have you know that I'm a very good mother."

"Oh, *I* know that," Leigh laughed. "In fact, that's exactly what I was just telling my friend Dixie at Mynt the other night. You seem to do it all, *and* have a good time, to boot—it's quite a talent!"

Katie cleared her throat. "Billie wants me to enjoy myself when he's out of town," she said.

"Of course he does—and the less said, the better! *I* know that. That's why I told Dixie she should keep the photos to herself that she took of you that night. She emailed me some of them—I must say, you looked so lovely. Was *that* one of Billie's designs you were wearing?"

Score one for Leigh—she could practically hear Katie melting down on the other end. *It's probably the first time she's ever regretted being photographed*, Leigh thought.

"Are you *threatening* me?" Katie asked bluntly.

"Oh, no, dear, no," Leigh said. "I'm only reminding you, *politely*—of course it was all innocent fun. Now, I have to run. Say hello to Adrienne for me, and to Billie—both Billies. You remind me, I really *do* need to call your husband; we haven't talked in so long, and he always gives me something fabulous for my silent auction. Now, I really must run."

She hung up without giving Katie a chance to reply. The gears were already turning; she had to show this little tart who was really in charge around here.

"Jeffrey!" she yelled.

"Yes, my Queen," replied her assistant, coming to the door with a big smile on his face. "What do you have for me this morning?"

"Jeffrey, I'm going to lunch at Joe's," Leigh announced. "I need a

reservation for three at two o'clock—see if you can get one right next to Adrienne Adams's table. I'll call Dixie and Lauren to join me."

Jeffrey didn't move, but just stood smiling. Leigh was puzzled.

"Jeffrey, didn't you hear me?"

"Of course, my Queen. I also heard every word of your conversation with Katie Parker, and have already secured your table for you. I thought two-thirty would be better—that way you could walk on their lunch and catch them red-handed—but I'll change it if you like. Dixie can't stay long, but is confirmed, and is bringing a copy of the photo she took of Katie that night. I placed a call to Lauren as well, but her cell went to voicemail so I called her office. She's apparently showing some high-roller a condo at the Icon, so she's practically across the street from Joe's. I left her a message to join you after her appointment, but you may want to call her just in case."

Leigh sat stunned a moment. The man was truly Australia's loss and Leigh White's gain. There was a reason he was the highest-paid assistant in all of Miami; it was frightening how well he knew her sometimes.

"Jeffrey, what—what would I ever do without you?" she sighed finally.

"Don't even think about that. You know I'd never leave you— you wouldn't survive twenty-four hours." They both laughed. "And remember," he added, "I would *never* let you be humiliated in print, but we all know how jealous and self-promoting some of these egomaniacs can be! So I've put in a call to my friend Joey, who works as Adrienne's assistant. I'll have a list put together of the people she's going to interview for your feature before you leave for lunch. How's that for the power of the *real* queens of Miami? I'm telling you, the gay mafia can make anything happen."

"You never cease to amaze me, Jeffrey," Leigh said. She knew she was lucky to have Jeffrey; he'd had an interview scheduled with

Gloria Estefan right after his interview with her five years ago. She'd hired him on the spot, and never looked back. "I think this year you may deserve more than just a bonus," she added. "Something like a trip, or maybe a new car—what do you think about that?" Jeffrey had been hinting for a while that he needed a new car, but couldn't quite afford the one he wanted. This was because he'd been paying off his boyfriend's debts for some time—against Leigh's advice, but Jeffrey was an angel and that was what Leigh loved most about him.

"Yes, my Queen—a car would please me," Jeffrey teased, his Australian lilt dropping into a posh British accent. "If my lady needs anything else, I'll be across the hall awaiting her command." They both laughed again as he bowed.

"Oh, Jeffrey, your boyfriend doesn't deserve you," Leigh said. "If I were gay and single, I'd—oh, never mind. I've got to get dressed for lunch." She scanned her schedule to see if there was anything that needed changing; her afternoon was free but for a facial appointment that Jeffrey could cancel. "Jeffrey," she called after him. "Can you—"

"I've already rescheduled your facial appointment," he called back. "Oh, and I almost forgot." He walked back into the room. "Here's a list of the messages that piled up while you were talking to Little Miss Slut Wife," he said sweetly.

"Thank you, humble queenservant," Leigh teased. "Now get back to work, so Her Majesty can get dressed."

***

While Leigh was getting herself together for lunch—white linen Stella McCartney pantsuit, French mani-pedi, Manolo Blahnik sandals—Billie Parker was in a meeting discussing his wife.

Billie was a street-smart businessman, and knew more than enough to protect himself against most threats to his prosperity, including his wife. His earliest precaution had been the ironclad

pre-nup he'd insisted on in their marriage; his latest now sat across from him in the form of Steve Senkew, private investigator.

"Thanks for meeting me on such short notice," Billie said. "Did you remember to bring the pictures?"

Steve gave him a wry look.

"Ha. Right," Billie said.

Steve presented him with a thick manila file. Inside was a treasure trove of evidence of his wife's shenanigans: transcriptions of phone conversations and texts, printed emails, typed observational reports, a dossier of photos. Billie opened the dossier. The first photo was of a very recognizable Katie, pinning a young man to a hotel mattress with her recently slenderized thighs. Her buttocks were in the air and her trademark sneer was plastered across her face. He turned to the next photo: a shot taken through a window, of Katie on her knees, hair pulled back, in front of a man with a huge bush. The man's head was cropped off, but his pubes created a wild Afro around Katie's head. Billie pulled it from the dossier.

"I'd like to keep this one for my personal files," he said.

"Of course, sir."

"For amusement only, you know," Billie smiled. The private eye smiled back.

"Of course," he said again. "Will that be all for today?"

"Yes—thank you, as always. I'll be in touch."

As the private eye closed the door gently behind him, Billie sank into his chair in exasperation.

He'd had a gut of his little wife, that was for sure. He'd long known she was slutting around; that wasn't the problem. He wasn't exactly the picture of marital fidelity himself. But he couldn't believe she was being so careless in public! They—he—had an image to maintain, after all.

How had she turned out such a nightmare? He felt a pang of

guilt, knowing it was he who had created this monster. She'd be working the third shift at Dairy Queen or styling hair in Selma, if it hadn't been for him; and that would probably have been better for the world at large.

Ugh! He'd have to get her out of the picture, and that was that. But timing was everything. He had to find a way to enforce the pre-nup on her *and* keep Little Billie, if it was the last thing he did.

It would most likely get ugly. He would probably have to pay Katie off, or threaten to take her to court and show a judge the vulgar photos he had of her. Yet if that was what it would take to keep Little Billie, he would do it. Billie would get custody of his son, one way or another. After the pre-nup, Katie would be desperate— and when he was done with her, she'd be humiliated, too. He had once loved a woman named Katie; but that was not the woman he was married to today. This Katie was poisonous, a toxic parasite on him and his son, and his need to be rid of her was more intense than his love for the other Katie had ever been.

He just had to figure out how to do it without involving his son in the conflict. The adoption behind his back had initially infuriated him; but Billie had quickly come to love the boy as his own. Part of it was simple softheartedness for Little Billie's situation. He'd never seen his wife treat the boy as anything but an accessory to her wan- nabe fame; and if nothing else, Little Billie certainly deserved better than his wife's empty ambitions and neglectful ways. But they'd hit it off quickly, and now he couldn't imagine being without the boy, or leaving him in the care of such a woman. Adoptive mother or no, he was going to ensure that Katie's days around his son were num- bered. She was certainly anything but motherly at home. Coming back just the other afternoon, Billie had found her sprawled across their couch in a thong lace panty and matching bra, with earplugs stuffed tightly in her ears, mask over her eyes, and an empty bottle of champagne next to her Lunesta on the nightstand. After taking a photo with his phone for his records and slamming the door in disgust, Billie had turned to find their son crawling free on the carpet, eyes wide in confusion.

She has to go, he thought again, clenching his fists; *she simply has to go.* He would publish her photos in the tabloids if he had to. With any luck she'd take her Botoxed, siliconized, lifted, tucked, tweaked and airbrushed self right back to where she'd come from. The thought made him smile.

He would run her out of town.

CHAPTER 14

LUNCH AT JOE'S

Got Jeffrey's msg. En route.

—Lauren

At precisely two-thirty, the door at Joe's Stone Crab opened, and in walked Leigh, Lauren and Dixie. The hostess, prepared by Jeffrey a minute or two in advance of their arrival, brought them directly to their table—two away from Katie and Adrienne's.

The effect was immediate. Adrienne was overly effusive towards Leigh and Lauren. Katie's red-faced "hand caught in the cookie jar" expression was worth getting out of bed for. The two women were just being served their appetizers; it was pretty clear they wouldn't be finishing them. The interview had obviously been disrupted; Adrienne seemed embarrassed, and put her notes away abruptly.

"Katie and I were just grabbing a quick bite," Adrienne said. "She was telling me all about her new jewelry line."

Leigh looked down at the printed photographs Katie had brought along to show her jewelry to Adrienne. The stuff looked like cheap, gaudy knockoffs of a QVC special, or flea-market costume accessories.

"Yes, she was telling me about it earlier, too," said Leigh. "I was so glad to hear about it; I really hope it takes off."

Katie, obviously thinking she saw an opportunity to seize, chimed in.

"I was just telling Adrienne how much I'd love to have you wear some of it for your Ocean View shoot," she said in a saccharine tone. "Have you had a chance to think about it?"

"It's lovely of you to offer, but I don't think it would go as nicely with what I'm wearing as some of the more *established* pieces I have—but of course, you must know that already!" Leigh turned to Adrienne. "Her husband has sent me some lovely samples from his next line; I was thinking of wearing one of those for the shoot. Which of them is your favorite, Katie?"

Katie turned bright red. It was obvious she hadn't seen the new line.

"Oh, forget I asked," Leigh said. "It must be so hard to pick, when it's your husband's work you're talking about—and he's *such* a talented designer! But anyway, how lovely to see you two here! Isn't this a wonderful restaurant, Adrienne?"

"Oh, I *love* Joe's," said Adrienne eagerly.

"So do I," said Leigh pointedly. "I know some people find it touristy, but that's ridiculous, don't you think? I think of this place as a Miami institution."

"It certainly is," agreed Adrienne. "And Katie said it was one of her favorites when I suggested it, so that worked out."

Leigh smiled at Katie, who was glaring at the tablecloth. "Well, I'd hate to interrupt you, ladies—we're going to take our seats. We'll try not to talk too loudly! Enjoy the rest of your lunch!"

The message had been sent. The three of them returned to their table and ordered drinks. When a good interval had passed, Dixie stood up to send a message of her own. She strutted over to their table.

"Oh, Katie," she drawled, as though in afterthought, "Ah just remembered—Ah've been holding onto somethin' for ya!" She loudly rummaged in her purse for a few seconds—just long enough, Leigh noticed with satisfaction, for Adrienne to come to full attention—and drew out a printout of one of the more incriminating of the photos of Katie from Mynt.

"Thoughtcha might want a copy for your scrapbook—that's a good one, Ah think!" she said, passing it carefully in front of Adrienne's sightline. Katie snatched the photo, fuming.

"How dare you wave that at me," she snarled. "You ought to learn to keep things to yourself."

"Oh, Ah know, honey, Ah know," Dixie lamented with a laugh. "But it's all harmless fun; you know Ah don't mean any harm. Ah'm just so *baaaad* when it comes to dirt like that!" She turned to Adrienne. "*You* know what Ah mean, honey, right?" She laughed again, and returned to her table.

Adrienne Adams was a lot of things, but she wasn't dense; she knew how to take a hint. When the three women walked in, the elephant in the room had been that she hadn't yet asked Dixie for an interview. But that was going to change now. She was careful not to bring it up with Katie, but Dixie's photo stuck with her through the rest of their lunch.

Granted, with Leigh within hearing distance, the rest of Katie and Adrienne's lunch didn't last long. Without any connection to her cover story, Adrienne was uninterested in Katie's efforts at self-promotion, and before long she'd trotted out an excuse to leave. Never one to be left alone at a table, Katie found an excuse of her own to strut out while Adrienne was handling the check.

As Adrienne was leaving, she discreetly handed her card to Dixie.

"It was a pleasure meeting you, Dixie," she said, barely suppressing a shriek at the chipped red polish on Dixie's split fingernails.

"Oh, the pleasure's all mine, darlin'," said Dixie with a smile, raising her glass to her as she walked out.

Once she'd left, the three of them laughed hard.

"Thank you, ladies, for that," Leigh said. "That was too perfect, and I couldn't have done it without you!"

"All in a day's work, honey," said Dixie with a smile, tossing back the last of her wine. "Now if y'all will excuse me, Ah've got to get goin'."

"What've you got going on today, Dixie?"

"Oh, er—Ah have some shopping to do before Howard comes home."

Leigh smiled; she knew exactly what that meant.

"All right, Dixie, see you soon."

"You betcha!"

Dixie tottered her way out the door.

Leigh turned to Lauren. She was actually glad Dixie had only been able to stay for a bit; since they'd arrived, she'd wondered about Lauren. Something was obviously up with her. *Hopefully not more Sassy drama,* she thought, steeling herself.

"You've been quiet today," she said. "Is everything okay?"

Lauren sat quietly for a while. *Oh boy,* Leigh thought. *Something's happened, all right.* When Lauren finally spoke up, she looked like she was going to cry, or perhaps scream in rage.

"I—I've found something out," she said.

"Found what out?"

"It's about Francisco."

"Oh no." Leigh's stomach tightened. "What is it?"

"I know why he's been so strange lately." Lauren suddenly slammed her fist on the table. "I can't believe it—it's such *bullshit!*"

"Okay, calm down and tell me."

Lauren took a deep breath. "I was looking for something on his computer—"

"Something?"

"Yes, something—never mind what. Oh fine, I was looking to see if he'd been emailing someone else."

"Lauren!"

"I know, I know. But he's just been so *weird* recently! And what I *did* find…God, Leigh, it's just as bad!"

"Why? What was it?"

Lauren looked sick. "Porn."

"Porn?"

"Yeah, porn. Tons of porn. He's got hours of it—*days* of it—stored right there, on his computer."

Leigh felt a wave of relief. *God,* she thought, *the way Lauren had looked, I'd thought she was going to say he was cheating on her.* "Well, so what?"

Lauren looked at her incredulously. "So what? *So what?* So he's been keeping a *porn* addiction from me, is so what! And that stupid algorithm—it was all just a cover-up!" She shook her head. "I mean, it's not *totally* fake—he's been working on that, too—but he was using it as an excuse to keep me off his computer and away from all *that!*"

"Do you know how often he watches it?"

"Of course I know—there are timestamps showing when the files were last opened! He watches it at *least* once a day."

"Okay, but—well, there's not much wrong with porn by itself, Lauren. Depending on the type, I guess. What sort of porn is he watching?"

"I mean, some of it was pretty straightforward—"

"*Some* of it? What was the rest?"

"That's what I mean! It gets worse, Leigh. Way worse."

"Okay, go ahead."

"Well, I kept looking, and I found a file on his computer—"

"Yes?"

"—and it was full of—ugh, God, they were videos of—"

She shook her head incredulously, unable to say it.

"Videos of *what?*" Leigh almost shouted. What could Francisco be watching that had Lauren so upset? Videos of men? Kids? Animals?

"Us," Lauren said disgustedly.

"*You?*"

"Yeah. Us."

"You guys…"

"Yes. Us doing it. Us making love. Us fucking."

"He's been secretly *filming* you?"

"Yeah. I found the camera! It was hidden in a goddamn book, with a wire running out the back and into the wall. There was a hole in the spine, right in the middle of the letter 'O' in the title, and the camera was there behind it."

Leigh couldn't help but laugh.

"It's not funny, Leigh!" Lauren's voice surprised her; she was close to tears. "All this time, he's been hiding this from me! And no wonder he seemed so distant and…showy; he was *performing!* And getting *me* to perform too! That's where all the dirty talk came from, and costumes, and positions…God, the whole thing is just sick."

Leigh inched her chair around the table, so she was sitting close by Lauren's side, and leaned in. "I'm sorry I laughed, Lauren; I see this is upsetting to you," she said gently. "But…aside from the fact that he kept it secret, is it really so bad?"

"How can you ask me that?"

"Well, you said yourself that most of the tapes are of you; you made it sound like he's been cheating on you."

"No, I don't think that—but—I mean, isn't this just as bad?"

"How so? Look, I remember you saying, back at Gena's fund-raiser, that you were actually kind of getting off on it, or getting into it, or something. Weren't you enjoying it before?"

"I was—but that was before I knew he was *taping* everything!"

"Is he showing the tapes to anyone else?"

"He says he isn't. I don't know if I believe him."

"Fair enough. But let's assume he's telling the truth—would it be such a problem, if he were just making them for himself, to watch later?"

"I guess not," Lauren admitted. "But he still kept it from me! That's *so* not okay."

"I know, honey, it's not. But as lies go—again assuming he's just been making the tapes for himself—it's not such a bad one, is it? It seems like one of those things you guys could work through, and come out stronger for. Especially if you can find a way to enjoy it together."

Lauren thought for a minute.

"I guess so…now that you say it that way," she said. "But how do I forgive him for lying to me?"

"Well, talk to him about it. Try to understand why he felt like he had to lie to you in the first place. He's probably pretty insecure about it, and knew you wouldn't like it if you heard."

"That's certainly true."

"But you *did* like doing it. If it's something you do together, or that he knows you accept about him, there's no need for him to lie about it." An image of Katie Parker popped into Leigh's head. "Unless he gets off on lying, which is another story," she added.

"I couldn't believe that about Francisco," Lauren said.

"Well, you know him better than anyone," Leigh said. "Try talking it out openly with him! See where it goes. If he's cheating on you, or using you, that's a deal-breaker; but otherwise, a little porn doesn't do much harm, and it might be something you can share with him."

"I'm still pissed at him for lying," said Lauren, "but what you're saying makes sense. He did seem really upset that I was so hurt by the whole thing; he kept saying he'd meant to tell me, but was afraid of what I'd say."

"Of course he was. Unless he's *really* been living a lie, he's the same guy you were married to last week."

"I guess so. I'll try talking to him today."

"Good! Give it a chance to turn around. These things sometimes do, you know."

"You're the best, Leigh."

The two friends hugged. As they let go, Leigh looked hard at her friend.

"This has been quite a lunch already," she said with a sigh, "but what do you say we order something?"

"I'm not hungry, to be honest," said Lauren.

"Oh, me neither." Leigh smiled. "I was thinking Chardonnay."

"Perfect," said Lauren, and the two women laughed.

CHAPTER 15

DIXIE CALLING

> Some lunch! Bet Katie hit the Valium after that one!

—Dixie

An hour and a few sobering cups of coffee later, Dixie was taking matters into her own hands. Wherever he was, Danny was going to have to wait.

"Hi there, this is Dixie Johnson, callin' for Adrienne Adams? She gave me her card today at lunch, and wanted me to call her as soon as possible."

Well, that hadn't been said, of course. But the invitation was implied, Dixie thought. Anyway, there was good clean dirt on the line here, and Adrienne knew she had it. She *had* to convince her to add her name to the list of people being interviewed for Leigh's feature in *Ocean View.*

"Ms. Adams is out of the office at the moment," said the receptionist. "May I take a message, or would you prefer her voice mail?"

Dixie thought for a second. She really hadn't anticipated Adrienne not being available, and wasn't prepared to leave a message. She wondered if the bitch was actually in the office and just not taking the call. Dixie couldn't trust anyone anymore—it seemed she was always being left out.

"Just leave her the message that Dixie Johnson, Dr. Howard Johnson's wife, called. We met at lunch yesterday at Joe's Stone Crab, where Ah was lunchin' with Leigh White. Adrienne's doing a cover feature on her—? Yes, well, Ah have some information that she might be interested in. Yes, she'll know what Ah'm talking about."

"And the name is Dixie Johnson?" asked the receptionist. "Would you like to leave you number so Ms. Adams can return the call?"

Of course I'd like to leave my number, you stupid girl, Dixie thought. "Yes, of course," she said, and rattled off her cell number. Dixie rarely used this number at all; only Leigh and her driver ever called her on it. But this was a call she didn't want to miss. "Didja get that? That's my cell number, so she can get me any time."

The receptionist read the number back to her.

"Yes, that's correct—now, do you expect Adrienne back soon?" asked Dixie, almost shouting into the phone. She wasn't sure why she was all worked up over this *Ocean View* thing, but it was more than just boredom. She had a lot to say, and wanted to be heard!

"I'm not sure when Ms. Adams will return to the office, but I'll make sure she gets your message. Thanks very much, Mrs. Johnson—have a good day." The assistant hung up without even allowing her to reply.

Well, of all the nerve! She'd have to mention that to Adrienne when she talked to her. There was no place in an office as prestigious as that of *Ocean View Magazine* for little snippy receptionists. She ought to be working the night shift at the Dairy Queen—pompous little bitch!

Ugh. This stress called for some likker! Dixie poured herself a big glass of white wine and thought about how she might spend her afternoon. Being deprived for the moment of her conversation with Adrienne, she found herself bored and horny as usual. Danny had better be around somewhere! He would make the perfect diversion. Why go to the gym when she could work off a few hundred calories romping in bed with him?

Howard had been paying more attention to her lately, which had proven a bit of a "careful what you wish for" situation. When he returned home at night, he usually found her one Xanax and a few cocktails too many for good sex; so he'd taken to ravaging her in the mornings, which wasn't exactly Dixie's cup of tea. She wasn't much of a morning person, and she usually was at least a little hung over from the night before. She passively complied to keep Howard happy, but it didn't exactly dissuade her from her extracurricular escapades with Danny the Faithful Driver. Midday sex was really the thing for her; and besides (she reasoned), it wasn't exactly fair to Danny to start depriving him now! After all, he'd been there when Howard hadn't, and it wasn't his fault that Howard finally wanted to have sex with her again.

Plus, truth be told, Howard was no Danny in the sack. Sometimes she felt guilty about treating her driver like a human dildo, but facts were facts, and if his dildo didn't have diamonds, it came with a lot of other benefits. The man was young, hung and insatiable, and every bit the sport-fuck she wanted in the afternoon. He was also paid well for his job, so she figured she had every right to utilize his highest potential. "An employee is an employee" was her philosophy.

Dammit, where is he, anyway? Dixie thought as she hung up from yet another unsuccessful call. First no Adrienne, now no Danny? It was enough to make her mind reel—and her vagina. Now what was she supposed to do? Happily, her friend Chardonnay never let her down; she poured some more for herself now. It was odd, though, she thought; she hadn't seen quite as much of Danny since he'd abandoned her to disaster that night. *Oh, that fateful night,* she thought. She remembered her peed-on shoe and shivered, her rampant horniness and nascent buzz deserting her for just a moment.

"Good morning, Mrs. Yohnson," said her housekeeper, Betty, as she entered the kitchen. Dixie was a bit startled; she hadn't expected her to be there. Sometimes she forgot Betty was there at all.

Betty, short for Beatrice, was an immigrant from Venezuela who spoke solid Spanglish and moved silently through the house five days a week. These were the two main reasons Dixie had hired her: she kept to herself and could barely understand English. And there was a lot of English in that household Dixie didn't need to have understood—or repeated. But the maid had had a little surprise or two up her sleeve.

One day, Betty had walked in on her and Danny going at it in the pool house. It had been pretty flagrant; Danny'd had her up against the wall, legs wrapped around him, with pool-cleaning implements scattered all over the place. Betty had turned quickly, as though she'd suddenly remembered something in the house, and ran out. Later, when Dixie had confronted her, the maid had smiled and said, in her broken English, that it was none of her business.

"Mrs. Yohnson," she'd said carefully, "you are all alone, in the *beeg* house. Your husband, he is never home. I understand. You are beautiful woman, and you have need. I will never say nothing to Mr. Yohnson—especially if I get the raise." When it came to money, her English was almost perfect.

"A raise?" Dixie had yelled. Then she'd stopped, and had laughed out loud. The nerve of the little minx! But God bless her—why not? She was a single mom, and if anyone deserved a little extra pay for keeping her mouth shut, it was her. Besides, it would be Howard paying for his own ignorance anyway!

"Of course," Dixie had said with a genuine smile. "You deserve one anyway, Betty; you're an excellent employee! Ah'll take care of it."

The two women had sort of bonded.

As a result, they'd begun to talk a little more when nobody else was around. At first, Dixie loved her as a loyal friend, but couldn't help thinking her a bit boring; after all, what could a housekeeper have to talk about? But then Betty had started sharing gossip with her, from the other maids and households in the neighborhood.

It seemed Betty could speak very good English when it suited her, a phenomenon referred to in Miami as being "conveniently bilingual." The local housekeepers had all learned that their bosses sometimes wanted them to understand English and sometimes didn't, and had become very adept diplomats as a result. Apparently they often shared gossip in the afternoons, when they waited for the bus together. Dixie learned that Betty, like many of the others, didn't have a green card—always a good thing to know, for a socialite with something to hide; though now that she'd given Betty her raise, it didn't matter much—but she'd also found out some pretty juicy dirt on her neighbors.

Still, she didn't particularly want to get into a conversation with Betty today. She had other activities in mind.

"Betty, have you seen Danny? Ah may need him to drive me to Bal Harbour for some shopping." She stared at her glass awkwardly. Why had she said that? Betty was in on the secret, and anyway Betty knew she never went to Bal Harbour to shop. She shopped online while drunk, which Betty knew because it most often benefited her—whenever Dixie bought too much, she wound up with a whole new wardrobe. On many such occasions, Betty would help her pick things out that she liked herself. Luckily for her, she and Dixie happened to be the same size—"voluptuously chubby" or "pleasingly plump," as folks called it in the South; "curves" up north; and in

Miami, just "junk in the trunk."

"Mr. Danny took the car to mechanic for the tune-up. He say for you to give him a call if you need anything."

They both knew what that "anything" might be. *A tune-up!* Dixie thought. *I'd better get him back here soon, so he can tune me up, too.*

"Thank you, Betty," she said. "Ah just hadn't seen him in a while—Ah was worried he wasn't workin' for us anymore! Grab me a new bottle, will ya? Ah'll just head up to the study and make a few phone calls."

She left Danny another message, telling him to come over soon. With any luck, she could fit in some Bal Harbour shopping with him before Howard got home. And if nothing else, there were always those session tapes. And Diamond Jim. She'd given her jewel-studded LELO dildo that nickname, and it had never let her down. Plus, she'd noticed the other day that Howard had brought home a new tape, labeled "B. PARKER." Billie's ramblings-on, no doubt about his gold-digging wannabe-socialite wife, had to be quite an earful!

Now that she thought of it, it would take Danny a few minutes to get here anyway—why choose? She'd have time to give Billie's tape a listen before he got here; and if Danny took his time, well, she'd just follow it up with another listen to Mr. Blackbird. There was nothing saying she couldn't have both Danny *and* Diamond Jim today.

Maybe it was good to be home alone, after all!

CHAPTER 16

JACQUES AND THE
ART OF GIVING

> It was my pleasure to meet you. I look forward to discussing my inventory and how it can generate money for your charity.

—Jacques

Leigh's phone rang nonstop all morning. Everyone in Miami and their uncle had heard about her blowout gala, and wanted to be involved. She tried to keep a handle on all of them. Some were from returning media partners, and she gave her attention to them; but most were from people jumping at the chance to get a little press for themselves, or a (non-existent) free ticket. Around noon, the calls started to taper off, as they often did; moochers and fame-seekers seemed to think that if they didn't reach you one morning, it was better to try the next.

Her last call, with the society writer from the *Miami Herald,* had lasted much longer than necessary, and her unfinished cup of tea was cold. Taking advantage of the momentary silence, she tried to finish her daily to-do list.

"Jeffrey, are you there?" Leigh shouted into the intercom.

"I'm here," replied Jeffrey. "Do you need something?"

"A salad or something," she said. The phone rang again; her appetite dropped away. "Never mind; the stupid phone's ringing again. Just some more tea, please. I'm losing my voice!"

"Do you need me to get that?" he asked.

"No, I'll get it. And never mind the tea; I seem to have forgotten my resolution. Hot coffee, please." She took a deep breath, and picked up the phone for the thousandth time. "Hello, Leigh White," she said in her business voice.

"Hello, Leigh," came a smooth, deep voice on the other end. "It's Jacques—Jacques Mercier. We met at your gala and then had lunch a while back, with your friend Lauren—?"

"Yes, of course—hello, Jacques, how are you?"

"I'm well, thank you. I was hoping to discuss a business proposition with you."

"All right," said Leigh warily, knowing that this would be a diplomatic situation. She'd been interested in speaking to Jacques from the beginning—the idea of getting some art for her gala auction had crossed her mind more than a few times. But she didn't want to upset Lauren; and though Lauren had been pushing—rather hard, actually—for her partnership with Jacques, his connection to Sassy continued to complicate things. She suspected Lauren was probably encouraging her to work with him, primarily in order to get him away from Sassy; but what if Leigh and Jacques struck a deal, and Jacques stuck with Sassy anyway? Under those circumstances, having him on the gala committee might make for even more drama with Lauren; and that, Leigh wanted to avoid at all costs. Ugh—it was all so petty!

At least *he'd* reached out to *her* though, Leigh reflected; that gave her some semblance of the upper hand in all this.

"I'm in the art scene internationally, and Miami is a hot market right now," Jacques said. "Your gala would be the ideal way to meet a few local art collectors, and help the charity at the same time. I thought it would be nice if we could meet for lunch to discuss some donation options."

Well, at least he went right to the point—Leigh liked that.

"My schedule's pretty crazy these days—what'd you have in mind?" she asked. If she could get a few high-end art pieces for the gala's auction out of the guy, a lunch meeting would be well worth it.

"I'm flying to Europe on Friday to select a few pieces to be shipped back to the States. I'd like to meet today or tomorrow to discuss some selections—that way I could acquire specific pieces for the gala during my trip, if necessary." He gave Leigh a moment to digest this, then asked, "How about tomorrow at two? You choose the place—not too noisy, so we can talk."

"Sounds good," Leigh said. "How about the Globe on Alhambra?—they have my favorite salad, and it's quiet and convenient for me."

"It's a date," Jacques said. "I'll bring some slides and a deal you won't be able to refuse." Leigh wasn't sure she liked the sound of that; she like to be in control, and this added to her nagging sense that this character already had something all worked out. She couldn't place what it was; maybe it was just a residual feeling from the "scorned Lauren" days. In any case, though, she wanted to size him up herself. She'd have to do some checking up on him before their lunch tomorrow, and maybe bring Jeffrey along to see what his instincts told him. She was a pretty good judge of character and a ball-breaker when it came to business deals, but she was enough of her husband's wife to know that the more background checking you did before signing, the better.

"Great—see you tomorrow," she answered. No sooner than she'd hung up, the phone was ringing again. "Good God! Jeffrey, will you get that? *Jeffrey!*" When he didn't answer, she picked up the phone with a grimace. "Hello, Leigh White."

"Leigh, it's Hugo," said the new caller. Leigh breathed a sigh of relief.

"A friendly voice, at last," she said. Hugo was a handsome African-American man in his early thirties, effortlessly classy, and filthy rich. He was a real-estate and marketing genius; every business venture he became involved with seemed to become instantaneously successful. He didn't work for money, though; he had plenty of that already. He liked the action, the thrill of working and playing hard. When he'd become one of the charity's media sponsors, he'd committed his magazine to working hands-on with it to make it a success. He and Leigh had become good friends since, and she counted him among the few people she could completely trust.

"Oh no," he said, laughing. "Has it been one of those mornings?"

"You know it! Everybody in the world is calling about the charity. It's already crazy, and the gala isn't for months!"

"You asked for it! Anyway, I'm just calling to give you a friendly little warning."

"Warning?" Leigh's stomach tightened. "About what?"

"Well, you know I'm totally behind you, and *I* know that any press you can get for the gala is good. But be careful with Adrienne Adams and this feature she's doing for *Ocean View.*"

"Why? What do you mean?" Hugo had always made a point not to criticize or badmouth other publications or their staff, and his frankness set off alarm bells.

"I've been hearing that Adrienne's calling around about you; it sounds like she's looking for a scandal angle for her interview."

"I was worried about that," Leigh said after a moment, "but I'd just assumed she was interviewing anyone she could. I didn't think she was pushing for that angle; she painted the whole feature to me as a promotional piece for the charity. Anything negative, or carrying the scent of personal drama or self-promotion, affects the charity—not to mention what it would do to the gala and fundraising efforts."

"No kidding."

"Are you sure that's what she's doing?"

"Well, she recently hired Johnny Hernandez, the photographer who shot you for our magazine last year," said Hugo. "You remember him?"

"Sure. And—?"

"And he called me, and told me that Adrienne has been asking him all kinds of pointed questions about you and the charity. She's digging hard for dirt, and even offered him steady work if he delivers."

"I can't believe it," Leigh said. "I knew I shouldn't trust her! I'd better call around and find out who she's already talked to. I mean, if she's looking honestly, I don't have anything to worry about," she added quickly. "There's no scandal for her to find. For goodness' sake, I like to be in bed by nine!"

"I thought so," said Hugo. "But remember, she's a reporter—honesty's not exactly at a premium with them! Anyhow, just giving you the heads-up; I'm sure you'll do the right thing. And you know I'm on your team, so whatever I can do, let me know."

"Thanks, you're a good friend," Leigh said. "How's Jennifer, anyway?"

"Who?—oh, Jennifer," replied Hugo, laughing. "She's history, I'm afraid. Another one looking for a husband, and I'm not quite ready yet."

"Oh, too bad! But you'll find the right girl, don't worry. It's just that this town is filled with gold-diggers, and you're a treasure! Not to mention you could buy the Treasury!" The mention of gold-diggers brought an important question back to mind. "Hey, while I have you on the phone, I have a question for you. I'm having lunch with an art dealer tomorrow who wants to offer some of his art for the gala. I'm not quite sure what he has in mind, but my gut tells me he isn't the type to offer me a deal unless he can make some money. You know the charity usually only accepts 100% donated items, but this one might be worth an exception, if his stuff is all it's cracked up to be. His name's Jacques Mercier—have you heard of him?"

"The name doesn't ring a bell," Hugo replied, "but I'm hardly an expert. Listen, I'll have my art writer do some research, and get back to you. I do know the art market isn't doing too well, and prices have dropped, so collectors with cash are buying like crazy these days."

"That's what I'm hoping—I'm just wondering what kind of deal he's going to offer," Leigh said. "I know he has to cover his costs."

"Well, one way or another, be careful," said Hugo. "I'll get back to you about it before your lunch. In the meantime, say hi to Brad for me! I've gotta run to a meeting, but let's all have dinner soon."

"Sounds good. Talk to you soon, love—and thanks for thinking of me!"

Leigh hung up and sat down in silence. There was a cup of hot coffee sitting in front of her; she hadn't even noticed Jeffrey when he brought it in. He loved to do that, and to rib her afterwards about her not noticing him.

The phone rang again. This time it was Jeffrey calling from the kitchen, to let her know he'd be gone for about an hour. While she'd been chatting on the office phone, he'd answered the private line and taken messages from Lauren, Lorraine, Katie, Brad and Adrienne. She wondered how Adrienne had gotten the number to the private line. Like having her cell number wasn't already enough! *I hate pushy broads,* Leigh thought. *And now add pushy covert broads.*

She couldn't forget to tell Jeffrey that she needed an escort to lunch tomorrow, and that they had some checking-up to do beforehand. They'd need to look closely into this Jacques guy. He'd said he'd be shipping art in from Europe. Could you just ship high-priced art to the U.S.? she pondered. What about the duty fees, insurance and customs? Surely he wasn't skipping any steps…?

She shook her head. As if she didn't already have enough to worry about, without being paranoid! With her having such a well-connected, powerful lawyer for a husband, anyone would be insane to involve her in something illegal. And even so, what reason did she have to suspect Jacques at this point? It wasn't like he was just *giving* his art away; that would have set off alarm bells. He was just another player, using the gala auction to get his foot in the Miami door. How was that so different from any of the rest of her friends?

The biggest difference, she thought with a smile, was that there was something in it for her, for a change. Depending on the deal, it could be a great opportunity for raising money, and bringing something new to the Charity Ball to boot. With the new publicity the *Ocean View* article would bring, and a fine-art auction to rival the best in the country, this year's Ball was really going to be something special. She let the excitement flood over her for a minute as she thought about it all. Sure, it was stressful—but damn it, it was going to be worth it.

This gala was going to be the *best!*

***

The following day began with a call from Hugo.

Jacques, as it turned out, had a very strong presence online, having dealt art worldwide for some time through a few private channels. Hugo had also been able to confirm his possession of the artworks he'd mentioned, by calling a few friends with access to dealership catalogues and private collection records. It looked like he specialized in minor works by major artists: a lot of his confirmed collection was comprised of sketches, prints and privately commissioned sculptures.

Jeffrey, for his part, wasn't able to turn up any dirt on the guy, either. He had a friend at the British Museum who was able to take a look at their last year's catalogue periodicals, and found Jacques's name featured prominently there. Only one of the works he'd mentioned to Leigh was listed with his name, but other minor works by the same artists were also listed.

Lunch proved to be no less a pleasant surprise. Jacques turned out to be the perfect gentleman; and true to his word, he made Leigh the perfect offer. Most of his pieces were modern, but he had a few minor works by the great masters of other generations: a Breughel printer's proof, a couple of oil sketches by Manet, some color-block tests from Mondrian. (Some of the pieces, Leigh saw on looking them up, had even been mentioned in Dottie the Collectista's blog—and Leigh knew she was a go-to resource for anything art.) Jacques explained that aside from modern works, this kind of art moved quickest on the market because it comprised the only works of the masters that weren't already in museums.

For the gala, he was willing to offer each piece at ten per cent over the lowest market value. The charity would get that extra ten percent, and Jacques would get his regular commission from the rest. Essentially, there would be a buyer's and seller's premium, as at Sotheby's and Christie's. It was the perfect arrangement. At the prices this art could sell for, collectors would go crazy—meaning big, *big* money for the gala.

Jacques would be flying the art in on his own plane, he told her with a wry smile, so he didn't generally have to pay shipping. This raised Leigh's eyebrows! She thought about the risks involved with customs, with airport security. But then, surely that was Jacques's concern and not hers—and he had every detail worked out. The way he packaged the artworks for travel, he said, there was no way of knowing them for authentic masterpieces; to the average customs agent—even if they inspected his cargo, which they rarely did—they would seem like nothing special. Apparently, all art dealers operated this way.

At his estimate, the collection Jacques was offering was valued at just short of twenty-one million dollars, with the charity taking ten percent. Leigh couldn't believe her good fortune. Indeed she was skeptical at first; but Jacques anticipated her concerns and suggested she deposit all of the money made from the art sales directly into the Charity's account. This would ensure that the Charity held no risk, and show that he trusted her to get him his share when she was able.

It was all Leigh needed to hear. It seemed Jacques's slate was completely clean, aside from his jilting Lauren for Sassy. That part was regrettable; classy as he was, Jacques didn't seem to have a taste in women to match, and it would have been nice to think less of the man who'd hurt her friend's feelings. But the deal was too good to turn down. The art would be great publicity for the gala, and the money—! It was hard for Leigh to wrap her head around that part. Brad wouldn't believe her good fortune and shrewdness in working out such a deal. She couldn't wait to share the news and start spreading the word. Maybe Jacques would even allow some of the art to be used in the photo shoot for *Ocean View!*

She had to pinch herself.

CHAPTER 17

MAN TO MAN

Glad 2 hear it! Good art is hard 2 come by.

—Brandon

Acouple of days after Leigh's meeting with Jacques, Brandon Westbrook was on his way to discuss an art deal of his own. Dressed down in vintage Dior slacks, crisply tailored shirt and understated gold wristwatch, he looked like any slim, well-heeled man out for a brisk walk in Wynwood. No one would have guessed that here was the Diva Lorraine Manchester in person; nor would they have imagined what sort of business the Diva might be up to. He'd taken care to park the Range Rover in a garage; there had to be a few people in the neighborhood who'd recognize it.

He strolled into the cool lobby of a renovated brick building, and took the elevator to the 12th floor. The elevator ran slow and loud; the hallway was clean and neat, but nondescript and industrial-looking. It was amazing what these artists were willing to put up with for their space! He walked up to 12E and rang the buzzer.

After a while he heard a cautious approach of feet, and a shadow crossed the keyhole. A moment later the door opened, and Brandon stood face to face with Arturo Veraz.

The trip to Europe didn't seem to have done Arturo any favors. Normally small, he looked drawn and nervous—tired, even—much less attractive than the last time Brandon had seen him. Still, there was something ingenuously handsome about his soft face and dark, soulful eyes—and Brandon smiled to think back on the smooth Cuban beauty the man had in his pants.

"I wasn't expecting you," Arturo said sheepishly.

"Obviously not," said Brandon. "May I come in?"

"Of course," said Arturo, and stepped aside.

Brandon walked into the loft, careful not to let his clothes brush against anything. You never knew where wet paint might be, in an artist's home. It was quite a large space, with high ceilings and big windows: a perfect place for a painter. The walls were exposed brick, the floors a rough wood with Persian rugs scattered around here and there. Easels were set up throughout the loft, displaying paintings in various stages of completion.

"I see you've been busy," Brandon said coolly, scanning the easels. There were quite a few nice ones—still lifes, a few portraits, one or two more abstract compositions—but the one he was looking for was nowhere to be found.

"Yes—I'm sorry I haven't called about yours," Arturo said hurriedly. "A huge job just came through."

"It's been quite a while, darling," said Brandon, still searching for his portrait among the canvases. "May I see it?"

"I—I haven't had time to work on it," said Arturo. "I'm sorry; this job was too big to turn down."

"Hmm," said Brandon, "I understand; though I *did* pay a pretty penny for it, if you recall."

"Yes, I know. I'm sorry," Arturo said again.

"So you say, sweetie, so you say," said Brandon mischievously. "But just how sorry are we talking, here?" He stepped closer, and put his hands on Arturo's shoulders. His voice raised to a feminine whisper. "I have a big job for you too, you know—getting bigger, in fact."

"I don't think so," said Arturo, looking uncomfortable.

Ah, hell. Brandon was feeling strangely horny this afternoon. "No? Perhaps you'd prefer it if the job were mine, like before— remember?" He reached a hand down and deftly cupped Arturo's crotch. Arturo jerked backward as though he'd been burnt.

"No—no," he said simply.

"Come on, sugar," Brandon purred. "That isn't what you were saying the last time we saw one another. Just a little lick." He made another reach toward Arturo's fly. This time Arturo took his wrist to stop him.

"It's—different—for me," he said, "when you're a man."

Brandon looked shocked for a moment. Then he laughed out loud, and it was the Diva's high, cold laugh.

"Oh, honey, you just lack imagination! Don't you know you get the best of both worlds with me?—a woman's mouth, and a man's understanding of what to do with it. But I won't push you." His voice dropped back into its deeper register. "The bottom line is this, sweetie: I've paid you good money for a painting. A very beautiful painting, of a very beautiful woman—namely, myself. You haven't done the painting. When do you intend to?"

"Soon," said Arturo. "As soon as I finish—"

"—this big job. I get it. And when is *that* going to be?"

Arturo thought a moment. "I'm sure I'll be able to finish it after April first. The paintings are needed before then."

"April first? Are you *kidding?* I paid you for this *months* ago!" Leigh's gala was on in mid-March, and he'd hoped he might offer to loan her the portrait to use as part of her after-party decorations. That's where the *real* insiders' party was going to be; and aside from being around celebrities, nothing made a celebrity of you quicker than being commemorated in the décor.

"I'm sorry," Arturo said, "but I really can't do it until this job is done. The people I'm doing it for, they're very"—he searched for the word with a troubled look—"insistent."

"And *I'm* not?" Brandon was livid. He looked around the room at the other paintings. "What makes *these* so damned important? And who are these 'insistent' people you're doing them for, anyway? You have a chance to paint *the* Diva Lorraine Manchester, and you're spending your time painting these"—he gestured disgustedly at the sketchy bright red-and-pink one nearest to them—"these blobby *flowers,* instead?"

"I'm sorry," said Arturo again, simply.

"You need to get your priorities straight," Brandon huffed, struggling to compose himself. There would be other uses for the portrait. Besides, he needed to get going. He wouldn't want to be late for one of Leigh's committee meetings—especially today's.

"Look, I have to go," he said. "But this thing better get done. I've paid you for it in more ways than one."

"I'll make it up to you, you'll see," insisted Arturo. "It's going to be an incredible portrait, I promise."

"It can't help but be that, honey, it's of me," Brandon spat back. "But I'm going to trust you one more time. You may be a hot mess, but you're talented, and I still want my picture. Just don't let me down again! I'm a sweetheart to my friends, but trust me, you *don't* want to piss off the Diva—I'm only as nice to people as they let me be!"

CHAPTER 18

THE NAKED COMMITTEE LEADER

> I'll be at the meeting. I have celebrity signed auction items left over from the IBS Foundation gala. Pffft!

—Mitchell

Leigh was at her over-the-top gala, loving every minute of it. The gala was packed with celebrity guests—Barry Gibb, Swizz Beatz, Broadway star Frankie Grande (who was expected to win a Tony), Lee Daniels—the famous director and Hollywood royalty behind the new show Empire—Courtney Love, and lots of others who had donated generously to the charity over the years.

Everything was picture-perfect as Leigh walked through the ballroom graciously acknowledging guests, posing for photos and giving the occasional hug and air-kiss to a friend or one of the high-rollers who had already promised to bid big in the auction. After all that stress, everything was going so wonderfully! She walked cautiously up the three steps to center stage, taking care not to trip in her new Manolo Blahnik strappy satin pumps, and grabbed the microphone, ready to address everyone.

The entire room gasped and went silent. The shocked crowd stared.

Leigh looked down, and a wave of unspeakable horror flooded over her. Aside from that thousand-dollar pair of strappy fuck-me stilettos, she was completely naked. Photographers swooped to the stage, and she was blinded by flashes.

She sat up in bed gasping. A classic naked-on-stage dream! She'd heard of actors and public speakers having such dreams, but she'd had never had one herself; it seemed so silly! Yet the dream had shaken her to her core. *Was it an omen?* she couldn't help but wonder. She looked over at Brad. He was sleeping soundly, and looked incredibly peaceful. Surely the dream was nonsense. The stress was just catching up to her a bit; there was really nothing new to worry about. She'd pulled off the gala nine times before—she could do it again in her sleep! So to speak.

Anyway, she'd never be so frivolous as to spend a thousand dollars on shoes—that was just insane!

***

Leigh's morning was again filled with phone calls, and every member of the new gala committee had already phoned her at least once. Brandon Westbrook had called three times for some reason; she'd missed the last two calls. She was sure it could wait; the group was supposed to meet at her house at two o'clock, less than an hour away. Jeffrey was supervising the preparations, so she'd have a bit of time to herself before everyone arrived.

"Everything's ready," he said as he walked into her office, closing the door behind him. "There are folders at each setting with the itinerary of the meeting—here's yours"—he handed her a manila folder—"and Michael has set up the bar. Oh, and Brandon's just arrived. Why is it that, as Brandon, he's always the first to arrive, but when he's Lorraine Manchester, she's always the last?"

Leigh laughed; the Diva always showed up as Brandon West-brook to the meetings. In part this was in keeping with his mantra of *No pay, no three hours of hair, makeup and wardrobe;* but Leigh suspected there were deeper reasons behind it. Brandon was the organized, managerial counterpart to the Diva's outsized theatrical personality; and without the pressure to perform, he was by far the more reliable committee member. It was an interesting dichotomy, and far from being unique to Brandon. A producer friend had once told Leigh a funny story about Snoop Dogg (or Snoop Lion, or whatever he was going by these days), that if you booked him as Snoop, he'd show up stoned, thugged-out and generally Doggish, with an entourage to match; but if you booked him by his real name, Calvin Broadus, he was punctual, sober and very businesslike.

"Well, Lorraine has to make an entrance, and Brandon likes to make sure he's in control," Leigh reasoned. "But still—so early! It's unlike him. And he's been calling me all morning! Tell him I'll be out in a second."

"Yes, my Queen. I'll alert you when everyone has arrived." Jeffrey knew that Leigh had no intention of emerging until the entire committee was present, with drinks in hand. Leigh White didn't wait for people, they waited for her; and besides, she'd make good use of the time beforehand.

"Thanks," she laughed as he bowed ostentatiously. "And don't you dare do any of that 'my Queen' stuff in front of this group of crazies. There may be a queen or two here, but I'm not one of them." They cracked up laughing.

"Yes, my Queen," Jeffrey said again as he ducked out. "If anyone calls, I'll tell them you're on the phone giving advice to Obama."

Leigh smiled to herself. She knew Jeffrey had it all under control, and loved it. He was organized and detailed, and didn't take any bullshit from the likes of the crowd they expected today. Her gala committee members were all pros at tossing it at him, but he always managed to toss it back. She looked over her itinerary, and at the list of committee members.

There was Lauren, of course, who—as was fitting for a shopaholic—usually volunteered to head the silent auction.

Mitchell and Scarlett would compete for attention through the whole meeting, and try to best one another with the lists of celebrities, mostly unrealistic, that they hoped to deliver to the event.

Brandon, acting on behalf of the glamorous Diva Lorraine Manchester, would insist on emceeing, which might become a problem if Mario Lopez offered to do it. Mario would obviously be the better choice—he'd done an incredible job at it before—but convincing Brandon of that would be somewhere between a splitting headache and a world crisis in diplomacy. Leigh thought of offering Lorraine the position of red-carpet hostess, in which she'd welcome all of the celebrities and VIP guests. That would certainly make her happy; the only problem was that as hostess, she'd suck a little too much oxygen out of the room. As celebrity-obsessed as Lorraine was, she tended to forget they were there when the red carpet was under *her* feet—at which point, everything became about her. To make matters worse, Julie Fogel, who'd done the global PR at Nikki Beach, had offered to assist; and because Julie was all business and the Diva was all show, the two of them never failed to clash.

Billie Parker had asked her to put Katie on the committee this year—probably more to keep her busy and out of trouble, than anything else. Leigh had regretted agreeing to it since the whole *Ocean View* debacle had blown open, but Billie had contributed a lot to her events in past years, and this year he was offering a Mars Suitland, one of his most talked-about couture dresses, for the live auction. Ah well; she didn't imagine Katie would show anyway, after their run-in at Joe's—and if she did, Leigh could always make room for her in some out-of-the-way subcommittee. Lavatory management, perhaps.

She'd hoped Brad could make it to the meeting, as he was always instrumental in bringing a general tone of sanity—and some prestigious donors—to the proceedings. Unfortunately he was in court today, defending someone or another in a capital case. Didn't the man know where he was *really* needed?

Jacques, the newcomer, would be giving a presentation on the art he was bringing to auction. Unfortunately he'd insisted on bringing Sassy along as well—under the assumption that she'd be helpful in ticket sales. Hopefully, if Lauren were given leadership of the silent auction, the two could be kept from fighting over everything else.

For the thousandth time, Leigh sighed and wished she were at least having more fun in all this; it was hard to play the clown while running the circus. The months leading up to a gala were filled with long days of phone calls and meetings, and late nights of schmoozing and promoting. Granted, she felt great that she'd managed to raise so much money over the years. Her efforts literally kept the school running, and its kids out of trouble. But the gala was a major job. It wasn't something too many people would ever understand, but organizing a charity gala of this magnitude was much like producing a Broadway show: there were a million parts to put together, and almost no room for error. In this case, however, Leigh wasn't only the producer of the show, but its writer, casting director, conductor, lead player, janitor and Chairman of the Board.

It was also quite a task to get her committee of friends to work together without killing each other. She was really the only common thread for most of them—or at least the only neutral ground. She'd always thought that the mixture of egos would prove explosive one day; each of them simply *knew* they were the most important person in the group, and wouldn't hear otherwise. And while all of them (well, all of them aside from Sassy) were instrumental to some degree in making the gala work, they needed a tremendous amount of hand-holding, schmoozing, wrangling, double-checking and follow-up from her in order to be kept productive.

Well, it was showtime, anyway.

As she grabbed her iPad and itinerary, she felt her phone buzz. It was Dixie. On an impulse, Leigh pressed "Accept," and immediately regretted it. What was she thinking?

"Hi, Dixie," she said. "Listen, I'm sorry, but I can't be long; I've got a—"

"Honey, yew ain't gonna *believe* this! Ah've just been listenin' to Billie Parker's session tapes!"

"Dixie, you—you *what—?*"

Leigh clammed up as a veritable flood-tide of gossip came through the receiver. She could barely understand Dixie's drawl at such break-neck speed, but what she heard was enough to make her eyes pop. Billie's affairs—his wife's—her plans to hang onto him—his plans for their divorce—a private investigator—! It was almost too much. Leigh felt a pang of sympathy for Billie, and hoped he was doing all right; but it was hardly disappointing to hear he'd had enough of that Botoxed backstabber of a wife. Getting rid of her would be worth a little therapy.

"Hang—hang on, Dixie," Leigh said, as she switched the intercom off. She didn't want to be interrupted in the midst of *this*.

Jeffrey came in discreetly. Leigh waved him over as she covered the phone's mouthpiece with her hand.

"The mob's all here, and already restless," he whispered. "And—"

"Very good," she whispered, cutting him off, "could you just have Michael set out a couple of bottles of wine, and tell the group I'll be with them in a minute?"

"Yes, my Queen," Jeffrey answered quickly. "I should tell you,

Brandon's waiting in the hall for you, and there are some—"

"I'll have to take care of that in a minute, Jeffrey," she whispered, pointing urgently at the phone. Dixie was just launching into the Parkers' pre-nup; she didn't want to miss this part.

"I think you—"

"Just a *minute*, Jeffrey—I'll be done soon, I promise. Hold the crowd at bay for me!"

"All right, my Queen," Jeffrey sighed. "Shall I offer the powder room for Brandon and Mitchell as well?" he added, then gave a roar of laughter.

Leigh nodded with a smile; this was a joke between them. The two would probably have snuck off already to perk themselves up, but Jeffrey always enjoyed shoving it in their faces. Mitchell had been in and out of rehab for years, but rehab is for quitters, as the saying goes, and he'd never been willing or able to stick with it. As for Brandon, he rarely used the stuff.

"Very good," said Jeffrey, and ducked out. She turned her attention back to Dixie.

"—and he said she's even tryin' out for a *reality TV show!*" Dixie was saying. "Can you *believe* that? She ain't even interestin' in real life, much less on TV! But she's sure gonna try and drag Billie along with her, just to get herself in everyone's faces."

"A *reality show?*" Leigh laughed. "God, that'd be just like her."

"Wouldn't it, though? She's sure it's gonna be nothin' but shoppin' and globe-hoppin', goin' out to fancy parties and showin' off her bod on the beach. She'd probably be perfect for it, now Ah think of it—you gotta have someone on there that people love to hate! Have *yew* ever thought about doing something like that, Leigh?"

"Not really my thing," said Leigh.

"No, I guess not," laughed Dixie. "But oh, another thing—!"

Leigh eyed the clock as Dixie went on, feeling bad for keeping her committee waiting. Everyone on it was busy and involved in lots of other activities—not to mention paying jobs—but she always expected them to forget everything else when they joined her for a gala meeting. All cell phones were to be off; all gossip was to take place before and after the meeting. Most of the group arrived early and stayed late, for that reason. But that was another reason she didn't quite like leaving everyone alone now. Because she usually didn't join them until it was time for the meeting, they were free to include her in the gossip. Usually her intercom brought her every word—even with friends, it was good to keep tabs on things—but now it sat silent. Who knew what they could be saying? She'd have to cut this short for now.

Jeffrey reentered. "Your humble court awaits you," he whispered with a smile.

Leigh held up her hand to Jeffrey, indicating that she wanted him to stay. "Dixie, darling," she said into the phone, "didn't you say you wanted to volunteer to help with my charity gala?"

"Weellll, yes!" Dixie's excited screech could be heard on the other side of the room. Jeffrey snickered. Dixie had repeatedly offered herself as a volunteer and desperately wanted to be on the gala committee, but she'd never shown up, so Leigh had stopped mentioning it.

"Well, I really should have insisted sooner," Leigh went on, "but we're having a gala committee meeting at my house in forty-five minutes. Why don't you come over and join the group?"

Leigh smiled through the torrent of enthusiastic exclamations on the other end. Jeffrey looked quizzically at her, then nodded appreciatively as he realized what she was thinking: she figured she could start the meeting when she got off the phone, and by the time Dixie got there, she'd be wrapping up. Dixie would scare everyone away with her gregariousness, and Leigh could keep her to finish telling her about Billie's session. It was really the best way to get the dirt today; if she didn't invite Dixie over, Dixie would just get drunk and pass out, and Leigh wouldn't hear anything more about it until tomorrow. And one thing was for certain: she couldn't let that happen, or she would never sleep tonight. Enquiring minds had to know.

"Great—you'll be on your way, then?" Leigh asked sweetly, as Jeffrey silently applauded.

"Ah sure will!"

"Excellent—see you in forty-five or so." She hung up with a flourish.

"Bravo, my Queen," laughed Jeffrey.

"Diplomacy was always my strong suit," Leigh said, rising.

"You'll need it in the next room, I imagine. Lauren already looks like she wants to skin Sassy."

"Ugh, I'm sure. I feel bad for having Sassy here in the first place, but Jacques insisted on bringing her. What's with all these people and their unwanted plus-ones?"

"I can't say I was too happy about it myself," Jeffrey said. "After going to such trouble to balance the seating arrangement, it pained me to have an extra person to take care of. I hope you didn't want me to make her an itinerary."

"Oh, no, darling—I'm glad you didn't! It'll get the point across that she wasn't invited, and it'll make Lauren happy. Such a dramatic bunch! Well, let's get this over with!" She started toward the door.

"Before you do," Jeffrey said coolly, "you should know that there are some photographers here."

"*Photographers?* What photographers?"

"They're from *Ocean View*. Apparently they wanted to get some early shots of the gala preparations."

This was getting to be too much for Leigh. "How did they even *hear* about this meeting? And why didn't you tell me they were here?"

"I tried, my Queen, a number of times," Jeffrey sighed. "You were on the phone. Now that I think of it, that must be why Brandon's been hanging around the door all this time."

"Of course," Leigh said. "He wants to be photographed escorting me in to the meeting. I should've guessed there were photographers here, from his early arrival. Well, nothing to be done about it now; just close the doors and make sure they leave once we've started."

"Certainly—I've already informed them that they could only stay until the meeting started. And I made sure Michael got some drinks in their hands, too, to keep them contained."

"Very good, Jeffrey, thanks."

Leigh glanced at herself in the mirror by the door, gave herself a nod and opened it.

On the other side were a small crowd of photographers and a very eager Brandon Westbrook. Brandon was quick on his feet, you had to give him that; he was somehow able to get beside her, with her arm in his, before the first flash popped.

"It's about time you emerged from your sanctuary," he said with a big, photogenic smile. "I just wanted to say hello before everyone grabbed you, and escort you into the drawing room in style. You know I'm your right-hand man—and woman."

Leigh just rolled her eyes.

They walked in together. The drawing room, situated just off the patio, was a large and elegant room, with an airy ceiling and high windows. Paintings and prints decorated the walls, giving it a comfortable, classy feel. This was the main room in the house that the Whites used for entertaining, and Leigh had given many intimate parties here, for hundreds of Miami's who's who. The contrast between the room's stately atmosphere and the invariably petty dishings of the gala committee never failed to strike Leigh;

but then, that was the real Miami, wasn't it?

There was a scramble when she and Brandon arrived; everyone wanted to be photographed with her before they actually sat down to start the meeting. *Ah well,* she thought, *at least the magazine will bring us lots of publicity and sponsorship money.* Once they'd had a few shots and a good group photo taken, Leigh nodded to Jeffrey, and he escorted the photographers out. It was bad enough having this gang of publicity-mongers on the committee; having journalists actually *at* the meeting would really be too much. Leigh didn't want any of their preparation details leaking to the press until everything was confirmed, and this year the pre-press for the gala had started before she'd even confirmed its date or location.

Once the photographers were gone and everyone had settled, she went straight to her seat at the head of the table, with Lauren and Brandon on either side.

"Good afternoon, everyone," she said. "Thank you all for taking time out of your busy schedules today, and please accept my apologies for keeping you waiting. I was just on the phone with my friend Dixie, whom some of you know. She's agreed to join our group, which I'm very excited about. She has connections to several celebrities she thinks she can get to attend." *Hopefully that'll pacify this power group,* Leigh thought. Someone would certainly question Dixie's place on the committee otherwise.

"Ooh, more celebrities, eh? Sounds good to me—you know I'm always up for more of them," said Brandon cheerfully. Lorraine Manchester loved celebrities more than anything, except perhaps being photographed with them. A lot of people, especially in Miami, claimed to be friends of celebrities, while in truth they were simply low-level stalkers, hanging around them in clubs and shoehorning themselves into photos with them when they were drunk. Brandon, on the other hand, truly was a friend to many of them; and Lorraine was friends with more. Not only was the Diva a lot of fun to hang around with after-hours, she never failed to attract photographers, and always had access to party favors. As did Brandon—as his sniffling now attested.

Scarlett was more skeptical. "That sloppy drunk housewife? Who exactly does she think *she* can get to come?" she sneered.

"It doesn't matter right now," Leigh insisted curtly. "We have our own celebrities to discuss. This year we have to pull out all the stops. It's our tenth gala, and it may very well be my last—I'd just say it is my last, but that's what I said last year." Pleasant laughter waved around the room. "Anyway, this is the culmination of ten years of passion and experience, so it must be the best gala ever. We must reach higher than we've ever reached before—and when I say higher, I'm talking donations." Again, the room ruffled with polite laughter. "So tell me: who are we thinking we can get?"

It was a hard reality of the charity-gala game, that celebrity appearances were essential. Stars not only brought publicity, they also attracted the money crowd—and money was what mattered in a gala. They really set the right tone. To get people to feel like throwing their money around—even people with more of it than they knew what to do with—you had to set up an atmosphere of fantasy-like opulence, where holding onto your money felt embarrassingly cheap; and nothing did that like celebrities. They made the guests feel like they weren't on Earth anymore, but in some glamorous alternate universe where money was of no consequence. For this reason they were the icing on the money cake, and Leigh knew it well. If she wanted to give her guests a magic carpet ride, she needed the big names.

"I think I can get my boy Flo Rida to perform," Mitchell announced, standing up with chest puffed out like he'd just laid down a royal flush. "His new single's hot, though it isn't out yet. I guess most of you probably haven't heard it—?" He directed this last question at Scarlett.

"I have; I don't think it's his best," she snapped.

"But he's a rapper," Lauren whined. "I hate rap music; it's all noise. Anyway, I don't think that's the best kind of entertainment for this money crowd, do you? These people don't know how to dance to rap. No one does, really."

"I love rap music," Sassy opined loudly, smiling at Lauren. "Besides, Flo Rida's hot, and he'll be a great draw to the young-money crowd. Besides, for the older crowd, he's a name—that's all they care about."

"It's never a bad idea to have a variety of entertainment scheduled," Leigh said, anxious to avert a blow-up between the rival realtors.

"Whatever—I think I can get Pharrell anyway," said Scarlett. "He's been doing a lot of high-profile charity work lately, and environmentalist stuff. He's recently partnered with an awesome recycled-textile company called Bionic—they do *amazing* work. Tell him about your charity, and with any luck he'll put on that cute little hat of his and break out into 'Happy' for you." Scarlett was sharp; she knew Leigh had always had an affinity for Pharrell and all his "help the world" views. She turned to Mitchell with a "told-you-so" look. "Leave it to the pros, sweetie," she added smugly.

"Well…why don't we make a list of who's available, and see who comes through?" Leigh asked. "That way we won't get bogged down in possibilities. And let me remind you, in addition to our friends we should be looking for celebrities who need to up their public image by doing something good. Has anyone we know been busted for anything juicy lately?" She thought she heard Brandon giggle. "No? Well, I've put Scarlett and Mitchell in charge of the entertainment arrangements, so if anyone else has any leads, please pass them on to those two."

"Or to the one of us with real connections," Scarlett smirked.

"Or the one with real tits," rejoined Mitchell. "I'll leave you all to guess."

"He's just jealous," said Scarlett cattily. "You know, Mitchell, you've been hanging around those bitchy models of yours for so long, I'm kind of worried you're becoming one."

"If you were hanging around them, you'd be coming too," Mitchell sent back.

"All right, you two," interjected Leigh, barely suppressing a smile. As usual, the rivalry was all show. She knew that the two actually made an unstoppable team: Scarlett had major connections through her involvement with various pop artists; Mitchell knew all the big-money guys who hung out with sports stars and models. Together they could make a party happen, and happen big. With any luck they could get Jason Binn to cover the event for Du Jour magazine while they were at it.

"Well, if Dixie's joining the group, why don't we see if we can get Britney?" asked Brandon mischievously. "I've heard that she's one of Dixie's husband's long-time clients, and has even more problems than we all know about. Word is, she's got—"

"Hey now—you know the rules," Leigh said sternly. "No gossip during the meeting. And Brandon, don't be calling a kettle black." Everyone laughed, Brandon included.

"You're right as always, Leigh," he said. "But I'm not the only one in this room who has some guilty pleasures! I'm sure I don't need to mention any names. Oh, Scarlett," he added, as if in after-thought, "would you add Courtney Love and Pamela Anderson to your list? They're bad-girl pop icons, and it'll make your crowd happy to have them at the event. I'm sure I can get both of them to come, and probably to donate for the auction, too."

"I know every manager of every store in Bal Harbour, Merrick

Park and the Design District," Lauren said proudly, "so unless anyone objects, I'll take charge of the silent auction subcommittee again this year. I can even reach out to the fine jewelry department at Neiman Marcus—you know, the Atlanta store is renowned for their estate jewelry."

Sassy seemed about to speak up, but a pointed look from Leigh shut her up. When no one else objected, Lauren went on.

"Great!" she chirped. "Go ahead and give any auction information to me, then—but *only* when you've confirmed a donation. And I mean *confirmed!* Brandon, last year your list of celebrities turned out to be practically worthless! We only received one donation from your list, and it was Katy Perry's sweaty bustier."

"Let's not get into that now," Mitchell said. "We need to concentrate on the cocktail party that Scarlett and I are planning. The idea, as you know, is to attract some new celebrities ahead of time, and formally announce the gala so we can start generating some press. I'm happy to announce that *Ocean View Magazine* has just confirmed that they'll sponsor the party, and print photos in the magazine."

"Wait—*Ocean View's* sponsoring it?" Leigh asked suspiciously. *How many pies is Adrienne trying to get her fingers in?* she thought.

"Yeah—what's the problem? It'll be great publicity."

"I know—I just—it would've been nice to hear about this before now, Mitchell. Is that what they were all doing here today?"

"Yeah, I told them about today's meeting," Mitchell said. "Sorry—I didn't think it'd be a problem. I only just spoke to them the other day."

"I bet," laughed Brandon. "Little Adrienne's been casting her net pretty wide lately."

"Well, anyway, they're offering to pay for it, and I think it's a good idea," said Mitchell quickly. "If they're covering it, I think I can have Heidi Klum come in to make the official announcement; she's shooting with them that day and they'll have her on retainer already. Please, though—nobody say a word about it until it's confirmed. If it all works out, we might be able to get her ex to perform for the gala."

"*Seal?* You're even dumber than I thought," Scarlett scoffed.

"Just like you to underestimate me, darling," Mitchell said sweetly.

"Well," Leigh went on, clearing her throat, "there's also the matter of the venue. We've had a few different suggestions so far, but no definitive offers; so I wanted to open it to the group. Any thoughts on venue?"

"I think the St. Regis would be a good choice," said Lauren. "My friend Lourdes Alatriste at Engel & Völkers has a major relationship with the decision-makers over there."

"Right—close to your *shops,*" Sassy smirked contemptuously. "Expand your territory a little, honey."

"And I suppose you've got something better in mind?" Lauren retorted.

"Definitely," Sassy spat back. "The Fontainebleau would be great for the event, and I think I can get a good offer there. I've worked with some of the managers before."

Leigh's ears pricked up at the name. Hadn't Adrienne been pushing the Fontainebleau on her before? Had she and Sassy met, too?

Scarlett cut in.

"The St. Regis could work out," she said. "I know some of the resort managers there."

"She means massage girls," Mitchell laughed.

"Nobody's talking to you, douchebag," Scarlett said.

"We have these pet names for each other, you see," Mitchell said to the rest of the room, smiling good-naturedly.

"I guess we'll just have to wait for the offers," Leigh sighed. "In

the meantime, give any venue leads to me, celebrities to Scarlett and Mitchell, and auction leads to Lauren. Now, I have just one other important new point on the agenda today." She gestured at Jacques. "Everyone, if you haven't already, I'd like you to meet Jacques Mercier. He's an art dealer, new in town, and has graciously offered some wonderful artworks for our auction! I think it's really going to be the touch that sets this year's gala apart from all the rest. Please, all of you, give him a warm welcome. Jacques, I believe you have a presentation for us—?"

"Yes, indeed," Jacques said, opening his laptop. Jeffrey switched on a projector and turned down the lights, and the group went uncharacteristically silent as Jacques began his presentation.

The collection was wide-ranging, and beautifully curated; in addition to the ones Leigh had seen photos of already, there was a huge Botero sculpture; an early Eric Fischl canvas and a piece of wall that Basquiat had worked on as a graffiti artist. ("That one is going to be hell to ship," Jacques quipped.) A few of the artworks, Jacques admitted apologetically, were in conservation and could not be photographed; but the works he showed were more than impressive enough to leave the rest of the committee speechless. This was only partly positive, Leigh knew; after all, this was a committee of type-A egos, and the others were obviously disgruntled that they were being upstaged by fine art. *Ah well,* she sighed to herself. They'd just have to deal with it. The art was the real star of this gala.

After Jacques's presentation was finished, Leigh stood.

"Thank you, Jacques," she said. "Now I want us all to break up and talk separately about our weekly goals; there's a lot to be done over the next few weeks, so let's try to stay organized and on top of everything. Grab a drink, or help yourself to the other refreshments—and thank you all again for coming!"

As the group broke for the bar and the "powder room," Lauren

made a beeline for Leigh.

"Can I talk to you a second, Leigh?" she asked.

Uh-oh, Leigh thought.

"Su-ure," she said warily; then she saw that Lauren was grinning.

"Don't worry," Lauren said, "it isn't about Sassy! I just wanted to say that I took your advice with Francisco, and it totally worked!"

Leigh could have danced with relief. "That's great! So you talked about everything?"

"Yeah—I won't go into it all, but yes, we talked, and we agreed to try to do the taping thing together."

"And—?"

"And it's been great so far! Like you said, it was fun for me before, and now that we've talked about it, it feels like there's this whole new level of intimacy there."

Leigh hugged her friend. "I'm so glad," she said.

"That makes two of us," agreed Lauren. "I've been so over the moon, I've even been looking forward to talking to Dixie about it! Speaking of whom—didn't you say she was going to be joining us today?"

"Yeah, I don't know where she is," Leigh said with genuine confusion. Dixie only lived a few blocks away; where was she?

As though on cue, Jeffrey appeared with the cordless phone.

"Leigh, it's Dixie," he whispered. "She told me she'd decided not to get out of bed, and I heard a man laughing in the background."

Leigh smiled. That Dixie got more sex than the lot of 'em!

CHAPTER 19

DO TELL

> Hi babe! Call me, I think I can get Mariah to come. Maybe perform...

—Joe Francis

A few days later it was business as usual, with ringtones and gossip flying left and right. Leigh and Jeffrey went over to-do lists and fielded the calls together from Leigh's breakfast nook, shouting "Incoming!" each time one of their phones exploded.

Lorraine Manchester was the first to check in, and the second, and the third. Leigh had evidently put the fear of God in her by mentioning Mario Lopez after the meeting yesterday; and even if Mario wasn't confirmed yet, she wasn't going to go down without a fight. There was little Leigh could say to reassure her, and truth be told, Lorraine's over-enthusiasm wasn't doing her any favors. Leigh already knew that she'd be a great help to the gala, and a much-needed volunteer as always; but Lorraine's constant calls, emails, texts and demands were getting out of control. Having already sent a few texts that morning, she was now calling again. Leigh couldn't believe it—it was the second morning in a row that she'd called before noon! It wasn't like her; she usually worked late at the clubs and partied until dawn, and very rarely called until late in the day.

When Leigh picked up, she didn't even say hello before launching in.

"Leigh, you'll never guess who might fly in for the gala," she screamed into the phone.

"Well, good morning yourself, Lorraine," Leigh said. "You must have someone pretty incredible to tell me about, to be calling so early. Weren't you out at a black-tie party last night?"

"Ohmygodyes—in the most *gorgeous* black velvet gown! I'll have to show you the photos. And I had the most outrageous thing happen to me; I'll tell you about it after. Or maybe I'd better tell you about it first; oh, *goodness!*"

"That's more like it! I'll hear your gala news after." She signaled Jeffrey to bring her another cup of tea, and settled in; these conversations were never short. "What happened?"

"Well, darling, it was like this. You know the party was at that beautiful mansion-house up on Ocean Drive? I was hostessing, of course, and doing the most *fabulous* job of it. There was a line out the door to be photographed with me, and I think I got carpal tunnel writing autographs. Well, halfway through the evening— around 1 a.m.—I excused myself to freshen up. The wife of the house, cheeky bitch that she is, asked me whether I'd be looking for the men's or the women's room; she thought she was so clever! (And they actually *have* both in that mansion house, you know.) Anyhow, I was ready for her. I said both of those were for the *guests*—and surely she could show me to something better!

"While she was trying to come up with something smart to say, her husband offered to show me to the master bathroom upstairs.

He had to use it too, he said; so he'd just wait and use it afterward, if that was all right with me. Such a *gentleman!* So I said yes, and let him show me up, *much* to the annoyance of the wife. Oh, that bathroom was *huge!* I could have fit half my wardrobe into it.

"Well, the husband waited in the bedroom outside while I sorted myself out and touched up my *maquillage.* Oooh, baby—but I was in for a surprise when I came out! He was lying on the bed—tuxedo pants *around his ankles*, darling, and he was *excited*—leaning up on his elbows, looking right at me! So I stop dead in my tracks, and he says, 'That's a good shade of lipstick on you; how do you think it'd look on *this?'* Ha! Smooth operator, dontcha think?"

"My God," laughed Leigh. "Did you do it?"

"Well now, you know me, darling; I don't kiss and tell!"

"All right, all right." Leigh knew her friend well enough to know that this probably meant she'd done it enthusiastically, and gotten a nice chunk of cash for it, too. "But that's quite a story. And I would never have guessed it of *him!*"

"Oh, you'd be surprised how many straight guys go for the Diva," said Lorraine; "or *supposedly* straight, anyway. But don't you worry, honey; wonderful as they are, my charms have never worked on Brad!"

Leigh laughed out loud again. "That's good to know! And now, dear, who's this all-important celebrity you had to tell me about?"

"Well," purred Lorraine proudly, "how about the one and only *Janet Jackson?*"

"Oh—?"

"Oh, yes! I just got off the phone with her—she's thinking of coming to Miami for a week or two, and I think I've convinced her that she needs to come to the gala while she's here."

"Did you ask her if she would perform?" Leigh prodded, laughing to herself. She knew very well that Janet would never perform at the gala; in fact, it would be a major miracle if the performer showed up at all. It wasn't easy to get stars, even ex-stars, to come out and play; and besides, one couldn't exaggerate Lorraine's liability to exaggeration. Still, it was fun to indulge the Diva sometimes. "She'd be a great addition—and it might even help reignite her career."

"Now Leigh," said Lorraine, not realizing Leigh was teasing her. "Janet is still a major star, and doesn't need any help with her career. I told her all about the charity, and she wants to help out as much as she can. She's talking to her people to see what she can arrange."

As Leigh well knew, when a celebrity says they're talking to their people, it's generally their way of saying no without letting it seem like the "no" came from them. It's a large part of what publicists, managers and agents are paid for: to give a star someone to blame with booking them on some project or other, in order to make them conveniently unavailable. Leigh had always thought it was a nice myth that celebrities had no control over their own lives; and a funny irony that the ones who had recourse to it the most always seemed to be the A-listers, who had the most freedom of anyone to do as they damn well pleased.

"I hope you at least asked her if she'd donate something for the silent auction," Leigh said, wanting to cover all the bases. An auto-graphed CD, photo or costume from someone like Janet Jackson sold for big bucks. She'd donated a leather jumpsuit three years previously to another charity event, and it had raked in fifteen grand.

"Don't you think it's a little early to ask that?" Lorraine said. "It's like assuming that she's not coming. You know I'll ask her for something fabulous if it turns out she's not available. By the way—speaking of something fabulous—you *must* see the new rings that one of my fans brought me last night. They're so gorgeous, and look so real! You must let me loan you one when I style you for your *Ocean View* cover shoot."

Here it comes, Leigh thought. Now even Lorraine was trying to weasel herself into the shoot. Leigh had seen before how this would play out. Once on set, she'd come off with a multitude of suggestions, all of which would include putting herself in the photo with Leigh. And rather than come as Brandon, she'd claim she was on her way to some gig afterward, and make sure to be decked out in full Diva attire.

"It's not too early for anything," Leigh insisted, letting the comment about *Ocean View* drop. "You have to think of everything! I'll let the committee know that Janet might be available as a performer; if nothing else, it could be a good bargaining tool in getting another big name on board." This was sure to shake Lorraine up.

"You can't tell anyone yet!" Lorraine shrieked. "If word gets back to Janet, she *definitely* won't do it. You don't know how she is—she has to control *everything,* and her people would have to make the announcement. She'd *kill* me if she thought I'd told anyone she was coming to Miami, without confirming it first."

Ah-ha, Leigh thought. As she'd suspected, it was all a bunch of fluff, spun up to get the Diva's foot in the door with her. This *Ocean View* story was really bringing out the wolves! Ah well, at least this one was actually her friend.

"Okay, I won't tell anyone until it's confirmed," she said. "Good work, Lorraine. It would be wonderful if Janet were even a celebrity guest at the gala. Make sure you bring all the news of what you're doing to the next committee meeting. You are still on for that meeting, aren't you?"

Another teasing question. Lorraine would never miss a meeting—or as she saw them, a way to work her way onto the gala stage.

"Of course I am, darling," Lorraine said. "How would anything get done otherwise? I hope some of the others are planning to pitch in with some ideas, at least on auction items—it gets so tiring when it's just you and I doing everything."

Leigh barely suppressed a laugh. This was the one thing every committee member could be counted on to say, and she just let them all think it.

"Too true," she said, "but there should be some good auction items this year. I think Warren Henry or the Collection will donate a wait-listed car again—you know how much the rich and famous love things in short supply. And there's Jacques's wonderful art collection, too."

"I meant to ask you—just who *is* this Jacques?"

For once, the question wasn't motivated by suspicion. The Diva simply felt she had to know everything and everyone who might be useful to her someday—even those who'd insulted her when she met them. Say what you would about her, Lorraine Manchester wasn't vindictive—except when it was good publicity.

"He's an art dealer. Recently moved here from France—or at least he's trying to move here; I think he's hoping the gala will put him on the map. Lauren introduced me to him when she was showing him properties; Sassy poached him from her. At first I was avoiding calling him because I didn't want to get more in the middle of that drama than I already was, just by being friends with Lauren! But he ended up calling me and we had lunch, and I have to say, the guy won me over."

"Careful, honey," said Lorraine. "For all you know, he could be using the art business as a front to bring in all sorts of stuff—meth, heroin, guns, who knows? That kind of thing goes on all the time in Miami. You'd better check him out before you get involved with him."

Leave it to Lorraine to add drama to the situation, Leigh thought. Of course, the story would be completely different if *she'd* been the one to introduce Leigh to Jacques; then the guy could have done no wrong. "Oh, I did—he checks out," she reassured the Diva. "His name's in the catalogue registry at the British Museum."

Jeffrey came back into the room with more tea, and pointed to his watch.

"Lorraine, darling," Leigh added quickly, glad for the excuse. "Jeffrey just came back and I have to get back to work. Let's talk later."

"Of course," said Lorraine. "I've got a busy day myself—I had to reschedule a photo shoot so I could make your meeting. I'm doing a spread with Dennis for *Miami Scene* magazine."

"Dennis" was, of course, NBA legend Dennis Rodman, who made more news off the court than on it. An infamous party guy and frequent visitor to the Miami clubs, Dennis had a larger-than-life personality and a huge smile full of gold and diamonds—just the kind of celeb that Lorraine loved to befriend. He was given the star treatment wherever he went, and since his trips to North Korea, an even broader mystique had surrounded him. It was the kind of fame that rubbed off on people around him, and the Diva knew it.

"That sounds like fun," Leigh said.

"Always, with that one!" said Lorraine. "He wanted to be my escort to the gala, but I told him I was hosting so I'd have to arrive early to the red carpet and introduce everyone."

Leigh smiled to herself. She knew very well that Dennis would never be Lorraine's escort; he always showed up with his own entourage. Plus, as eager as Lorraine always was to be photographed with him, Leigh knew she wouldn't want to be tied to any one celebrity at such an event; she'd want to be footloose and fancy-free, flitting around meeting other stars. Still, he was always a good guest to have.

"Well, say hello to him for me," Leigh said.

"I will do," said the Diva. "By the way, about one of your new additions—Dixie. Honestly, I don't see what she has to contribute. She'll be wasted for the meetings, and we won't be able to get anything done."

Leigh couldn't believe that Lorraine, of all people, was questioning Dixie's value. Five years ago, Leigh had faced the exact same disbelief from the other committee members when she'd told them that a notorious local drag queen was going to be joining the group.

"Dixie's husband always spends a lot of money at the gala," Leigh said, "but more importantly, she's eager to volunteer her time and help however she can. You know we need all the help we can get."

"Well, she'd better pull her weight—and she has a lot of weight to pull," Lorraine said. "She certainly has plenty of time on her hands; she's been calling me every day to talk about every little thing. She wanted to chat my ear off yesterday, but Pamela is in town and we were meeting for lunch."

Leigh rolled her eyes. She knew for a fact that Pamela Anderson was in Vegas, because she'd talked to a friend who'd seen her there last night, appearing as an assistant in a magic show at one of the hotels. Leigh could never understand the career choices of that one; but her name was still in the press and she always looked fabulous.

"I'll have to hear about that another time, Lorraine," Leigh said. "Jeffrey calls. Bye for now, all right?"

"Big kiss, darling," Lorraine said, and hung up.

"Do you see what I have to put up with?" asked Leigh, looking right at Jeffrey. "Everyone expects me to drop everything and chat with them whenever they call. I don't think people realize how much we work!"

"It's your job as Leigh White," replied Jeffrey. It was a phrase Leigh had repeatedly said to him early on, and these days he took every opportunity to throw it back at her. "Anyway, while you were chatting with our dear Diva, the stylist for the *Ocean View* cover shoot called again. She needs to schedule a fitting to organize the clothes you're going to be wearing. Adrienne also emailed the final advance copy for the article, for your perusal."

"That should be fun," Leigh mused darkly. With all of Adrienne's digging, she couldn't help but have a bad feeling about the article. Leave it to a journalist to put a negative spin on charity!

"No doubt," Jeffrey went on. "The photographer's assistant also called—he has to reschedule since he has another booking with a *Vogue* shooting. Angelina Jolie, I think he said it was."

"How *does* the woman do it?" Leigh asked sardonically. "I can't imagine she and her husband have much time to speak to one another, with so much going on between them."

"Well, speaking of husbands named Brad," Jeffrey said with a smile, "yours also called. He wants to know why the photographer's assistant is calling his office. I didn't say anything about it, but I presume you haven't told him that he's to be in some of the photographs?"

"Ugh, I forgot," Leigh said. "Can you do that for me? Just call his office and tell him how important it is that he be in a couple of shots. Tell him it'll help the charity so much. If he asks to talk to me, tell him I'm getting a massage. God, does that man hate having his photo taken!"

"A true rarity in this town, my Queen," smiled Jeffrey.

"Especially with my friends! Speaking of which—incoming!" Leigh looked at her phone as Jeffrey bowed discreetly out.

"Hey, Lauren," she answered.

"Leigh—I have to talk to you!"

Get in line, Leigh thought. Ever since she'd announced her last gala, it seemed like everyone from the valet to the Mayor wanted a piece of her. But there was an urgency to her friend's voice that caught her attention. "What's up?" she asked.

Lauren got right to it. "You know Francisco and I have been… well, making those tapes together now."

"Sure," Leigh said. "You said it was going well."

"It has, yes," Lauren said hurriedly, "but that isn't the point. It's the maid."

"The *maid?*"

"Yes! Francisco and I were out, and we'd accidentally left the camera running—"

"In the daytime?" Leigh chuckled. "Are you filming in the *mornings,* now, too?"

"Never mind that," said Lauren. "The point is, Jacinda had Dixie's maid Betty over for coffee while she was cleaning the kitchen, and we caught their whole conversation on tape!"

"In the *kitchen?*" Now Leigh couldn't hold back her laughter. "Wow, Lauren, you've really come around to this taping thing, haven't you?"

This time Lauren had to laugh a little, too. "Will you leave the damn taping thing alone?" she said. "This is serious!"

"Okay, okay. We'll talk about your new hobby another time. So what'd the maids say?"

"They were talking about Jacques!"

Leigh felt her stomach tighten. "*Jacques?* What on earth would your and Dixie's maids have to say about Jacques?"

"Well, it wasn't really about Jacques," Lauren backtracked. "I think it may have more to do with Sassy, actually. I think she's setting him up."

Ah, the familiar story, Leigh thought, relaxing. "How do you figure that? Did the maids say that?"

"They were talking about some Mexican guys that Jacques has been hanging around with—Dixie said they were at that Mynt party with Sassy."

"Oh, yeah," Leigh said. "They were all over her there. But Jacques was there, too."

"Exactly! I think they're Sassy's friends, helping her pull something on Jacques. Jacinda recognized them from Mexico; that's what she was telling Betty about."

"Okay, but what makes you think these guys are doing anything wrong?" Leigh asked. "Surely it isn't just that they're Mexican; I mean, you and Francisco are both Mexican."

"*Which* is how we both knew who the maids were talking about—when they said these friends of Sassy's are connected to the Garcia family!"

"The who?"

"They're a big secret-crime organization in Mexico," Lauren explained. "Everyone knows about them. You name it, they're into it: drugs, guns, illegal immigrants—I don't even want to know what kind of scam Sassy's got them involved in. I told you that woman was bad news; she's like a virus!"

"I thought we were done with this rivalry stuff, Lauren," Leigh sighed. "What happened to the high road?"

"Leigh, this is serious," said Lauren. "If Sassy's got the Garcias working with her, who knows what she's trying to pull?"

Leigh bit her tongue to keep from going off. This was getting ridiculous. Now Lauren was resorting to hearsay from a maid?

"Look, Lauren, what do you want me to do about it? Until she does anything wrong, we can't exactly run to the feds."

"Of course not."

"Well, what do you suggest I do, then? Kick her and Jacques off the gala committee?"

"No!" cried Lauren. "Well, maybe *her;* but I actually think it'd be better to keep Sassy close, so we can try and dig up some evidence on her. Plus, she goes wherever Jacques does, so definitely don't kick him off or he'll be on his own. I think you working with him is the right thing to do—it gives him some business connections that are independent of her."

Leigh had to admit to herself, that sounded pretty reasonable. But she was still unconvinced that this wasn't all just the usual histrionics from Lauren.

"Okay, dear, I'll do what I can to look out for Jacques," she said with another sigh. "And we can try to keep an eye on Sassy in the meantime. But don't let it sideline you! Remember what you stand for!" Lauren didn't really stand for anything besides high-end shopping and buying and selling houses, but there was a point to be made here. "You have your own life to think about."

"I know, I know," said Lauren, "and I'm thinking about it, I promise. I just wanted to let you know. I don't want anything happening to Jacques, or you."

"Thanks," said Leigh. "I'll keep a watch on her."

"Great," said Lauren, sounding relieved. She'd be okay, Leigh knew; she just needed a little friendly backup. Cheap women rarely hung around, and Sassy was the biggest one-trick pony of them all. Still, Leigh had other things to do today than talk mess about her.

"So now, not only are you and Dixie hanging out, but your maids are, too?" asked Leigh. "Glad I could connect everybody."

"Yeah," said Lauren. "Dixie's a funny one. I don't know what she's going to do for your committee, but she's certainly a good person to gossip with."

"That she is," Leigh agreed. "And speaking of gossip—I'm all over the place today, but we should get together sometime so you can tell me more about your video escapades with Francisco."

"Not on your life," laughed Lauren. "What happens in that bedroom—"

"—and kitchen—" Leigh pointed out.

"—*stays* there!" The two laughed together. "All right, Leigh, I'll let you go," Lauren said. "Thanks for listening, as always."

"Of course. Talk to you later."

They hung up, and Leigh stood, feeling as though she'd been swinging a hammer all morning. It was high time for a bath.

Her phone buzzed again. She closed her eyes, her thoughts darkening as she picked up.

"Leigh White," she said curtly.

"Leeeeeeeigh!" Dixie's voice came through.

"Dixie! I was just talking about you."

"About mah sex life, no doubt," Dixie said with wild laughter. "Ah'm so sorry Ah missed yer meetin' the other day, but Ah had important things to do."

"I heard!"

"Yeah, well, what can Ah say? It's good to have mah driver back. Ah won't miss the next one—yew can count on me!"

"I know you won't, Dixie; I'll make sure we have a place set for you."

"Graaaate! Ah knew yew'd understand. Say, listen: Ah was callin' because it just occurred to me: that Jacques, you know, he really seems like a good guy, and—"

"Jacques again!" Leigh said. "He seems to be on everyone's lips today. Don't tell me: you think Sassy's out to get him, too?"

"Well, if yew say so," Dixie said. "*Ah* was just going to say, he seems like he'd be a really great guy to work with! He's so cultured and fancy; Ah hope you can find a way to work with him somehow."

"Then you'll be glad to hear he's on the gala committee," Leigh laughed. "He's going to be auctioning off a bunch of high-end art at the gala, and donating the proceeds. The guy must really have a stellar collection; he's giving us some really valuable stuff."

"Oh, Ah'm so glad! He seems like such a nice man—and cute, too! Give him a good foot to stand on, and he'll be over that Sassy gal in two shakes. Well, Ah'll make sure my faaaat rich friends'll be ready to buy some art! Talk to ya later!"

"All right, Dixie—bye for now."

That Dixie, Leigh thought with a smile. It was clear that Lauren had put her up to that—funny, that those two had found common ground!—but coming from Dixie, in her sincere manner, it was touching nonetheless.

That woman really did have a heart of gold.

Meanwhile, a neighborhood or two away, Dixie made her way downstairs to her husband's home office.

Danny was back in her saddle again; and though he'd been a bit quick lately—Dixie had started calling him her "Irish Minuteman"—he had certainly restarted her engine. He was out today, though; she'd have to take care of herself.

She went straight to her favorite section of tapes on her husband's shelf. Today was an "R. Blackbird" day: the rough Australian voice aroused her deeply. She reached up, took out a tried-and-true tape and slipped it into the machine.

She walked back across the room and closed the door. Reclining deeply in Howard's chair, she put the headphones on over her snarled and puffed morning hair. She then reached into Howard's sideboard. This was piled high with files he never used or added to, creating the perfect hiding place for her beloved Diamond Jim. She took out the blue velvet presentation box—anyone would suspect the box held a beautiful set of crystal or china—and placed it on the middle of the desk.

She leaned back in Howard's chair and opened the box slowly. This was an important step; she never tired of that first glimpse of the pleasure-giving wonder, nestled in petal-soft fabric and glistening with precious metals and rock. Cradling it in her hand, she hit Play.

"…Ah love plump women," "R. Blackbird" was saying. "So soft… yeah, the bigger the better, mate… those huge, long arses…

oh, I *loved* me first babysitter. God, was she a big, beautiful woman. Reminded me of my mum… I loved her, too. Not like that, of course, but man, she smelled sweet. So sweet. I always liked the big burds but me blokes made fun of me, told me I wanted to fock librarians and shite. No, sir. I fock the big ones for the great ride."

At this moment, Howard's voice came on over the tape with an observation, whispered into the microphone as his client ruminated. "Subject is overly attached to the soft flesh of his early caregivers." *Ha!* Dixie thought. *Ain't nobody better in the sack than a Momma's boy that thinks you're his Momma—you can get him to do anything.*

"I met this one burd on set," the sexy Australian star continued. "Man, she was *big*. She wore black stretchy pants and long shirts. I could see the dimples on her arse when she leaned over. Her tits went on for days. I watched her for weeks. I couldn't believe it—no one was paying any attention to this juicy burd!"

The deep, raspy voice surrounded Dixie. She knew every word to this story by heart, and it never failed to make her wiggle all over Howard's chair in arousal.

"She made Li'l Ross big—real big," he went on. "I took her in the trailer. Aw, well, it wasn't *my* trailer, mate: it was Eddie's. But I took her in the trailer. I laid her out on that long couch by the tiny stove—ah! She was a real beauty, a P.A. That's a production assistant, mate. Come out of the woodwork, they do; they're all over the damned set.

"Oh, I focking loved her focking pink flesh! She had that fat that rose above her knickers—oh, it was so good. Her bra, I played with it with me fingers. Made it jiggle. Put my mouth on it and blew, licked all around the edges. That thing was under some tension, believe me! I put me hand in her hair and stroked it, telling her how I was gonna do it to her. I twisted her hair up in me fist and pulled her head back, and sorta mouthed her neck. Ah, she liked that! She started wiggling so I twisted her hair harder, and harder, and told her to strip for me.

"She took her clothes off real slow, and got down on the floor. Shy—so shy. They always are. When she was finished, she just looked up at me with those big dark eyes…aw, I loved it, mate! Raw! All that white, pink flesh for me own purposes! I told her she had to be extra quiet. Set trailers ain't the best spot for a quick shag, 'specially not with a big burd like this one; they're all just made of tin. She nodded, and got to workin' on Li'l Ross. I remember it, her head going up and down slowly, those rolls on her neck just oozing pink flab.

"I don't know where it comes from with me, Doc…but all I wanted was that flesh. There were just piles and piles of it, everywhere my hands touched. I stroked her neck and worked my way down to her tits. Jeez, Doc! They were huge! They almost hit the floor when I pulled her up. I cupped 'em in my hands and told her how pretty they were; I buried my face in 'em. Oh, I was lost, mate! I must've petted her hips and ass and bush for five minutes or so. I had to pull her stomach up just to get to it all. Oh, mate, she quivered all over! By the time I'd finished stroking her, her eyes were closed. That burd was on another planet.

"That's when I made my move. I had to; I couldn't wait anymore. I ain't no Ron Jeremy! I told her to get on her hands and knees on the couch, and mounted that P.A. like she was a big strong horse! I pushed it in, and got to sliding in and out real fast, mate. I felt like I was riding something amazing—big and out of control. She kept moving that gigantic arse up and down, quicker and quicker; I gave her a big slap on it, and she made a real deep moan for me. I had a handful in each hand, mate—and there was so much more! Me cock felt like the Opera House on fockin' New Year's Eve!"

The tape went quiet for a moment. The ragged breathing of "R.

Blackbird" was all that could be heard. This was Dixie's favorite part. She leaned back and moved the LELO more quickly, matching her own ragged breathing to his. Within a few seconds, a hoarse shout that sounded like *"FOCK YEAH!"* was heard by Betty, downstairs in the kitchen.

The smooth, quiet voice of Dixie's husband, came back onto the tape. "And how did you resolve your encounter with this woman?" he asked.

"Well, Doc, that was a funny one," said "R. Blackbird," his voice uneven. "Someone knocked on the trailer door, and I just popped right off her and went and answered it."

Yeah, Mr. Raspy-Voiced Aussie Superstar was sexy, Dixie thought—sexy, and probably stupider than a red worm. Orgasms always cleared her head, and that had been a good one. She found herself thinking strangely critically of "R. Blackbird" as she straightened up the desk and put her LELO away. *Really?* she thought. *An international star that lives to motorboat plump nobodies that remind him of his nanny and mother?*

Ah well, she thought. Marry smart and screw dumb—that was Dixie's motto.

CHAPTER 20

GALA MAYHEM

Flo Rida? The whole state's coming?

—Brad

After weeks of meetings with the Fontainebleau, the South Beach Ritz-Carlton, the St. Regis and others, a deal was finally made with the Eden Roc. Eden Roc, a luxury resort and spa as rich in history and scandal as the neighboring Fontainebleau, had just re-opened following a two-hundred-million-dollar renovations project. David Siguaw, their Director of Sales and Marketing, made Leigh an offer that she simply couldn't refuse. All high-end hotels know the value of an A-list crowd and national press, and this one knew better than most.

"Jeffrey, have we had a call back about the entertainment?" Leigh asked. "I need that confirmation." Her voice startled her a bit; it was rough-sounding and she couldn't seem to avoid talking fast, like she was panicked.

"Leigh, I think you need a break," Jeffrey said from the doorway of her office, looking at her with the concerned expression of a mother with an overwhelmed child. "I brought the last message to you while you were on the phone with Jacques. The entertainment has been confirmed, and the lineup is typed and sitting on your desk under your other messages."

"Oh my God," Leigh said as she looked over the list. "I can't believe we're getting all these people to perform! Natalie Cole, Lady Gaga, Patti LaBelle…" Her head swam. Last year she'd had Rick Ross, Dionne Warwick and Pitbull perform, and she'd thought she'd never get another lineup to match it. "This is incredible! Why didn't you tell me?"

"My Queen is going into meltdown mode," Jeffrey said, shaking his head. "I waved it right in front of your face when I brought it in, but you waved me away!"

"Sorry, Jeffrey," she answered. "This has been a day from hell, and I still have so much more to do! All the publications want to photograph the art ahead of time, and since it won't arrive until a night before the gala, we only have slides for them. Jacques is driving me crazy with the details of each piece, but the charity needs that sales commission. All twenty-one million dollars of it! We need to promote it now, Jeffrey—we may already be too late! I'm a nervous wreck just thinking about it. And—oh my God," she said suddenly. "Jeffrey, have we arranged for extra security for the art?"

"Yes, that's been taken care of," Jeffrey sighed. "We even—" He stopped talking as Leigh's cell phone rang. She handed it to him in disgust.

"I can't deal with this, Jeffrey. Here, you answer it."

"Leigh White's cell phone, may I help you?" Jeffrey intoned.

"Jeffrey, put Leigh on. Ah need to talk to her," Dixie's voice boomed out of the phone. Jeffrey handed the phone over gingerly, like it was dirty.

"What is it, Dixie?" Leigh sighed.

"Ah've sold another table of ten, but it has to be close to the stage," Dixie said in a rush. Dixie had turned out to be a good soldier after all; she'd gotten a list of her husband's above-board celebrity clients, and was selling tables to them like a Girl Scout selling cookies. It seemed none of them could say no to her; a lot of them were buying tables or donating money even if they weren't planning to attend.

"Dixie, you know we've already sold all the tables," Leigh told her wearily. "There isn't any room left—we have a waiting list! Most of the press isn't even allowed to sit for dinner. Sorry, but you'll have to call them back and cancel."

"But it's Flo Rida and his plus-one, with a party of eight! A *rich* party of eight!" Dixie screeched. "You *have* to find room for 'em! They'll be big spenders."

"What? Flo Rida? I can't believe it!" Leigh's voice rose to a frenzied pitch. "Is he one of your husband's clients?"

"Yew know Ah'm not supposed to say!" Dixie cried. "Even mah husband's celebrity patients deserve their privacy. Anyway, he bought a table for ten. He's a big star; you oughta kick someone out! The press'll eat him up. *Ah* would eat him up, if Ah had the chance! Besides, he's an art collector, so he might bid on something."

"Okay, I'll find a place for him up front," Leigh laughed. "Just don't sell any more tables!" She turned to Jeffrey. "Table for ten for Flo Rida. Up front," she whispered. Jeffrey had charge of the seating chart, and had skillfully arranged the guests at tables according to rank, celebrity and wealth.

"But my Queen, the ballroom is already overbooked and the tables assigned," he sighed. "There's no room. Whom do you want me to throw out? The Martins? Joe?"

The Martins happened to be the wealthiest guests who attended the gala each year. They'd dropped three hundred thousand for the Ferrari at last year's auction. "Joe" was Joe Francis of "Girls Gone Wild" fame, who'd been like family with the Whites ever since Brad had kept him from going to jail on a wrongful charge. He had a heart of gold, and year after year, he came through in grand style with celebrities, entertainers and big spenders for the gala.

"Jeffrey! Don't you dare touch those tables," Leigh said, raising her voice a bit higher than she'd intended. "You know how important they are! We'll figure it out; we always do." She started to say something else to Jeffrey, but caught herself when she realized that Dixie was still on the phone.

"Sorry, Dixie," she said. "We'll figure out something. I'll talk to you later, okay?"

"Okay, darlin'," said Dixie. "Remember to take a break today! Talk to ya later."

They hung up and Leigh let out a big breath.

"Don't worry about the table for Flo Rida," she told Jeffrey. "I'll arrange it somehow."

"All right," he said on his way out the door. "I'll go start the—"

But Leigh's phone was ringing again, and she missed the end of what he was saying. "Hello, Leigh White," she answered.

"Leigh—where are you?" It was Adrienne Adams, sounding strangely flustered. "We're waiting for you at the studio! Greg flew in today from Paris for this shoot—you know Greg Lotus; we're super lucky to have him, but he's on a really tight schedule. Our hair and makeup people expected you half an hour ago. You'd better get here soon!"

Leigh's stomach sank. She'd gotten so wrapped up in other preparations, she'd forgotten her photo shoot!

"I'm so sorry, Adrienne," she said. "I had an emergency here at the house. I'll be there in ten minutes."

"Okay—just hurry! See you soon!"

Leigh hung up in a daze. She couldn't believe she'd forgotten about the shoot; it had been booked for weeks. She'd even had an appointment for a facial yesterday, but had had to cancel it—ugh, she was in no condition to be photographed now! But she knew she couldn't back out. At least her nails were freshly done and looking great with a new color, Ferrari Red. Plus the makeup artists for *Ocean View* were the best in town, and if worse came to worst, the photo could always be retouched. Katie Parker had taught her a thing or two about that! But nowadays, everyone was airbrushed in magazines anyway; they even did it with the top models. The covers of *Vogue* and *Cosmopolitan* were looking more and more like digital paintings of models than photographs of them, and Leigh sometimes didn't even recognize the faces of old friends staring out at her from them.

"Jeffrey!" she yelled. "How did you let me forget the *Ocean View* shoot?"

Jeffrey magically appeared in the doorway with her hot-red crocodile handbag.

"Don't blame me," he said. "I reminded you three times today while you were on the phone, and each time you waved me away! I even dropped a copy of their latest issue on your desk while you were talking to Jacques, hoping you'd get the hint. This is what I mean—you need a break."

"I'm not going to get one," Leigh said miserably.

"Well, not at the moment, anyway; there isn't time. I just started the car—here's your handbag."

"I thought we were going with the black croc bag—?"

"That was before you had your nails done bright red; this'll match better. They'll have everything else at the studio. Between Edward, Duber and Tony, they'll make you look like a supermodel.

You can touch up your hair in the car. I'm driving—you're a wreck waiting to happen."

"Jeffrey, I love you," she said, rushing out to the car.

***

On the ride over, Leigh's mind wouldn't stop racing. She called Brad to try to calm herself down, but just ended up telling him about the amazing lineup of stars who had volunteered to perform at the gala, and getting herself all worked up again.

"We should have brought a list of the performers for *Ocean View*," she said to Jeffrey when she'd hung up.

"It's in the media packets I prepared," he said. "There's one for the magazine and one for you—look in your Birkin." As usual, Jeffrey had taken care of everything; not only had he switched bags for her, but he'd organized the new one's contents perfectly.

"Jeffrey, I'm speechless," Leigh said as she opened one of the folders.

"Don't worry, you'll have plenty of opportunity to reward me after this is over," he laughed. "You owe me *big time!*"

"I know it, dear," she answered. "And don't *you* worry, either— I have a big surprise for you!" Unbeknownst to Jeffrey, Leigh had booked him and his boyfriend a two-week vacation at a holistic retreat on the Greek island of Zakynthos. She'd arranged the vacation to coincide with the two weeks after the gala, when she and Brad usually went on their own annual getaway. It was quite a trip; even with her organizational skills, setting it up without Jeffrey's help had been a nightmare.

Leigh jumped out of the car and forced a smile as she headed for the door of the photography studio. Adrienne was outside waiting for her, looking panicky. A very sour-faced, square-shouldered man stood behind her in the doorway, looking uncomfortable in dark pants and sweater.

"Leigh!" Adrienne shouted as she came up. "Everyone's waiting for you. Did you get the final copy I sent you for the feature?"

"I did, thank you," said Leigh. "It looks great." She bit back the word "actually." After all Adrienne's back-alley dealings with her gossipy friends and frenemies, Leigh had read the article with a horrible foreboding. But for all that, it had been clean as a whistle—utterly factual and dirt-free. She'd had to read it twice to be sure. "I think it'll bring a lot of good attention to the charity, so thanks for the opportunity. And sorry again for being late."

"It's all right. You already look great, but come this way and let's have hair and makeup take a quick look at you."

"Okay." Leigh waited for Adrienne to introduce the sourpuss behind her, who was looking at Leigh very intently. When she didn't, Leigh extended her hand to be polite.

"Hello, I'm Leigh White," she said.

"I know who you are, Mrs. White," the sourpuss said, shaking her hand stiffly. Leigh, a little taken aback by his rudeness, glanced over at Adrienne.

"Oh—excuse me," said Adrienne uncomfortably. "Leigh, ah, this is Stan Corinne. He's my new assistant."

"Pleased to meet you," said the man unpleasantly.

"Likewise," said Leigh.

"Let's head in, shall we?" said Adrienne. "We've got a lot to do."

They all went in, Stan eyeing her the whole way like he thought she might steal something. What was *with* this guy? When he stepped aside, Leigh caught a glimpse of a slim wire running from the man's ear down through his sweater. He was wearing an earpiece, like a club bouncer or Secret Service agent. Weird. She looked around, but didn't notice anyone else on Adrienne's crew wearing one. Weirder!

Fortunately, at this point I'm used to weird characters, she sighed inwardly as she let them lead her in. She widened her smile as a troop of assistants flocked around her. In an instant she felt the familiar prodding and pulling of stylists as they gave last-minute tweaks to her hair and makeup, teasing and unteasing, wiping off a bit of makeup here and reapplying it there. She settled into the chaos around her, letting it overpower the swirl of gala-related thoughts careening through her head. It was almost reassuring; with any luck, they'd be able to make her look a little less crazy than she felt.

Only a few more days of this madness, she thought. *Then—never again!*

CHAPTER 21

THE BIG NIGHT

> Where's the disappearing Jacques?
> Trashy Sassy is still trying to sabotage
> us! LOL.

—Lauren

The noonday Miami sun fell on the massive awning at the entrance to Eden Roc. Beneath it stood Leigh Anatole White, phone in one hand and clipboard in the other, awaiting the arrival of her committee. After endless preparations and back-to-back meetings, the day of the gala had finally arrived. Somehow, everything had fallen into place yet again.

Storage at Eden Roc had become tight as auction items arrived from all over the country: ball gowns from Zac Posen, Bulgari, Dior, Tom Ford, and Jean-Paul Gaultier; luggage sets from Gucci; two complete sets of golf clubs from Callaway; Harry Winston wristwatches; and on and on.

Art handlers had brought in Jacques's art over the last few

days; and watching them unpack it, Leigh had been ecstatic. The twenty million dollars' worth of art would truly lend the event a gravitas it had never had.

Celebrity guests had confirmed in droves. The red carpet was to be televised nationally, with *Extra* host Mario Lopez welcoming the guests. God, Leigh loved that man's dimples! At the last minute, Mariah Carey had agreed to perform a couple of songs a capella, and they'd scrambled to make room for her on the performance schedule. This party was going to go down in history!

Now, incognito behind her Dolce & Gabbana sunglasses, Leigh was all business as she supervised the final preparations. The New World Symphony and a singer from the Florida Grand Opera were already warming up and doing a sound check. Jeffrey, who had his own clipboard filled with lists, was overseeing the receipt of the last few auction items.

Dixie, Mitchell, Scarlett and Lauren arrived within minutes of each other. Like the leader of a Zero Dark Thirty rescue mission, Leigh checked off their names and handed them separate lists of tasks. They accepted their missions like dutiful agents, nodding earnestly. Leigh wished she had a tiny cassette tape to burst into flames at the end of her instructions, but all that happened was that Dixie broke a heel.

Having attended to the heel, Dixie was the first to start her project of setting up the check-in table at the front doors, where guests could sign in. Mitchell and Scarlett, cell phones glued to their ears, walked through the ballroom putting numbers on tables and checking off their own guest lists. They were the real party pros in the group, and moved with practiced speed and efficiency. Lauren, looking proud as a peacock and quite official in her Bluetooth headset, took command of the volunteers working with the committee members to unpack items and set up tables for the silent auction. She had exquisite taste and a real flair in this kind of thing, and would make sure all the displays reeked of sophistication.

Brandon, uncharacteristically, was almost half an hour late. When Leigh took off her sunglasses and gave him a look, he knew not to try an excuse. The crew had a lot to accomplish before the first person walked the red carpet tonight at 7:30—not to mention the fact that Brandon would have to leave early for his three-hour transformation into Lorraine. He followed Leigh around sheepishly while she ordered the others about their business, until she sent him outside to wait for the Rolls-Royce that was being auctioned off that evening.

Katie Parker took advantage of her committee status to arrive early. She had convinced a handsome security guard to volunteer to watch over some of the silent auction items, and now stood flirting with him. *Anything to keep her out of my hair,* Leigh thought. There were a few other guards there anyway.

"Leigh!" Jeffrey shouted as he ran up to her on the ballroom stage. "The Rolls-Royce isn't arriving until six. Brandon's outside with his friend Ricky, waiting for it, but I think he heard me talking to someone about it, and now he's pestering me to let him leave to get glammed up. Should I just send him home?—he doesn't want to be here anyway. The flower arrangements are arriving at two, the ice sculptures will be placed on the tables at seven and I've delegated volunteers to light the candles five minutes before the ballroom doors open. By the way, Brad called twice—he said he couldn't get through on your cell, surprise surprise—and Univision called to confirm."

He looked to Leigh, waiting for a response. After a moment Leigh noticed him and turned, taking her phone from her ear at the same time.

"Sorry, Jeffrey—I've been on the phone with Mariah's manager," she said. "What were you saying?"

"You didn't hear a thing, did you?" Jeffrey said in mock disgust.

He repeated his list of messages, while Leigh checked off a few lines on her clipboard.

"All right, thanks," she said. "Tell Brandon he can help you unload gift bags from our cars instead of waiting for the Rolls—you know where those go. Actually, send him and Ricky to do that, and you go find the engineer to get the lights set up."

"Got it." Jeffrey rushed off just as Mitchell walked up.

"I need to go back to the office and do some damage control with one of my promoters," Mitchell said. "The tables are all numbered, and Scarlett will stay to make sure the volunteers do their jobs." He pointed over at Scarlett, who was on the phone with her usual Victoria Beckham pout. How a woman could look that surly when she was married to a body like Beckham, Leigh had never been able to imagine—but then, Scarlett wasn't.

"Okay," Leigh said. "Just check in with her to make sure everything gets done."

Looking out into Eden Roc's "Pompeii Ballroom," Leigh had to quell the anxiety that threatened to rise within her. In just a couple of hours, this practically empty room would be packed with fabulous guests expecting first-class everything. More than packed, in fact: the room had a banquet capacity of 750, but she'd had the crew add two more tables of ten to accommodate extra guests. There was so much work to do! *Okay, one thing at a time,* she reminded herself.

She walked through the ballroom, checking each table number against her list to make sure they were placed properly. This was always where her promoter friends had to be checked up on. Sure enough, Mitchell had placed all of *his* tables near the front, to curry favor with his clients. Some things never changed! She sighed and moved the numbers around in order to put the big spenders and high rollers closest to the stage, where they could ogle the performers and bid big.

Slowly the ballroom underwent its metamorphosis. A team from Ellie's Flowers and Natural Impressions Design set cream-colored candles and explosively colorful flower arrangements throughout the room, transforming it into a wonderland of white and arresting color. Technicians tested lighting and sound equipment, shouting orders and specifications to one another. The committee and volunteers had finished their own tasks, and were now double-checking one another's work. Jacques, away overseeing the art handlers' last shipment, was the only one missing from the group. Everything was coming together with an unprecedented smoothness. *Guess that's ten years of experience for you,* Leigh thought.

Or perhaps she'd spoken too soon. "Leigh!" Jeffrey called as he rushed towards her.

"What is it?"

Jeffrey, normally calm and collected, seemed frantic. "The Rolls-Royce is too big to fit in its assigned area," he said. "The parking attendants say they won't be able to valet cars with it there. The only thing we can do is to put the Rolls where the red carpet was supposed to be. The Rolls guy and the valet captain are yelling at each other—what should we do?"

Leigh thought for a moment. Of course this would happen now! She had only a little over an hour and a half to check over everything, drive home to get herself camera-ready for the evening and return with Brad. There was no time for big problems like this.

"Make the switch," she ordered. "We have no choice. The rest of the crew is leaving, and I've got to get home and change."

"All right," Jeffrey said anxiously. "What should we do with the—"

"Just make it work, Jeffrey!"

He stiffened, and turned to go. For an instant she actually considered adding "Apologize to Jeffrey" to the bottom of her to-do list, then caught herself.

"Jeffrey," she said, "I'm sorry for snapping. I couldn't have done any of this without you, and you know I love you. I'm just finishing up here, and I have to get out of here soon. I'm sure you have a handle on it—I trust you."

Jeffrey smiled.

"It's all right, your Majesty, I'm used to it," he grinned. "Go ahead—I've got my stuff in the committee suite, so I can stay and sort this out."

"Thanks, Jeffrey. See you shortly."

She finished her tour of the ballroom and other areas, checking off everything to herself one more time. *Silent auction items—check. Bar—check. Other bar—check. Guest registration—check. Other other bar—check. Rolls—check. Red carpet—not as good as where it was before, but check.* A volunteer already sat arranging the guest lists at Dixie's check-in table, and a PR assistant was stationed at the media check-in. It was time for her to go.

She took one more look at her clipboard, pushed her sunglasses back up her nose and stepped outside, to where the valet already had her car waiting. Her gown would be waiting for her at home, too, as would her husband. Everything was prepared. It was the only way to make these things work. And the Tenth Anniversary Charity Ball *was* going to work—it just had to.

On her way home, she fought the urge to get on the highway and just keep driving.

***

The full moon shone, enormous and dazzling, in the Miami sky. Even the stars seemed brighter on this gala night, as though struggling to compete with the jewels and shining smiles below. A cool breeze from the water blew past the grand boats docked across the street from the luxurious Eden Roc.

Next to the limo line organized to drop V.I.P. guests off at the door of the hotel, photographers surged forward behind the velvet ropes as Brad and Leigh stepped out to make their grand entrance on the red carpet. The more seasoned photographers chuckled at the newbies as they jockeyed for position, knowing that the best pictures of the couple were yet to come. Year after year, the couple did the same thing: Leigh would rush inside and check on everything while Brad stood outside waiting for her, greeting other guests as they arrived. After a short time, Leigh would then rush back out onto the red carpet to meet, greet and observe—and, of course, look fabulous.

This time, though, the two gave an early photo op, taking their place at the top of the stairs and looking down on the red carpet and its mass of photographers. The Diva Lorraine Manchester, already posing in front of a list of gala sponsors, waved up at them. Leigh had to laugh to herself. That Diva had never met a camera she didn't like, and she was so quick to the red carpet, she was practically on it before it had been fully unrolled.

Leigh was dressed in a spectacular floor-length silk taffeta-and-tulle red strapless gown embellished with delicate embroidery. This was one of Billie Parker's newest designs and, from the look of the photographers, it was going to be a lucky thing for Billie that Leigh was loyal to her supporters. What Leigh wore to her gala tended to boost careers, and even Billie's wasn't beyond boosting; these photos would be priceless for his PR.

Leigh's hair was pulled up in an elegant French twist—not her favorite style, but the best way to display the diamond-drop Jeffrey Rackover earrings she was wearing. Together, the earrings were 100 carats; Brad had joked they could be seen from the moon. This pair of stunners would hopefully be auctioned off tonight, but Leigh planned to bask in their glory until the very last second. Whoever bought them would have to take them off her ears, with her kicking and screaming all the way.

"You know, you're looking beautiful tonight," Brad said with a cheeky smile. "We should really do this more often."

"How about we switch, then?" said Leigh back, waving at the photographers. "You deal with criminals, liars and unjust accusations, and I'll be the defense attorney."

"No way—your job's too hard," laughed Brad.

"Speaking of which, I'd better get in and double-check everything," said Leigh. "Hold down the fort for me! I'll be back in a minute."

She rushed inside, where she narrowly avoided running into Jeffrey.

"Oh, thank God you're here," he said. He'd changed into a sleek tuxedo, but still wore his tense expression from earlier. "Jacques has a security guard standing watch over the art backstage, and he won't let anyone back there—even the performers!"

"I'll handle it," Leigh said. Jacques had called her when the art had arrived, and she was happy to hear the art was safe backstage, but she hadn't figured on his security guard being so senseless. While the art was certainly the main moneymaker for the gala, performers had to perform, and the big-name ones wouldn't put up with that kind of nonsense. Every one of them thought they were the most important person in the room. "Anything else I need to know?"

"Not that I can think of right now," Jeffrey answered. "I've got everything else working smoothly, and you look beautiful. You can go ahead and do your walk-through but everything is set up; the volunteers are in place at the silent auction and the ballroom looks incredible."

"Thanks," Leigh smiled. "I'll handle the art situation. Brad's out front and Lorraine seems to be handling the press." They both laughed out loud.

"It's going to be a great night," Jeffrey said. "Let me know if anything comes up."

"Will do. Oh, by the way, where's Jacques? I haven't talked to him since this afternoon when he called."

"He's at the bar," Jeffrey said, pointing in the direction of the big crowd already gathering in the center of the lobby. Leigh scanned the drinkers and spotted him standing alone at one of the mini-bars set up under the giant mural of a 1950s bathing beauty that accented the renovation of this Morris Lapidus-designed hotel.

"I see him," Leigh said. "Tell Brad where I am, and that I'll be back as soon as I work the art issue out."

As Jeffrey left, Leigh turned and walked toward Jacques. He looked tense. Perhaps he was nervous about making such a grand entry into Miami's elite; it certainly was a lot to handle at once.

"Good evening, Jacques," Leigh said, approaching him.

Jacques seemed startled for a moment. "Ah—good evening, Leigh!" he said, slipping quickly back into his smooth demeanor. "The great night, it is finally upon us, eh?"

"It is," Leigh agreed. "I'm just going around making some last-minute adjustments. I'm told your security guard isn't allowing the performers backstage—not a good thing, with some of these divas. Would you mind telling him he has to move aside for them, and for the stage crew?"

Jacques responded with a string of French curses, uttered under his breath.

"I am very sorry, Mrs. White," he said, his face becoming very grave. "I did not think he would be such a fool—I'll take care of it right away."

"Let's go together," Leigh said. "I need to check on things back there anyway."

The two of them headed backstage. On the way they ran into

Valerie Zucker, the event's publicist. She was dressed in a black cocktail dress with spaghetti straps and an empire waist—pretty much her uniform for events like this.

"Leigh, you look amazing!" she gushed. "The room is beautiful, and I nearly fainted when I saw the list of artworks for the live auction. This is really going to be some night!"

"Thanks," Leigh said. "I hope I survive it." She turned to introduce Jacques, but he'd already rushed ahead. *That's what I like to see,* she thought, *a real go-getter.* "Listen, I'll have to talk later, Valerie—we're on our way to check on the art backstage now."

"Sounds good; see you later!"

Leigh came backstage and looked around. Paintings and sculptures were arranged neatly on rolling displays, ready to be wheeled out onstage. Jacques was over by the wall with the security guard, giving him a quiet but seemingly very serious dressing-down. When he saw her coming, he turned.

"I'll take care of the art," he said. "Surely you have enough to worry about here. We'll rope off an area for the performers, and I'll stay to make sure the art is protected."

"Thanks," Leigh said, and left them to their preparations. *I suppose if I were responsible for millions of dollars' worth of art, I'd be acting a little strangely too,* she thought.

She walked out onto the stage to take a look at the room in its entirety. The lights dimmed just as she reached center stage. She could just see waiters moving among the tables, and hear the soft clink of silver and glassware as they finished their preparations. Soon, she'd be taking bids for the live auction from this very spot.

The room truly *was* magnificent. Each table had a beautiful donated centerpiece of mixed exotic flowers: some of the type you'd see in a Monet—yellow irises, lupins and tulips—and others, like flaming red-and-yellow orchids and soft white plumeria, that you'd expect to find cascading down walls and rocks in Hawaii. The blossoms were difficult to find, and had been flown in by the floral designer from around the world. A three-foot ice sculpture of the number "10," carved in a graceful shape, stood also in the middle of each table, commemorating the gala's milestone. Every place setting had a miniature signed Domingo Zapato lithograph in a Tiffany frame. White branches and tree limbs spanning four feet high were arranged about the room, interwoven with tiny white lights and bedecked with small roses here and there. Sudden bursts of color and twinkling lights on the white walls added to the candles, candles and more candles to create a softly lit Cinderella room, within which the women would look even more enchanting and the men would feel even more like big-spending Prince Charmings. Of course, if that wasn't working, each table was also prepared with champagne and a bottle of Grey Goose on ice, to enhance things a different way.

Leigh greeted everyone she passed as she made her way back out through the lobby and to the front entrance. Outside, the crowd was arriving en masse. A line formed in front of the check-in tables as people entered the hotel, the gentle hubbub of their talk mingling with the classical music and popping of corks. Waiters wove to and fro with trays of Dom Pérignon donated by the Mariano Foundation, one of the night's big sponsors.

Leigh was on her way to the press line when she ran into Lauren and Francisco, who were giggling together like a couple of high-schoolers.

"Hey, you two," she said, smiling. "Having a good time? You'd better be, Lauren—you asked for this!"

"Oh Leigh, it's come together beautifully!" Lauren said. "It's already the event of the year, and everyone is talking about it. I've never had my picture taken by so many photographers at once!"

Inwardly, Leigh breathed a sigh of relief. Lauren would be the first to tell her if anything wasn't perfect.

"Yes, it's quite a night—and you look gorgeous! I'm not even going to try to guess what you're wearing," Leigh joked. "Lauren's done a great job," she added to Francisco. "Your wife's a girl with hidden talent."

"She certainly is," he said, his brown eyes twinkling. Lauren punched his shoulder playfully.

"All right, you two, go inside and enjoy!" Leigh laughed. "I'll talk with you later—I have to find Brad!"

She rushed through the crowd and made her way out the door and into the reception area. It was like stepping into a movie scene; all of a sudden, cameras and lights were on her. Trying to remain poised as she looked around, she spotted her husband. He was being photographed with Katie and Billie Parker. *Poor Brad*, she thought. As much as he hated the pomp and circumstance of these things, he was always willing to take one for the team—and posing with the Parkers was taking more than one.

Katie was covered in jewels—some, obviously of her design, much tackier than others—and wearing a black satin gown that fit her like a glove. The neckline was cut extremely low, leaving practically nothing to the imagination as she twisted her torso this way and that. Billie had on a black tuxedo with a muted paisley bow tie, red silk cummerbund and red smoking slippers. Each dressed to the max, they looked mismatched as a pair—typical of Miami couples that tried too hard.

"Don't you two look lovely?" Leigh said as the photographer walked away. "You guys should join the cocktail hour before everyone goes into the ballroom." She wanted a moment to talk to Brad without Katie preening next to them.

"You look lovely tonight," Billie said as he reached over and gave Leigh a kiss on the cheek. This didn't go unnoticed by Katie, who struggled to keep her photo-face.

"Thanks to your beautiful gown!" Leigh replied. "I'll see you during dinner—but go ahead in! I have to keep this red carpet moving, so we can get everyone inside."

"Shouldn't we wait to make sure the photographers have all the shots they need of us?" Katie asked in Billie's direction, craning her neck to peer over at where Scottie Pippen and his lovely wife Larsa were arriving with an entourage. Billie had just locked eyes with Ellie Ramirez, the South American beauty from last year's gala, and looked like he couldn't wait to get away to talk to her.

"If you want," said Leigh, "though the magazine photographers are waiting inside."

"Okay, we'll see you there," Katie said, already dragging Billie off behind her.

Brad had already been pulled off to pose with yet another couple. As Leigh followed him, photographers walled her off for a shot of her with Scottie and Larsa in front of the step-and-repeat backdrop featuring the evening's sponsors. She posed with the pair for a couple of seconds before Lorraine Manchester jumped into the shot.

"Hell-looo, darling!" said the Diva, ostentatiously air-kissing her and edging in next to Scottie. "Nothing like a nice *tall* man to make you feel like a woman, eh?"

"One more shot! This way, Leigh! Over here, Scottie!" the photographers yelled over one another. Leigh flashed a smile, but was thinking of a million other things. She actually liked the new placement of the red carpet and the Rolls-Royce, the latter of which was showcased under spotlights right in the front of the hotel. *That should get the bidders' attention,* she thought, wondering at the same time if anyone else in the world had ever thought about such things while sandwiched between an NBA star and a drag queen.

"*Our* dear friend Dennis will be here soon, Scottie," Lorraine was saying unctuously to the Dream Teamer. "You be a doll and send him over to me when you see him, will you? Oh, and there's Pamela!" she screamed before he could respond. "Let's get some photos with her!"

Pamela Anderson had just arrived with the designer Richie Rich and a huge entourage. She looked as voluptuous as ever, squeezed into a hot-pink satin high-low that was, no doubt, the first of many outfits she would wear throughout the evening. The ex-*Bay Watch* star certainly pulled it off. Leigh was still astonished that Lorraine had actually managed to get her to show up. Still, it would have been nice to know about it before the last minute; they might have arranged some sort of fundraising stunt with her. Pamela was always up for a good party and a good cause. Still…Leigh's mind raced. Maybe they could sell big donors pictures of themselves with her—men would pay well for that, especially if she'd sit in their laps! Depending on the guy, that could get mighty lucrative. Pamela was known to have a soft spot for bad boys, and they had a hard spot for her.

Leigh slipped off the red carpet while Lorraine posed with Pamela and Richie Rich. Getting past the line of photographers, she noticed that Brad, finally free, was waving her over.

"Hey, honey," Leigh asked as she caught up to him. "Took a while to get to you! How's it going?"

"Okay," said Brad, looking a bit dazed. "Adrienne was looking for you a minute ago—who's the guy she's with? He doesn't look like he's having a bit of fun."

"I don't know," said Leigh. "Maybe it's her new assistant? I met him briefly at the shoot; he's a pretty dour-looking guy."

"Maybe so." Brad looked around uncomfortably. "Hey, look, I think we should probably get the obligatory photos over with, before it gets too crazy around here."

Poor Brad! Leigh thought with a smile. The man was so sweet to indulge her in this. He was also right; everyone wanted their photos taken with the power couple, and they usually separated and mingled during the rest of the party. They often sat at separate tables, too, to accommodate more VIP guests—*if* Leigh sat at all; it seemed there was always something that needed adult supervision. Since this was to be her last gala, Leigh had originally arranged for them to sit together at the center table; but some last-minute big-spending additions had confirmed, forcing her to split them up again. Hopefully they'd get to catch each other during dinner; both of them were usually too busy with guests to eat anyway.

"Right you are, dear," she said. "I'd say we—"

"Hello, Leigh!" came a friendly voice from behind her. It was Eric Milon, the former owner of the Miami hotspots Privé and Mansion. Eric, a former model, had just arrived with his beautiful on-again-off-again ex-wife Stacy, who looked amazing in a black strapless cocktail dress and an exquisite diamond pendant. *Leon's of Beverly Hills*, Leigh guessed admiringly.

"Hello there, Eric," Leigh smiled. "Stacy—lovely to see you! Brad, let's have a picture with these two." She smiled at her husband with a "gotta start somewhere" look.

A photographer was more than ready to oblige them; the two couples were picture-perfect.

"All right, quick," said Leigh once she'd guided Eric and Stacy inside, "let's get one together before anyone else rushes up." They smiled into the camera together. "This one's for the twins."

"Just another picture of date night, for them," laughed Brad. He looked around again, holding his wife close. "It's a beautiful crowd, honey," he said. "You've done it again."

"*We* did it again," Leigh said. "And anyway, it ain't over yet! If the auction goes the way I hope it will—"

"It will," Brad said. "You're going to raise a ton of money for those kids. That Rolls is going to bring in a bundle, and that art—! I had a look at some of it before; it looks incredible."

The mention of the art brought Leigh's mind back around to business.

"That reminds me, honey—do you mind greeting guests for a bit, while I find Jeffrey? I need to make sure everything's okay backstage."

"No, go ahead," Brad said. "I'll be right here, smiling for the cameras and crying inside." He gave her his trademark "boy, isn't this fun" look.

"You're the best, sweetie. I'll be back!"

"That's what they all say," Brad sighed, a mock-tragic look on his face. "Tell our boys I loved them!"

Leigh turned to go in, stifling her laughter as another couple came up to be photographed with Brad, and another two lined up behind them. Bless the man, he'd probably rather be swimming with alligators than schmoozing.

A loud Southern voice floated over to her from the check-in table. "*There* you are!" called Dixie. "Leigh! Come over here for a photo!"

Leigh headed over to where Dixie stood with Howard. Dixie looked pretty good, considering the flush she already showed in her cheeks; but Leigh soon realized she shouldn't have told her what she was going to be wearing tonight. Dixie's gown, a black floor-length velvet number embellished with lace and glittering rhinestones at the waist and straps, looked like a knock-off of the one Billie Parker had designed for Leigh. She'd probably bought it online or on one of those late-night shopping shows like QVC or HSN, and had the lace added to match Leigh's. Poor Dixie! She tried so hard to fit in. Howard, on the other hand, wore the same custom-made tux—which somehow managed to look like a rental—that he wore to every event his wife dragged him to.

"Hello, Johnsons," Leigh said, greeting both of them with a

kiss. "So glad to see you here! Howard, have you seen any of your patients in the crowd?"

Howard smiled good-naturedly at the joke. "Oh, Leigh! I won't say—but if there were one place I'd be likely to run into them outside of the office, this would be it! Congratulations on the turnout."

"Thank you," Leigh smiled. "And Dixie, that's a *beautiful* gown! We could be sisters tonight."

"Ah know! Of course, mine ain't no Billie Parker; yew know that *anti-fat-ist* never makes sizes above a 12? Ah've never appreciated that kind of discrimination—and it *is* discrimination! BMI is DNA, just like skin color."

"Here we go again," laughed Howard. "Dear, you know I love you the way you are, and so do your friends."

"Well, *Ah* know that! Ah just gotta call it like Ah see it, and that kind of discrimination ain't just anti-fat, it's anti-*American!*" Her voice dropped to a conspiratorial whisper. "Y'know, Ah've always known that a size 0 had somethin' to do with North Korea; Ah just cain't figure out what."

"Well, you look lovely," Leigh said with a smile as she posed with the couple. "It looks like it's going to be a great night; make sure you two bid during the auction!" She winked at Dixie, getting a saucy wink in return. It was always a good little arrangement with the Johnsons: Howard brought the black AmEx, and Dixie brought Howard.

"Excuse me a moment," Leigh said. "Jeffrey's waving for me."

She walked up to her assistant, who had a pained expression on his face.

"What's wrong?" she asked, with a sinking feeling. "Is it the art? What's going on backstage?"

"Oh, no, that's been resolved; Jacques dealt with it," said Jeffrey. "But now Mitchell and Scarlett are inside the ballroom, moving table numbers. I tried to tell them that all the table assignments were set, but they wouldn't listen to me."

"I'll take care of it," Leigh said, her relief quickly giving way to annoyance. "They did that earlier and I moved all the numbers back! Go out front, will you, and check with the publicist about celebrity arrivals."

She rushed into the ballroom. She should have known Mitchell and Scarlett would cause trouble; for all their rivalry, they tended to band together like thieves when it came to keeping their groups happy.

"Leigh!" Mitchell yelled when he saw her. "Someone messed with the table numbers since this afternoon. I have VIPs coming! They need to be seated up front."

It was a classic last-minute problem; Mitchell and Scarlett's idea of a VIP was simply different from Leigh's. Their VIPs spent big bucks in clubs on bottles of Grey Goose and Cristal, but weren't likely to bid on any big-ticket auction items at a charity. Still, it was worthwhile to remain calm. Mitchell had sold a lot of tables, and he and Scarlett were sponsoring the after-party next door at the Fontainebleau. She needed them happy—just not at the expense of the big donors and the charity.

"Mitchell," she said patiently, "the whole *room* will be filled with VIPs tonight, and you know the table assignments have been confirmed for some time. You can't change them now."

"I just changed a few," Mitchell said, grabbing her hands. Mitchell had a habit that when he talked to someone, he held their hands in his—a way of ensuring he had their attention. As he grabbed Leigh's, she noticed Scarlett was still switching the numbers on a front table with another table on the far side. She almost wished the two were fighting again.

"Now look, we should all be outside on the red carpet, posing with the celebs and our VIPs," she said, as Scarlett came over to join them. "Let's go—we need to get a photo of the three of us together anyway." These two were impossible; she'd just have to get a seating chart from Jeffrey and put the tables back the way they were supposed to be once they were distracted with the guests and cameras.

As she led them from the ballroom toward the front door, a red-haired woman wearing a long black beaded gown came swishing towards them. This was Beverly Horowitz, freelance columnist for the *Miami Herald*, who covered the event—and wore the same dress to it—every year.

"Leigh!" she burst out happily. "Lovely party!"

"Hi, Beverly," Leigh said, not wanting to stop long. She knew that if she didn't excuse herself quickly, Beverly would probably complain about the press being seated all the way in the back of the ballroom this year. *Wait'll she sees* her *seat,* Leigh thought, remembering that she'd had to place her behind a column to make room for someone. Ah well—that she made room for any press at all was a big deal. "I'm just taking Mitchell and Scarlett outside for photos now; I'll make sure we have the *Herald* photographer take one for you guys." They all knew Lesley Abravanel, the main lifestyle and gossip columnist for the Herald, was somewhere in the room; hopefully this would keep everyone on their best behavior.

"All right," said Beverly. "I saw the *Ocean View* piece, by the way—the photos were beautiful! I've been trying to find Adrienne to talk to her about it. I saw her briefly with someone—is that her boyfriend? He didn't look like he was enjoying himself much."

"Oh, you must mean her new assistant, Stan something."

"Assistant?" Beverly looked confused. "Adrienne doesn't have any new assistant."

Leigh stopped. "Are you sure? I met him at the photo shoot, and she introduced him as her assistant."

"I mean, maybe…but we lunch together pretty regularly, and I'd think she would have told me."

There was an awkward silence. Scarlett tugged at Leigh's arm, bringing her back to the moment. "The red carpet awaits," she said.

"Right," said Leigh, snapping out of it. "We'd better get outside, Beverly. I'll catch up with you later, okay?"

"Sure! It's a wonderful turnout, darling!" said Beverly as the three of them walked away.

Weird, Leigh thought, wondering what the deal was with Adrienne. Probably she just hadn't told Beverly about the guy; these journalists were never as close with each other as they made it sound. Or maybe she didn't intend to keep him long. Leigh couldn't blame her for that; the guy didn't seem like typical assistant material.

In any event, it was "on" time, so out came the smile as Leigh walked through the lobby. Mitchell and Scarlett rushed ahead to be photographed with Sean Combs Diddy, these days and his beautiful date. Sean was one of the rare cases in which gala VIP and club VIP coincided. In addition to being a rapper, producer, actor, and entrepreneur, he was a philanthropist and a big spender, and helped make any party happen. And everyone loved his mom Janice, whom he usually invited too, and who was the perfect guest at a party. Leigh would make sure he'd keep his seat up front when she undid Mitchell and Scarlett's havoc; he'd probably bid on the Rolls, at least.

"Hello, Sean," Leigh said after the superstar had posed with Mitchell and Scarlett.

"Hello yourself, lovely lady," he said back, flashing a winning smile. "Good to see you again! We need to get a photo together."

Leigh smiled. Like any good businessman, Sean knew that you always have your photo taken with the hostess. She smiled for the camera and tried not to be distracted by the mob scene outside. When she could, she excused herself and made her way out, through one photo-op after another.

Outside the crowd was swarming around the red carpet area to get a glimpse of Mariah Carey and Queen Latifah. Just having the two here was a coup; but it got better. The two had arrived at the same time, and hearing that Mariah had offered to sing, Queen Latifah had agreed to welcome the guests and introduce Mario as the night's emcee. The photographers were going nuts, as was Lorraine Manchester, who seemed to be on a non-stop mission to be photographed with them. The two pop goddesses didn't seem particularly interested, turning their favor instead on their adoring fans and the legions of media representatives on the scene.

The national press attendance at tonight's gala was unheard of for a local event. Behind the ropes, all the major entertainment press were there: *People, US Weekly, Entertainment Tonight, Haute Living Magazine, E! Television, Univision, Deco Drive, TMZ, DuJour Magazine*...you name it. The BBC was even here, because Craig David, a major R&B star in the U.K., had performed last year, and was returning this year as a guest.

As Leigh walked down the steps, she glanced over and saw Brad in the same spot she'd left him, bravely doing battle against the Beast with a Thousand Flashbulbs. What a trooper! He was now being photographed with Joseph Nelson and his wife. Leigh smiled to see them; if Sean didn't buy the Rolls, then Joseph surely would. He was a billionaire and an avid collector of cars and women; tonight he had wife number five on his arm, and who knows how many mistresses waiting who knows where. Each wife seemed to get younger as he got older, and always left the marriage with a fortune, a baby and an incredible collection of jewelry.

Leigh posed for a few shots with Mariah and Queen Latifah, and continued on her rounds. She greeted Joe Francis, and had a few shots taken with him near the wall of photographers on the red carpet. Not that she'd doubted he'd show, but she was glad he'd made it; besides being a good friend, Joe was a well-dressed, handsome man with the charm of an A-list actor, and his presence made anywhere relevant. Leaving him she said hello to a few other guests who'd just arrived; then passed a contortionist performing on a platform, and shuddered a bit to see her fold herself backwards, tightly in half. It was about how Leigh felt right now, herself.

The cocktail-reception area, just outside the closed ballroom doors, was now filled with guests collected everywhere in drinking, chattering cliques. Everywhere Leigh looked was a grander, more fabulous group. Everyone was meeting-and-greeting with manic energy, and the ladies were all checking out each other's gowns, jewelry, shoes, hair, mani-pedis and perfumes in that strange combination of mutual admiration and snarky competitiveness that seemed to be the norm at these things. Some people just stood surreally in silent groups, smiling out at the rest of the room as if they were waiting to be photographed.

Leigh noticed Jacques standing alone at a side bar, fidgeting a little with his drink. It occurred to her that she hadn't seen Sassy all night, and the thought troubled her. Where was she? Surely there wasn't anything to what Lauren had been saying about her—?

She was brought back to reality by the bonging of the bell chime that signaled the end of the cocktail reception. In five minutes the ballroom doors would open; that gave her five minutes to change the table numbers back that Mitchell and Scarlett had switched. She rushed to the ballroom, where Jeffrey stood outside, sipping a glass of champagne.

"Jeffrey!" she shouted. "What are you doing? We're working here. I need you to stand watch at the door until I finish changing the table numbers back. If Mitchell and Scarlett come around, keep them away! Do you have the original seating arrangement?"

"Of course." Jeffrey handed her a chart, printed pocket-size.

"Great. Now give me that glass; I'm the one who needs a drink!"

Leigh grabbed the glass of champagne and downed it.

"No rest for the weary," sighed Jeffrey.

Leigh rushed into the ballroom and quickly changed the numbers on the front-row tables, looking around the spectacular room as she did. The tables were set; the Eden Roc staff poised and ready. All she had to do was sell a few million dollars' worth of art, jewels, cars and designer gowns, and she could go home happy. She took a deep breath and walked over to the doors, where the staff captain was waiting. She nodded, and the doors were opened to a gasp and cheer from the crowd.

As her jubilant guests filed into the ballroom, Leigh grabbed Jeffrey and pulled him over to the back bar.

"Text Brad and tell him we'll meet him inside," she said. "We can't go through that crowd again. For now, let's have a toast; we're long overdue. Two glasses of champagne, please," she motioned to the bartender.

"Feel free to drug mine with something," Jeffrey quipped. "Or better yet, hers."

"It'd be wasted on me," Leigh said.

"Make mine a double, then," Jeffrey laughed, looking at his phone. "Brad's on his way, and Lil Wayne has just arrived with his entourage. Joe's handling it."

"Great," Leigh said, raising her glass. "Here's to our biggest and best gala ever!"

They toasted, and took a moment to look around the room as they collected themselves.

"I can't believe this is the last one," Jeffrey mused.

"Me neither," Leigh agreed.

"What ever are we going to do with ourselves?" Jeffrey was smiling, but there was a serious note underlying his question. Admittedly, over the past months Leigh hadn't had time to consider it at all. But then, it wasn't her way to ask questions like that; there was always something to be done.

"Oh, I'll think of something," she smiled back.

"My Queen always does."

"She does indeed." Leigh took a deep breath. The crowd surged through the ballroom doors, already beginning the chaotic search for place cards. It was time to get back to it. "In the meantime, we have work to do!"

"Yes?" Jeffrey said, straightening to attention.

"Get out there and make sure everything is going smoothly with the silent auction; this is a bigger-money crowd than ever, so let's milk it for what it's worth." She thought for a moment. "And let me know if you see Sassy anywhere. I've got to work the room while this crowd's coming in."

She took her glass and glided off through the room, greeting guests and making introductions. The room filled quickly and Leigh greeted everyone like an old friend, putting on her utmost hostess charm. She enjoyed making everyone feel like they were the most important person in the room, and (if she could say so herself) she he had quite a knack for it.

Across the room, she saw Real Housewife of Miami Lisa Hochstein (along with her husband Lenny, a plastic surgeon credited with many of the "enhancements" on prominent display at tonight's event) and chuckled to herself. Lisa had always seemed to her to be one of the show's more likable cast members, a girl who just wanted to have fun; and Leigh couldn't help but think she'd know something about the rumors that had been circulating lately about the show's future. Talk around town was that the show's renewal was in limbo—that a couple of the more accomplished, classy wives had felt that they were "swimming with the skanks," and proud Miamians, eager to exchange the trashy image of the show for one of fun and glamor that would showcase the best of the city, were calling for the show to drain the swamp. Leigh thought about going over and getting the scoop from Lisa; but remembering herself, she decided to leave it to the reporters. She'd read about it in the paper next week—and besides, since when did she have time for that kind of reality-TV gossip anyway?

Waiters placed caviar services on the tables as the guests found their places. As always, the mood of the crowd was fickle at this point. Everyone was already a bit toasty from cocktails and champagne, but where that took them depended on the person. Compliments about the beauty of the room were invariably punctuated by complaints about the seating arrangements. Leigh's favorite line in this situation, "There's not a bad seat in the house and everyone here is a VIP," generally worked; but if it didn't, she could fall back on the more punchy, "At least you *have* a seat—this year the attendance is so high, my husband and I have to stand."

Out of the corner of her eye, she caught what seemed to be one of these "damage-control" situations, going on a few tables over. She walked over and intervened in the conversation. Jackson Fuller, one of the charity's biggest donors, was unhappy with his table number. He'd always had table number one, and this year he'd been edged over to table two—hardly fair treatment, for someone of *his* generosity.

"Oh, Jackson," Leigh said, hoping to placate the millionaire, "you know we all appreciate your support! We just had to move people around, and knew we could rely on our best friends most."

"Of course, of course," sniffed Jackson. "But isn't there any way to—"

"Top the competition? Sure there is—bid big!" She winked broadly at him. "I promise you, nobody'll care what your table number is then; they'll be too busy trying to keep up with you."

"But I—"

"I know, I know—*you* don't care what people think; you're above all that. But some people are very competitive in these things, and your bids turn that competition into good karma for everyone."

"Yes, well, my table—"

"I knew you'd understand! It really is *so* good to have people like you on board, Jackson; I feel we understand each other perfectly. But you'll have to excuse me; I believe I'm needed at another table. You wouldn't believe how many people come to things like this to complain. That's why keeping everyone happy is a full-time job! Big kiss, Fuller!"

She wandered off through the room, continuing to chat up guests as the last of them were seated and dinner was served. The meal began with an arugula salad with roasted beets, goat cheese, candied pecans and aged balsamic vinegar; this was followed up by a tender filet mignon served on a bed of mashed potatoes, paired with seasonal vegetables and a small lobster tail. Between Thierry's Catering and the Eden Roc's five-star in-house chef, every mouthful was exquisite, or at least looked it—as usual, Leigh had no appetite now and probably wouldn't even be hungry until many hours later, when she had taken off her gown and makeup and was curled up in bed in her robe, too exhausted to be bothered.

Once Heather McDonald, who had agreed to open the evening, had welcomed the crowd and cracked a few jokes, she introduced Leigh, who walked out to center stage and took the microphone.

"I'd like to thank all of you for coming to our tenth annual Charity Ball gala," she began. The crowd burst into applause. It was only now that she really got a good look at the sheer number of people here. It had been an incredible turnout.

"All of our galas have been such special events for me, and for our charity," she went on, once they'd settled, "but this tenth gala is particularly special for me. Many of you have been with us for years, some even since the beginning; and I don't have to tell you that ten years is a really incredible milestone." The crowd applauded again. Suffice it to say that, she had decided; she'd considered announcing at the gala that this would be her last, but had decided against it. It would only dampen the mood, and invite a whole new round of protests.

"So many people have given their time and energy to bringing this gala to fruition. I couldn't possibly thank you all to the extent that you deserve; there's just too much to say. But I do want to extend a special thanks to my beloved husband, Brad White. Darling, I simply could not have done any of this without you. Thanks."

The crowd erupted again into applause, this time interspersed with "awww"s. Leigh caught Brad's eye where he was sitting, and smiled as he mouthed, "I love you." Leigh could practically feel the room glow with warmth and togetherness.

Time to get down to business.

"All of you here are already familiar with our charity, and what we do," Leigh went on, "so I won't take up your time explaining it. Instead I'm going to commence with our live auction—our tenth and biggest yet!"

The crowd couldn't restrain its excitement, and cheered again. She could practically see people shifting in their seats, anxious to begin warring over who could throw down more of their money, faster. *This is going to be a cakewalk,* Leigh thought.

Just as she was about to announce the first item of the liveauction, there was a commotion as Diva Lorraine Manchester strutted out onto the stage with a cocky nod, hamming it up and throwing ostentatious kisses to the crowd. It was clear she was going to be the belle of the ball, whether invited or not.

Heather leaned into the microphone. "Hey Diva, you're blocking my view!" she said. The crowd roared.

Leigh was stunned; but, she realized, not particularly surprised.

This kind of stunt was her friend Lorraine through and through—and besides, the crowd was eating it up. Smiling in acquiescence, she took the microphone back.

"Ladies and gentlemen," she announced, barely suppressing a laugh, "tonight we are honored to have in attendance the glamorous Diva Lorraine Manchester, who will be assisting us with the auction."

Lorraine waved at the cheering crowd and gave Leigh a look that said, *You won't regret it—after all, we're here to make money!*

"Now," Leigh resumed, "on to our first item!"

***

The room was hot and the competition fierce at the Charity Ball live auction. Every item Leigh announced got an immediate response, and her volunteers scrambled to retrieve the winning bidders' information. The designer gowns and jewelry were especially hotly contested; a beautiful diamond pendant, displayed on top model Joanna Krupa, nearly caused a riot. It looked as though Joseph Nelson was going to get the Rolls for a steal at $300,000; then Jackson Fuller threw in another $300,000 to double it—a subtle reminder that table number one was wherever he wanted it to be.

Jacques's artwork was saved for last. The crowd was especially impressed with the art, and excited by the chance to snap up some lesser-known masterworks at auction price. Practically every piece brought on a bidding war, and the final sale prices were phenomenal. A major philanthropist, Arthur Benjamin, bought a small Monet ink drawing for $350,000; a scribble on a napkin by Picasso—from the days when the great artist was paying for his meals with such drawings—went for $170,000. Dixie, who'd been drinking since before she'd put on shoes today, cheered on the bidders like she was hollering at a football game.

Leigh did her best to keep calm in the midst of the frenetic bidding. In this she was bolstered by the antics of the Diva, for whom other people's money was nothing but a number, and no bid was high enough. There was only one moment when the Diva seemed lost for words, and it wasn't at a bid. They had just brought out a new batch of paintings, and Lorraine stopped mid-caper, actually doing a double-take at one of them. This was especially strange—not only because Leigh had *never* seen the Diva lose her stage composure, but because it was such a middling painting that she seemed to be so smitten with. Leigh had never known the Diva to be particularly into art to begin with. What was it about this one—a red-and-pink oil sketch of flowers by Manet—that could have struck her? Bemused, Leigh made a mental note to ask her later.

All told, the live auction brought in a total of just over twenty-two million dollars. While Leigh knew that the charity would only receive a portion of the artwork's sales, she was ecstatic; her gala had never raised anywhere near this much money. Her head spun as she walked offstage, leaving Queen Latifah to come up for the microphone. It was a good thing she'd agreed to announce Mariah; Leigh had completely forgotten.

She felt like a woman in a dream as she walked through the ballroom, looking for Brad. The greetings of her guests fell muffled on her ears, and she hardly responded. She was in daze. Twenty-two million dollars! That would mean over two million to the charity—on art alone! She couldn't believe it; Jacques and his art had changed everything. It was only now that it occurred to her that she hadn't seen the man since earlier in the evening. Surely he was out schmoozing with the art buyers; if there was ever an opportunity for him to network, this was it. He could hardly have made his entrance onto the Miami art scene with a bigger bang, and his million-dollar premium seller's commission was nothing to sneeze at either.

Where might he have gone? Was he nervous around so many celebrities—? He certainly hadn't ever seemed it, with all that high-powered "Jay and Bey" talk. She scanned the crowd looking. Perhaps he was backstage? But she'd just come from there.

She felt a warm hand on her shoulder.

"Leigh," said Brad, wrapping his arms around her. "Great job on the auction. Everyone was so impressed with those items, especially the art! It was like watching a championship fight, with all those bidders yelling out. You must be so happy, darling; congratulations."

Leigh was still reeling. "I think I need to sit down," she said weakly.

"Right here, dear," he said, guiding her into an empty chair. He looked hard at her. "Are you all right?"

"Yes—yes, I'm fine," she said. "I'm just a bit overwhelmed." She grabbed a chocolate left behind on a dessert plate next to a tray of Divine Delicacies custom cakes, went to pop it in her mouth, and thought twice, reaching instead for Brad's champagne glass. "I just can't believe we raised so much money—and it was so easy! It seemed almost too easy."

"People just really wanted to come through for you, honey," said Brad warmly. "It's a great thing. And it's only fitting, after all your hard work. Are you sure you're all right?"

"Yes," she smiled. Now that it was sinking in, and Brad was reassuring her, she felt better than all right. "I'm fine—thanks, darling."

"Great." He kissed her gently. "Now let's go stand in the back and listen to Mariah—I don't want to miss her, and I know you don't either!"

They made their way to the back of the room and stood hand-in-hand as Mariah walked up to take center stage. She was singing unaccompanied, and only for a short set; but her voice was as exquisite as ever and the crowd was mesmerized. She dedicated her last song to the kids in need, and thanked everyone for coming and supporting such a great cause.

When Mariah had left the stage to thunderous applause, Patti LaBelle stood up at her table and sang her way, without a microphone, to the stage. Again, the crowd went wild and stayed that way. When she'd finished, Leigh's friend DJ Tracy Young took over and got the younger crowd moving, while the older folks made their way to the door for their gift bags. These were filled with hundreds of dollars' worth of specialty merchandise and gift certificates, donated by various local retailers; and the only gift bags to rival them were at the Oscars.

While Leigh was checking with Jeffrey to make sure all the bidders' information had been collected and the silent-auction items were slated for delivery, Dixie stumbled over to her and grabbed her in a clumsy embrace.

"This has been the best gala ever," she slurred. "Ah was still reelin' from Dionne Warwick last year, then you pull this off! How *do* yew do it, year aftah year?"

"I had a lot of help, Dixie," Leigh laughed, "including from you! I'm so glad you've had a good time."

"Oh, the best," Dixie said. She leaned in mischievously. "And Billie Parker's enjoyin' himself too, by the look of him! He's outside flirtin' away with that dark-haired babe he's been eyein' all night, and it looks like it's goin' great! Guess Katie's too busy courtin' the photographers to notice, huh? Anyway, we're headin' home, darlin'—congratulations on a job well done! Ah'll call ya tomorrow."

Howard wished Leigh goodnight, and helped his wife out the door. *Is Danny driving tonight?* Leigh wondered idly. It was a bit of a strange sight, seeing Dixie out so early.

Leigh couldn't help but envy her the early exit. She was feeling the long night already, and the party would continue for many, many more hours. Now it was time for Mitchell and Scarlett to shine, and treat their VIP club crowd like royalty. Everyone from the gala was invited to the after-party next door at the Fontainebleau, but it certainly wasn't everyone who was interested in the hard-party atmosphere that would prevail there. For her especially close friends, Leigh had set up a small pre-after-party cocktail hour in the penthouse suite upstairs. All of her favorite people would be there, and a lot of them at the after-party; but all Leigh wanted was to get home and out of her clothes and shoes, and eat something. Hopefully she'd be able to get a moment to order something from room service.

Joe Francis caught up to her at the door, flanked by his entourage—among them Lance Bass, David Cooley and the whole L.A. crowd.

"Hey, congratulations on a great night!" Joe said. "You raised some serious bucks there, lady."

"Couldn't have done it without you," Leigh smiled.

"I'm rounding people up for the VIP suite—you coming up?"

"Yeah; grab your group and bring them up to the penthouse in five. This party's just getting started!"

"All right, see you soon! I've got that 'Real Mr. Housewife' blogger coming—he'll get the success of the after-party all over the blogs!"

Leigh sighed with exhaustion as they left, marveling to herself at how press-savvy her friends were. The job of a hostess was seemingly never done. Lorraine Manchester took the stage to announce the after-party, and Leigh felt a surge of gratitude. *God bless that Diva Lorraine,* she thought. *She may have a hell of an ego, but she's exactly what I need to help me play hostess and keep the energy going.* If only she could leave it all up to the Diva, and disappear.

The thought brought her back to Jacques with a sudden chill. Where *was* he?

CHAPTER 22

AFTERMATH

> Hey Jacques. Where's my fucking art?

—Scarlett

Despite her exhaustion, adrenaline still pumped through Leigh's body as she and Brad made their way up to the penthouse suite, where room service had set up a half-dozen bottles of Perrier-Jouët on ice. She quickly changed into one of her favorite party dresses, a less formal short cocktail dress by Marc Jacobs. The simple dark-blue sheath was stunning, especially at this late hour and with the long diamond earrings she'd brought to replace the pair of Jeffrey Rackovers she'd auctioned. In the new clothes she felt refreshed and energized, and it was a good thing, too—the night was just beginning for the small crowd heading up.

"This has been the best yet," Brad said, taking off his jacket and walking to give her a kiss. He handed her a glass of champagne. "Let's toast to a wonderful night, and a very successful gala—

all ten years of it."

"Wonderful idea," said Leigh, raising her glass.

Before they had a chance to take a sip of the delicious bubbly, there was a knock at the door.

"Here we go," Leigh laughed. "Quick—here's to us." She quickly took a sip before she opened the door.

"It's party time!" Joe yelled from the door, where he stood surrounded by his entourage. "And I see our hostess has changed for the all-night party." He led his group into the room after giving Leigh a big kiss.

"Congratulations on a great night," said Lance Bass as he hugged Leigh. Lance was there with his husband Michael Turchin, an amazing artist who had donated a major piece of work for the auction that was bought by Real Housewife—and well-known classy dentist—Karent Sierra.

"Thank, Lance—and thanks again to you, Michael! The artwork really stole the show tonight."

"I'm just happy to have had a spot up there with Picasso and Monet!" Michael said. "That was really something, Leigh."

Everyone headed straight for the champagne and Lance handed out glasses as Joe poured. Joe was just about to make a toast when the door flew open and in came Lorraine with a group of her friends, including Pamela, her husband Rick Salomon and Richie Rich. Behind them was another group, among whom were Lil Wayne and his entourage. For a few seconds, entourage gridlock created a strange mob of famous people at the door.

Spirits were high, and the champagne flowed amidst the delicious Indulge desserts sent from New Jersey by Kathy Wakile. When the initial supply of bubbles ran out, Joe called and ordered twelve more bottles. Leigh didn't hear the call but was too happy to be upset when the bottles arrived at the door. Joe often had this problem; he was so used to partying with high-rollers and being comped for everything, the thought never seemed to cross his mind that someone might have to pay for things when he ordered them.

"Let's toast to Leigh," Joe called out loudly to the room, which cheered in agreement. "I can't believe I bought a fuckin' Warhol tonight!" He raised his glass and downed it in one gulp, an amazed look on his face.

"Does anyone need a bracelet for the after-party next door?" Lorraine shouted over everyone's head, brandishing a handful of rubber Electric Picks bracelets. "It's going to be a mob scene over there, and although I know none of you will have any problem getting in—hi, Gaga!—the bracelets ensure VIP status and top security."

Leigh was grateful for the help, but also knew better than to think it was *just* help. This was simply Lorraine's way of making sure she'd met each and every celebrity in the room. Why else pass out bracelets with iPhone at the ready, taking pictures along the way? But seeing the Diva reminded her of something else.

"By the way, Lorraine," she said, when she was able to pull the Diva aside for a moment, "I never figured you for an art fan! That was quite a long look you gave that red-and-pink painting tonight onstage tonight."

The Diva brightened.

"Oh, that! Honey, I was just surprised that you had one of my friend's paintings at auction! I mean, *I* know my friends are fabulous, but I didn't know he'd made the big time."

Leigh didn't understand. "Surprised? What friend do you mean?"

"Oh, but of *course* it's a fabulous painting," the Diva went on. I was just so caught up in strutting my stuff up there, I didn't hear you say his name, is all."

"Who? Manet?"

"I mean, of course I heard you talking about *money,* darling. No,

I mean my friend Arturo, the painter."

"I—I don't—" Leigh began, now thoroughly confused.

"Sorry to interrupt, honey," said Brad, leaning in to Leigh.

"That's all right," Leigh said, shaking her head. "I'm not sure what Lorraine was talking about, anyway—seems like she may have started partying a bit early tonight. What's up?"

"Someone's locked themselves in the bathroom," Brad whispered, giving Leigh an apologetic "Hey, they're your friends" look.

"I have no idea who's in there," Leigh said.

"Has anybody seen Pamela and Rick?" yelled Lorraine to the room, taking the chance to duck out of Leigh's question. "I want to round up my crew to go next door."

"Oh—check the bathroom," Leigh said. "Brad's just told me someone's locked in."

"Those two are so bad," laughed Lorraine. "With everything they've been through, they still can't keep from getting it on wherever we go." Lorraine rushed to the bathroom and started knocking on the door.

"Leigh!" Billie and Katie had arrived arm-in-arm, looking uncomfortable together. Katie avoided Leigh's glance and Billie went in for a warm hug.

"What a great night," he said. "I can't believe I picked up that Mondrian—it was a steal! Where's that dealer who got you all the art? He did a great job tonight; I'd like to shake his damn hand and talk to him."

"That's Jacques," Leigh said, "and if you can find him, I'd sure appreciate it. I haven't seen him since the beginning of the evening! I invited him here, but he hasn't showed; he must be at the club next door already."

"Well, you certainly did a good job putting him on your committee," Billie said. "We're meeting friends next door at the party, so we're going to have to rush off—sadly, I must add. Right, honey?" He not-so-subtly nudged Katie, whose attention had wandered over to where Tony Bennett and Lady Gaga were talking animatedly about something.

"Of course—right," she said sullenly.

"Congratulations again, Leigh! We'll see you later!" Billie said, pulling his wife behind him.

As they rushed out the door, Leigh wondered if they were really heading to the party or going their separate ways. Playing the loving couple all night for Miami society and the cameras, when you were that much at each other's throats, must be exhausting.

"Us too—we hate to leave, but we must; the paparazzi are waiting," said Lorraine, her group gathering around her. She was certainly right; by now there would be a ton of paparazzi clustered outside the club, and a handful of roving photographers inside.

"All right," said Leigh. "I'll probably be joining you in not too long. Joe," she shouted over to where Joe was sitting, flanked by a model on one side and his longtime girlfriend, Abbey, on the other. "Is Mariah coming?"

"No," he said. "She had another appearance at the Mansion, so she had to rush off. She's leaving early tomorrow anyway."

"Well, maybe we should all head over, then," Leigh suggested. The party in the suite was still going, but Leigh thought it might be a good idea to wrap up here, and move on before anyone decided to settle in too much. She sometimes thought she should set up a volunteer-funded expense account just to handle the costs incurred by her hard-partying friends after the gala—Joe being the foremost offender.

"Sounds good," Joe agreed enthusiastically, and leaned forward to shout to a group by the bar. "Hey Wayne! Ready to party?"

***

It was a 20-foot walk from the Eden Roc to the Fontainebleau. As Leigh's VIP guests arrived at the official after-party, a crowd inside the Fontainebleau lobby jammed up against the doors to the club, hoping to get a glimpse of the celebrities. The frantic look on some of their faces was too much, and it made Leigh feel instantly exhausted again. Fortunately, Mitchell was waiting for the group, and pulled all of them through the crowd while several photographers snapped pictures. Leigh had to hand it to Mitchell at times like these; when it came to nightclubs, he could part a sea of groupies like Moses.

Inside the club, Scarlett rushed up with Sal, Miami's most well-known scene photographer, and welcomed the group into the club. Sal started pulling people together for a group photo, and Scarlett pushed herself into the middle between Joe Francis and one of his models, knowing that way she couldn't be cropped out. Some paparazzi photographers would pose any group of people as long as there was a celebrity in the group, and crop out everyone but the celebrity and a person or two, for realism's sake. Two-person photos sold better than group shots, and were much easier to wrap stories around—as Scarlett had learned from Cubby, a local press guy.

When Sal had finished, Mitchell grabbed Leigh's hand and led her and her group to their table. Lorraine and some of her people were already sitting.

"It's about time!" the Diva boomed. "Welcome to our Queen of the Night!"

"Someone's having a good time," Leigh said. The Diva had been at it since the seven o'clock red carpet, and was still bursting with energy. Her secret was well-known; long ago Jeffrey had told Leigh that "Lorraine's waiting" or "Lorraine's in the bathroom" was pretty common slang outside the States for one of those party-favor moments. "Everyone happy?"

"Absolutely!" said Mitchell. "Only—where's our art god, Jacques?

I have a table reserved for him, and no one seems to have seen him."

"That includes me," said Leigh. She panned the room for him, but couldn't spot him in the seething crowd. "I'm actually a bit—"

But Mitchell had already gone off with Scarlett for some reason. *Promoter ADHD,* Leigh thought.

"Hey sweetie, are you going to sit down, or shall we walk around and see who's here?" Brad asked with a nervous look. He wasn't at all fond of large crowds, particularly in over-packed clubs, but was used to escorting his wife around when she needed to make the "see and be seen" tour.

"Let's sit," Leigh said. "I'm afraid of what I might see! I can already see more than enough from here."

Scarlett returned with Sal, and after posing the table for a few more photos—Lorraine insisting on being in the center "because of her height"—she leaned down to Leigh.

"Hey, have you seen Jacques?" she asked. "I need to talk to him."

"That's the question of the evening," Leigh sighed. "Sorry, no."

"Don't you think it's odd that he's made himself so scarce? I haven't seen him since the cocktail hour."

"It's definitely odd," Leigh said. "You would have thought that he would have used the auction as a networking opportunity. Everyone wants to meet him."

"He's not answering his phone, either," Scarlett went on. "But he promised me a print for introducing him to my celebrity clientele, and I want to make sure I get it. I put my friends on the line for him; he'd better not use me and skip town without paying up!"

Scarlett rushed off into the crowd again, leaving Leigh stunned. It had made her nervous to see the usually street-smart Scarlett so suspicious, but that last comment hit like a ton of bricks. What did she mean, *skip town?* Did she know something, or suspect something, that she wasn't letting on?

"Leigh, have some champagne," Brad insisted, handing her a flute with a strawberry floating in the top. "Lorraine got you one of her specials. Have you heard from Lauren? Are they coming?"

"No, they're heading home. She said something about an early meeting in the morning, but I'm not sure I buy it." Leigh pulled out her phone to check on her calls, realizing she wouldn't have heard it even if Jacques *had* called. The music was so loud in here, one had to yell to be heard.

"How long do you want us to stay?" Brad asked. Now that they'd made their appearance and been photographed by the requisite half-a-dozen photographers, Brad was more than ready to leave.

"We'll get out of here soon," Leigh said distractedly, scrolling through her calls. She had calls from Lauren, Dixie, Scarlett, Mitchell, Jeffrey, Lorraine and even Sassy, but nothing from Jacques. How strange! Was it worse than strange—? He'd disappeared without a word, which was weird; and getting a call from Sassy was even weirder. One would think she'd be here preening like a peacock, but she too was nowhere in sight.

"Leigh," Joe said, looking up from his phone, "a few of us are talking about heading over to Elleven in a bit for some food—want to join us?"

Food—yeah, right! Leigh thought. Elleven was one of Miami's hottest—and most expensive—stripclub-and-nightclub combos, and while they did have a 24-hour kitchen, there were always other reasons to go there. In all probability, Lorraine would make it through the whole night without eating a bite—of food, anyway. Leigh was starving, but she knew if she went with *that* crowd, food would be a long time coming.

"I'll pass tonight," Leigh said. "It's been a long day, and I'm looking forward to bed! Brad and I are going to leave soon."

She turned to see Jeffrey running up to her, pushing his way excitedly through the crowd.

"Leigh," he said breathlessly, "I just saw Sassy downstairs, making out with Thomas Kramer! I thought she was with Jacques—have you seen him yet?"

"Thomas *Kramer?*" she said. "Now this is getting too weird. No, I haven't seen Jacques all night—where'd you say you saw Sassy?"

"By the front entrance; it looked like she was on her way out."

"I don't get it!" Leigh said. "I'd at least have thought I'd see her and Jacques at the after-party! Listen, Jeffrey," she said in a low voice, leaning in. "Do you think anything…fishy…is going on with those two?"

"Isn't it always?"

"No, I don't mean like that—I mean, like, something we should be worried about."

"Worried about?" Jeffrey considered it. "I don't think so; I mean, what would it be? Jacques just earned you a ton of money—a lot more than he earned himself."

"I know, I know; it's just weird that he's not around. Isn't it?"

"Not necessarily; I'm sure there are plenty of explanations. He could be someone who doesn't do well in crowds, or maybe he and Sassy are fighting, or he's having wild, filthy sex with his next fling in her car, or something."

"You're right," Leigh thought, thankful for the reassurance. "I think I'm probably just edgy from tonight."

"You've been edgy from tonight for a long time, my Queen," Jeffrey smirked. "Have you eaten anything?"

"No; but Brad and I are going to head out soon."

"Good." He put a hand on her shoulder. "You should; you don't need to be here. You've got a whole mob of promoters and celebrities here, keeping each other busy—it's hard to say exactly who's promoting whom!"

"All right, I will," she sighed. "If anyone asks for me—"

"I'll tell them you sent me for them personally, to bid them goodnight." Jeffrey smiled. "It's under control, my Queen."

She laughed and returned his theatrical bow. "Thanks, Jeffrey—you're the best. I'll see you tomorrow, okay?"

"Bright and early." They hugged tightly, and he held her by the shoulders. "Hey—we made it, huh?"

She smiled at him, suddenly fighting back tears. "Yes," she managed. "We made it."

CHAPTER 23

BASKING IN THE GLOW OF SUCCESS

> Love my necklace! And Howard is so happy with his picture. Lunch soon?

—Dixie

The phone rang on Leigh's bedside table, waking her from a sound sleep. She cursed the shrill sound as she awoke; but remembering the dream she'd been having, she stopped herself. It was the same dream she'd had every night since the gala.

In it, she wandered through her house, all of her walls covered with art from the gala auction. She then discovered, by an unplaceable feeling, that she was alone in the house. She tried a door, then another, then another, all in vain—the doors were all locked. Her phone rang, but she was unable to find it. A panicked feeling washed over her, and this was usually when she'd awoken.

This time, the phone really was ringing. An omen, she thought, as she grabbed the receiver from the nightstand.

"Hello," she said, trying to sound alert.

"Good morning, Mrs. White, it's John Temple from the *Miami Herald.*"

"Good—good morning, Mr. Temple, how are you?"

"Fine, fine. Listen, I was hoping to schedule an interview with you for the art section—we'd like to talk about the success of your gala this year. We're also trying to locate your art dealer, Jacques Mercier, for an interview. Any idea how we might reach him?"

At the mention of Jacques's name, Leigh's stomach sank. She still hadn't heard from him herself.

"Um, listen, Mr. Temple," she said, "can I speak with you another time? I'm in the middle of a meeting." She looked at the clock on the bedside table. It wasn't quite 9 a.m.

"Of—of course," Mr. Temple said dubiously.

"Thank you," she said before he had a chance to go on. "I'm sure my assistant has your number; he'll get back with you. Goodbye!"

She hung up and pulled herself out of bed, shivering a bit as she did. Why was Jacques's disappearance troubling her so much? All the artworks sold in the auction had been delivered to their bidders, and the money had all changed hands without incident. Nobody had been disappointed; on the contrary, everyone was raving about their purchases. Why should it bother her so much that Jacques had gone off-radar? He was probably off celebrating. But it seemed incredibly unbusinesslike of him. Here he was, with just the opportunity he'd been looking for to promote himself and his business in Miami, and he was nowhere to be found. And she'd set up all those connections for him!

That was probably a big part of her concern, she reflected as she started up a cold shower. Jacques's disappearance cast a strange light on her recommendation of him. But wasn't there another worry kicking around in her mind—something more sinister? Could he be involved in something shady? Had something happened to him?

She remembered what Lauren had told her about his connections—or were they Sassy's connections? She couldn't remember. But she hoped nothing that bad was going on.

Refreshed by the cold shower, she told herself to calm down. Nobody blamed her for Jacques's vanishing act, nor did it reflect badly on her. She was just overstressed and under-rested. It didn't help that the media hadn't let up since the gala. The Ball been a phenomenal success—the "pinnacle of Miami's social season," as the press was calling it—and her phone hadn't stopped ringing with press inquiries. Naturally, the mysterious Jacques was at the center of a lot of them, and she hated not having an answer—but it wasn't her problem. He just needed to show up and explain himself.

Anyway, she had plenty to do to keep occupied in the meantime. Ever since the gala, other charities had been calling her, trying to entice her to raise money for them; and everyone who'd bought art through her auction was calling to invite her and Brad to their private unveilings. There was a ton to do. Still, she always suffered from a certain after-gala depression, and this year she had it bad. She imagined it was similar to what an addict felt, going through withdrawal; or perhaps a mom, wandering through an empty house after the last kid left for college. It was partly because her own house was empty—her boys had left for baseball camp a couple of days before the gala—but there was something else. Her cure for this feeling had always been to get started on the next year's gala; but this time, there was no next year. Without that occupation, she realized she felt empty and purposeless, and the endlessly ringing phone seemed to mock her.

"Jeffrey!" she called out, walking towards his office.

"My Queen," Jeffrey said. She jumped and turned around to find him walking towards her with a cup of hot tea.

"Jeffrey! You startled me!"

"Apologies," he sang. "Are you ready for another glorious day?"

"You're certainly chipper today," she smiled, appreciating the contrast of his mood to hers.

"I am," replied Jeffrey, "and you should be, too! Tomorrow I leave for my vacation, thank you and Brad very much! He told me this morning; I can't thank you enough." He smiled earnestly at her. "Anyway, you won't see me for two weeks, and that is what's got me so chipper. During which time, by the way, I expect you will take a vacation yourself, as you always do."

"I hadn't planned it this time," she sighed. "There's just been too much going on."

"Well, you'd better, and quick," he said in mock seriousness. "This business will make you sick otherwise. Anyway, it can't be *so* hard; you planned such a fabulous one for me! I half-suspect you've been holding out on me this whole time, and are completely capable of doing everything yourself after all. Oh, will this phone ever stop *ringing?*" he half-asked, half-shouted, rushing back towards his office.

Leigh, dazed, walked back out towards the kitchen. Hopefully breakfast would settle her stomach. Absentmindedly she grabbed a yogurt out of the fridge and sat at the table. Going to open the yogurt, she found a Post-It stuck to the top.

Let's get away from all this craziness (it said).
You deserve a break. Call me when you can!
Love, Brad

Laughing, she put the yogurt back and dialed Brad.

When he picked up, his voice had that little tremor it always had when he was going to surprise her. Despite his cool courtroom demeanor, he was usually pretty bad at surprises with her. Besides the tremor in his voice, there was a crooked little smile he always broke into—she called it his "Here It Comes" smile—that showed his hand from miles away.

"Hey, honey—guess what?"

She laughed; she could practically see the "Here It Comes" smile over the phone. But just hearing his voice made her feel better; he really was her rock. It was amazing how quickly her mood changed with him around.

"Oh, man," she said. "I'm not sure I can handle any surprises today."

"Well, never mind then," he said. "How would you like to hear about the latest in judicial reform? Spoiler alert—there hasn't been any."

"Okay, okay," she said, "what is it?"

"I," he said magnanimously, "in my infinite wisdom and benevolence, have decided you and I need a vacation, and a break from the relentless Miami sunshine. To that end, I have booked us a suite for a week at the Beverly Wilshire—"

"Ha, you sneak!"

"—where we can enjoy the relentless L.A. sunshine instead, and you can spend far too much money on Rodeo Drive. How does that sound?"

"That sounds wonderful, darling. When?"

"We leave tomorrow."

"Oh," she said, the anxiety returning. "I'm not sure I can—"

"Honey," he said calmly, "you say this every year, and you know you *can* leave this soon. The arrangements are all made; the boys are away at camp and Jeffrey's leaving tomorrow anyway, so it's perfect timing. You need this; I need this. This is a Gone Fishing trip, Leigh." She smiled. "Gone Fishing" was Brad's code for a complete break from regular life—no texting, no calling, no emailing, no gossip, no local news. "Besides, the flight's at 9:45 in the morning, and I'm afraid I'm simply too busy to cancel it! All you have to do is pack your bags and give the maid a week off. Aside from that, there's nothing that can't wait."

She knew he was right. The fact that she had nothing pressing to do was one of the things that was making her so anxious in the first place. Brad always knew when it was time to step up and take control. God, she loved him for that.

"Yes, sir," she sighed happily. "You're right, of course. Brad—I love you."

"I love you too, darling," he said in a soft voice. "I'll talk to you later on. Now go pack!"

As she got off the phone, she realized she felt better already. A week in L.A. would be the perfect thing to chase away her post-gala blues. Dinner at the new Palm, lunch at Spagos, pampering—! She thought of what she needed to do before she left. Whom would she call? Lauren? No, she was on her way to New York. Dixie? What for?

No one, she decided.

"Jeffrey—" she called, but stopped when he came in through the door.

"I know; Brad already told me. I've already taken care of the most time-sensitive pending stuff, like the early bills from the Eden Roc and the wire transfer to Jacques for the art—minus the charity's commission, of course—and I spoke to Doris, too. Don't worry about any of it! Just go pack."

He gave her a big smile and walked back out.

"Thank you!" Leigh called after him. She sat down at her desk and opened her appointment book. The miracle of a blank page met her eye. Today was empty. She really did only need to pack.

Her cell phone rang, shaking her from her haze. It was Jacques.

"Hello, Jacques!" she almost shouted into the phone. "So good to hear from you; Jeffrey's just told me the wire transfer's gone through. Hello? Jacques, hello?"

The line was silent, then went dead.

Leigh called him back, her mind racing as it rang. Was he in a remote area? Had his battery died? Was it him calling to begin with?

Nobody answered.

Jacques, it seemed, wanted to make the calls, not receive them.

CHAPTER 24

REENTRY

Landing 14:30, JB 435. Assemble 14:00, Domestic checkpt. Notifying local support.

—Stan Corinne

The time away in Los Angeles was just what the doctor ordered. Leigh spent half of each day in the spa at the Beverly Wilshire. There she was given hot-rock treatments, facials and body scrubs, and had sheets of collagen placed on her from head to toe.

Rubbed, scrubbed and burnished, she then spent her afternoons at the pool reading, or out shopping on Rodeo Drive and the Beverly Hills Golden Triangle. Melrose had never been her scene, but this was just right. Shopping and window-shopping here were a daydream for her—a much-needed daydream. And there was a new art gallery that she was anxious to visit, New Vision gallery, right across from her old favorite restaurant Craig's.

While Miami carried every great fashion designer on Earth—hers being Rene Ruiz and Gabriella Arango—and she always found great new pieces by designers there, it was nothing to compare with Rodeo Drive and the over-the-top L.A. scene. All of her favorite stores were here: Savannah in Santa Monica, Maxfields, Hermès, Harry Winston. Benzes, Rolls-Royces, Lamborghinis and Range Rovers with tinted glass lined up in perfect order under the towering palms. Celebrities and paparazzi kept up their endless dance, seemingly at an understanding with one another in this city of fame and make-believe. Leigh bought an Alexander McQueen gown—a whopping $3,000 at half price—the dramatic green color and thick bejeweled waist of which made her feel like she wasn't of this world. It was hypnotic, heavenly.

This would be her new life, she decided. No more stress, no more drama—at least for a little while, she'd take a break from her hectic social life and the stress the charity had brought her. Life would be about Brad, their twins and herself—and many, many more such vacations.

All that week, Leigh didn't touch her phone or watch the news once. She went from penthouse suite, to spa, to pool, to car, to boutique, and back to the suite again. She and Brad ate dinner out twice and went to her favorite gay bar, the Abbey, where they ran into the most fabulous group—Ross Mathews and his partner, the stylist Salvador; David Cooley; and the TV producers from Purveyors of Pop—and had the most fun she and Brad had had in months. On each of the other nights, they sprawled in bed with room service and a rented movie.

It was perfect.

***

478 messages.

Tanned and rested, seated with Brad in first class for their flight back to Miami, Leigh had just kicked off her pumps, wrapped a blanket around her legs and leaned back with the first of many drinks she had planned for the trip home. On a whim, she'd decided to check her cell phone while they waited on the runway.

Some whim!

She sighed, turning the phone off again. Of the 478 voice and text messages she'd picked up in their nine days away, most, she knew, would be from people who knew very well she was away on vacation. Most would be asking her for something, or seeking her attention for some reason. Requests for lunch dates, press calls, raves about the gala, invitations to unveiling parties—all her normal/abnormal routine. Nothing had changed.

God, she thought, *I'm not ready to face this again.*

She turned to look at her husband. He was reading the *Wall Street Journal* and sipping a Scotch on the rocks, utterly absorbed. From the first time they'd ordered Scotch together when they'd met, he'd always ordered it right alongside her. They'd been on the same page ever since.

Brad looked up and met her smile.

"Hey, good-looking," he said, raising his glass to hers. "Ready to head home?"

"I was just thinking," she replied, "something like the opposite."

"Checked your phone, didn't you?"

"Mea culpa."

"Ah well, it never lasts forever," he laughed. "That's why they call it a vacation, dear."

"I know, and it's been so lovely," she said, kissing his hand. "Thank you for organizing it, Brad. I'm just anxious I won't be able to keep this good feeling going."

"So you're anxious about being anxious."

"I guess so, yeah."

"Well, you know what I always prescribe for that." He raised his glass again and they laughed. "But seriously, sweetheart, things are going to be different now."

"How are you so sure?"

"Everyone knows this gala was your last. That, at least, is a huge change."

"I know, but—what if I've made the wrong decision?" She frowned. "While I'm working at it, I'm so sure it's the last thing I want to be doing; but once it's over, I wonder if I'm just being selfish. What if I *shouldn't* want to be done?"

Brad smiled. "Well—whether you should or shouldn't—if you want to, you can always pick it up again," he said. "It's your life, honey. So what if you change your mind? That's what all this is—changing your mind. You aren't here to make the right decision or bust; there might not even *be* a right decision. You make the decision you *can* make, and if it turns out not to make you happy, you make another one. And you know you have a lot of people on your side, pulling for you."

"Do I?" she asked.

"Well—at least me," Brad said. They laughed again. She pulled him in for a kiss.

"You'll do," she said.

Brad and Leigh walked hand-in-hand up the jetway and into the terminal. As they walked towards the baggage claim, Leigh noticed a crowd of photographers waiting on the other side of the security checkpoint.

"That's funny—was there someone famous on the plane?" she asked.

"I didn't notice any." Brad laughed. "You know, I bet they're here for you."

They burst into laughter.

They walked through the security point. A crowd had gathered there with the photographers, who now began snapping photos wildly in Leigh's direction.

"You've got to be—" she began, when she spotted a familiar face in the crowd. *What's Adrienne's assistant doing here?* she wondered in a blur of confusion. *Is Adrienne responsible for all these photographers? But if so, where is she?*

The man she knew as Adrienne's sour-faced assistant stepped forward. A badge hung around his neck. It was only then that Leigh saw he was flanked by a group of police officers.

"Leigh Anatole White," he said, taking hold of her arm.

"Stan! What's happening? Where's—"

"You are under arrest for fraud," he continued, not heeding her as he slapped a pair of handcuffs on her wrists. "You have the right to remain silent. Anything you say…"

The rest of the words blurred as a policeman took her by the shoulders and guided her away from Brad. She stared at the policeman, mouth open. Brad was yelling. They ignored him, and led her away as he followed them to a police car outside the terminal doors. All the while photographers danced around them, snapping flashbulbs in her face. Reporters shoved tape recorders and microphones toward her, barking questions at her. The crowd of tourists and returning travelers gawked.

Brad. She could barely hear his voice over the commotion; what was he saying? A policeman was holding him back; they were arguing. She looked up at her husband in bewilderment as they opened the cruiser door to shove her into the back. *Like they do with criminals,* she thought vaguely. What could possibly be happening?

"I'll meet you at the police station!" he shouted as the door slammed shut.

CHAPTER 25

STARS AND BARS

> Where are you? Call me and let me know how I can help.

—Dr. Howard Johnson

t was surreal, Leigh thought. It felt as though she'd had eyes on her from when she touched down in Miami. First the cameras, then the police; and now every woman in the holding cell she'd just been thrown into was trying to stare her down.

"Whatcha in for?" the woman next to her asked.

Leigh shook her head. How could someone be asking *her* that question? What was she doing here? This was a bad dream, a nightmare.

"Honey, I'm talking to you," the woman said again, this time a little more forcefully.

"Sorry, I'm in a bit of a daze," Leigh answered. "I was arrested for fraud."

"So the rich bitch got caught," said a tough-looking woman in a blonde wig. "About time one of you did. You know, there's no maid service in here, honey; you'll have to make your own bed." The woman laughed, her eyes continuing to hold Leigh like she was her next meal.

"I'm sorry. I don't feel like talking," Leigh said.

"Oh, I'm sorry," said Blondie mockingly. "I didn't realize you were upset. Please, let me visit another time."

Leigh's head spun. She'd never been inside a prison cell—it had always been *her* rescuing people from them. Where was Brad? How long would she be kept here?

Stan Corinne, as it turned out, was no editor's assistant. He was with the FBI, who had apparently worked with local authorities to bring her in. He'd told her at the station that they'd been looking into her for months, and that she was being charged on multiple counts of art fraud. Beyond that, they weren't giving her any information yet; but she knew that was exactly the number of paintings Jacques had contributed to her auction.

Jacques! The combined sales from the art had amounted to millions. Had it been stolen? Forged? If all of it had been hot, she knew she was in big trouble; to protect the charity she'd deposited all of the sales checks in the charity's account herself, and authorized transfers for Jacques's commission and expense costs. Jacques hadn't carried out any of the transactions alone; she had been responsible for all of it. How could she have let this happen to her friends, her charity, her name?

Hopefully Brad would have some idea of how to make this right.

It was Friday night. Brad always said Friday nights were the worst time to get arrested: judges weren't available to hear cases until Monday morning. At the thought, a sick panic rose in her stomach. She didn't know what she would do if she had to stay here all weekend. She remembered Dixie's beautiful Manolo Blahnik pumps, covered in pee.

"Hey, honey, it's not so bad," said a woman with a black eye, standing next to her. "Your husband'll have you out in no time, I'm sure. You have a husband, don't you?"

"Yes, thanks," Leigh said weakly.

"Well, then," said the woman, who then turned away, apparently satisfied.

Leigh felt despair wash over her. What about her friends who had bought all that art from her? What must they think of her? Could they ever trust her again? How could she have been so stupid?

If she and Brad couldn't make this right, they'd lose everything: her freedom, their money, their house—everything! She'd be sent to prison, and he'd be ruined. Who'd want to hire a defense attorney with a wife in prison? Her charity would go under, and the school would enter bankruptcy. The students—all of whom were depending on the school to change their lives—would have no future. Her and Brad's children would be left without a mother, their future grandchildren without a grandmother. Her new McQueen dress would languish without a wearer!

She couldn't imagine how the press must be covering all this. She remembered the reporters yelling at her and the photographers pointing their cameras at her as she was led out of the airport—it was like a scene from some bad movie. It had been less than a week and a half ago that the same photographers and reporters were sucking up to her at *her* charity ball! How had it flipped around so quickly? Fraud? For God's sake, she barely broke the speed limit most days! It made her nervous to take more than one free sample at the grocery store!

She looked up at the woman in the blonde wig, who was still staring at her like she was a ham sandwich. Leigh could no longer hold back her tears, and soon she was sobbing uncontrollably.

Evidently a crying ham sandwich was a different matter. "Knock it off, honey, it's all right," said the woman with surprising gentleness.

"No, it's not," Leigh sobbed. "I'm in big trouble."

"Honey, we all are," said the woman. "You'll get out of it, you'll see."

"What makes you say that?"

"You have friends, don't you? As long as you have somebody out there pulling for you, you'll be all right in the end."

Leigh felt a stab of shameful gratitude to hear Brad's words echoed in her cellmate's. Even the meanest girl in the pack was sympathetic to her.

"I just—I just don't know what I'm going to do," she said. Anger rose within her at Jacques's perfidy. "I've been duped, completely duped—by a—scumbag con man."

"Well," grinned the woman, "then you better stay strong, sister. If nothing else, you got a scumbag to bring down with you."

***

"Leigh White, come with me, please—you're being released."

Leigh roused herself awake. An officer stood at the cell door.

She joined the officer, looking up at the hall clock, and pinched herself to make sure she wasn't dreaming. How was it possible that she was being released? As miserable an experience as it had been, she'd been here less than four hours.

As it turned out, her black-eyed cellmate had been right. Brad had used every connection and pulled every string to get her out. Every favor he had out in Miami, he'd called in for her. The judge had called a special hearing to expedite her release. The bail bondsman had worked with Brad to post her $500,000 bond. The head warden himself had brought out her personal items for her to sign for.

Yet even her Jeffrey Rackover jewelry and Gucci belt seemed unimportant to her now. She felt dirty, tainted. What did it matter that she was being released? Her reputation, her life, was ruined. Who was going to have anything to do with her now?

She felt like collapsing when she saw Brad walk into the booking area. He put his arm around her as she picked up a pen to sign her release papers.

"Honey, I got you out as soon as I could," he said. "It's a real mess, but we'll talk about it later. For now, I just want to get you home. Are you okay?"

"All things considered," she said, trying to get her hands under control. Her signature looked like the line on an EKG machine.

"It's going to be all right," he said softly.

She could only smile weakly at him as he led her down the hall.

"We'll take the rear entrance," he said, nodding to an officer. "There's press swarming all around the front."

The car was waiting just outside the door. Brad quickly opened the door for his wife. As she got in, she had a brief flashback to being put in the police cruiser, and closed her eyes.

"I'm sorry," she said. "I've really ruined everything."

"You didn't ruin anything," said Brad. "Don't worry, honey. We'll figure it out."

He put his hand on her hands, where they were clutched together in her lap.

They drove home in silence. When they turned down their street, Leigh saw a cluster of news vans and photographers gathered in front of their house. A bit closer, and she saw that their yard was had become a satellite city, with cameras, lights, cables, microphones and batteries strewn everywhere.

"Get down, honey," Brad said. "I'm going to drive right into the garage."

As they came down their driveway, photographers and reporters swarmed around the car, tapping on the windows and shouting questions.

"Leigh, did you think you'd get caught?"

"Mrs. White, how long were you planning this?"

"Leigh, give us a photo."

"Smile for the camera! Brad, this way!"

Brad brought them slowly into the garage and closed the door behind them. They sat in the car for a moment looking at each other in disbelief as the press yelled outside, pounding on the garage door. After a moment, Brad broke the silence.

"Well—nice to know they're not just fair-weather friends, huh?" he said.

In spite of herself, Leigh laughed.

"It's true," she said. "I recognized a bunch of them from the gala."

"I tell you, babe, we're keeping their whole industry going."

"At least Sal wasn't there."

Brad laughed. "On a Friday night in Miami? He's got better things to shoot."

She looked at him tearfully. "Brad, what are we going to do? It just seems so hopeless—I don't know how to prove I wasn't responsible for any of this."

He took her hands again. He'd never seen his wife look so lost; it wasn't a look he could bear.

"Well," he said firmly, "first we're going to go inside and get you something to eat."

"Okay, that I can do."

"Then we're going to get in our own lovely bed, and have an excellent night's sleep."

"I don't know how I'm going to sleep at all," she said sadly.

"You'll do fine," he said. "I, for one, intend to fall asleep counting handcuffed Frenchmen." He looked through the windshield. "Anyway, one way or another, we're going to need to rest up. Because the next step is, we're going to find this Jacques son of a bitch, and make him pay for this."

CHAPTER 26

WHAT—AND WHO—IS REAL

> So sorry you have to go through this. I'm here if you need me.

—Scarlett

Early the next morning, Brad White crept downstairs in slippers and a cautious attitude. Approaching the front door, he looked through the window with a wary eye. It seemed he was early enough; no reporters yet. Moving as quietly as he could, he opened the front door and reached a hand out for the newspaper.

"Mr. White!"

"Just one comment, Mr. White!"

He just had time to shut the door as a camera clicked. Outside he heard the muffled voice of a reporter, shouting something at the door.

"Can't fault them for laziness," Brad sighed, pausing in the foyer. They must have camped out overnight. He turned the folded newspaper upwards to glance at its headline.

HIGH-SOCIETY PHILANTHROPIST ARRESTED IN ART FRAUD SCANDAL

With a roll of the eyes, he tossed it onto the kitchen table and started back up the stairs.

***

"Leigh! My Queen! Wake up!"

Leigh blinked awake, her head a strange mixture of confusion and dream. What had she been dreaming? She remembered Brad coming in to kiss her on his way out to work. What day was it? Wasn't it Saturday? Ah, yes, now she remembered—he was going in to the office to pull some files, and start trying to track down Jacques. Her life was ruined. Right.

She leaned up on her elbows. A trim figure was busying itself with pulling aside the shades. Sunlight flooded into the room, illuminating a neatly dressed, very evenly tanned Jeffrey.

"Jeffrey! What are you doing here?"

"I'm here to help you fight the war, of course," said Jeffrey. "You didn't think you could beat a fraud charge without me, did you?"

"But how—what about Zakynthos?"

"I flew back the moment I heard."

"I—I'm so sorry I ruined your vacation, Jeffrey."

"Oh, that's nonsense! We had a lovely time, and it was thanks to you anyway."

She sat up fully. "Are there—are there any reporters outside?"

"Any reporters! There's a mob, a whole savage tribe! They're crazy—they surrounded my car when I started to pull in the driveway, chanting all sorts of questions at me. I don't even think they knew who I was! They were a bit too much for me, so I pulled out and parked around the block. I had to climb through the neighbor's yard to get here! How're you holding up?"

"I—I don't know," Leigh said. "I'm a bit overwhelmed." She took a deep breath. "Thanks for coming, Jeffrey. This is all so terrible—I don't know who I can trust!" Her eyes welled up with tears.

"Now, stop that," Jeffrey said, sitting beside her. "That's not the Leigh I know. The Leigh I know is a strong woman, who won't stop until she's proven her innocence to the world. We'll get to the bottom of this, I promise you."

"I don't know how! Even if we find Jacques, which is doubtful, how do we prove that I was conned? I was supposed to be in charge of the whole thing, and I let him right in under my nose, like an idiot."

"You can't blame yourself for that; he was very well vouched for."

"That's true."

"And Brad says we'll find him—he's got a whole team of private investigators working on it for him."

"I certainly hope they find him."

"They will. But in the meantime, what can we do? Surely there's got to be some way to make good with the buyers—to get them their money back?"

"Yes—yes, I suppose we should let them know we're working on it," Leigh said numbly.

"Great," said Jeffrey. "Well, why don't I start by putting together a list of everyone who bought one of Jacques's pieces, and how much they spent? Then we can contact everyone today and let them know we're going to make it right somehow. We have to at least show that we're on top of this on our end."

"Okay, that makes sense."

"The rest is going to depend on finding Jacques, and sticking the charges to him instead of you—and we'll cross that bridge when we come to it."

"Okay," Leigh said again. She put her hands over her eyes.

"I just can't believe this mess!"

"Believe it," said Jeffrey. "Every queen's got to deal with insurrections from time to time! Now come on, get dressed. I'll get the coffee brewing; we've got work to do."

***

Their afternoon of calls didn't put Leigh's mind much at ease. Most of them ended in messages being left with assistants or over voicemail; few people wanted to talk to her. The police had made their last few days hell, too, questioning and cross-questioning them about their art purchases, and with the incendiary work of the media and the wildfire spread of gossip, by now most of the social set were suspicious that she'd planned the whole thing.

Brad called periodically during the day to catch them up on what was going on. He had his whole legal team working on the case, along with the investigators he'd hired to track down Jacques and research his background. Through his sources and a few of Jeffrey's connections, they slowly managed to piece together an explanation of what had happened.

The whole thing had come to light, apparently, when one of the winning bidders—a multimillionaire named Howard Reynolds—had taken his new Picasso etching to a Sotheby's representative to have it appraised for insurance purposes. This was a routine procedure, involving photographing the front and back of the work, and filling out forms regarding its history. To the untrained eye, the Picasso had every characteristic of authenticity. Not only was it signed, but it also had a label and seal of authenticity from the Musée d'Orsay, as well as an inspection seal and stamp from Christie's. When the representative from Sotheby's looked it over, however, something seemed not quite right about the Christie's stamp. It looked a little *too* perfect, he thought; so he looked closer—and found that the stamp, the seals and the label were as fake as the etching itself.

Howard Reynolds had immediately called his attorney, who'd called the police. Word had spread fast among the A-listers, many of whom worked with the same attorneys. Soon every bidder was having his art inspected, and all of it was turning up fake. Dealership-catalogue entries in Spain and France were revealed to have been forged, as were the periodicals in the British Museum. It seemed it was no mean feat to check out copies of such records and replace them with forgeries.

All fingers pointed to Leigh and Jacques. Jacques's involvement was unquestionable; but with him missing, Leigh was the only one who could be charged with the crime. And she looked undoubtedly like the scam's middleman, if not instigator. All the money that had changed hands had gone through Leigh—Jacques, she realized, had made sure of that—and it was the going opinion of law enforcement that they'd been working together, in whatever capacity, for some time. Stan Corinne and his FBI team had received a series of anonymous tips over a year ago, tipping them into some suspicious activity at Leigh's charity, and had followed her and Jacques's movements from very early on. All of Adrienne's interviews with her friends, it turned out, had been at Stan's direction, and all of them revealed that she'd been working with Jacques—meeting with him privately, taking his calls, giving him a seat on her gala committee—for months.

"Leigh, Lauren's back from New York. She's on the phone in your office," called Jeffrey, sounding as though he were announcing a lottery win.

Leigh scrambled for the phone.

"Lauren, are you back?" she asked.

"Of course—Leigh, darling, what's going on? I mean, I've heard the news from several people, but I know it isn't true! Give me your side of what's happened."

"It's all so unbelievable," Leigh sighed. "I was arrested at the airport, and they held me for four hours before Brad could get me out. Jacques has completely disappeared, and they're charging me with fraud!"

"So it really is that simple," Lauren said. "But everyone knows you wouldn't get involved in something like this willingly! How can they charge you?"

"It seems not everyone knows me as well as you do, or cares to. They just need someone to bring down, and there seems to be enough circumstantial evidence for them to do it."

"But you would never do this—you don't even need the money!"

"Try telling that to the people who busted Bernie Madoff. What's need got to do with it?"

"But the charity—you've never benefited from that charity, all these years! Hasn't it *cost* you money to run it?"

"Yes, but that's exactly what they'd say to prove I *did* do it!" Leigh gritted her teeth in frustration. "God, Lauren, the whole thing is so humiliating! The press is all over the place, and nobody trusts a word I say."

"Well, I do," Lauren said. "Listen, I'm coming over. We can brainstorm about all this; I'm sure I've still got some of the phone numbers Jacques gave me when he first arrived. One was a Mexican number; I remember that. He also gave me the number of a gallery owner in Santiago de Cali, where he sometimes lived."

"That'd be great; I'm sure Brad could use those. He's got detectives trying to track Jacques down. But I don't know if you should come over. I'd love to see you but there's a mob outside—the press has been keeping a 24-hour vigil, trying to get a stupid shot of me leaving. I haven't left the house since I got back; they're like vultures, waiting for you to die!"

"Oh, fuck them. Let them take my picture, I don't care. I'll shoot 'em the finger when I walk by! You need me, and I'm coming, and that's that."

Leigh could have cried from gratitude.

"Okay," she said. "Thanks. Park around the corner and come to the side door—you might be able to make it without them seeing you."

"All right," Lauren said. "Sit tight, doll! I'll see you soon."

Leigh hung up and wiped her eyes. Cooped up in her house, with the press and all of Miami's who's who turning on her, she'd felt more alone than she ever had. Yet she still had her husband, she still had her assistant, and she still had her best friend. The fight wasn't over yet. She may be a prisoner in her own house, but the fight wasn't over.

God, did she want her old life back! The life where decisions were about what to wear to lunch; where they made bets about Dixie crashing the next party; where the gossip was harmless, and always about someone else; where fraud was pretending not to know when the Diva swiped things from her closet, and fakery was just what everyone did sometimes. This wasn't *her* Miami, this place of drawn curtains and mug shots; things had gotten far too…real.

She looked up to see Jeffrey standing in the doorway, his eyes wide.

"Pick up line two," he said, his voice almost a whisper. "It's Brad. They've found Jacques."

CHAPTER 27.

EXTRADITION

I heard on the news they got him. Thank God!

—Lance Bass

rad White sat at his desk, waiting in a fog of strange anxiety. From the moment Leigh had been arrested, he had been tirelessly at work; now, normally cool and collected under pressure, he struggled to keep his composure as he waited to hear back about their witnesses.

It had been days since Jacques Mercier had arrived at the Dade County Jail, to a minimum of fanfare. Brad's investigative team had tracked him down to a tiny village near Veracruz, Mexico, where they, the Miami police, the FBI, the Mexican police and the Mexican government had worked together to arrest him and extradite him to the U.S. Even with so many after him, he'd nearly escaped. Having managed to steal a French passport, he'd posed as a French tourist at the border, and was only narrowly caught boarding a boat for Panama. Having been taken in at last, he arrived again in Miami in the middle of the night, shackled to a runaway drug dealer, and was taken straight to his new lodgings.

Inside sources at the jail had kept Brad abreast of Jacques's new life. Apparently early on among his many attempts to make bail, he'd reached out to Sassy, who'd refused his calls. Conditions at the already-full jail were harrowing; at first Jacques had been given a cell to himself, but as the jail took on other inmates, he was forced to share his ten-by-ten-foot cell first with two, then with three other cellmates. Throughout all this he was indignant and supercilious, treating the guards with disdainful obedience. In response, his complaints were ignored, and Jacques himself left to wait while Stan Corinne and his team sorted through their evidence against him. Most of those arrested and sent to Miami-Dade were out in a day or two, having made bail quickly for petty crimes. The authorities took their time with Jacques.

His story, however, remained troublingly consistent. His claim from the outset was that Leigh White had manipulated him. She had used his art connections, he claimed, to authenticate fake art without his knowledge and push it through her auction, in order to fleece her wealthy connections for their money. Her plan, according to him, was to launder most of the money through her charity, which by now trusted her implicitly with its expenses; and pay him a commission to insure his silence, a percentage of which he would kick back to her. He could never have initiated the scheme himself, which relied so thoroughly on Leigh's connections—much less carried it so far.

This story changed the situation of the defense considerably. With so much of the case against Leigh now hinging on circumstantial evidence and her "co-conspirator" Jacques's word against hers, Brad knew it would be crucial to provide a strong cast of character witnesses to fill out Leigh's credibility for the judge, and testify to her innocence. Her charity volunteers and past donors were first on the list—he knew they would testify to how tirelessly his wife worked, and how devoted she had always shown herself to be to the underprivileged. Yet her friends would be indispensable witnesses in this regard as well—particularly those who had served as members on her gala committee.

Having spent a good deal of time and consideration drawing up his witness list, Brad had passed it on to Katherine, a young lawyer from his firm, to start setting up individual interviews. He wanted to meet with each of them separately, to discuss strategy and how they might best contribute to Leigh's defense; he also figured that one on one, it would be easier to stress each witness's personal responsibility. Leigh had been there for all of them over the years, at the very least as a strong shoulder to cry on; and both of them had helped each and every one of them out of some difficult situation or another. Rarely had she ever asked for help from anyone. Now, for the first time, she desperately needed it. Her friends had to come through. Of *course* they would come through.

The phone rang.

"Katherine," he said, grabbing a pen. "Give me the run-down. Who have we got?"

"Well," she said, getting right to it, "let's begin with Billie Parker. He says he won't be able to commit."

"What? Why not?"

"He says he's taking Little Billie to meet his grandparents while Katie's gone."

"Meet his grandparents! Great. So Katie's gone too?"

"Yes—she's taking an extended spa vacation, apparently to get in shape for the upcoming launch of some sort of jewelry line."

Brad gritted his teeth. "All right, go on; she probably wouldn't have been much help anyway. Brandon Westbrook, a.k.a. Lorraine

Manchester? How about him?"

"The Diva has a gig somewhere, as host of a gay-pride party. Supposedly she can't miss out on the opportunity, as it could lead to—"

"Oh, for heaven's sake, I don't care what it could lead to! Go on."

"Scarlett Ruiz has been consulted on a new nightclub opening in Austin, Texas. She claims she wishes she could be here, but that she can't risk a reputation for flakiness in the nightclub world."

"Well, we wouldn't want to tarnish her reputation! I suppose she felt Mitchell could stand in for her?"

"She did, as a matter of fact."

"And?"

"Mr. Hudson has actually been consulted on the same nightclub. He told me to call Scarlett."

"Jesus!"

"Dr. Howard Johnson has a speaking engagement in Jacksonville that falls during our scheduled trial date."

"All right. What about his wife?"

"Dixie plans to go with him and take advantage of the seminar's personal trainer and nutritionist."

"*What?*"

"She said something about dropping twenty pounds before her class reunion in Tennessee."

"This is unbelievable. This is the same Dixie for whom Leigh and I got out of bed and spent the night helping to get her out of trouble? My God, if Leigh knew about this, she'd be heartbroken! Speaking of which," he added somberly, "not a word about this to her, Katherine! All problems come to me."

"Of course."

"Okay. Now what about Lauren Altamira?"

"Mrs. Altamira's husband is scheduled to appear at a scientific conference in Germany. Lauren claims she needs to be there with him—"

"Are you *kidding?* She's supposed to be Leigh's best friend!"

"—but said she'd skip the extra week they were going to spend skiing there, so she could return early and offer moral support after the verdict."

"How generous of her!"

"Sassy Davilon—"

"Sassy! Don't tell me *she's* the only one showing up!"

"She says she would be happy to give any information that would be of help."

"She's Jacques's girlfriend! I don't want to step into any surprises with her. Besides, even if she were completely forthcoming I don't think she'd have much to tell us. But if we don't depose her, that leaves us with nobody!"

"That's not quite true—your wife's assistant Jeffrey is also available."

"Ah." Brad rubbed his eyes and took a deep breath. "Well, that'll be helpful, as long as the prosecution waits to indict him as an accomplice until *after* we get a chance to take his testimony."

"Yes, I suppose so."

Brad sighed heavily. "Well, thanks anyway, Katherine. Looks like we'll have to work out a different strategy here. Set up deposition appointments for the two we have, and I'll give you a call later today when I've had a chance to think things over. And remember— mum's the word!"

"All right, Brad, take care."

Brad hung up and slammed his fist against the desk. Oh, this was great. True friendship, Miami style! All it took was one bit of scandal, and the whole gang of vultures had turned on her. He couldn't believe it—after all she'd done for them! Leigh had advanced their careers, patched up their relationships, talked them through rough spots of their own; and *this* was how they repaid her?

Now what the hell were they going to do? Depend solely on the *evidence*? He knew the system far too well to rely on that. The *who* outweighed the *what* every time in this town; they could have all the evidence on their side and still lose without character testimony. Dammit, where was everyone when you needed them? The whole thing had him questioning his faith in people.

The intercom buzzed.

"Mr. White," his assistant called in, "Jeffrey is on the phone. Shall I put him through?"

"Of course," Brad sighed. He picked up. "Hi, Jeffrey. What's going on?"

"Brad! I think we may need security at the house."

"Security? Why, has something happened?"

"Not exactly—not yet. But we're completely surrounded by press; it's a total circus! Their cameramen are standing on ladders, or the tops of vans—anything to see over the shrubs!—and there are crowds of people gathered around, just gawking at the house."

Brad smiled at Jeffrey's alarm. "Oh, they'll lose interest when they realize there's nothing to see."

"I don't think so!"

"Come on, Jeffrey. It's not like Leigh's on trial for murder."

"It doesn't matter! Most of them seem to be there just for the cameras."

"Just for the—"

"Yeah, I think most of them don't even care what's going on; they just see the news crews and want to be on TV. I'm telling you, these people are crazy—they'll do anything for a little fame!"

Brad felt the light of inspiration dawning on him.

"Jeffrey—that's it!"

"What's it?"

"You're a genius!"

"Well, I could have told you that…but, er, why so, if you don't mind telling me?"

"I'll have to tell you later! I've got to make some phone calls."

"But the house—"

"Just sit tight, and don't speak to anyone," Brad said. "I'll be on my way home soon!"

He hung up, and immediately dialed Katherine back.

"Katherine! All those witnesses—they all know how to reach you, right?"

"Of course; I left them my personal number as well as the office info. But why? None of them are available."

"They will be," he laughed. "Just don't turn your phone off in the next day or two, okay? You're going to be hearing from every last one of them soon."

***

Jeffrey and Leigh waited inside at the Whites' house, shades drawn against the media circus outside. Jeffrey sat on the couch with a newspaper; Leigh paced back and forth nervously.

"My Queen, you're going to wear a hole in the carpet," Jeffrey said.

"What do you think is taking him so long?" Leigh said, ignoring him. "You spoke with him hours ago."

"An hour and forty-five minutes," Jeffrey corrected.

"Whatever. Didn't he say he was on his way home when you spoke to him?"

"Yes. But he said he had some calls to make, too, remember." Jeffrey looked up from his newspaper. "Seriously, Leigh, you've got to calm down. There's nothing we can do right now. You need a distraction. Why don't we turn on the news?"

"No—no news! I can't stand seeing all this nonsense anymore."

"It can't *all* be about you."

"I know…I just couldn't take it if it were. Besides, you'd be surprised! Surely there's something worth covering in Syria, or West Africa, or somewhere—but they keep coming up with new things to say about my stupid case instead! Things are really sad when people are more interested in a social scandal than Ebola, or beheadings, or things like that—God, it makes me sick! What are people thinking?"

"The irony of a wealthy woman defrauding a charity just makes for a juicier topic, I suppose," Jeffrey said mildly.

"Now, don't *you* side with them, too! It's all unbelievably trivial. Do you know they're only just now searching for whoever Jacques hired—whoever *Jacques and I* hired, supposedly—to forge those paintings? I mean, it's ridiculous! They've all been so quick to accuse me, and they haven't even found the person who—"

"Leigh! Jeffrey!" Brad shouted from the side door.

"Oh, thank goodness," Leigh said. "Honey! I was just wondering what—"

"Quick, turn on the news!" said Brad, giving his wife a quick kiss as he rushed in.

"Funny, we were just about to," said Jeffrey, handing Leigh the remote with a smirk.

Leigh rolled her eyes. "Do we have to? I'm sure it's just going to be more—"

"Trust me, it's worth seeing," Brad interjected. "Turn it on!"

Leigh switched on the TV. The seven o'clock local bulletin was just beginning.

"—where local Republicans are speaking out against what they consider the President's latest attempt to push the nation into socialist bankruptcy: a new health initiative for the homeless. But first, breaking news in the Leigh White art-forgery case."

"You see?" Leigh cried. "What did I—"

"Shh, listen!" said Brad.

"I'm standing outside the district courthouse," the local reporter was saying, "where Judge Martin Tarlow has just issued the announcement that the upcoming trial of Leigh White, the prominent Miami socialite recently accused of twenty counts of art fraud, will be the first in the district to allow near-unlimited courtroom coverage by news and entertainment media."

"What?" screamed Leigh and Jeffrey at once.

"Just wait," Brad said eagerly, turning up the volume.

"—a historic first for the district," the reporter continued, "which has traditionally only allowed certain partner agencies into the courtroom during trial, and in many cases kept all reporters out altogether. According to Judge Tarlow, complete transparency is something our justice system has been needing for some time; and this case is the perfect opportunity to try removing those limits, and allowing any and all news-media outlets a chance to cover the story."

"How can they do that?" Jeffrey whispered.

"As you can see behind me, a number of entertainment-news stations are already here setting up media kiosks around the courthouse," the reporter was saying, "and there are reports that media-sponsored stylists and hair-and-makeup artists will be offering their services gratis to participants in the trial."

Leigh, completely aghast, couldn't keep quiet any longer.

"This is insane!" she shouted, switching off the TV in horror. "How could the judge sell the trial out like this? A *perfect opportunity?* This is my *life* we're talking about here! And Brad—wouldn't he have to have permission from the defense to do such a thing? How on earth did he get such an idea into his head?"

"I put it there," Brad said.

There was a clatter as Leigh dropped the remote. "You *what?*"

"I put the idea there," Brad repeated. His smile was the sort usually reserved for boys who'd just planted something disgusting in a teacher's desk drawer. "I suggested it to Judge Tarlow, and he jumped at it."

"You suggested—*that?*"

"Yep! And the media kiosks. The sponsored stylists weren't my idea, but I did think they were a particularly nice touch."

Leigh and Jeffrey stared at him, each wondering in their own way whether the man had gone off the deep end.

"All right, Brad," Leigh said deliberately, "I'm sure I'm not going to guess, so I'll just ask: why did you do that?"

"I, my dear, am simply taking care to secure my witnesses," Brad said.

"What do you mean?"

"Let's just say a few crucial people were going to need some extra persuasion to show up at the courthouse."

"Extra persuasion? Who would we want as witnesses, who would need publicity to come?"

"Never mind that," Brad said, backtracking. If there was ever an appropriate time to tell his wife that all of her friends had backed out on her, this wasn't it. He'd keep it to himself for now. "Just trust me, okay?"

Jeffrey was looking at his iPad in disbelief. "It says here that literary agents are already tweeting out book-deal offers for anyone involved in the scandal, and talent scouts are going to be in attendance throughout the trial," he said. "Andy Cohen's already got a live feed running online, and Perez Hilton's put up a link to the coverage on his blog. Harvey Levin from TMZ says they'll have a courtroom presence, too."

"I don't know, honey," Leigh said. "It seems a bit extreme to me."

"Just trust me!" said Brad again with a laugh. "As your attorney, I think I know what needs to be done here. And as your husband," he added, "I think it's high time we poured you a glass of wine, drew you a bath with those rose-scented salts you insist you like so much, and settled in for the night."

"But—"

"No buts! Attorney's orders."

"Yes, sir."

"Good." He glanced at his phone, and a smile lit up his face. "Looks like I've got a few messages from Katherine; something tells me I should take those first, and join you in a minute. And in all seriousness, you two," he said, turning an appropriately somber eye on both of them, "no contact with the outside! Jeffrey, over the next few days, you're to take messages only. No questions, no answers—circle the wagons! Consider the White household to be on lockdown. You are not to discuss anything with anyone."

"But honey," Leigh said uncertainly as Brad started toward the kitchen. "*Anyone?* Even my friends?"

Brad barely suppressed a laugh.

"*Especially* your friends!" he shouted back to her.

CHAPTER 28

LAUREN DRAWS THE LINE

> Sorry L, running a little late. Be there in a few.

—Dixie

Dixie headed into Mariposa with a heavy heart. *Lord,* she thought, *of all the days to skip drinkin'!* But calories were calories, and if she wasn't going to have that personal trainer to help her, she'd need to make her own cutbacks. It wasn't every day you got to be on TV!

The hostess looked up brightly when she came in. It was Suzanne, the same hostess she'd met the last time she was here.

"Dixie! So good to see you again."

"Oh, hi, Suzanne!" Dixie said. "Good to see you, too! Yew know, Ah'm actually here to meet—"

"Your friend from last time, of course," said Suzanne. "She's already waiting for you. I gave you guys the same booth."

"Great, thanks! Same booth, huh? You're really buckin' to give me that, what do you call it, *déjà voila.*"

Suzanne brought her back to the table, where Lauren was ordering a drink from the waiter. He turned around as Dixie arrived, and Dixie felt her *déjà voila* increase by a jump.

"Hi, Dixie!" It was Bobby, their same waiter from before. "Glass of Chardonnay, right? Or shall I just leave the bottle?"

"Oh, er, no thanks, Bobby," Dixie said. "Ah'll just have a, uh, glass of cranberry juice."

"Cranberry juice?"

"Yeah—uh, with a straw."

Bobby nodded, looking a bit concerned, and left to get their drinks.

"Dixie, thanks for coming," Lauren said.

"Of course, honey," said Dixie, settling in. "What's on your mind?"

"Well, it's this trial of Leigh's."

"Ah thought yew and Franklin weren't going to be there."

"Francisco," Lauren corrected. "He's not, but I've decided to come back from our trip early. I just changed my ticket today. I thought I should show my support," she added quickly.

"Well, that's a funny thang—you know, uh, Ah felt the same way."

"So you *are* going to be there? You aren't going with Howard up to Jacksonville?"

"No, Ah—Ah decided that would be too selfish of me."

"That's so good of you," Lauren said, looking at the tablecloth.

"Yeah, well, you know," Dixie trailed off.

Bobby returned with their drinks, and the two women sipped them in an awkward silence. Lauren was the first to break it.

"So—did Brad already depose you?" she asked.

"Yeah, he did."

"And did you tell him?"

"Tell him what?"

"Oh, you *know* what!" Lauren hissed. "About the tapes! Did you tell him about what your husband's patient Cavalleri said on those tapes, about Sassy and Jacques?"

"Of *koorse* not! Why would Ah tell him that?"

"Because it might bear on the case, that's why!"

"Oh, Ah'm sure it's completely irrelative."

"Let Brad decide that!"

"But what if Ah'm just confusin' things? Ah wouldn't want to, y'know, lead him astraight."

Lauren looked hard at her. "You're worried about Howard finding out!"

"Well, yeah, if that's what you're askin'—"

"But he won't even be in the courtroom!"

"There's going to be all sorts of TV cameras there—or, uh, so Ah've heard."

"Dixie, you *have* to tell Brad what you know! This could mean Leigh's future!" Lauren lowered her voice. "If you don't, I will."

Dixie's eyes flew open in surprise. "Yew—yew wouldn't!"

"Try me! I'll be under oath, remember; I'll *have* to tell what I know!" Lauren's eyes glowed with a sudden inspiration. "And I'll tell Howard about Danny!"

"Lauren! Yew know that ain't right; don't do that!"

"I won't—*if* you tell Brad what you know, and agree to testify to it in court."

"Oh, Gawwwd," Dixie moaned. She took a deep pull off her cranberry juice, remembered it wasn't alcoholic and glared at it in disappointment.

"Dixie, Howard probably won't even be watching the trial," Lauren said. "He's not the type to go in for sensationalism like that. Besides, it's in service to a good cause! This could make the difference between Leigh walking, and Leigh going to jail. Don't you want to help her?"

"Of koorse Ah do," Dixie mumbled.

"Then you'll do it?"

"Yeah, Ah'll do it." Dixie fiddled with her straw sulkily before looking fiercely at Lauren. "But not a *word* of this to Howard! Everyone else can hear about it, but Ah don't want none of it makin' its way back to him."

"Agreed," Lauren said. "You just make sure you own up to everything about Sassy, and I won't breathe a word of it to him."

"Okay, then."

The two of them sat silently for a minute.

"Ah'm not sure Ah'll be able to keep from drinkin', if Ah'm gonna be sayin' all *that,*" Dixie said finally.

"Oh, you'll be fine," said Lauren. "Just remember, it's now or never! We need to help Leigh out of this mess. This is a critical juncture, Dixie."

"A clinical *what?*"

"A moment of truth. A time for action!"

"Oh, right." Dixie couldn't see what that had to do with clinics, but she supposed she could see Lauren's point. "Ah guess it is. Ah'd feel bad if Ah didn't do mah part. And besides, like yew say, Howard probably ain't gonna be watchin' anyhow."

"No way. He's got better things to do. And if he hasn't found out about you and Danny by now, it's not like he's suspicious to begin with."

"Yeah." Dixie looked down guiltily. "Ah think Ah may be done with that anyhow."

"With Danny?"

"Yeah. It's not as fun as it used to be, and Ah just feel bad about lyin' to Howard."

"I understand," said Lauren. "But just think of it that way when you testify. You'll get the best of both worlds—it'll make you feel better to fess up publicly to what you were doing, and you won't even have to have Howard around to hear it!"

"Ah guess that's true. As long as Ah don't have to say anything about Danny."

"Of course not—that wouldn't help Leigh anyway. And just think, afterward, you'll be so glad to see Howard."

"That's true too," said Dixie, glowing with the thought. "Ah guess it'll be kind of like a new start. Ah've been wantin' that for a while."

"That's *exactly* what it'll be," said Lauren, gesticulating with her wine glass for emphasis. "Leigh goes free, you and Howard end up happy like before—I'm telling you, you come clean, and I promise you everything will turn out right in the end."

"All right, then," said Dixie. She nodded solemnly. "It's a deal."

And the two friends shook on it.

CHAPTER 29

THE TRIAL BEGINS

> Leigh, my thoughts are with you. You know my family and I are no strangers to a media circus! Stay strong.

—Natalie Cole

The day had come.

Brad and Leigh awoke to an empty house. Their twins had finished up at baseball camp, but in order to spare them the media insanity in their front yard, they'd sent them to stay with their cousins outside of Orlando. The boys loved their cousins and were happy to go; for them it was just another vacation. Thankfully they were still in preschool, so none of this would register much for them.

Ironically, the lawn had emptied not long afterward. The media vans camped out on their street had all relocated to the courthouse the day before, leaving only one lonely news crew lingering out front. Their reporter seemed so disheveled and eager, it was almost painful turning him down; but taking an interview was the last thing the Whites wanted to do on their way to trial, so they gunned it past him.

They drove to the courthouse without a word, all of their senses frazzled with anticipation. Their stomachs seemed butterfly enclosures; their hearts, intolerable bongos; their Mercedes four-door, a Datsun hatchback. Yet no anxiety would prove equal to the reality of the situation. As they neared the courthouse, their jaws dropped at the scene that had unfolded there.

The courthouse's surroundings had become a carnival. All around the building, news vans were stationed, some practically on top of each other. Photographers and reporters milled around by the hundreds. Hot-dog stands and other food vendors were everywhere. Hawkers shilled T-shirts with pro- and anti-Leigh slogans printed on them—*FREE LEIGH: IT'S FOR A GOOD CAUSE!* and *REAL BARS FOR FAKE ART* were apparently the most popular—and fake Picasso etchings were available for $25, official stamp and all.

Along the side of the building, security had roped off a walkway for the lawyers and witnesses to enter, and a separate entrance for court staff and jurors. All along the velvet ropes, reporters and photographers lined up, firing questions and flashbulbs at everyone who entered.

"It's a wonder they didn't spring for a red carpet," Leigh mused as they pulled up.

"Some people here seem to think they did," smiled Brad. He pointed over to a particularly busy area. "Look who's here."

Leigh squinted to see through the crowd, then put her hand to her mouth. "Oh my God. Is that—?"

It was. Diva Lorraine Manchester, towering over the crowd in a fierce platinum-blonde wig and understated three-inch black stilettos, stood in full courtroom drag—slinky black Chanel pants suit, gold pendant earrings, red nails—preening and posing for the crowd. Mario Lopez, back with *E! Entertainment News*, held a microphone out to her.

"Miss Manchester, hello again!" he said, flashing those winning dimples. "Would you mind introducing yourself for the folks at home?"

They heard the Diva's piercing voice over the crowd, loud and clear.

"Of course, Mario! I am Miss Diva Lorraine Manchester: entertainer, performer, singer, hostess with the mostess, emcee, celebrity, model and best friend of Leigh White."

Brad stifled a laugh. Leigh stared, not sure whether to laugh or cry.

"I see," Mario said. "You're looking fabulous today."

"Thank you, Mario—I'm wearing Chanel, of course, top to toe," the Diva said, giving a slow turn for the camera. "On occasions like this, a girl has to class it up; you might say it's a civic duty."

"Of course, of course. And what do you have there?" Mario gestured at something hidden behind the crowd.

"These are yellow roses, Mario, in honor of Leigh—she's from Texas, as her best friends know."

"I see," Mario said. "And I suppose this means you're here in support of Leigh; what do you think about the trial?"

"Oh, it's a crime, darling, a crime!" moaned the Diva with a tragic gesture. She leaned in to the microphone. "Leigh White is innocent, and we're going to prove it!"

The crowd around them cheered. Leigh sat stunned.

"All this for me?" she said, choked with emotion. "I—I don't believe it."

"I was just thinking the same thing," Brad said with a smile. "Come on, let's head in."

***

Brad and Leigh got out of the car and went straight for the side door reserved for court staff and jurors, where press and onlookers could be held in contempt of court for over-meddling. *Ultra-VIP,* thought Leigh as the crowd surged against the ropes. She and Brad held hands and kept their chins high, Brad firmly repeating his mantra of "No comment, no comment" as cameras and microphones were shoved across the barrier into their faces.

"Leigh, how long will the sentence be if you're convicted?"

"Brad, how does it feel to be defending your wife?"

"Leigh, who are you wearing right now?"

I am wearing a conservative St. John suit, comfortable three-inch Lisa Pliner shoes, the double strand of pearls I got when my twins were born, small clip-on pearl earrings, a Kelly box leather handbag and Chanel No. 5, you idiot reporter, thought Leigh darkly as she smiled and kept walking. What silly details to dwell on!

The courtroom door opened, and a sea of faces turned toward them. A pin hitting the floor at that moment would have resounded like a rocket. Happily for the eardrums of all present, none did.

Leigh and Brad took their seats, and the bailiff stepped forward.

"All rise—the court is now in session, with the Honorable Judge Martin Tarlow presiding!" he bellowed.

Everyone stood as the judge entered. The Hon. Martin Tarlow had a calm, controlled look about him: piercing eyes behind tortoiseshell glasses, a firm-set chin, thick salt-and-pepper hair buzzed short in a military style. To Leigh he looked like a stuffy Republican without a sex life. The thought filled her with terror.

In a curt tone, he told everyone to be seated. Leigh leaned forward, overwhelmed with tension. She felt paralyzed with fear—frozen in time, underwater somehow. She felt like a wreck: her jaw was sore from clenching the night before, her eyes dry, her hands shaking, her knees weak, her breathing shallow. She thought back on all her years of hard work, all her years of helping others; of paying her own way, fighting the good fight, doing the right thing. She thought of meeting Brad, of delivering their twins, of organizing her first gala. She thought of helping her brother Gerald. Was he somewhere watching all of this on television? Was all this going to go up in smoke?

She looked at the jury; they sat still and impassive, but for one man in the back, resolutely picking his nose. These people held her fate in their hands; would they see their way to justice? Had Brad sufficiently prepared his witnesses? Would they even observe proper courtroom decorum? She thought of her life in Lorraine's hands—in Dixie's—in Katie Parker's—and shuddered.

At that moment she looked over at Jacques, and felt her blood run cold. He reminded her of a serial killer, he looked so completely at ease. Was he so confident in his story? He looked over at her and smiled, and she looked down in disgust.

Judge Tarlow peered at the jury through his glasses, and politely addressed them.

"Ladies and gentleman of the jury, we will now begin our joint trial of the State of Florida versus Leigh Anatole White and Jacques Mercier, each charged with conspiracy to defraud the community by knowingly and willingly selling forged artwork. The state's opening statement will be presented first, followed by that of the defense. The two defendants, though both charged with conspiracy, have separate counsels and the right to present their independent defenses, and so will be represented in two opening statements and two lines of cross-examination during the trial. Let me remind you, for now, that these opening statements are not to be considered evidence, but as an overview of what the prosecution and the defense plan to present during this trial. I further remind you that, despite the *overwhelming* presence of media representatives here"—he looked sternly around the courtroom, where reporters were furiously scribbling—"you are not to discuss this case, or any evidence or testimony presented during this trial, among yourselves or with anyone else, throughout the duration of the trial. Having said that, and taking it as understood by everyone present, we will now begin with the prosecution's opening statement."

"Thank you, Your Honor," came a bellow from the other side of the room. Leigh jumped, and looked over at its source for the first time. Brad had described the prosecution team for her, but this was the first time she'd seen them.

Mr. Silvers, the tall, 40s-ish male prosecutor, appeared to be an all-American jock type. He had muscles everywhere, and the perfect cheap dark-blue polyester suit for them to poke through. Every hair was in perfect place—"coach hair" was the term Leigh knew for it—and his shiny, perfectly dimpled blue tie screamed fatherly self-assuredness and Ivy League intellect. To female jurors, he would appear handsome, wholesome and authoritative. And if that weren't enough, right alongside him was his female counterpart, the icily pretty Ms. Defoe, whose blonde hair and blue eyes—staring out beneath a pair of perfectly shaped, sultry dark eyebrows—would be apple pie for the men. Brad had told her about this, too; the prosecutors were wary of Leigh and Brad's husband-and-wife team drumming up sympathy among jurors of both genders, and so had taken care to provide their side with a pair to rival them. Devious, the way these things worked! Make no mistake about it—these prosecutors were calculated, and had covered every base.

"Ladies and gentlemen of the jury," Mr. Silvers began, "all of you are familiar with the concept of charity. Charity, ladies and gentlemen!—by which I mean, of course, selfless generosity, and the assistance of one's fellow man. It is charity to which we turn for a salve and healing agent in our society, when our other safeguards fail. It is, some would argue, the very glue of society itself.

"Yet even this selflessness is sometimes perverted, ladies and gentlemen, and used to serve selfish ends. Imagine the brazenness, the outright audacity, of such a thing! Imagine the re-appropriation of money intended for charitable ends—given freely in the goodness of the givers' hearts!—to the purchasing of boats, and clothes, and fancy vacations! Imagine luring out these generous givers with priceless artworks, ramping up the prices with appeals to their charitable spirit; and when the time comes to deliver, sending them off with clever fakeries instead!"

The female prosecutor, Ms. Defoe, brought out a large board with images of all of the forged artworks on it. Mr. Silvers gestured at it forcefully.

"Here, ladies and gentlemen of the jury, is a representation of the extent of this crime. Twenty works of art—all supposed priceless masterworks, and *all* forged! A run down the list of artists will convince you of the audacity of this fraud." He gestured at the images as he recited. "Picasso. Mondrian. Basquiat. Monet *and* Manet. Renowned artists, the great recognized treasures of our culture—passed off in cheap imitation! Or shall I say *expensive* imitation? For so these imitations turned out to be: over twenty million dollars' worth, and all as worthless as the canvas they were painted on.

"Imagine these flagrant, premeditated misdoings, ladies and gentlemen of the jury, and you will have the whole substance of Leigh White and Jacques Mercier's appalling conspiracy against the Miami community.

"Today we the prosecution intend to demonstrate to you the how, the why, the when and the where of that conspiracy. That its participants take up separate corners of the defense, and disavow responsibility for one another's misdoings, is only a sign of their thorough treacherousness. There is no honor among thieves, ladies and gentlemen; and these two have turned on each other as readily as they turned on their society.

"At bottom, the cause is the same: self-interest and greed.

"For Jacques Mercier, it was simply an opportunity to bilk high society out of millions. He had no connection, no allegiance to Miami, or indeed to America. He is a newcomer to both; and based on his many relocations over the past years, it is difficult to see to what society, if any, he feels responsible. It is this, among other qualities, which made him desirable as a co-conspirator in Mrs. White's scheme, and which delayed his capture. Yet here he stands, and we will bring him to justice, if only for a secondary role.

"Leigh White's transgression, on the other hand, was a far more heinous one. For years, Mrs. White has been a key player in the very community she set out to defraud. She spent a decade building the trust of her victims, and enjoying her spurious charity's many ancillary benefits along the way. Whether she had always planned to use her charity for criminal ends (as we believe), or decided to do it somewhere along the way, there is no denying that in the end, it was a source of tremendous financial and personal gain for her; it put her on the inside with the rich and famous, lent her the ear of the wealthy and powerful, and ultimately put her in the ideal position to perpetrate a fraud of epic proportions. It will be argued that, being rich already, she would not have needed the money she stole; but all too often our richest citizens are those with the fewest scruples about grasping for more, and her high status only makes her guilt more poignant.

"Indeed, this flagrancy of her crime is, beyond a doubt, its most offensive feature. Fake art for real; fraud for friendship; selfishness for charity! These substitutions would have an almost artistic fittingness to them, were they not so insultingly obvious. Can any of us look at this charity of hers, and not see it for what it was—a way to feed her inflated ego, to control people, to have her picture in all the magazines and newspapers, to be seen as a present-day Mother Theresa? Do any of us not recognize the trappings of vanity, of insatiable self-serving greed, where we see it? What else could such conspicuous do-gooding be, but a cover-up for selfishness on a grand scale? Ladies and gentlemen, it pains us to believe it, but that is precisely what we see—right here in front of our eyes.

"We the prosecution feel this to be as plain as day, and we hope that by the end of our trial, you ladies and gentlemen of the jury will recognize the truth, and deliver a verdict of 'guilty,' both for Leigh White and for her partner in crime, Jacques Mercier."

***

Leigh listened to the prosecutor's diatribe in disbelief. The prosecution couldn't have gotten the story more wrong if they'd tried. Could anyone really believe such a thing of her? It horrified her to reflect that, as Brad had often told her, such accusations were made of innocent people every day—and enough of them believed to put many of them in jail.

The judge motioned next to Jacques's court-appointed lawyer, and she rose. Marcia Fischer, whom Brad had seen in action before but never argued against, was a small, round woman with mousy hair and the face of a fighting bulldog. As she stood, Leigh saw an expression of innocent concern plaster itself across Jacques's face, as though he couldn't believe any of this was happening to him. His lawyer had obviously coached him to look victimized while she spoke. Leigh stifled a sound of disgust.

In a lackadaisical tone, Ms. Fischer addressed the jury.

"Ladies and gentlemen of the jury, what you have just heard is true in many particulars. Yet it doesn't quite get to the *heart* of the truth. You have heard my client, Jacques Mercier, referred to by the prosecution as Mrs. White's 'partner in crime,' her 'co-conspirator.' A crime indeed it was, and a conspiracy; but our two defendants were no more partners in it than Mrs. White's attorney and I are now.

"The truth, ladies and gentlemen, is simply this: that Leigh White, having concocted the scheme for charity fraud which we have already heard so colorfully described by the prosecution, then contracted my client, Mr. Mercier, to import high-end copies of artworks into the U.S. Such copies—decorative artifacts, as they are called in the art world—are very common. They are found, for instance, at vendor stands outside many famous museums.

"They are also perfectly legal, for private use; and that is all Mrs. White told my client they were for. He had no idea that she planned to pass them off as originals, much less sell them for millions of dollars to her charity donors. When Mr. Mercier attended her charity gala, as a guest, he was appalled to see the copies on auction, and attempted to stop Mrs. White from displaying them. But it was too late. She threatened to implicate him in her scheme if he told anyone about it, and alleged various evidences—some of which, no doubt, her attorney will bring forth today—in proof of his supposed complicity.

"I ask you now, ladies and gentlemen of the jury, to put yourself in my client's place, and imagine what you might do. You are a foreigner, new to the city and the country. The woman in whom you, like so many, have placed your trust, has just implicated you, without your knowledge, in a scam of incredible proportions. Yet she is no foreigner; in fact, she is as connected as they come. Her friends are rich and powerful; her husband is a famous, well-regarded attorney; the media is in her back pocket. You are at her charity gala—itself one grand, ostentatious display of her power and control. What, ladies and gentlemen of the jury, do you do?

"Well, I can tell you what my client did. He sat by, helpless, as

Mrs. White shamelessly auctioned off his decorative artifacts to her unsuspecting guests; he made himself scarce for the rest of the gala; and then he left town, hoping to put the whole sordid affair behind him, and alert the authorities when he could drum up enough proof of his innocence. Notice, ladies and gentlemen: Mrs. White still hadn't paid him for the artifacts he'd imported for her, but Mr. Mercier didn't care; he simply wanted to get as far away from the crime and Leigh White as possible.

"Yet Leigh White's manipulation was far from finished. Over the following days, she wired a sum to Mr. Mercier's bank account. This, he assumed, was his commission; but he was in for a shock. That sum, ladies and gentlemen of the jury, exceeded Mr. Mercier's agreed-upon commission by nearly *a million dollars!*

"Now, if you are wondering, as my client did, why Mrs. White would do this, the answer is simple. In overpaying Mr. Mercier, Mrs. White sought first to secure his silence with a bribe; and second, in case the bribe failed, to use him, yet again unbeknownst to him, as a money-launderer. She knew if he didn't take the money, he'd want to return it to her as quickly as possible; and would be willing to return it in whatever form she wanted, just to have it gone. She could ask for it in cash, in property—in gold bricks, if she wanted to!—and if he didn't want to look like a knowing accomplice, he'd do exactly as she said.

"When he saw the situation he was in, Mr. Mercier fled, to buy time. At the time of his capture, at the instigation of Mrs. White's hired thugs, he was attempting to return to his native France, in a last desperate effort to find support for his cause and put all this behind him.

"This is the kind of relationship that really existed, ladies and gentlemen, between Leigh White and my client. It was no co-conspiratorship, no partnership. It was a one-sided, manipulative, top-down scam, plain and simple, with Mrs. White at the wheel and everyone else playing catch-up. It was, in short, exactly the sort of relationship Mrs. White is used to being in, where she has all the connections, and calls all the shots. Even before the arrival of my client on the scene here in Miami, Mrs. White's charity was under suspicion; and the fact that Mr. Mercier was caught up in her illicit behavior, was simply a matter of his being in the wrong place at the wrong time.

"This is what the evidence will prove today, ladies and gentlemen of the jury," the bulldog concluded simply, "in our pursuit of a commutation of sentence to Leigh White, and a verdict of 'not guilty' for Jacques Mercier."

***

A wave of murmurings ran through the court as everyone digested this last version of the story. It was the exactly the sort of ante-up that most of them had hoped for. The socialite linking forces with the con man had been good, but the foreign art dealer, ruthlessly victimized by the Miami power-player? This was too rich!

Leigh sat stunned. She'd never heard such an outlandish accusation made against her in her life; the prosecution's take had been almost reasonable by comparison.

Fighting back tears, she took a deep breath as Brad stood to address the jury. The room fell silent with anticipation, as everyone waited to see how her husband would speak to her defense. Leigh realized with a strange thrill that she shared in their suspense. She and Brad had discussed the particulars of the case only to the extent that it was necessary, and even she didn't know what he planned to say. Would he betray any emotion? Would he acknowledge her as his wife?

"May it please the court?" Brad said. The judge motioned for him to begin.

"Ladies and gentlemen of the jury," he said, not moving from the table where his wife sat, "you have just heard two very different opening interpretations of our case today. In some points they seem as different as two sides of a story can be. They do have one particular thing in common, however; and that is that they are both entirely in error as to the nature of Leigh White's involvement in the situation at hand.

"The evidence will show, ladies and gentlemen, that Leigh White's only part in this fraud was as its principal victim. Like its other victims—a great many of them long-standing, dear friends of hers—she was ruthlessly conned by Jacques Mercier, a man with a history of such cons, who took advantage of her generous and trusting spirit as he would anyone's, and used her friendships, her connections and her very dedication to the Miami community against her. The details of this con are what our trial is all about, and you will see those clearly enough as we proceed.

"Yet Jacques Mercier's last and biggest con is one that, to some of you, remains invisible. It is going on as we speak. It is, in a word, the trial of Leigh White itself; and make no mistake, though she stands to suffer most for it, you, ladies and gentlemen of the jury—and *you,* people of Miami"—he gestured out at the crowd—"are its *real* victims. From *that* con, I cannot save you. But the truth can, and I am confident that it will.

"Ladies and gentlemen, you have already heard a great deal today, and I won't take up your time with yet another long story. You don't need to hear it, any more than I need to say it. The evidence will speak for itself. Plainly put, the stories of Mr. Silver and Ms. Fischer are long and overwrought for the same reason that many others are: they are making up for a lack of truth. The truth need not be so dramatically embellished. It need not be so emotionally charged. The truth, in many cases, is simple; and Leigh White's is such a case."

He gazed around the courtroom, and for a long moment seemed to look into the eyes of everyone present. The silence was electric. Returning his eyes to the jury he reached out, and without taking his eyes away from them, placed his hand on Leigh's shoulder.

"The evidence, as I say, will speak for itself," he said, "and we will get to that soon enough. Yet for now, among the long stories, the empty suppositions, the sheer *non-facts* of Ms. Fischer and Mr. Silver, let *this* fact speak loudly and plainly for itself, too: that I, who know the faults and perfections of this woman better than anyone alive—that I, who along with our children have the most at stake of anyone but herself, in the outcome of this decision—that I nevertheless stand by Leigh White now, in unfearing defense of the truth, and defense of you; and say to you, as certainly as I will ever say anything, that my wife is innocent!"

***

The silence in the courtroom broke dramatically as, overwhelmed by the earnestness of Brad's speech, a good part of the audience began to applaud. Judge Tarlow, however, was having none of it. Calling for silence, he thanked the prosecution and the two defense councils, and instructed the jury to return after an hour-long recess for the beginning of the trial testimony, reminding them sternly that there should be no discussion of the trial among them.

Soon the jury had filed out. Jacques and his lawyer went to the office the court had provided for them, just a little ways down the hall from the courtroom. Brad and his team assembled in their own private office, a few feet outside the courtroom door, and emailed their list of defense witnesses, reminding them to be in their assigned seats outside the courtroom in exactly one hour, prepared to be called in.

Brad went back in once the emails had been sent, to check on his wife. Leigh sat stoically at the defense table, taking deep breaths and trying to calm herself down. Brad sat with her and put his arm around her shoulders.

"Honey, everything's going to be fine," he said.

"I just couldn't believe those opening speeches," she said, looking stunned.

"I don't know—I thought mine went over pretty well," he smiled.

"Oh, yours was wonderful, darling. I just had no idea the other two would go so far to throw me under the bus. Especially Jacques! I mean, talk about an imagination!"

"I know. But that sort of thing always sounds stronger in the opening statements. The evidence will make pretty short work of their argument."

"So everyone's going to make it to testify?"

"I'm sure most of them are already here. They knew when they were supposed to show up, and we just emailed them all a few minutes ago to remind them."

"Good," she sighed. "I just want it to be over."

"I know, honey, and it will be soon. The judge has already informed me and the prosecution that if we can establish your innocence with our witnesses, Jacques's trial with the state could possibly be carried on separately—a lot of his case rests on setting you up as the fall guy, and I think the state's evidence is a lot more ambiguous than anyone's willing to say right now."

"Well, that's good, I guess." Her eyebrows knitted. "Provided everyone comes through for me."

"Oh, they will, honey; don't you doubt that. I've talked to all of them, and they all know—" Brad trailed off as he looked up and noticed the bailiff and guards conferring by the door. He caught the words "pandemonium out there."

"Hang on a sec, sweetie, okay?" he said. "I'm just going to step outside a minute."

Brad left Leigh at the defense table, and walked out of the court-room and through the side door to the outside. Coming around to the front of the building, he looked out over the sea of reporters and photographers. His jaw dropped.

In every direction he saw one of his witnesses, talking eagerly to a separate squadron of reporters. Mitchell and Scarlett, Billie Parker, Dixie—every last one of them was completely surrounded by press, smiling for the cameras. Katie Parker was holding up some sort of hideous jewel-encrusted thing, turning her face to different photographers as she spoke, as though she were a model on ShopTV. Lauren appeared to be handing out her business card. All of them were dressed to impress—and *not* as though they were there for a serious trial.

What the hell were they thinking? He'd made it perfectly clear with each of them that they weren't to speak to any press during the trial; he'd even told them to enter through the side door, so they couldn't be cornered. His wife's life was on the line, and these people thought it was the pre-party for the Emmys! Far from remaining discreet, they were working the press like the rent was due tomorrow. Exasperated, he ran back inside to rally his team, hurrying them outside to help him retrieve their witnesses.

It was going to be a long day.

CHAPTER 30

ASSISTING THE TRUTH

> Good luck today, handsome! Zakynthos (and I) miss you.

—Jonathan

The lunch break was soon over, and everyone filed back in to resume the trial. Losing no time, Brad called in his first witness and the clerk stood to announce the name.

"The court calls Jeffrey Kruger to the witness stand!"

Jeffrey strutted in with the confidence of a model and looks to match, decked out in Tom Ford couture and monogrammed navy velvet bedroom-slipper–type shoes. Pity Billie Parker hadn't made sure he was dressed in one of *his* suits! All the fashion and pop websites were going to eat him up, Leigh thought with a smile to herself—to say nothing of the boy-blogs. As he was sworn in in that sexy Australian accent of his, she could practically hear gays around the country sighing.

Brad approached the stand.

"Mr. Kruger," he began, "would you kindly state for the jury how long you've been Leigh White's employee, and what it is that you do for her?"

"Well, I've been working with Leigh for twelve years," Jeffrey said. "As for what I do, I'm technically her executive assistant, which in her case means I keep her life together in about a thousand ways."

The courtroom audience tittered. Brad went on.

"So you would say you organize Mrs. White's affairs—keep her appointments in order, make and receive calls for her, that sort of thing?"

"Yes, that sort of thing."

"And this has included working with her charity, and the annual gala in particular?"

"Oh, certainly, every year. If I had a nickel for every time she told me she couldn't have pulled it off without my help, I'd be able to start my own."

"So you would say you know the goings-on of Leigh White's charity gala pretty much inside and out, would you?"

"Along with most other goings-on in her life, yes."

"Do you enjoy working for Mrs. White?"

"Very much so," Jeffrey said. "She's a very good employer, a very hard worker and a wonderful woman."

"Wonderful in what way?"

"She's incredibly generous, and highly motivated to help people. Working with her charity has been especially rewarding for me; I've been amazed at how much we've been able to do for those kids."

"Interesting." Brad turned abruptly, his face suddenly serious. "Mr. Kruger, would you tell me the names of everyone seated at table two, at this year's gala?"

"Let's see," said Jeffrey, scarcely missing a beat, "the Baileys, the Murcianos, Gloria and Emilio Estefan, Frank Amadeo. Steven

Mariano and John Brant were originally there, too, but we moved them to table one this year." He thought a minute, then grinned. "Oh, and the Fullers, of course."

"Of course," smiled Brad. "And table nine?"

"That was our PR table," Jeffrey recalled. "We had Sarah Greenberg, two reps from Rogers and Cowan, and a couple from Harrison and Shriftman and the Black Sheep team, Integrated PR, and Lizzie Grubman."

"And how many white candles were purchased for the gala?"

"This year? Well, we bought twelve hundred, but we only ended up putting out nine hundred and one."

"Nine hundred and *one?* What was the extra one for?"

Jeffrey snickered. "To replace one from Table Nine that…two of our guests brought into the bathroom with them."

The courtroom laughed.

"I see," Brad said. He looked around playfully at the courtroom audience before turning back to Jeffrey on the stand. "Mr. Kruger," he said, not quite succeeding in returning his face to its former seriousness, "what type of shoes, and in what color, is my wife wearing right now?"

"Objection," Mr. Silvers cried. "I don't see how any of this is relevant, Your Honor."

"Let's find out," said the judge, who seemed almost amused. "Overruled."

"She's wearing her black three-inch Lisa Pliner heels," Jeffrey answered without hesitation. Dozens of faces in the audience lit up with the glow of touchscreens as this crucial bit of information was tweeted out.

"I don't believe they're visible from where you're sitting, Mr. Kruger," Brad said, walking around the stand to demonstrate. "Are you quite sure?"

"Absolutely," said Jeffrey. "I knew she would want them for today, so I had the insoles replaced on Friday at noon—actually, right before I stopped by the dry cleaner's for the shirt *you're* wearing."

"Well, never mind me," Brad said, barely keeping from laughing along with the rest of the courtroom. "These shoes—has Mrs. White had them for long?"

"Lisa gifted them to her three years ago, after the gala that year."

"I see. So Mrs. Pliner was a guest at the gala?"

"Yes, she and her husband Donald have been regular donors to the charity for some time."

"And how much do they donate, generally?"

"Our VIP Couple Package—twenty-five hundred, consistently."

"Every year!" shouted Lisa Pliner from where she sat in the courtroom, and the room tittered again.

"Mr. Kruger, I think you've adequately demonstrated that you have a handle on things," Brad said in a clear voice, when it had quieted again. "Do you recall the first time you ever heard of Jacques Mercier?"

"At the gala last year," Jeffrey replied. "He was there as a plus-one; Sassy Davilon brought him along and introduced him as her date."

"When did the notion arise of him working with the gala?"

"Oh, not until we were well into our preparations for it. I remember he called her wanting to show her some slides, and she had me make a lunch appointment for them for the following day."

"Would you say it was clear that she was already sold on the idea of working with Mr. Mercier?"

"No, not at all. She had me and another friend do some research into his credentials before she even met with him."

"What sort of research?"

"Well, I have a friend at the British Museum, who looked

Jacques up in their catalog periodicals for me. Her other friend, Hugo, did a more extensive check on him—online, as I remember, but also through art-world connections of his own."

"And did you turn up anything suspicious about Mr. Mercier, in these researches of yours?"

"If I had, I wouldn't have sent Leigh to lunch with him."

"Did Hugo?"

"Not at all."

"What did you, personally, find out from your friend at the British Museum about Mr. Mercier?"

"He told me that Jacques was legit—that he was listed in the museum's catalogs, and that one of the artworks that he'd mentioned to Leigh was listed with his name. He was also associated with different artworks by a few of the same artists he'd brought up with her over the phone."

"No further questioning, Your Honor," said Brad.

***

The prosecutor approached the stand.

"Mr. Kruger," he said, "you've just been mentioning some background research you and this other friend of Mrs. White's conducted on Mr. Mercier. Was that at Mrs. White's instigation?"

"Certainly," said Jeffrey.

"So she had suspicions about working with him from the beginning."

"Objection," said Ms. Fischer blandly. "Leading the witness."

"Sustained," said the judge.

"All right," said Mr. Silvers. "Mr. Kruger, how would you characterize your employer's attitude toward Jacques Mercier, before she first met him to discuss his working with the charity?"

"Unsure of him," said Jeffrey carefully, "and a bit cautious of working with him."

The prosecutor leaped on this. "Cautious? Why?"

"Jacques had angered Leigh's best friend Lauren by taking his business to his girlfriend Sassy, and Leigh was reluctant to put herself in the middle."

"No other reasons?"

"She thought he seemed a little slick."

"A little slick," repeated the prosecutor sternly. "As in, suspicious?"

"Objection," said Ms. Fischer again.

"Overruled," said Judge Tarlow.

"Yes, I suppose she did seem to think him a little suspicious," said Jeffrey.

"Yet she agreed to work with him anyway."

"Why not? We didn't *find* anything suspicious about him."

"You don't seem to me to have looked very hard," said Mr. Silvers. "Don't you think it seems a little hasty of your employer, Mr. Kruger, to jump into a twenty-million-dollar partnership on the basis of two people's opinion?"

"No hastier than accusing her of fraud, on the basis of one person's," Jeffrey returned mildly. A laugh ran through the courtroom.

The prosecutor, a bit flustered, tried another tack.

"Mr. Kruger," he said, "are you under the employ of anyone besides Mrs. White?"

"No," said Jeffrey.

"So you must be paid well for your services, I take it?"

"I can't complain."

"No, I don't suppose you can," said Mr. Silvers. "Is it not true, for instance, that after this last gala was over, your employer sent you on a particularly lavish trip? To one of the Greek isles, I believe?"

"Zakynthos, yes," said Jeffrey.

"All expenses paid?"

"Which ones do you think she should have left for me to deal with?"

"Yes or no, Mr. Kruger?"

"Yes, of course all expenses paid," Jeffrey said. "It was a thank-you trip for my help with the gala."

"That's quite a big thank-you."

"It was a big gala."

"Indeed it was," said Mr. Silvers pointedly.

Jeffrey's expression was indignant. "If you're suggesting that she was buying me off, she wasn't," he said. "Leigh always gives me a bonus of some sort for my help with the gala."

"I never suggested anything of the sort—though it's an interesting idea," said the prosecutor condescendingly. "But even if she wasn't buying you off, Mr. Kruger, do you believe your employer never keeps anything from you?"

"No, of course not."

"What makes you so sure of that?"

"Besides the fact that she is a dear friend, and like family to me," Jeffrey said, "I don't know how she could."

"Because you're so closely involved with her schedule, her activities, her appointments, and so on?"

"Yes, that's right."

"So you don't believe she would be capable of deceiving you."

"In so many words, no."

"And yet she managed to surprise you with an all-expenses-paid trip to Zakynthos, with all flights, hotels, tours and even a spa package, booked in advance."

Jeffrey flushed as he saw the trap he'd fallen into. "Yes," he said, "but that's—"

The prosecutor smiled. "And all without your knowing."

"Yes," Jeffrey had to say again.

Mr. Silvers leaned in to the stand. "I'd say your employer might be a bit more capable of hiding things from you than you're giving her credit for," he said, and turned to the judge before Jeffrey could respond.

"No further questions, Your Honor," he said smugly.

CHAPTER 31

A WOMAN'S INTUITION

> Bitch, what r u doing on Court TV?!?

—Randy

"The defense will now call its next witness," said Judge Tarlow.

"The defense calls Mr. Brandon Westbrook to the stand," called the court clerk.

As one, the room turned, and there was a general outcry as, looming large in an enormous wig and heels, and exploding with red and hot-pink accents, Diva Lorraine Manchester walked her slowest-motion sashay down the aisle. She looked left and right, smiled and waved, winked and grinned for all her worth; and the audience in the courtroom went nuts for it. Judge Tarlow could hardly bring himself to call order, the scene was so surreal, and sat speechless as the Diva took the stand.

"Do you swear to tell the truth, the whole truth and nothing but the truth?" the bailiff asked.

"You betcha!" said the Diva with a wink.

Brad stepped up to begin his direct examination.

"Thank you, (ahem) Mr. Westbrook"—the jury broke into laughter—"for testifying on behalf of the defense today. I have just a few questions for you—"

"Oh, take your time, Mr. Brad, I have all day," said Lorraine, to another peal of laughter. Looking directly into one of the three courtroom cameras, she added, "I spent *hours* getting myself together today; I wouldn't want to cut my visit short."

"Mr. Westbrook—" Brad began again.

"Please, Mr. Brad, if you wouldn't mind, call me by my proper name, the Diva Miss Lorraine Manchester. I wouldn't want the folks at home to be confused."

Brad looked over at the judge, who shrugged.

"All right, Ms. Manchester," Brad went on. "Would you please tell the jury how long you've known Leigh White, and specify your relationship to her and her charity?"

"Why certainly—it will be my pleasure," said Lorraine, pulling out a hand fan detailed with pink lace and fanning herself ostentatiously. "And if I may, right at the beginning I'd like to say to the people at home just how important it is to clear our dear friend Leigh's name."

She turned toward the nearest camera, whereupon the judge, coming out of his spell, interjected.

"Excuse me, Ms. Manchester, but it won't be necessary to speak to the audience at home," he said.

"Oh, all right—if you insist, Your Honor, darling." The drag queen looked straight across at the judge, waving her fan slowly in front of the camera. The judge squinted suspiciously at the front of it.

"May I ask," he said, "what is written on your fan, Ms. Manchester?"

"Oh, don't you mind that, Mr. Judge, Your Honor—it's just the name of my website, DivaLorraine.com, where I sell my eyelashes, wigs and makeup. Right now there's a special on hot-pink—"

"Please proceed with your questioning, Mr. White," the judge said loudly as the courtroom chuckled and the cameraman zoomed in for a close-up of the web address.

Brad braced himself at the podium.

"Ms. Manchester, how long have you known Leigh White?" he asked.

"Oh, you know how long we've been best friends, Mr. Brad," she said. "Years at least, though I feel I've known her forever."

"And what is your relationship to her charity?"

"I'm an indispensable part of it, of course," the Diva said. "Leigh always taps me to announce at her galas, and bring in the A-list talent. That's why I have a seat on the committee—"

"The gala-planning committee, you mean."

"—yes; because Leigh knows that when it comes to lining up stars, there's nobody like the Diva. I work a lot of hot parties, you know, emceeing and presenting on the red carpet, so I'm friends with everyone, absolutely *everyone*. I understand them, so they trust me. When Tyra Banks is in town, who do you think she calls to dish? The Diva Lorraine Manchester, of course. When my dear friend Dennis Rodman was on his way off to North Korea, who do you think it was who told him about the detention camps, and the American prisoners there? Me again, darling—over lunch. You know, just the other day I was talking to Giuliana, and she said I was—"

"So you've worked as a hostess for Leigh White's charity gala?" interrupted Brad.

"Oh, *thousands* of times," the Diva said. "And I'm happy to do it, because you know what?" The Diva put on her best humble look. "I've been *so* blessed—I just have to give back somehow. And besides, my dear friend Leigh and her charity deserve the best, and there simply is not anyone else like me in the biz. Promoters all over the city know my dedication. You know, *this*"—she encircled her face and body with a sweeping gesture—"takes endless hours to put together each day! But I have it down to a science. You know, on DivaLorraine.com—"

"That's quite all right, Ms. Manchester," Brad said with a sigh. "I'd like to move on, if I may, to the charity gala itself. You were on the committee for this gala from its first meeting, correct?"

"That is correct, yes."

"And do you remember Jacques Mercier being part of that meeting?"

"Oh, yes I do. I had a bad feeling about him from the beginning."

"Did you? Why so?"

"Oh, I don't know, Mr. Brad—but a woman's intuition is never wrong. You know, years back, when my friend Pamela Anderson first started dating that Rick Salomon, I said to her—"

"Did you tell Leigh White about your suspicions?" Brad cut in again.

"Well, I asked about him, yes. She told me she'd looked into him, and he was squeaky-clean, so I forgot about it."

"I see," Brad said. "And on the night of the auction—do you remember seeing Mr. Mercier then?"

"No, not at all," the Diva said. "But I was *so* busy, Mr. Brad; I'm sure I could easily have missed him. You know I was working the red carpet *and* helping with the stage auction, and posing, of course—everyone always wants their picture taken with me. I'm a big 'get' for the press, that way. Anyway, it was stressful going so quickly from one to the other, but I knew Leigh needed me—just having me on that stage makes the money move, honey!"

"I'm sure that's true," Brad said. "What about at the after-party?

Did you see Mr. Mercier there?"

"Oh, no; but again, I was *working,* darling. A woman's work is never done. Besides, that was a *fabulous* after-party—no place for a sleazebag like him! Like I said, I knew about him from the beginning. And Mr. Brad, you know what else? I knew those paintings were fake the moment I saw them all in court earlier today!"

"I see," Brad sighed, returning to the defense table. "Well, as helpful as your intuition has been today, Ms. Manchester—"

"Oh, no, darling, it wasn't intuition this time," Lorraine said decisively. "This time it was simpler than that; I recognized one of the paintings at the auction."

Brad almost fell over his chair. The judge, the prosecution, and the whole courtroom leaned in.

"What—what was that, Ms. Manchester?" Brad asked.

"I'd seen one of those paintings before," Lorraine said, enjoying the attention. "Though it was different when I saw it."

"How do you mean, *different?*"

"It wasn't finished yet."

A gasp arose in the courtroom. The judge's eyebrows seemed to raise up to the top of his head.

"Ms. Manchester," Brad said, trying to keep his voice steady while his heart beat triple-time in his chest, "let me make sure I understand you. Are you saying you saw one of the forged paintings that Jacques Mercier brought in to Leigh White's auction—which *he* passed off as original artworks—while it was in the process of being forged?"

"You heard it from these hot-pink lips, Mr. Brad."

"Where did you see it?"

"At the home studio of the artist who was painting it, Mr. Arturo Veraz."

"Arturo Veraz?" Brad asked to confirm for his team, who were already searching the Internet for an image.

"That's right."

"And how did you come to be there, Ms. Manchester?"

"Well, Mr. Brad, you know I've always had an eye for art. I met Mr. Veraz some time ago, and thought I should commission him for a portrait of the most glamorous subject I could think of, the Diva Miss Lorraine Manchester herself! Well, I paid the man (and then some, honey, you can believe that), and next thing, he goes off to Spain or France or somewhere, and I'm left without my painting. Well, the Diva didn't like that at *all;* so when I heard he was back in town, I popped around to his place, you know, just to check on how it was coming along. And what do you think I saw there, but all kinds of paintings—and not a *one* of Miss Lorraine! Oh, honey, I was *heated.* He hadn't done anything, and he said he couldn't until April!"

"April!" Brad repeated. "After the gala?"

"Objection," said the bulldog, looking a little uncomfortable. "Counsel is testifying."

"Sustained," said the judge. "Go on, Mr. White."

"All right," Brad said, his mind racing. He looked over at the prosecutors, who were sitting very still.

One of Brad's team rose and handed him an iPad with a Facebook photo of a man on-screen.

"Ms. Manchester," Brad said, holding out the device for the Diva to see, "is this Arturo Veraz, the artist of whom you've been telling us?"

"Yes, Mr. Brad," said Lorraine. "That's definitely him."

Brad showed the image to the judge. "Your Honor, I'd like to submit a printout of this picture to the court as evidence in connection with Mr. Westbrook's testimony, pending the arrival of this new potential witness."

"You may," said Judge Tarlow. "For now, the present witness's recognition of Mr. Veraz is noted. You may proceed with your questioning, Mr. White."

"Thank you, Your Honor." Brad turned back to the Diva.

"Ms. Manchester, did this Mr. Veraz say why he couldn't do your painting until April?"

"He said he had to finish a big job for someone." The Diva waggled her head back and forth scornfully. "Imagine—the nerve of the man! Big job, ha! To put the Diva second to—"

"Did he say who the other person was?"

The Diva gave her enormous wig a haughty toss. "Doesn't matter—next to Miss Lorraine, they're nobody!"

The courtroom laughed.

"But did he *say* who it was?" Brad pressed her.

"No, and I didn't ask, either," the Diva sniffed.

"But you recognized one of the paintings later, at the auction?"

"Yes—an ugly little thing, with red and pink blobs for flowers!"

"And you're sure it was the one you saw in Mr. Veraz's studio?"

"Oh, absolutely, Mr. Brad."

"So you saw it once in Mr. Veraz's studio, unfinished; and again, finished, when it was being sold at Mrs. White's gala auction?"

"That's right," the Diva said. "And I did a double-take when I saw it, too."

Brad barely avoided doing one himself. "Ms. Manchester," he said, "why didn't you bring this up earlier?"

"I thought my friend had just gotten a piece into Leigh's auction somehow," the Diva said. "I didn't realize it was supposed to be by someone else until Mr. Prosecutor there showed it to us in court."

Mr. Silvers' eyes went wide. "So," Brad said, smiling, "when you saw it at the auction, you'd just thought your friend had happened to have gotten a painting up there, alongside works by Picasso and Mondrian?"

"Why not? He's painting *me*, isn't he?" said the Diva proudly.

"I told you, I have an eye for these things, Mr. Brad. I know a great artist when I see one. Besides, it's not unusual for the charity to auction local artists' work."

"Thank you, Ms. Manchester," Brad said earnestly. *Better quit while I'm ahead with this one,* he thought, and turned to the judge on his way back to the table. "No further questions, Your Honor."

***

"The prosecution may proceed with questioning," said the judge.

The female prosecutor, Ms. Defoe, rose to question the Diva, and the men on the jury stared outright. Ms. Defoe was already a beautiful woman, and next to the over-the-top drag queen, she looked as slender and elegant as a supermodel.

"*Mr.* Westbrook," she began, launching the masculine title at him like a rocket, "it sounds like a rather complicated life you lead."

"Don't you know it, Mrs. Prosecutor," Lorraine said, to light laughter from the audience. "Day in, day out—sometimes even *I* wonder how I do it."

"I'm sure you do! All this promotion, emceeing, hostessing—I assume it usually takes place at nightclubs?"

"The *best* nightclubs," Lorraine corrected her.

"Of course," said Ms. Defoe. "And when you aren't *working* at these nightclubs, what are you doing there?"

"Oh, I'm *always* working, darling—working, or working *it.* "

"Late nights?"

"No later than four or five a.m., most times."

"That must be very difficult to keep up."

"Only the strong, darling."

"I see." Ms. Defoe's expression became hard. "Mr. Westbrook, do you use cocaine?"

"Objection," Brad called. "The question is inflammatory and irrelevant."

"Overruled," said the judge. "Mr. Westbrook, please answer the question."

"Oh, I had been known to take a bump or two when the music was slow, years back, when I was much younger," the Diva said dismissively.

"So that is a yes."

"Yes, but I really prefer strong black espresso these days."

"And what time do you sleep until, Mr. Westbrook?"

"Oh, until the late morning, mostly; I also get a beauty nap in the afternoon. And I usually follow *that* up with a Sudden Youth facial, if you'd like to know that too, Mrs. Prosecutor." The Diva made a show of scrutinizing Ms. Defoe's face, adding, "I don't see any smile lines to speak of, but it'd do wonders for your browline."

The courtroom laughed again. Ms. Defoe smiled icily.

"Thank you, Mr. Westbrook; I'll remember that," she said. "Now another question about this interesting life of yours, if I may. I imagine you meet a lot of people out at these clubs every night; is that true?"

"Oh, thousands," said the Diva.

"Some of them famous, I would assume."

"Very many of them, darling."

"Is that so? Would you say you associate regularly with celebrities, Mr. Westbrook?"

One could practically see the Diva's eyes light up to be asked such a question in front of so many people. "Definitely, darling, without a doubt!" she said.

"How many celebrities would you say you know well?"

"Oh, too many to count," said Lorraine, rolling her eyes as if she were overwhelmed by the mere thought of it.

"Really! You really don't think you could give a number, even as a guess?"

"No way, honey—I'm sure I would leave someone out, and we can't have that on camera!" The audience laughed and the Diva, encouraged, went on. "This is what my life is like, honey; this is what the Diva deals with on the daily. Give a number? Ha! I can't even keep some of these people straight when I see them."

"I was wondering about that," said Ms. Defoe coolly. "Even celebrities?"

"Oh, *especially* celebrities!" Lorraine scoffed. "When you know as many of them as I do, honey, trust me—they start to blur together."

"Well, then, I imagine regular people haven't got much of a chance," said Ms. Defoe.

Realizing her mistake, the Diva backpedaled. "I don't know about that, Mrs. Prosecutor," she said hastily. "Remember, for me, regular people are the exception."

Ms. Defoe ignored her and went on.

"So let me get this all straight, Mr. Westbrook," she said. "You take drugs, you sleep erratically, and you meet so many people, you have a hard time keeping them straight. This doesn't sound like a set of qualities conducive to clear recognition."

The Diva smiled. "What can I say, darling? I'm full of surprises."

"So we have seen," said the prosecutor. "But in light of what you've just said, it seems to bear asking again: are you *quite* sure the painting you saw in this Mr."—she looked at her notes—"Veraz's studio was the same one at Mrs. White's auction?"

"Oh, yes, Mrs. Prosecutor—as sure as I am fabulous."

"Well, you are undeniably sure of *that,*" said Ms. Defoe. "But isn't it true that you could be mistaken?"

"That I'm fabulous?" The Diva laughed hard. "Anyone can see that, honey."

"I will rephrase," said the prosecutor. "Isn't it true, Mr. Westbrook, that you could be mistaken as to the painting in Mr. Veraz's studio?"

The Diva leaned forward, her wig looming over the prosecutor's head. "No," she said simply.

Ms. Defoe was unfazed. "Some may disagree," she said, speaking out to the room; "but for the time being, let's assume the paintings were one and the same." She turned back to Lorraine. "Did you not say to Mr. White, five minutes ago, that at the time of your visit to Mr. Veraz's studio, you were unaware who the client was, for whom he was painting the work in question?"

"I couldn't say."

"You couldn't say?"

"I'm not sure *how* long ago it was that I said that," said the Diva sweetly.

The audience in the courtroom laughed. Even the judge smiled, in spite of himself.

"But you *were* unaware who the client was?" Ms. Defoe pursued.

"That is correct."

"Nor did you ever find out subsequently."

"No, I didn't."

"Mr. Veraz never mentioned the name of Jacques Mercier in connection with the painting?"

"No."

"So your conclusion that the painting was made at the request of Mr. Mercier, and not that of Leigh White, or both of them together, is entirely speculative."

"No, honey, it's based on facts."

"Which facts do you mean, Mr. Westbrook?"

The Diva looked down on Ms. Defoe with a withering smirk. "The fact that Leigh is an honest babe," she said, "and the fact that Jacques is a lying sleazebag."

The audience in the courtroom erupted in laughter. Leigh felt tears coming to her eyes as she silently laughed along with them.

"Order, please! Order in the courtroom!" Judge Tarlow boomed.

Ms. Defoe returned to her table as the room quieted again. "I don't believe we need any further questioning, Your Honor."

"Thank you, Ms. Manchester; you are free to go," the judge said.

"Well, thank you, Judge." The Diva stood up delicately, and carefully extracted herself from the stand. "It's been real, and it's been fun—can't say it's been real fun—but what's a girl to do? Now if you'll excuse me, Instagram and Twitter await; I've got followers to make happy. 'Bye, darlings!" She strutted back out of the courtroom, fanning herself and throwing kisses to the jury box as the audience lapsed back into laughter.

As she pranced out of the courtroom and out to the front steps, the audience inside could hear her loud voice—proclaiming, by turns, the innocence of Leigh White and the originality of the products available on DivaLorraine.com—*especially,* darling, the hot-pink lip gloss.

CHAPTER 32

DIXIE TAKES A STAND

> Don't forget!!! If you don't say it, I will.

—Lauren

Outside the courtroom, the day's remaining witnesses sat silently awaiting their turns to testify. Mitchell and Scarlett sat resolutely ignoring one another. Billie Parker tapped his foot impatiently, waiting for his wife to arrive. Dixie sat nearest the door, bored and anxious, and occasionally put her ear to the door to see if she could catch any of the testimony.

"Oh, this is *torture,*" she whispered to Billie. "How much longer do you think we're going to have to wait out here—how d'you call it—semestered like this? Ah haven't kept from talkin' for this long, since Ah don't know when!"

"I don't know," Billie whispered back, "but I think you're next. Brad told me you would go before the rest of us."

"Please, no talking during the trial," said an officer standing near them.

Dixie sat back miserably. It was bad enough that Lauren was pressuring her into telling the truth about that Cannellini fella, and Howard's tapes—she'd texted again to remind her—but no *talking* in the meantime? That was just cruel and unusual. *And* her Chardonnay buzz was starting to wear off from lunch.

Gawd, there were so many reporters and cameras everywhere! The knot formed in her stomach again when she thought of what she had agreed to say; but then, Lauren was probably right. Howard had never been much of a news watcher, and besides, he was at his conference. The odds of him tuning in to Court TV while she was on the stand were beyond slim; and nobody was likely to report on the details of witness testimonies otherwise. Still, all this waiting was murder!

The courtroom door opened, and one of Brad's team emerged, scribbling notes on a pad. Dixie tottered to her feet to accost him.

"Oh—excuse me, Ah'm Dixie, one of yer witnesses," she told the young man. "Um, would you mind tellin' me if Ah'm goin' in to testify soon?"

"They're in a short recess now," he said, "but you'll be in the next group. There's just one other person ahead of you. Excuse me," he added, extracting himself before she could ask him who the other person was.

"Sheeesh," she said, sinking back into her chair and putting her head in her hands. If she'd known it was going to be this long, she'd'd've gotten in a solo round of Spanx Time with Diamond Jim beforehand! That probably would've relaxed her a bit.

She was just weighing the possibility of slipping out for another glass of Chardonnay at the diner across the street, when she heard steps in the hallway, and a familiar voice.

"Dixie!" the voice said; and Dixie looked up.

It is often said, by people who have undergone some kind of

terrible trauma, that in the moment that the shark attacks, or one's parachute doesn't open, or the airplane takes a sudden turn for the downwards, one experiences a sort of disconnection with oneself. One sees one's whole life flash before one's eyes, and everything looks as though it is seen distantly, through someone else's point of view.

That, in a nutshell, is what happened now to Dixie, at the moment she looked up. Not before then, exactly; for in the split second before that moment, there had been a distinct flash of hope in her mind, that the owner of the voice would turn out to be someone other than the person she thought it was—a clever impersonator, perhaps. But it had turned out to be *exactly* the person she'd thought it was; and somewhere between the memories of her first glass of wine and her first kiss flashing before her eyes, his hand on her shoulder brought her back down to earth.

"How—Howard!" she managed.

"Hello, sweetie," Howard said gently, sitting down in the chair next to hers and kissing her.

"What—what on earth are *yew* doin' here?"

"The conference was called off early, so I came back to testify," he explained. "Brad deposed me over the phone yesterday."

Dixie felt as though her brain were melting. "Testify? Does that mean *yew're* the one goin' before me?"

"I suppose so—I'm taking the stand next."

"Huh," she said, the feeling slowly draining out of her.

"Guess Brad wanted us to go up one after another."

"Ahah."

"Lucky thing I made it here on time, huh?"

"Lucky, yeah."

"I haven't got much to say about the whole thing, but Brad says anything helps."

"Uh-huh."

"Hey, listen," he said. "I was thinking, if you're going up after me, I'll just wait in the courtroom while you testify, and we'll go home together afterward. How's that sound?"

Dixie looked at him in slowly dawning horror.

"Yew'll wait—"

"In the courtroom."

"The same one *Ah'm* in?"

"Yes, of course."

"While Ah—"

"While you testify."

Dixie's eyes went wide. This was a nightmare—it couldn't be happening!

"Oh, no, no, no," she mumbled, grasping through the fog for an excuse. "No, Ah mean—Danny—Danny's got my car anyway—Ah'll just have him wait with—"

"Oh, I actually just spoke with Danny outside," Howard said brightly. "I told him he could bring your car home, and take the rest of the day off."

"Well, isn't that kind of yew," Dixie said.

"After all," Howard added, "it isn't so often that we see each other in the daytime."

"No, that's true," Dixie said.

He looked at her with a mischievous smile, and leaned in to whisper. "You know, after seeing you on that stand, I have a feeling I'll be in quite a mood."

"Ah—Ah'm sure yew will," Dixie said to the floor.

"Howard Johnson?" said a clerk, approaching them.

"Yes, that's me," said Howard cheerily.

"We'll be resuming soon; please take your seat and wait to be called."

"Very good."

"Ah think Ah need to use the restroom," said Dixie.

"All right, darling," said Howard, kissing her again. "If I don't see you before I go in, I'll see you after your testimony. Wish me luck!"

"Oh, ah, sure." Dixie smiled back weakly as she rose. "Break a leg, honey."

***

Howard Johnson's testimony was short, but sweet. The entire court could see the relief on Brad's face as he finally found himself questioning a completely credible witness. The good doctor—friend and confidante to so many celebrities and powerful Miamians—answered every question like an expert. He spoke clearly and definitively, never departed from the point at hand, and managed to put things in remarkable perspective. Despite having spent many thousands of dollars at Leigh White's auction on a necklace for his wife and a forged print for himself, he insisted on her innocence, and related the history of their friendship in great detail. He described her dedication to her charity over the last decade, and dismissed as preposterous the notion that she would ever defraud her donors, many of whom had been friends for years.

After a lackluster cross-examination by Mr. Silvers, who didn't seem to want to risk being made a fool of by so unimpeachable a witness, Howard was dismissed and the clerk rose to announce the next witness.

"The defense calls Dixie Johnson to the stand!"

The side door opened, and Dixie poured through. It seemed she might have forgone the restroom for a visit to the diner across the street after all; she wavered visibly on her way to the stand, and had to place her steps very deliberately to get there in one piece. The bailiff caught hold of her arm to swear her in, at which point she steadied herself against the stand, put her right hand up, and before he could say anything further, said with a pained expression, "Yep."

Having been more or less properly sworn in, Dixie then flopped down in her seat with a loud "Phew!" that sent a laugh rippling through the courtroom. She smiled along with her audience for a moment, then, seeming to remember something, looked between her hands and the TV cameras with a comically worried expression until Brad approached the stand.

"Mrs. Johnson," he began, "how long have you known Leigh White?"

Dixie held her hands in front of her and counted on her fingers for a moment before giving up.

"Oh, years and years," she said. "My husband and Ah have been attenders at her gala since the beginning."

"So we've just heard," said Brad. "And would you say you and Mrs. White are good friends, outside the gala?"

"Of *koorse*, yew know that! We get together and gossip on the regular."

"What do you and Mrs. White gossip about, Mrs. Johnson?"

"Oh, this and that—yew know, what so-and-so was wearin' the other day, who's cheatin' on who, that sort of thing. Real House-wives–type stuff, mostly."

"I see," said Brad. "And did Jacques Mercier ever come up in your gossip?"

"Sure, a whole bunch."

"Oh? In connection with what?"

"Well, he—that is, Ah—"

There was a noise from the back of the courtroom. Dixie looked up just in time to see Howard closing the door behind him. *Oh, it's too soon anyway,* Dixie thought, and went on.

"Well, one of Leigh's other friends had a bug in her bonnet

about him runnin' off with that Sassy gal, so he came up that way a few times."

"Lauren Altamira, you mean."

"Yep, Lauren Altavista. She brought him round to lunch once, too—"

"You mean Mrs. White did?"

"No no—Lauren did. Ah think she was tryin' to impress Jacques. Not in a romantical way, see, but professionally—she's a realtor, like Sassy, and when Jacques started datin' Sassy, he stopped doin' business with *her.*"

"I see. So Lauren brought him to lunch to try and win back his business?"

"Ah guess so. But that Sassy gal showed up anyway, and snuck off with him before too long."

"When was this, Mrs. Johnson?"

"Oh, almost a year ago. It was pretty soon after last year's gala."

"And do you remember any of the conversation that took place before Ms. Davilon arrived? Did Mrs. White seem to know Mr. Mercier well?"

"No, not well," Dixie recalled. "He didn't seem to know anyone too well. He said he was new in town."

"Did he say anything about his art business?"

"Well, he talked a pretty big game. He said somethin' about sellin' to Jay and Bey—"

"To whom?"

Dixie closed one eye and scrutinized Brad through the other. "Now, Ah know yew lawyers are a hard-workin' bunch, but you ain't going to tell me you never heard of Jay-Z and Beyoncé."

"Ah," said Brad with an abashed smile, as the audience chuckled. "Right, of course. So Mr. Mercier claimed to have sold art to—to them?"

"Yeah."

"Did he seem to be trying to win over Mrs. White with such claims?"

"Objection, Your Honor," said Ms. Fischer.

"Sustained," said the judge. "No conclusions, Mr. White."

"He did seem to be, though," said Dixie.

"Ladies and gentlemen of the jury, please disregard that answer," said the judge. "Mr. White, you may proceed."

"Mrs. Johnson," Brad continued, "do you remember Mr. Mercier saying anything else during that lunch?"

"Not really," Dixie said. "Leigh and Lauren got up to use the restroom, and Jacques and that Sassy gal started pawin' all over each other. Ah had to get up too, just to keep from gettin' anything on me!"

The courtroom laughed.

"And when you came back?" Brad asked.

"They were gone by then."

"I see." Brad paused a moment. "You said a minute ago that Ms. Davilon 'snuck off' with Mr. Mercier. Did you believe at the time that she was actively trying to keep Mr. Mercier from the rest of you?"

"Um—" Dixie hedged. "Ah guess—Ah thought she was tryin' to get him away from Lauren, yeah."

"As a matter of professional rivalry?"

Dixie looked at her hands again. "Yeah, mostly," she muttered.

"I'm sorry?"

"Ah said—"

Dixie looked up, and her eyes met Lauren's in the audience. Lauren nodded urgently at her, as though to say, *Go ahead, say it!* Dixie faltered a moment before finishing.

"—Ah said, yes, that's all Ah thought it was."

Lauren's expression changed from insistent to furious. Dixie looked away.

Brad went on.

"Mrs. Johnson, you were on Mrs. White's last gala-planning committee, were you not?" he asked.

"Ah was, yes."

"And what was your role on that committee?"

"Leigh thought Ah would be able to bring in some celebrity guests."

"And why did she think that?"

"Well, my husband—associates with quite a few, in his line of work."

"As patients?"

Dixie caught Howard's eye in the audience. He looked distressingly cheerful to her. She looked down again.

"Patients, or former patients," she said hesitantly. "Some just as friends, these days."

"I see." Brad paced back and forth, then suddenly turned. "And did you ever meet anyone in that connection who knew Jacques Mercier, or had anything negative to say about him?"

"M—meet?" Dixie stammered, her heart pounding. "Personally, yew mean?"

Brad leaned in. "Yes, Mrs. Johnson."

"No—Ah mean, not personally—" Dixie began—and stopped short, a cold sweat breaking over her as she suddenly remembered what Lauren had said. The—what do you call it—the clinical junction had arrived! The moment of action! It was now or never!

She swallowed hard and took a deep breath. "But—"

"That's all right, Mrs. Johnson, that will be all," Brad sighed, walking back to the defense table. "No further questions, Your Honor."

CHAPTER 33

ADMISSION IMPOSSIBLE

> Car's at home like you said. Let me know when you need me again.

—Danny

Dixie sat thunderstruck.

No further questions? But she hadn't had a chance to say *anything!* She looked out at the audience to see Lauren shaking her head angrily. Oh, no, no… Didn't she see that Dixie had *meant* to say it? Surely she wouldn't…but Dixie knew by the look on her face that she would. The evidence was too important. But surely the only thing worse than having Howard find out about her indiscretions from her was having him find out from someone else—that would be a double betrayal on her part! He would never forgive *that*—but what could she do now?

Dixie was shaken out of her despair by the formidable sight of Mr. Silvers approaching the stand. It occurred to her then that she was still *at* the stand, and she looked around, confused. Was she supposed to leave it now? Was Mr. Silvers coming to escort her out? No—it didn't seem so. Then it hit her: he was going to *question* her. Her cross-examination! There was still time!

"Mr. Prosecutor, you may begin," said the judge.

At these words her buzz fell from her like a heavy cloak; and Dixie sat upright, ready to bravely speak forth the truth, and hold her tongue no longer.

"Thank you, Your Honor," said Mr. Silvers. "Mrs. Johnson—"

"Yes, Mr. Prosecutor," she said eagerly.

"—where were you just now, before you came into this courtroom?"

Dixie let out a breath of frustration. "Oh, now, what kind of a question is that?" she said.

"Please answer the question, Mrs. Johnson," said Judge Tarlow.

"Ah was out in the hallway, of course, with the other witnesses."

The audience laughed.

"You know that isn't what I mean, Mrs. Johnson," said Mr. Silvers. "Did you go out while you were waiting to be called up?"

"Well, yes, if yew must know," Dixie sniffed. "Ah went to the diner across the street. But what does that—"

"And how many alcoholic drinks did you have there, Mrs. Johnson?"

She looked shocked. "Just what are you incineratin', exactly?"

"Please, just answer the question."

"One or two."

"Which was it? One, or two?"

"Oh, Ah don't remember. What difference—"

"You don't *remember*, Mrs. Johnson? You seemed perfectly able just now to remember the ins and outs of a conversation you had almost a year ago with Mr. Mercier! What's happened to that memory of yours?"

"They must've made them one or two drinks stronger than Ah thought," Dixie snapped back. "But," she went on, as the courtroom burst into laughter, "that's not important anyway. Why don't yew ask me—"

"On the contrary, Mrs. Johnson," interjected the prosecutor. "I'd say it's very important indeed. Are you in the habit of drinking excessively?"

"Yew mean, one after another? How in hell else am Ah supposed to do it?"

"I mean *to* excess, Mrs. Johnson."

Dixie scoffed. "Well, if *two* is excess, then yes, Ah suppose Ah *am* in that habit."

"And what about passing out?"

"What about it?"

"Do you pass out often, from drinking?"

"Oh *Gawd,* no," Dixie laughed. "What sort of a lightweight would Ah be? That only happens once a week, twice tops."

The courtroom laughed louder still.

"Once a week, twice tops," the prosecutor repeated loudly, smiling at the jury. "I wonder if that sounds like credibility to you, Mrs. Johnson?"

"There ain't nothin' incredible about it," said Dixie. "If yew want to hear somethin' incredible—"

"Perhaps there isn't," interrupted the prosecutor, "but it all sounds like a very uncertain frame of mind, from which to accuse Mr. Mercier of any criminal behavior that you don't equally ascribe to Mrs. White."

"Well—" Dixie began.

"Objection!" cried Ms. Fischer. "The witness has made no such accusation."

"Well—" Dixie began again.

"Sustained," said the judge. "Please keep it direct, Mr. Silvers."

"Very well," said Mr. Silvers, turning back to her with an unctuous smile, "though I am beginning to doubt, Mrs. Johnson, whether *any* of what you've said can be taken but with a grain of salt. You've said, for instance, that you were on Mrs. White's gala committee. Do you remember who was present at the first meeting of that committee?"

"No," Dixie admitted.

"Interesting—another fault in your memory, Mrs. Johnson?"

"No, there wasn't no way Ah *could've* remembered that," Dixie said indignantly. "Ah wasn't there."

"Oh, you weren't *there!* And where were you for that first meeting, Mrs. Johnson?"

Dixie hesitated a moment. "Ah was at home."

"Well!" laughed the prosecutor triumphantly. "This sounds like quite an inside position you had on Mrs. White's committee."

"Ah *was* on the committee!" Dixie cried. "Ah just couldn't make it that day, is all. Now—"

"Are you quite sure?" smirked Mr. Silvers.

Dixie stared at him in fury. The nerve of the man, to question her like this—and when she had such important things to say! "Yes, Ah'm *sure,*" she said. "Now, if yew'll just let me—"

"You say Leigh White wanted you on the committee for your celebrity connections," Mr. Silvers interrupted, strolling leisurely past the jury. "Did you actually deliver any such connections, Mrs. Johnson?"

"Yes—yes, Ah did."

"Such as—?"

Dixie bristled. "Ah'll have yew know Ah brought Flo Rida to that gala, and a bunch of others, too!"

"I'm sure you did," said the prosecutor with infuriating condescension. "And how did you say you managed to make those connections?"

"Through my husband," Dixie said through gritted teeth.

"Your husband, the psychiatrist?" said Mr. Silvers. "Surely none of these were his *confidential* clients."

"No, of *koorse* not," said Dixie quickly, seeing her chance, "but Ah—"

"Those would be the ones on the *inside,*" suggested Mr. Silvers.

"Ah'm plenty on the inside!" said Dixie. "In fact—"

"I think we can all see how the case actually lies, Mrs. Johnson," interrupted Mr. Silvers again, turning a cruel eye in her direction. "You are the wife of a prominent doctor; you spend a lot of your time intoxicated, as you are now—"

"Objection!" Brad cried, as Dixie's face turned bright red. "He's badgering the witness, Your Honor."

"I'm willing to overrule that, for a hostile witness," said the judge. "Continue, Mr. Silvers."

"As I was saying, Mrs. Johnson," said the prosecutor coldly, "you know a few celebrities, perhaps, through your husband, but not in any level of depth—just enough, it seems, to gossip about them with your friends. And one of the friends with whom you gossip about such *trivial* matters—none of which seem to pertain to the case at hand—is Leigh White."

Dixie's mouth gaped open, but no sound came out.

"Idle hands do the devil's work, Mrs. Johnson—as does a bored housewife. And you are very used to having your idle gossip heeded. But a courtroom is no place for gossip; and a trial is no place for someone on the *outside* to make claims for guilt or innocence."

The courtroom had gone dead silent. Mr. Silvers turned his back on Dixie, who had now turned a deadly pale, and went on. "One might be tempted to wonder if you were even as close with

Mrs. White as you've suggested, Mrs. Johnson. I, for one, have a—"

"Ross Blackbird likes to fuck fat girls!" Dixie exploded.

The courtroom sat in shocked silence. All that could be heard was the sound of Dixie's breathing as she struggled to regain composure.

"What—what was that, Mrs. Johnson?" asked the prosecutor finally.

"Oh, yeah, *now* you're listenin'," Dixie said. "Ah think you heard me just fine, Mr. Prosecutor. This whole town's like that—all gossip! Nobody has a minute for anyone, but as soon as someone dishes some dirt, everyone's all ears! Well, there's some dirt for you, Mr. Prosecutor—he's one of my husband's patients, yew know. The *confidential* kind."

"What are you—what exactly are you saying, Mrs. Johnson?" Mr. Silvers asked in perplexity.

"Ah'm sayin' Ah know more than yew think, because"—she gulped in the silence—"because, Gawd help me, Ah've listened to some of my husband's session tapes!"

There was a general gasp in the courtroom as Dixie looked out into the audience and found Howard's shocked face.

"Ah'm sorry, darlin', Ah just couldn't stop myself," she said to him, wringing her hands, "and Ah hate myself for it, but Ah had to tell it like it is today, because mah friend's life is on the line. Ah've heard all kinds of things—about all kinds of people! And Mr. Prosecutor"—she turned back to the stunned Mr. Silvers and pointed a shaking finger at him—"yew oughta know, and yew too, jury people, that on one of them tapes Ah heard a man talkin' up a lot of shade about Jacques and his girlfriend Sassy, and he was a man with a criminal past, too, Mr. Cavatelli or somebody, sayin' Jacques was in over his head with that one; and Ah can say more about it, but y'all are going to have to *listen* to me!"

"All right, all right—one thing at a time, here, Mrs. Johnson," said the judge, trying to restore quiet to the courtroom. "For now, I'd like to call an emergency conference with the entire counsel, please."

Brad, Mr. Silvers and Ms. Fischer approached the bench, and they conferred for a few tense minutes while the courtroom murmured and Dixie sat with her head down, mortified.

The conference broke up, and the judge spoke.

"Given that Mrs. Johnson's latest information was not included in her deposition, and is of a confidential nature not suited to open court, we have elected to strike from the record the most recent portion of her testimony under cross-examination," he said. "She will be allowed to provide this information to myself, and all three head counsels, in a private deposition by telephone at the end of today's proceedings, and we will consider whether what she has to say is of sufficient relevance to be admitted as evidence in our final advisements. For now, Mrs. Johnson," he added to Dixie, who looked thoroughly at sea, "the prosecution has no further questions for you. You are free to go, pending our call later this evening."

"Free to—to go?" Dixie asked, stunned. "Yew mean all that was for *nothin'?*"

"That remains to be seen, Mrs. Johnson," said the judge. "For now, however, that will be all. Mr. White, please prepare for your next witness."

Dixie stepped down and made her way out the side door in a haze, not quite sure what had just happened. The courtroom hubbub ceased abruptly as the door shut behind her. How could that have gone so badly? But it had, it *had!*

She heard footsteps coming toward her down the hall. Looking up dejectedly, she saw Howard running toward her. Her heart sank.

"Howard, Ah'm so sorry," she began, the tears already beginning to flow. "Ah know yew'll never forgive—"

"Darling, it's all right," Howard said, wrapping his arms around her tenderly. "It's over now. Are you okay?"

"Am *Ah* okay?" Dixie asked incredulously. "After all that— yew—" A flood of guilt washed over her as she looked up into her husband's face.

To her astonishment, she found only warmth and concern there.

"You seemed so upset," Howard said. "I couldn't stand to see you that way, dear."

Dixie struggled with disbelief. "Yew—yew aren't angry?"

"Of course not," he said with a smile. "You said it yourself: your friend's life was on the line. I would have brought up that tape myself, if I'd remembered it—it simply hadn't occurred to me."

"But—but the others—" she faltered.

"Dixie," he said gently, taking hold of her shoulders, "you're my wife, and I married you for who you are. Of course I want things to be completely open between us; but if they aren't, you aren't the only one to blame! We're partners, darling, and we'll get through it as partners."

Dixie felt a weight drop from her that she hadn't known existed. Leaning into him, she felt an incredible gratitude for her husband. How had she forgotten this man—the person he *really* was?

"Howard, Ah just—Ah feel like such a fool," she trailed off.

"You did the right thing. And you didn't do anyone any harm." He chuckled. "Ross tells everyone about his conquests. You hardly revealed anything he wouldn't be happy to reveal himself. If what you said gets around, believe me, no one will be happier about it than him."

Dixie smiled tearfully up at him. Then a serious look crossed her face.

"Ah'll never do it again, Howard, on my life," she said. "Never."

"I trust you, darling. I'll keep the tapes at my office downtown, if you think it'll be tempting; but I saw how upset you were, and I trust you." He smiled to himself. "And you know, truth be told, it'd be nice to have someone to talk to about some of these things—naming no names, of course."

"Oh, Howard, Ah want to be that for yew! Ah feel Ah've been so selfish, for so long."

"Not at all, darling; and if something's making you feel that way, it's never too late to change. Today the Johnsons make a new start!"

"Cheers to that," Dixie smiled.

"Now, dear," Howard said, grabbing his coat from the chair, "let's get on our way home, shall we?"

"Yes, please," Dixie said. Home had never sounded so good to her.

"Great; I'll drive. I know I'm no Danny, but—"

"Oh, thank Gawd for that!" cried Dixie, and she meant it.

CHAPTER 34

APPEARANCES AND REAPPEARANCES

> God, SO boring!!! Think I got some ok exposure out of it tho. See u at home.

—Katie

After such startling testimonies, the next few witnesses were bound to be a bit less remarkable. True, each dwelled on their undying love and adoration for Leigh and her charity—if only for as long as it took to get to a suitable opportunity for self-promotion—but most of them just…hadn't witnessed as much.

Mitchell and Scarlett each used the gala as a starting point for long discourses on the celebrities they'd brought there as guests over the years, and the careers they'd helped launch or reignite that way. They both name-dropped the various clubs they promoted for, and managed to slip in their contact information for anyone in Court TV-land who might be looking for a VIP reservation in Miami sometime soon. True to their main interest, they also spent a disproportionate amount of time eyeing two young female jurors. Much to their chagrin, it was impossible to tell which of them (if either) the jurors favored.

Katie Parker entered the courtroom with an entourage of two nannies and a number of stylists. Handing off Little Billie ostentatiously to one of the nannies, she explained how she'd rescued the boy—now dressed in a miniature custom cut of one of his father's suits—from dire circumstances abroad, not long after last year's gala. She then took the stand and managed a truly astonishing number of references to her inclusion in the *Ocean View* article and her write-up in *Haute Living* magazine, the brands of makeup she endorsed, and the various pieces of jewelry she was wearing right now. Among the latter she wore a number of bracelets on one wrist, which clanged together throughout her testimony. To many in the room this distraction seemed accidental—until she began to separate the bracelets slowly on-camera while explaining that they were of her own design, and would be featured on her up-and-coming ShopTV appearance. Leigh White was hardly her favorite person these days—a fact which, she assured the court, had nothing to do with Mrs. White's inexplicable and hurtful rejection of her jewelry for the gala—but she was convinced that the woman was innocent nonetheless. She'd even considered tapping Leigh for the reality show she'd just signed a contract for, but she just didn't think it'd work now. Her contract had included *travel*, after all—and she wouldn't want to pull Leigh out of the Miami that loved her, for all those trips to Beverly Hills and Aspen that she was sure she had coming up. Her star was rising!

Her husband Billie took the stand last. He, too, was sure of Leigh's innocence, and could vouch for her ignorance of Jacques's true intentions. His primary connection to Leigh's gala, he candidly admitted, was through his brand, which had donated a number of suits to the charity auction over the years—one of which designs, yes, he happened to be wearing today. A number of major department stores already carried his designs—he artfully managed to mention Neiman Marcus and Bergdorf, among them—but the exposure he'd gotten from his partnership with the charity was indispensable. As a result he'd been able to dress a number of major celebrities in his couture wear, including Mario Lopez, Ross Mathews—here Brad cut him short. By now the self-promoting agendas of his witnesses had Brad pretty much on his last nerve.

Through all this, the press had a field day. Each witness was "kind" enough to give interviews on their way in and out of the courtroom, name-dropping and product-propping all the way, and Middle America was on the edge of its seat. Would the socialite philanthropist supermom and her big-shot lawyer husband be able to fight their way clear, or go down in flames?

Once Billie's testimony had wrapped up, Leigh excused herself to the restroom and Brad called Jeffrey over.

"Hey Jeffrey, do me a favor and drive Leigh home, will you?" he said. "I'm going to be here for a bit going over strategy with my team, and I know it's already been a long day for her."

"No problem," said Jeffrey. "How're you doing with all this?"

"So far, so good, I think," Brad said, managing a smile. "Tomorrow's really going to be the deciding day, but we'll definitely have a lot more to work with than we had this morning."

"That's good. I imagine Leigh will want company, so maybe I'll see you later?"

"All right, Jeffrey. Thanks so much, for everything. You did a great job today."

"Just telling it how it is, Mr. White!" Jeffrey said, with a mock salute.

Once the Whites had had a chance to say goodbye and Jeffrey

and Leigh had left, Brad went over to the defense's temporary office, where his team was waiting for him.

"All right," he said with a sigh. "Before I meet with Dixie Johnson, I wanted to see if you guys were already on this Arturo Veraz guy. What have we got on him?"

"We've found information on where he lives, and have contact info," said Katherine, "but so far we haven't been able to get hold of him."

"Damn!" Brad said, looking at the photo they'd printed out. "What I wouldn't give to have *that* guy on the stand. Ah well, hopefully Brandon's story will count for something with the jury anyway. How about Sassy Davilon? She's starting to look pretty useful after all."

"Another blank—nowhere to be found."

"All right, well, keep trying. Any ideas as to why Jacques's lawyer hasn't come up with a single witness yet?"

"We'd all been wondering that," said another young lawyer. "All we can think of is that they're hoping the prosecution can keep Leigh in the hot seat, and let us play our hand out."

"We've been pulling for them to recognize Leigh's innocence this whole time," said Brad, "but we need to find a way to pin it solidly on Jacques, too. Keep trying with this Veraz guy, and hopefully Dixie will have something we can use."

He was reaching for the door to go when he heard a soft knock from the other side. Opening the door, he found himself face-to-face with a man whose pleasant, calm smile seemed to cover up a lifetime of hard experience.

"Can I help you?" Brad asked.

"I think I may be able to help *you*, Mr. White," the man said. "My name's Steve Senkew—I'm a private investigator."

"Oh, thanks, but we've already—"

"I'm not offering my services, Mr. White," Steve said. "Not in that way, anyhow. I'm already working for one of your witnesses— Billie Parker—on some personal matters I came in today to meet with him, but showed up early and caught most of your other witnesses beforehand."

"All right," Brad said, not sure where this was going.

"I was particularly interested by the testimony of Mr. Brandon Westbrook—the Diva Ms. Lorraine Manchester, as he asked you to call him."

"You've got a good memory," Brad said.

"Rather," Steve smiled. "Mr. Westbrook brought up a Mr. Arturo Veraz during his testimony, and confirmed his picture when you showed it to him—do you happen to have that picture handy now?"

"Sure," Brad said, handing it over to him. "It was just the clearest image my team was able to find online."

"Well, that's him, all right," Steve said after a moment's glance at the photo.

Brad's eyes shot open in surprise. "Do you mean you know him? Can you help us find him?"

"I think I can do you one better than that. Look, I understand you've got to talk to that Johnson woman now," he added, "but I have time to stick around for a bit, if you can get the go-ahead to depose me for tomorrow."

"Depose you! Why, what's your connection to all this?"

Steve smiled again.

"An entirely accidental one, but I imagine you'll want to hear about it, Mr. White," he said. "Let's just say Mr. Veraz isn't the only stranger I've happened to recognize today."

CHAPTER 35

DAY TWO, DECADENT TRIAL OF THE DECADE

> You've got this. Just tell them the truth! That's all you can do.

—Francisco

Leigh arrived at court the next day feeling exhausted and on-edge. She'd tried to relax with a long bath and a massage the night before, but had made the highly questionable decision to watch TV afterward while she waited for Brad to come home, and it had sent her through a roller-coaster of emotions.

It seemed every station was airing footage about her trial, and most of them had "exclusive" press interviews with her friends to show, too. Leigh had watched them one after another with a strange mixture of amusement and horror. Did no one have any shame? Was Katie really *still* shilling those hideous bracelets of hers and talking about becoming a reality TV star? How had Billie managed to get on *Nancy Grace* already—and spend *that* much time talking about his new women's line? Had Dixie actually mentioned Weight

Watchers and girdles on her way out? And did all those wigs Lorraine had sewn together really look like *that* in the daylight? It was a wonder the bailiff had let her into court in that thing, she'd thought, laughing hysterically in the tub; it looked like raccoons might come out of it at any moment.

Yet there was an ugly thought beneath the ridiculousness of the whole thing. Were these really her friends, living it up on TV while she faced the possibility of years in prison? Dixie had given interviews after her testimony, most of which she spent talking about her struggle to lose weight; and Leigh had actually seen the Diva on the courthouse steps, passing out business cards with little blonde tassels attached to promote her line of wigs! Even Lauren was doing interviews about Miami real-estate investment versus art investment as a long-term strategy. Did these people really care what happened to her at all? Surely they did, in some way; they'd all spoken out on behalf of her innocence. But there was so much self-serving there, and so little tangible gain for her case!

To make matters worse, when Brad had finally come home he'd been obviously excited but very tight-lipped; he was willing to say there had been new developments, but like a kid afraid to jinx himself, refused to say much about what they were. All he'd done was tell her not to worry, kiss her goodnight, and fall instantly and unceremoniously to sleep, leaving her to toss and turn much of the night through. She couldn't blame him, of course—he'd been working so hard, and had so much to keep straight in his mind—but it hadn't helped her relax.

Now, back in her seat at the defense table, Leigh wondered what her husband could have up his sleeve. The other lawyers looked grim, as though hyper-conscious of the fight the day would hold for them; but Brad seemed somehow more energetic, more confident, than he had the day before. What was he planning?

Once everyone had settled in and the judge had addressed the jury and counselors on the proceedings of the day, the clerk stood to announce Brad's first witness of the day.

"The defense calls Lauren Altamira to the stand!"

Lauren looked very impressive as she entered the courtroom. Sleek and elegant in an all-business Valentino ensemble and minimal jewelry, she looked as though she were on her way to a power lunch somewhere. Her expression was the same self-possessed look she wore when she was talking a client up to a big sale. Seeing her, Leigh immediately felt reassured.

Once Lauren had been sworn in, Brad lost no time in approaching the stand.

"Mrs. Altamira," he began, "can you state for the court what it is you do for a living?"

"I'm one of the top realtors, here in Miami," she said proudly.

"What sorts of property do you represent?"

"Generally high-end residential and corporate spaces; a few premium condominiums and some downtown commercial properties."

"I would imagine these properties of yours are fairly expensive?"

"Yes, you could say that; though my clients generally don't," she said. "With *my* connections, I'm able to get a lot of breaks that other realtors aren't."

"I see." Brad waited a moment before continuing. "How long have you known Jacques Mercier, Mrs. Altamira?"

"Since he arrived in Miami, a little over a year and a half ago," she said.

"And how were you first acquainted?"

"He came on as a prospective real-estate client of mine, in the market for one of the condominiums I mentioned."

"A fairly high-end property, would you say?"

"Rather, yes."

"So he must have had quite a line of credit to secure your attention."

"No, actually, it was our understanding that he would be able to pay in cash."

"But you ran credit reports on him, I assume."

"I did. His credit ratings were very good; but since we never transacted any business, I was never able to put his claims to the test."

"Do you mean to suggest that you had some question of them, Mrs. Altamira?"

"Not in the beginning; but since then, yes."

"So your opinion of Mr. Mercier has changed since you were first acquainted with him."

"Oh, absolutely. I encouraged Leigh to work with him for a long time."

"Had he approached her before that, with the intention of working with her?"

"Yes, definitely."

"And had she known him before he had approached her in that way?"

"No, definitely not. Not many people in Miami knew him before that."

"Was your change of mind about Mr. Mercier due to anything in particular, aside from the proceedings directly involved in this trial so far?"

"Yes," Lauren said.

"And what was that?"

"A few months ago, I caught surveillance-camera footage of my maid speaking with another maid about a few Mexican men one of them had seen around town, who turned out to be associates of Jacques's."

"Allow me to stop you a moment, Mrs. Altamira," Brad said. "How was it established that they were Mr. Mercier's associates?"

"Well, my maid said so, for one," Lauren said carefully, "but it corroborated something my friend Dixie Johnson had already told me—she'd seen them all together at a party soon after Leigh's gala last year, and her driver Danny had spent time with them all there."

"So independently of what Dixie told you about Jacques and these Mexicans, your maid and this other maid spoke on a surveillance camera about the same association," Brad reiterated.

"That's right."

"Was that all they said about the matter?"

"Not at all," Lauren said. "My maid, Jacinda, recognized the men from back home in Mexico, as operatives of the Garcia family."

There were a few isolated gasps in the courtroom. Leigh looked out into the audience to where Stan Corinne was sitting. He seemed to be typing something very enthusiastically on his phone.

"And who are the Garcia family, for those of us who are unacquainted with the name?" Brad asked.

"They're a famous crime syndicate in Mexico."

"And how do you know this, Mrs. Altamira?" Brad asked, over the commotion Lauren's answer had spread through the courtroom.

"My husband and I are from Mexico, originally."

"Understood." Brad paced in front of the stand. "So just to repeat: Dixie Johnson had told you before of having seen Jacques Mercier associating with the same Mexican men you later heard your maid speaking about, as not only connected with Jacques Mercier, but with a known crime syndicate in Mexico?"

"That's correct, yes."

"And was Mrs. White, to your knowledge, aware of any of this when she met, and agreed to work with, Mr. Mercier?"

"Absolutely not."

"Your Honor, I don't believe I have any further questions for Mrs. Altamira," Brad said; and giving a curt nod to Lauren, he sat.

***

The courtroom was reeling as the prosecutor approached the stand. Many of the audience had already begun to suspect Jacques from the other bits and pieces of testimony against him, and this latest allegation from Lauren seemed very serious.

"Mrs. Altamira," he began, "you are a very close friend of Leigh White's, are you not?"

"I am indeed," Lauren said.

"For many years?"

"Yes."

"I see," said Mr. Silvers in an insinuating tone. "I'm sure you'll forgive me, then, if I question your story a little. It is, after all, quite a story. You told Mr. White a minute ago that you'd obtained all of this information from a surveillance tape in your home, correct?"

"Yes, that's correct."

"And yet, to my knowledge, no such tape has been entered into evidence. Why not, Mrs. Altamira?"

Lauren looked a bit embarrassed. "It was taped over, shortly after I saw it."

"Given the importance of what you saw there, why would you tape over it?"

"I—I didn't think it would be necessary."

"I see. You thought the fact that you'd seen it would be enough."

"Yes."

"Just as you thought the testimony of your maid would be enough?"

"I don't see any reason to doubt her."

"Don't you, Mrs. Altamira?"

"No, of course not! She's been with us for years."

"So you're saying you trust her implicitly?"

"Yes."

Mr. Silvers narrowed his eyes at her. "Then why, if I may ask, Mrs. Altamira, did you have a surveillance camera on her in the first place?"

Lauren's eyes widened. "I—I didn't—that is, the camera wasn't there for her."

"No?" Mr. Silvers pressed. "Where, if I may ask, was this alleged footage taken?"

"In our kitchen lounge area."

"The kitchen lounge area!" he said to the jury. "Not the most usual place for a surveillance camera, Mrs. Altamira—unless you're worried about someone, say, walking off with your silver."

"It wasn't for Jacinda!" Lauren insisted. "Francisco and I trust her completely. The maids sometimes gather there and watch tele-novelas while cleaning."

"Then what was it there for?" the prosecutor asked.

"It was—" Lauren faltered, her face turning a deep red.

"Yes?"

"It was for—private use."

Mr. Silvers leaned in, curious. "What *kind* of private use, Mrs. Altamira?"

"The kind that doesn't pertain to this trial!" Lauren exploded. The whole courtroom laughed uproariously.

"All right, Mrs. Altamira," Mr. Silvers relented. "But the question of your maid's reliability in all this remains. How long has she been in you and your husband's employ?"

"Eight years," Lauren said haughtily.

"And before that, do you know where she worked?"

"In Mexico—she came here to work for us."

"Legally?"

"Objection, Your Honor," said Brad. "The question is irrelevant, and unduly weighted by all the press here."

"Sustained," said the judge.

"Still," Mr. Silvers said, "we're talking about the word of an immigrant from Mexico, who may have any number of reasons, or none at all, for saying what she did about the men in question."

"If you're saying that the word of an immigrant is not as good as someone else's," Lauren said, barely containing her scorn, "you'd be better off not questioning me at all, Mr. Prosecutor."

The prosecutor backtracked. "Let me ask you about something else, Mrs. Altamira," he said. "You said that this tape corroborated what Dixie Johnson had told you, about the same Mexican men associating with Jacques at a party. Is that right?"

"Yes."

"Yet if I remember right"—he looked at his notes—"you said that party was 'soon after' Leigh White's gala last year, which would have placed it months before the appearance of this surveillance tape of yours. Correct?"

"That's correct."

"Did these men strike you as suspicious then?"

"They did, yes."

"Then why did you continue to, in your own words, encourage Leigh White to work with Mr. Mercier?"

Lauren hesitated. "I didn't think they were with him at first."

"Oh?" The prosecutor's eyes widened. "Whom did you think they were with?"

"I thought they were friends of Sassy Davilon's."

"Ah—Mr. Mercier's girlfriend," Mr. Silvers reminded the jury. "And, if I'm not mistaken, a fellow Miami realtor."

"Yes, that's right."

"As successful a realtor as yourself?"

Lauren laughed bitterly. "Ha! Hardly. She's only been here a couple of years! From what I heard, she came here after a breakup with some wealthy guy and got into real estate with his money. Believe me—she is *not* at my level of relevance in this town."

"But since then, she's been fairly successful, hasn't she?"

"I couldn't say," Lauren sniffed. "I don't follow people who use her kind of tactics."

"Perhaps not, Mrs. Altamira; but I believe Dixie Johnson did mention yesterday that there was a sort of rivalry between Sassy and yourself, centered around Mr. Mercier's business. Is that true?"

"Yes," Lauren admitted.

"And that you brought Jacques to lunch with Leigh White to impress him, in an effort to try to win back his business?"

"I did, yes."

"And you recommended him to Leigh White as part of the same effort?"

Lauren sighed deeply. "I admit that was part of my motivation, yes," she said. "But Sassy—"

"And am I right in assuming that these efforts to regain Mr. Mercier as a client failed?" the prosecutor interrupted.

"Yes," Lauren said, "and I'm glad they did."

"Still, that must have been very frustrating for you, initially—was it not?"

"It was, yes. But I'm not willing to use Sassy's slutty tactics, as I stated earlier."

"Frustrating enough to implicate Mr. Mercier solely in this affair?"

"No—that's ridiculous."

"Is it, Mrs. Altamira?"

"Yes!" Lauren shot back fiercely. "Besides, *everyone* knows his girlfriend's no good—it isn't just me!"

"Yet that's just hearsay, just as your story is, and bears not at all on your friend Mrs. White's guilt or innocence," the prosecutor said. "Let me spell it out for you. You say your maid—whose own word we have no reason to believe—was caught on a surveillance tape—which is apparently no longer in existence—associating Jacques Mercier with a few Mexican men—of whom we have no record—and associating those men with a crime syndicate in Mexico. Beyond being insubstantial hearsay, all of this says nothing as to your friend Leigh White's involvement in the scam in question; yet *you* can still sit here and tell us she was *absolutely unaware of it* when she entered into partnership with Mr. Mercier. On what grounds can you possibly make that claim, Mrs. Altamira?"

"I just—I know she wouldn't have worked with him if she knew," Lauren said weakly.

"Which is why you didn't tell her then, when you were trying to get his business back; and why you *are* telling us now, after it didn't work out for you."

"No—I—" Lauren spluttered furiously.

"Objection!" Brad said. "Your Honor, the question is argumentative."

"Overruled," said the judge. "Proceed, Mr. Silvers."

"That's all right," said the prosecutor smugly, as Lauren fumed. "I think we've made our point here. No further questions, Your Honor."

CHAPTER 36

MEMORY SERVES

> Leigh, been watching this trial thing on TV.
> This is C-R-A-Z-Y.
>
> —Joe Francis

Leigh wasn't sure how to take what she'd just heard. Throughout Lauren's entire testimony Brad had looked calm and collected, occasionally jotting notes down for himself, but otherwise looking on the whole spectacle with a more or less disinterested eye. Did that mean it had gone well?

She leaned over to Brad. "Is that testimony going to count for anything?" she whispered.

"Oh, definitely," he whispered back, "but it's a drop in the bucket."

"What do you mean?"

He looked at her with a twinkle in his eye. "It's still all coming together for me, honey—but just you wait. The next one's going to be even better."

"Who's—"

"You don't know him."

"I don't know him?" Leigh looked at her husband incredulously. "Who don't *I* know in this town?"

"Shhh—just wait and see!"

"The defense will call its next witness," Judge Tarlow said, and the clerk rose to announce the name.

"The defense calls Steven Senkew to the stand."

Leigh looked over as the door opened and a complete stranger walked in. The man was of medium height and build, with a boyishly handsome face and a calm demeanor about him. Yet while he was being sworn in she realized that she sensed something else there, too, that she couldn't quite put her finger on. His calmness seemed like the calmness of someone with nothing to prove. Inexplicably, the thought occurred to her that the guy had seen some things in his day, and the thought made her just a little uneasy. But Brad seemed happy he was here; and when she looked over at the prosecutor, she was pleased to see that the newcomer's presence seemed to be making him uneasy, too.

Brad got up and approached the stand.

"Mr. Senkew, what is your profession?" he asked bluntly.

"I'm a private investigator," Steve answered clearly.

"For what sorts of clients?"

"Mostly private contentions."

"Meaning—?"

"I work for a lot of jealous spouses." There was a burst of light laughter.

"You told me before that you have a particular trait that has suited you for this sort of work over the years," Brad went on. "Would you mind telling the court what that trait is?"

"I have what most people call a photographic memory. It isn't quite the accurate term for it, because my memory isn't simply visual."

"Do you mind if we test that, for the sake of the court?"

"Sure, go ahead."

"You were in the courtroom audience yesterday, were you not?"

"I was, yes."

"What color tie was Mr. Silvers wearing?"

"A rather shiny light-blue one."

Everyone glanced over at Mr. Silvers, who nodded bemusedly.

"Of course, the day's proceedings were televised, so quite a few people could probably have answered that," Brad said. "How about that gentleman"—he pointed to a friend of his he'd noticed in the audience the day before—"in the courtroom audience. Did you see him yesterday?"

"Yes," Steve said, squinting, "He was wearing a yellow collared shirt." He pointed with his finger, counting something. "He was sitting, I believe, three seats closer to the aisle from where he is now."

"My wife isn't with me today!" said the man, and everyone laughed.

"How about the substance of what was said—do you remember things like that?"

"Usually, yes."

"Do you remember the testimony of Brandon Westbrook, a.k.a. the Diva Lorraine Manchester?"

"Thoroughly."

"I have here a copy of the official court transcript of that testimony," Brad said, holding out the transcript for the judge. "Would you mind telling us, Mr. Senkew, what was the first objection registered during that witness's testimony?"

"Ms. Fischer objected to your testifying," Steve answered.

"Did Judge Tarlow uphold it?"

"He did."

"And the second?"

"You objected to Ms. Defoe's asking Mr. Westbrook if he used cocaine, a question you—though not Judge Tarlow—considered inflammatory and irrelevant."

"Very true," Brad smiled.

The judge looked up from the transcript.

"Mr. White, we'll take your witness's word for this ability of his," he said. "There's no need for any further stage-antics in this courtroom. Proceed with your questioning, please."

"Thank you, Your Honor," Brad said. "Mr. Senkew, did you ever see the defendant, Jacques Mercier, before you saw him in this courtroom yesterday?"

"I did, yes."

"When and where was that?"

"March 27th of last year, at Miami International Airport."

"And what was he doing there?"

"He was meeting the gentleman Mr. Westbrook referred to as Arturo Veraz, who had just returned on British Airways flight 1588 from Madrid."

A gasp ran through the courtroom. Ms. Fischer glanced briefly at Jacques, her face inscrutable. Leigh wasn't sure, but she could have sworn she saw a ripple of tension run through Jacques's jaw.

Brad returned to his table, and held up a printout of the photo of Arturo Veraz from the day before.

"Are you saying you saw Mr. Mercier meeting this man at the airport?" he asked.

"Yes, that's right," Steve said.

"What did they seem to be doing?"

"Mr. Mercier had apparently just returned on a separate flight from somewhere, and was meeting Mr. Veraz at his gate."

"Did you witness any part of their interaction?"

"Yes; as soon as they met, Mr. Mercier began to berate Mr. Veraz."

"How did Mr. Veraz take that?"

"Quietly; he seemed decidedly in the inferior position."

"And after that?"

"The two left together. I was there on separate business, so I didn't pursue them further."

"But you would say it was clear from what you saw, that the two men knew each other?"

"Oh, certainly."

Brad smiled. "I have no further questions," he said.

***

The whole courtroom was abuzz now. Leigh was astonished.

"Where'd you pull *him* out of?" she whispered to Brad when he'd sat.

"He turned up yesterday, completely by coincidence!" he said. "Isn't it incredible?"

"It's definitely that; I'm just hoping it's not too incredible to make a difference here."

"Oh, don't worry about that," he said with a sly smile. "I've got a few more cards up my sleeve."

She looked at him, bewildered. Before she could say anything, Ms. Defoe got up to begin her cross-examination.

"Mr. Senkew," the prosecutor began, "you say that yours is a photographic memory?"

"It's what people commonly *refer to* as photographic," he corrected her, "but the term isn't quite fitting. Photographic memory specifically refers to eidetic memory, which is shorter-term than mine is."

"I see. Then you're familiar with the research into such things, Mr. Senkew?"

"One tries to make sense of one's oddities."

"Then you must know of the scientific skepticism surrounding the concept of photographic memory."

"I do."

"Many cognitive scientists deny the existence of such a thing."

"Indeed they do," Steve replied. "I've read a few of their papers, as a matter of fact. I can't speak to the validity of their research, but I *can* tell you exactly what I was wearing and what the weather was like on the days I read them."

The audience laughed.

"But has this recollection of yours never been wrong, Mr. Senkew?" the prosecutor asked.

"Not that I can remember," Steve quipped, to more laughter.

Ms. Defoe buckled down. "What exactly were you doing at the airport, on the day you claim to have seen Mr. Mercier and Mr. Veraz together?" she asked.

"I was following someone."

"Who?"

"That is confidential, and not relevant to the case at hand."

"Are they here in the audience today?"

"Ms. Defoe," said Steve slowly, "this case is being televised nationally, so it doesn't matter if they're here or not."

"I just wish we had *some* sort of corroboration for your story."

"Which I have already given you, and the rest of the counsel, in private, in the form of my court deposition," Steve said coolly; then added, "Or have *you* forgotten?"

"I haven't," said Ms. Defoe as the courtroom chuckled again. "Only, it seems rather coincidental to me, Mr. Senkew, that you happened to see, and remember, Mr. Mercier and Mr. Veraz at the very moment that you were following someone else, all those months ago."

"If you had a memory like mine, you'd notice coincidences like that all the time," Steve said. "It's a pretty small world, and if you remember everyone you see, you're bound to recognize a few of them in some other connection."

"How long do these memories of yours last?"

"Oh, it varies. Usually a few years, sometimes more. A lot of them show no sign of ever disappearing."

"And this doesn't weigh down your mind at all?"

"It hasn't seemed to yet."

"Was there any connection between Mr. Mercier and the person you were following at the time?"

"None that pertains to this case."

"But you admit that there was some connection?"

"For the purposes of this case, I admit nothing of the kind. What it concerns you to know, Ms. Defoe, is that I *most certainly* saw Mr. Mercier in conference with Mr. Veraz—of whom a *strong* connection has been posited to the fraudulent artworks in question—at a time decidedly prior to Mr. Mercier's involvement in Leigh White's gala."

The prosecutor turned away in frustration.

"I have no further questions, Your Honor."

***

The judge spoke up over the clamor in the courtroom, a look of exhaustion on his face.

"Ladies and gentlemen of the jury," he said, "we're about to take our lunch break for the day. Thank you for your patience this morning. Let me remind you again, that you are not allowed to discuss the case among yourselves! Enjoy your lunch; we'll reconvene in two hours. Until then, you are dismissed."

Brad started to rise, to join his team on their way out the door. Leigh grabbed hold of his sleeve.

"Honey, you have to tell me how we're doing before you go," she said. "I'm just too anxious to be kept in the dark. That testimony seemed really, *really* good—just tell me we've got them a *little* bit on the run at this point!"

"Oh, if we haven't yet, we will soon," Brad said, his eyes glowing.

"What do you mean? Have you got more to add to this?"

"Darling," he said, kissing her forehead, "you ain't seen nothing yet." He leaned down to take her hands in his. "There are a few holes I still haven't figured out in all this, but I do have one more witness, and I promise you, what he has to say is going to be dynamite."

"Who is he?"

"I can't tell you that—or it'll be a better surprise for you if I don't."

"Do I know him?"

"Yes and no. Just wait and see, honey; you'll love it, I promise. Now, I need to go talk with my team—we're still trying to dig up Sassy. I'll see you after lunch, okay?"

"Okay."

Without another word, he was gone.

Despite Brad's enthusiasm, Leigh was far too wound-up to eat. Instead, she ducked into one of the private rooms, checked her email, called to check on the twins, had a Perrier and thought about the future. In less than a few days she'd either be home again, struggling to find meaning in a changed life, or—but that was unthinkable. She struggled to keep her anxiety at bay. Yet Brad seemed so sure of their case; why was she so terrified? Why couldn't she just trust that it would turn out as he said?

She knew the answer, of course. It wasn't that she questioned Brad; it was just so difficult having so much of her life outside of her control. It had always been her greatest fear, and now she was facing it; she felt helpless, useless—a feeling she'd taken the utmost care to avoid since she was a little girl. She thought again of her brother, and their childhood; and a new sadness overwhelmed her. Without Gerald, she might never have learned to work so hard for what she loved. His irresponsibility had been a gift to her. Where was he now? He had needed to learn to take care of himself, a thing he couldn't have accomplished with her there to take care of him. But did he know how, beyond her protectiveness, she'd loved him for who he was? Could she make him see it, with her own life in ruins?

She cried until there were no tears left; and when she could cry no more, Leigh White put her head on her folded arms and fell into a deep sleep. If she dreamed, she did not remember her dream; and when she woke, it was to the sound of Jeffrey's voice.

"Leigh, wake up!" he said, gently shaking her.

She slowly raised her head to look at him. He looked absolutely overjoyed.

"What're you so happy about?" she asked, his smile spreading to her face.

"It's the next witness—Brad says we have a miracle!" he said.

"We do? With the last witness?"

"Second-to-last. This one's a new one, apparently." He helped her up. "Anyway, come on, you'd better get a move on—court is in session!"

She got up and hurried into the courtroom. Brad, looking as excited as she'd ever seen him, was utterly engrossed with a new page of notes, furiously scribbling new ones in the margins here and there. She found her seat just as the bailiff spoke up.

"All rise…court is now in session, the Honorable Judge Tarlow presiding."

"Thank you, and welcome back, everyone," said the judge, sitting. "Let's get to it—the defense, you may call your first witness."

CHAPTER 37

HE SAIED, SHE SAIED

> Um, who's the suit? Looks rich...

—Jeffrey

"Your Honor, I request a sidebar," Brad said as he approached the bench.

A tense, whispered conference followed between the judge and the three counselors. Leigh strained to hear them, but couldn't make out anything but "staying at the W Hotel in Miami" and, to her surprise, Sassy Davilon's name. After a few moments, the other lawyers seemed to capitulate, and Brad returned to his table.

"What—" Leigh started to ask.

"The defense calls Mr. Mahmoud Al Saied to the stand," called the clerk. The door opened and an extremely well-heeled Middle Eastern man entered, wearing an exquisitely tailored light-grey suit and an expression of calm self-possession. Leigh struggled to remember if she'd seen him before, but could come up with nothing.

She wanted to ask her husband about him; but as soon as this Mr. Al Saied was sworn in and seated, Brad was out of his chair like a rocket.

"Mr. Al Saied," he asked, and even his voice betrayed a quiver of excitement, "would you please tell the court who you are, and why you've contacted me to testify today?"

"Certainly," said Mr. Al Saied. "I am a businessman and investor from Dubai, and now reside between that city, London and New York. I came to Miami this week, for a few days of meetings, and have been following your trial on television. I must say, the coverage of it has been rather…inescapable."

The courtroom laughed, and Mr. Al Saied went on.

"I was watching the trial last evening from my hotel room, and the broadcaster showed a photograph of a woman whom I recognized right away."

There was a ripple of whispering in the courtroom as Brad spoke up.

"Who was the woman you recognized, Mr. Al Saied?"

"It seems she now calls herself Sassy Davilon."

"And what connection to you have to Ms. Davilon?" Brad asked loudly as the ripple turned into a tidal wave.

Mahmoud Al Saied took a deep breath.

"Several years ago," he said, "I had a relationship with her—my first. We lived together for two years. After that time, my family—a prominent one in my country—was concerned that I might marry her, and had her thoroughly investigated, as is customary among many of our aristocratic families. Much to my shame and regret, our investigator discovered that the woman you call Sassy, whom I knew as Sameetha, was a former male model and dancer who had undergone a sexual conversion."

The courtroom erupted in a collective gasp of surprise and an explosion of speech, and the judge pounded his gavel for order.

When silence had returned, Mr. Al Saied continued gravely.

"It may be wondered why I had not known of this earlier. For my part, I can only elicit my profound inexperience in such matters; yet the operation had been a very successful one, with particularly convincing results.

"In any event, our culture is far from accepting such things, and I was devastated. I felt I had been living a lie, and looked for any way to believe it wasn't true—or at least convince my family that it wasn't. I confronted my beautiful Sameetha, who claimed it was a lie, a fraud perpetrated by jealous rivals, and begged me not to cast her off. I didn't know what to do. I was desperately in love with her, and wanted more than anything to believe her; perhaps I would even have overlooked her deception if I could have convinced my family to accept her. Yet Sameetha was only biding for time. Some weeks after the investigator told us of her secret, she forged checks, stole hundreds of thousands of dollars of my family's money, and fled the country."

The courtroom gasped again. Brad pressed on.

"What happened next, Mr. Al Saied?"

"The last word I received from Sameetha was a letter threatening, in the coldest terms, to publicly reveal what the investigator had told us, and ruin my family's standing in the Middle East. Her plot worked; fearing public scrutiny and censure, my family abandoned the search for her, and gave up any intentions of retrieving the money she'd stolen. If it may be said modestly, it was not a great deal of money to us."

"What caused you to speak out today?" Brad asked.

"My father had a weak heart, and not long after the ordeal with Sameetha, he passed away. A few years later my mother joined him, and I have since increased our family fortune through my own ventures. I had no intention of pursuing Sameetha; but with both of my parents gone, and a more independent view of my own life, I no longer had any reason to keep silent about her, either; and when I saw the trial on television, and how she was involved in ruining others' lives, I decided to expose her for the fraud she is."

"*It's a lie!*" screamed Jacques suddenly, leaping to his feet. The jury all looked as though they'd been goosed; these were the first words he'd uttered through the whole trial.

Leigh looked over at Jacques, and gasped. He looked as though he were on the brink of losing it entirely. His face was bright red, and contorted to a mask of fury as he pointed a shaking finger at Mahmoud Al Saied. "What you're saying is impossible—it's a damn lie! I would never do…that…with a man!"

"Control yourself, Mr. Mercier," said the judge sternly.

Mr. Al Saied remained composed, and answered Jacques coolly. "I would have liked to believe that myself, believe me," he said, "but take my word, my friend: a little serious thought will convince you in time."

With a noise of inarticulate rage, Jacques threw aside his chair and rushed at the witness stand. Brad moved in to block his way, and Jacques collided roughly with him; but readied by his first outburst, the bailiff and police were quick to pounce, and threw him easily to the ground. Jacques foamed at the mouth through a torrent of curses as they handcuffed him. The courtroom audience stood in noisy excitement, reaching their phones out for photos.

"Order in the court!" the judge shouted, throwing down his gavel. "Order—I *will* have order!"

"I don't fuck men!" Jacques raged. "I don't! She's a woman! She's—"

Writhing under the policemen's grasp, he began to convulse, his curses turning to hyperventilating gasps.

"Bailiff, have the defendant removed, and see that he's given proper medical attention," said the judge.

Once they'd done so, and some order had been restored to the courtroom, the judge turned to Brad.

"Mr. White, if you have further questions, you may proceed," he said.

"Thank you, Your Honor," Brad said, smoothing down his jacket. "I do indeed. Mr. Al Saied, do you have any reason to suspect that the person you call Sameetha is involved in the present fraud?"

"Only that I can attest to her criminal background, and in more ways than one."

"How else?"

"In my family's initial researches into her background, they discovered a fairly diverse criminal past, with a network of questionable associates. We gave up our searches early, as I've said, but what we saw was very suggestive."

"I see," said Brad. "Mr. Al Saied, you've been very helpful today. I know what you've revealed so far has been painful enough, and I have only one further question for you. Does the name Joseph Cavalleri mean anything to you?"

Mr. Al Saied looked surprised.

"Actually, it does," he said. "That is the name of one of the men we turned up in our early researches."

"As an associate of Ms. Davilon's?"

"No, as one of her former lovers, when she'd been a man."

The courtroom gasped yet again.

"Thank you, Mr. Al Saied," said Brad, nodding slowly as he thought over what had been said. "Your Honor, I have no further questions."

"Mr. Silvers, you may proceed with questioning," said the judge.

The prosecutor stood. "Your Honor, the prosecution does not wish to credit the relevance of this latest testimony by questioning it; but only to point out to the jury that its connection to this case is entirely unestablished, and to request a motion to disregard it on the grounds of irrelevance. Mr. Al Saied's relationship with Ms. Davilon has nothing to do with Leigh White's fraud."

Ms. Fischer rose quickly too. "Your Honor, we agree. Whatever Ms. Davilon's past or present, Mr. Mercier's guilt is in no way implied in his romantic association with her. In light of this, we too request the opportunity to file a motion to disregard this testimony."

"I will consider such motions as I receive them," said Judge Tarlow, rubbing his eyes. "For now, I'd like to get to the end of this, if we may. I'll be issuing a subpoena for Ms. Davilon's private deposition; in the meantime, Mr. White, I believe you have one more witness for us."

"I do, Your Honor," said Brad, a note of triumph creeping into his voice.

"Very well, Mr. White, please call your witness," said the judge, suppressing a yawn.

Brad looked over at his wife. The "Here It Comes" smile lit up his face.

"Your Honor," he said, "I call Gerald Anatole to the stand."

CHAPTER 38

MIAMI TURNAROUND

> Not sure what we're doing with that one.
> Looks like the plan's changing.

—Lila Defoe

Leigh clapped a hand to her mouth. Tears filled her eyes as she watched her brother stride confidently into the courtroom.

It had been years since she'd seen him. She had only bitterly accepted the fact that she couldn't help him until he helped himself; but it looked like he'd more than helped himself in the meantime. He looked well—terrific, really. Gone was the tough-guy James Dean look of his youth, but he was every bit as handsome and confident-looking in slacks and a sportcoat as he was in rolled-up cuffs and a T-shirt.

He smiled warmly at his sister as he was sworn in; then, steeling himself with a look of relaxed determination, he took the stand.

"Mr. Anatole, please tell us your relation to the defendant," Brad said.

"She's my older sister," Gerald answered.

"How long has it been since you've seen her?"

"About six years."

"Were you close in childhood?"

"Yes and no. We always got along; but she took care of me, and that was pretty much a one-way street."

"You had a troubled youth, Mr. Anatole?"

"I was arrested seven times before the age of twenty-one."

"And what do you do now?"

"I'm a security guard, and I volunteer for a few nonprofits."

"Quite a turnaround, no?"

"More than I can say." Gerald's voice cracked with emotion as he added, "I owe it all to my sister."

"And what is it that you do as a volunteer, these days?"

"I counsel prisoners back home in Texas."

"What sort of prisoners?"

"Oh, any that need help with work-release, prison life, you name it."

"Would you please tell the court what prompted you to call me, Mr. Anatole?"

"Of course," Gerald said. "In my volunteer work, I deal with a lot of illegals—mostly people waiting to be deported, but some who are caught for various crimes in the States and jailed for a while before they're handed over to the border authorities. Well, I was running a counseling session inside, and I had these two Mexican guys who were just a total handful."

"How do you mean, a handful?"

"I mean, they were just completely disrespectful of the system, and me, and everything. They'd been caught jumping the border—apparently they'd been really cocky about it. The cops had suspicions that they'd been involved in some minor thefts on the way, so they were being held for a while; and they just didn't care one bit about it."

"Didn't care about being arrested?"

"Right. They seemed to have all the time in the world; like, once they got out, they were set."

"Did they say anything to indicate why they had that attitude?"

"Oh, definitely. All they wanted to do was talk about it. I didn't pay much attention to them, at first; you know, a lot of guys on the inside brag about their crimes, and the last thing you want to do is gratify their big talk by listening to it. I tried to tell them my usual thing, about starting over and second chances and all that. But nothing I said to them was getting through. They didn't regret anything. They said they were looking forward to being deported and returning to their families; they wanted to build a soccer field for their hometown."

"Where did they plan to get the money for that?"

"That's exactly what I asked them, thinking it'd take the wind out of their sails a bit. But it got them going instead, and in addition to bragging about their connection back home to a certain 'powerful family'—"

"The Garcia family?" Brad interjected hopefully.

"I didn't ask," Gerald said. "But they didn't dwell on that much. That was more how they got started, rather than how they'd hit the big time."

"And how was that?" Brad asked.

"They told me they'd just helped to set up an American socialite in Florida. They said they'd run some sort of elaborate scam on a bunch of rich people, and set one woman up to take the fall."

"Surely they didn't orchestrate all this on their own?" said Brad suggestively. The room had gone utterly silent; and but for their voices, the only sound was the tapping of the court stenographer and the quiet hum of the video cameras.

"Oh, no," said Gerald. "Their job had been easy, they said: mostly go-between stuff, and creating online aliases for their boss to make his story plausible. This boss of theirs—a rich partner in the scam—they said he knew everybody and everything, and had money waiting for them in Mexico."

"So it was their partner's scam, and he hired them on to help him carry it out?"

"Yes, that's right."

"Did you happen to ask the identity of this partner of theirs?" asked Brad, looking pointedly over at Ms. Fischer.

"I did."

The silence was deafening. Brad leaned his elbow on the stand.

"Who did they say he was, Mr. Anatole?" he asked.

Gerald's voice rang out clearly in the stillness. "They told me his name was Jacques Mercier."

A pent-up gasp ran through the courtroom, followed by a general racket of people whispering to each other, tapping out texts and tweets on their phones, and snapping pictures of Jacques's lawyer, whose fighting-bulldog face had drooped even further into a comical pout.

"Quiet, please!" the judge shouted. "Order in the court!"

The hubbub only grew. The judge banged his gavel and called again for order, but to no avail. The crowd seemed on the verge of going completely out of control, when Brad spoke up again.

"Mr. Anatole," he said loudly, "did these prisoners have anything further to add about their partner, Mr. Mercier, or the scam they'd managed here in Miami?" The noise in the courtroom settled immediately.

"Yes," said Gerald. "They said Mr. Mercier was a Frenchman who lived in Mexico City. They'd met him through their connection with the Garcia family, who'd sponsored a few of his early efforts. His favorite scam was to sell art to rich people—with most of them, they said, art was particularly easy to fake. Mr. Mercier would move somewhere with a lot of money floating around, get in with the society there, get drunk with drivers and housekeepers and gardeners and pool boys to learn more about their bosses, and sell people on bogus art. He was very good at covering his tracks, and he had a sense of style that made him very convincing as a high-society man.

"Their latest job had been in Miami, and they said it had gone over especially well. They said everybody there was so used to being lied to and scammed all the time, they didn't see a real scam coming."

The courtroom laughed uproariously, and more phones lit up as the line was tweeted out. Brad walked past the prosecutor's table, and gave the two counselors a knowing look.

"This is all very interesting, Mr. Anatole," he said, still looking at the prosecutors, "but I have to say, these guys giving you all this information, practically unsolicited—it just sounds a bit too good to be true. I don't suppose you happened to collect any, oh, I don't know, collateral proof of what you're telling us?"

"Oh, these guys were convinced their deportation was going to pull them out of the fire," Gerald said. "They didn't mind telling me all about the operation in detail, as many times as I wanted to hear it—including when I'd started to record them on my phone. I've brought a copy of my recording with me today, and entered it with the judge before I was sworn in."

The faces of the prosecution dropped. Ms. Fischer, already dealt a blow by Jacques's exit, turned white. Whispers ran through the courtroom again, but quieted as the crowd waited to hear what Brad would say.

After a moment, he spoke up.

"Well, thank you, then, Mr. Anatole," he said, a look of quiet triumph on his face. "You've been extremely helpful. I have no further questions, Your Honor."

In the silence that followed, Mr. Silvers stood stiffly.

"Your Honor," he said, seeming a bit dazed, "the prosecution requests a short recess to review this, uh, this new evidence of Mr. Anatole's." He looked over at Ms. Defoe, who nodded grimly. "Pending that review," he added quickly, "we have no further questions."

The courtroom erupted into a chaos of noise and flashes. Gerald stood and walked out gracefully as the photographers shouted over one another, trying to get him to stop for a picture. The judge sat back with a helpless gesture as the bailiff called for order.

Watching Gerald go, Leigh burst into tears. The story that had begun in Hewitt, Texas had come around and completed itself. Her little brother had come to her rescue.

***

Judge Tarlow called for a short break, during which Brad took a Scotch with his team, Leigh and Gerald sat catching up on some of their lost time together, and Jacques—mildly sedated and visibly shaken—was returned to court under police escort.

When they resumed, Brad was granted an opportunity to summarize the position of the defense.

Jacques Mercier, he began by saying, had concocted the entire scheme in partnership with Sassy Davilon. This had taken place long before Jacques had been introduced to Leigh White, but had targeted her charity from the beginning. Using Sassy's connections to the Miami scene, they'd contrived to bring Jacques to Leigh's gala and introduce him to everyone, intending months later to propose a partnership with the charity.

Having set the trap for Leigh early on, Jacques had contracted Arturo Veraz—whom Brad suspected was one of Jacques's long-time associates—to forge his artworks for him, and had taken a number of transatlantic trips with the artist to museums, galleries, libraries in England and Europe to fill out the background of their fraud. It was on one of these trips that Steve Senkew had spotted them together; and the painting Brandon Westbrook had seen in production at Veraz's studio was in fact the painting later sold at auction at Leigh's gala.

Because of Jacques and Sassy's partnership, Lauren Altamira had been correct in her assumption that Jacques's Mexican associates were working with Sassy. However, because of her prior working relationship with Jacques, she'd failed to see his involvement in the scheme until long after she and Dixie had encouraged Leigh to work with him.

The tape Dixie Johnson had heard, of her husband's patient Cavalleri, didn't have quite the significance she and Lauren had thought, but it was crucial to the story nonetheless. Cavalleri, it seemed, had been a lover of Sassy's before her sexual conversion; and his comment that Jacques was "in over his head with that one" had only to do with the secret of Sassy's gender. Contacted for further comment, however, Cavalleri admitted that he had first met his lover in mandatory counseling after they were both arrested for larceny. He'd assumed that her new lover was aware of *that* part of her character.

Having brought the loose ends together, Brad asked that, if the prosecution's evidence did not obviously contradict this interpretation—and the material evidence submitted by Gerald Anatole—the court consider dropping the charges against Leigh White, and resume its charge of conspiracy against Jacques Mercier and Sassy Davilon alone.

The prosecution—and, much more vehemently, Ms. Fischer—objected to the proposal. The prosecution claimed that the charge of conspiracy had room for all three; while Ms. Fischer said it ought to be left to the jury to decide whether the "flimsy" evidence against her client was enough to implicate him.

Leigh held her breath as Ms. Fischer sat and the judge prepared to make his decision. The courtroom sat in suspense, only the hum of incoming texts breaking the silence. Judge Tarlow made a few notes for himself, looked out sternly into the audience and began.

"It is true that there is always room on a conspiracy charge for as many perpetrators as may be reasonably shown to have taken part in it," he said. "And as for the weight of the present evidence against Mr. Mercier, I agree again, in saying that it should be the work of our jury to make the final pronouncement of his guilt or innocence."

He looked over without expression to where Leigh and Brad were sitting. Leigh felt as though her heart had stopped. The silence was almost unbearable. She felt Brad take hold of her hand under the table and squeeze it.

"And yet," the judge went on, "I am also in agreement with Mr. White. The State's evidence that I have seen—collected in partnership with Agent Corinne and his team—is as well suited to his interpretation as to the others, if not much better; and the additional testimonies of Mr. Saied and Mr. Anatole, as well as Mr. Anatole's material evidence, are, it seems to me, quite decisive. The fact that the additional suspects implicated by these testimonies, Sassy Davilon and Arturo Veraz, have yet to be located, stands in my opinion as further support for Mr. White's interpretation.

"In light of this, and pending any further discovery from those persons, at such time as they are apprehended, the court agrees to drop the State's charges of fraud against Leigh Anatole White, and continue to address these charges as they apply to Jacques Mercier and any associates he may be proven to have worked with. Mrs. White, you are free to go."

The response in the courtroom was immediate. The audience erupted into shouts, cheers and camera flashes. The press assembled there immediately began to text and tweet out the judge's decision, and climb over each other for photos. Selfies were being shot everywhere. Judge Tarlow sighed wearily.

"Order in the courtroom, please," he shouted. "Our trial is not over yet, ladies and gentlemen—we need order, please! Order in the court—order in the court!"

"Ladies and gentlemen, the judge has called for order!" said the bailiff.

Some of the audience quieted a bit; but the press, already given too much free rein, was not to be calmed down. Bloggers, having long since broadcast the decision, raced to be the first to give their opinion about it. Photographers leaned in over the railing and snapped pictures of Leigh, who wept with relief as Brad grabbed her in a tight embrace. A round of applause started somewhere in the audience, amid which the judge spoke up over the chaos.

"I'm going to call for another short recess here, in hopes of restoring decorum to this courtroom," he said. "Those of you who can't control yourselves here, take this opportunity to excuse yourselves from the proceedings. Please don't force me to have any of you detained on contempt; we have enough on our plate as it is. You are free to go, Mrs. White," he repeated, gesturing toward the side door.

Overwhelmed with relief, Leigh could barely walk and clung to Brad as they made their way out. Jacques, still white and shaking, barely acknowledged them as they passed. But he had his own problems: in another moment the bailiff had him handcuffed and led out a separate way, to wait out the recess in an adjoining room.

In the hallway Leigh and Brad met Jeffrey, beaming with excitement.

"What an incredible turnaround!" he said, hugging them both. "I can't believe it's over!"

"I can't really either," said Leigh. She turned to Brad. "I mean, it *is* over, right, Brad? I'm really free and clear?"

"You're really free and clear," Brad said. "Sometimes it actually does just work out like that—not often, but sometimes."

"I just can't believe the judge was ready to move on."

"Well, they still have Jacques to go after, and now Sassy and Arturo Veraz, too. They know not to waste time with insubstantial accusations when they have real ones on hand. And besides, those last couple of testimonies were game-changers."

"No kidding! Which reminds me—" Leigh looked around, but saw no sign of Gerald. "Jeffrey, my brother—where is he?" she asked.

"Gerald's on his way to your house, my Queen," Jeffrey smiled. "I gave him the spare set of house keys; he'll be waiting for us there."

"Oh, good," Leigh said. "We should have your team over too, Brad. You all did such an amazing job with this."

"Of course," Brad said. "I'll go ask them if they'd come over this evening."

Leigh turned to Jeffrey again. "And everyone else—Dixie, Lauren—I've got to get all of them together to thank them. Can you—"

"I've already texted everyone to make sure they keep their evening free," said Jeffrey, looking at his phone. "I thought I should discuss the other particulars of the celebration with you, but I do know we're low on champagne, so I took the liberty of ordering two cases to be delivered."

Leigh could only laugh.

WRAP-UP ON THE OTHER SIDE OF TOWN

> Found a new spot to try.
> Wanna go today?

—Ray

"This place's been upside-down since 2000," Hooter said with a glance over his tackle box at the oily water sloshing in the causeway.

"Earlier'n dat," his friend Ray shot back, looking around for the sock he'd been using to lift the grill lid.

"Worse now," Hooter averred. "'Publicans everywhere."

"It's Florida. We always got pelicans."

"Not what I said," Hooter scowled. " *'Publicans.* Place just got nasty with them in 2000 with all that hanging chads voting business, and they ain't left since. Hell of a lot worse'n pelicans, Ray."

"No 'publican took my sock," Ray countered.

"You know," said Hooter reflectively, "just driving here, I saw a lady panhandling for a boob job. I gave her twenty-five cents."

"No!" Ray laughed, crouching over to pull off his other sock. "Whatcha think that'll get her? Half a nipple?"

"And they caught some hairy dude running around Walmart, too," Hooter continued, warming to his subject. "Seems he was a sex offender and had on see-through shorts. Nobody did *that* 'fore the 'publicans came. And then Rudy Eugene—"

"Ah, forget Rudy Eugene," Ray said. "How about dat fake dentist kissing those women's rear ends? Now *he* was clever. He was looking in their mouths, and they'd never expect him to wind up down dere."

"Might be we oughta try dat," Hooter allowed. Both men laughed.

"Hey, pass me dose tongs," said Ray, lifting the grill's lid carefully.

Hooter stood and handed over the battered tongs, which Ray used to press the little pile of white-hot coals down. "Dese're just about ready to cook on," Ray affirmed.

"Good, I'm hungry," said Hooter. "I was going to start in on my sangwidge—I can't believe we caught one so early, though!"

"It's a better spot than last time," Ray said proudly.

"Yeah, it is."

"Pretty good-sized snapper, too. Hey, you watch dis thing for a minute, while I wrap up the rest." Ray set half the fish on the grill, and began to wrap the other half in newspaper to tuck back in the cooler. He paused a moment in his work.

"Hey, you remember dat art-fraud case?" he asked.

"'Course," answered Hooter. "Two weeks it was on every channel, damn thing! That Frenchie went up for it, and they caught that tranny, too."

"Yeah, I heard dat! They caught her at the border, makin' a run for it. You hear she was dressed *as a man?*"

Hooter nearly spit out his beer. "No way! So, like, disguised like what she used to be?"

"Yep," Ray said. "Brought her in kickin' and screamin'. Wonder how that Frenchie felt, stickin' his weiner in the forbidden bun! She'll do some time for *dat* little stunt, and for rippin' off dat A-rab guy, too."

"You think she goes in male prison, or female?" Hooter wondered.

"Female, I guess," said Ray.

"Yeah? Why do you figure?"

"Well, she's a woman *now*, ain't she?"

"I guess so, yeah," said Hooter. The two pondered the point in silence for a moment before Ray remembered what he was going to say.

"Well, anyway, look here," Ray said, holding up a sheet of the newspaper he'd been wrapping the fish in.

"Whassat?" asked Hooter, squinting through the grill smoke.

"Gossip column for the *Herald*," answered Ray. "They did a 'Where They All At Now' sorta thing. Here, see how the other half lives." He cleared his throat and read.

"Brandon Westbrook, a.k.a. Lorraine Manchester—"

"That's that drag queen, right?" Hooter interrupted with a laugh. "I heard he was sellin' wigs and tits now, to all the other drag queens!"

"Yeah, yeah; here it is—*a.k.a. Lorraine Manchester, now supervises his own company, Diva Lorraine, full-time. The company has just announced a new line of high-end heels in plus-sizes, and hopes to follow it with a formal-wear collection."*

"Good job for him! Or her, or whatever," Hooter said. "Who else they got in there?"

"Everybody, listen. *After his widely publicized split from his wife, Billie Parker*—dat's the fashion guy, with the suits—*gained custody of deir son, and is rumored to be engaged to current girlfriend, supermodel*

Ellie Ramirez.—Whoo! Same life, different wife, huh? Some things never change. Dat's dat South American babe, y'know—guess now he's got a real model, and not a wannabe one. Lucky guy! Anyway— *Billie's soon to be ex-wife Katie Parker*—dat's the hot one, with all the Botox—*is reported to be filming her own reality TV show. Her ex-husband is said to have helped negotiate the contract for the show, a rags-to-riches story dat will have her returning home to Selma, Alabama to retrace her small-town roots."*

"Ha!" Hooter cried. "Sounds like fashion boy was smarter'n she thought! Bet she wasn't countin' on *that.*"

"No way," Ray smiled. "Hell, bet she thought she was goin' to Hollywood! But dey script all that reality TV stuff, you know."

"'Course they do," agreed Hooter. "Go on."

"Gerald Anatole has been offered a job as a private invextigator in Palm Beach County with top firm 'The Waking Eye,' and has worked for defense attorney Brad White a number of times. He was recommended for the job by fellow trial witness and famed investigator Steven Senkew, who said he appreciated Mr. Anatole's courtroom demeanor during the trial. Lauren Altamira—"

"I thought *she* was the hot one," said Hooter, poking at the fish with a fork.

"She was okay," Ray agreed. *"Lauren Altamira, recognized by* Forbes Magazine *as one of the nation's top realtors and honored on its cover last month, continues to do a thriving business in Miami. She claims that her association with the trial has brought her a whole new set of high-end clientele."*

"I bet it did!" Hooter said. "I'd buy a house offa that broad, if I had the dough."

"You'd buy *somethin'* off her, sure," said Ray.

"Wasn't she the one videotapin' in her house, and not sayin' what for?"

"Yeah, that's her."

"Hell, I know what *I'd* be doin' it for, with that one!" Hooter laughed.

"Well, she's a lady wit class, and you're a pre-vert. Anyway, listen: *Scarlett Ruiz and Mitchell Hudson*—who was dat again?" Ray asked, puzzled.

"Don't remember," said Hooter.

"Well, whoever dey were, the paper says right here—dey *were approached by a group of young entrepreneurs in the nightclub business, and offered partnerships and a full staff to open a much-anticipated chain of nightclubs, reportedly called Not Guilty.*"

"Bullshit," said Hooter quietly, turning the fish. "But good for them, I guess."

"*Dr. Howard Johnson has, of course, gone on to fame as America's psychiatrist, Dr. Howard*—You know, I saw dat!" Ray exclaimed. "He's like the new Dr. Phil. I just didn't know dat was him, since he's got hair now."

"Oh, they can do all sorts of things on TV," Hooter agreed.

"*His wife Dixie has been offered a spokeswoman's position at Weight Watchers, based on the success of her series of inspirational YouTube videos*—"

"You gotta be kiddin' me! Why would she wanna be skinny? I kinda like a girl with some meat on her—I never did understand all that girdle talk when she was bein' interviewed on TV."

"*—and by coincidence, deir driver, Danny, now works for Billie Parker's supermodel girlfriend Ellie.*"

"That's gotta be a good job," mused Hooter. "Drivin' a supermodel around? Man, wonder if that guy gets any."

"The driver? Forget it!" laughed Ray.

"I don't know; I bet that Dixie was pretty accommodatin'."

"Hell, maybe. But here's the assistant: *Jeffrey Kruger has been approached by a number of publishers for a tell-all memoir on Miami society and working for Leigh White, but says he is 'waiting for the right offer.'"*

"Well, he oughta."

"Guy's gotta know where the bodies are buried! And I guess this here is about the husband: *After successes in a number of high-profile class-action lawsuits, Brad White agreed to join President Obama's advisory committee for the Attorney General of the United States, as part of the President's new juvenile action program. He has recently been nominated for Attorney of Our Generation, by the International Trial Attorneys Organization."*

Hooter whistled. "Not bad for a lawyer—I still never met one I liked, though."

"Nah, me neither."

"What about the main lady?"

"Leigh White retired from her charity, and is reputed to be in talks with an unspecified television network for production of her own series. Guess da TV thing is what everyone does next, huh?"

"Guess so," Hooter said. "Is that everyone?"

"Yep, dat's everyone." Ray twisted off the tab from his beer can and flipped it into the water. "I remember they caught dat fake artist, too."

"He doing any time?"

"I don't think so. Think he just got a slap on the wrist, so far."

"Figures," said Hooter. "It just figures. You know, Ray, sometimes I wonder if anything's real in this town," he went on philosophically. "Fake boobs, fake art, fake money, women and men turnin' into each other left and right—you can't be sure of nothing!"

"No, dat's true," Ray agreed. "You know what ended up happenin' to dat art, right?"

Hooter shrugged. "Everybody got their money back, didn't they?"

"Yeah, but the *art.*"

"No, I never heard."

"Oh, then you'll like this. It's all famous now, because of the trial, so they just got it all together and auctioned it off again!"

"You're shittin' me!" Hooter laughed. "The same people?"

"Same people, same charity, just without dat woman—they sold it as trial souvenirs this time."

"They make any money off it?"

"More than they made off the real stuff!" Ray grinned. "Amazin' what people'll pay for a little touch of TV fame. Or maybe some of 'em just have too much money to—"

"But you see, there?" Hooter shouted. "Fake art's just as valuable as the real stuff, and the phonies are all celebrities. They always said Miami was a sunny place for shady people!"

"Yeah, yeah," Ray agreed. "Still, though, everybody got what dey deserved in the end, don't you think?"

"Hell, sure." Hooter smiled. "I'm still thinkin' about that tranny tryin' to sneak outta town dressed as a man!"

They chuckled together as Ray raised his beer.

"I'm tellin' you, man, only in Miami-town—and here's to it!" he said.

Hooter shook his empty can. "Hang on, I gotta get a new one," he said. "Easy come, easy go. You get this fish offa here, will you?"

Ray divided up the fish between two rolls; and having toasted, the two men started in on their lunch in silence. Once or twice, a seagull's cry came through the far-off noise of traffic. As they finished, Hooter leaned back in the morning sun, satisfied.

"You know, they got it pretty good," he mused, "but we got what *we* deserve, too."

"How'sat?"

Hooter's eyes widened. "Man, you ever catch a snapper like

that before? It was huge! And so early in the day—we hardly waited for it!"

"It's a good spot," Ray said again modestly, flicking a fish bone into the water.

"It's a *great* spot," insisted Hooter.

They looked out over the calm of Biscayne Bay. A few boats, their hulls a blinding white, were already out in the even brighter surf. Gulls in a crowd careened above the surface and dipped down, the afternoon sun flickering strobe-like through their wings. Behind them, the city shone bright too, a wonderland of strange possibility.

"You know, I wouldn't trade this town for any other," said Hooter quietly.

Ray smiled.

"Me neither, buddy," he agreed. "Me neither."

ACKNOWLEDGMENTS

Thank you to the following people for your help in getting this book completed, I am forever grateful for your support and talent: Megan Trank, Eric Kampmann, Felicia Minerva, and the team at Midpoint Trade and Beaufort Books; with special thanks to James Carpenter; James "Cubby" Clark; Jason Clarke; Erin Hosier; Integrated PR; Jenna Menking. To everyone that read the advance copy and enthusiastically recommended it, thank you! Your opinions matter.

Thank you to the dazzling city of Miami and its unique cast of characters, a city I call home, and especially to you the reader.

Thank you to Roy, Rj, Freda, Dottie, Wolfie, Whisper, Buddy, and my Texas family.

This book is dedicated to all my "loyal friends," my puppies that have passed on and are now living on the other side. I miss you!

—Lea Black